SEP   2013
CLAYTON FOR STACKS
31012003940009
A FIC BORNIKOVA, PHILLIPA
Bornikova, Phillipa.
Box office poison

P9-COP-015

Georgia Law requires Library materials to
be returned or replacement costs paid.
Failure to comply with this law is a
misdemeanor. (O.C.G.A. 20-5-53)

CLAYTON COUNTY LIBRARY SYSTEM
FOREST PARK BRANCH
4812 WEST STREET
FOREST PARK, GEORGIA 30297-1824

BOX OFFICE POISON

BOX OFFICE POISON

phillipa bornikova

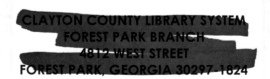
CLAYTON COUNTY LIBRARY SYSTEM
FOREST PARK BRANCH
4812 WEST STREET
FOREST PARK, GEORGIA 30297-1824

TOR®

a tom doherty associates book

new york

This is a work of fiction. All of the characters, organizations, and events portrayed in this novel are either products of the author's imagination or are used fictitiously.

BOX OFFICE POISON

Copyright © 2013 by Melinda Snodgrass

All rights reserved.

A Tor Book
Published by Tom Doherty Associates, LLC
175 Fifth Avenue
New York, NY 10010

www.tor-forge.com

Tor® is a registered trademark of Tom Doherty Associates, LLC.

Library of Congress Cataloging-in-Publication Data

Bornikova, Phillipa.
  Box office poison / Phillipa Bornikova.
      pages cm
  "A Tom Doherty Associates book."
  ISBN 978-0-7653-2683-6 (hardcover)
  ISBN 978-1-4299-4890-6 (e-book)
  1. Motion pictures—Fiction.   2. Motion picture actors and actresses—Fiction.
3. Women lawyers—Fiction.   4. Vampires—Fiction.   I. Title.
  PS3602.O765B79 2013
  813'.6—dc23

                                                        2013015151

Tor books may be purchased for educational, business, or promotional use. For information on bulk purchases, please contact Macmillan Corporate and Premium Sales Department at 1-800-221-7945 extension 5442 or write specialmarkets@macmillan.com.

First Edition: August 2013

Printed in the United States of America

0 9 8 7 6 5 4 3 2 1

This one is for George (Railroad), who said I might be pretty good at this screenwriting thing, encouraged me to try, introduced me to his agent, and guided my first tentative steps in Tinsel Town. Thanks, George, I couldn't have written this book without your generosity and friendship.

Acknowledgments

I had a lot of help writing this book: Daniel Abraham, Ty Frank, and Walter Jon Williams, who helped me with the initial plot break, because I can't do these without a blueprint. My friend and lawyer, Christie Carbon-Gaul, who talked to me about arbitrations and sent me the AAA Commercial Arbitration Rules and Mediation Procedures. Ian Tregillis, for being my beta reader and letting me talk through scenes when I got confused and who offered sage advice on how to fix problems. Thanks to you all.

BOX OFFICE POISON

1

I looked out the plane's window at Los Angeles, and it looked like any other airport. No palm trees in evidence. No movie stars strolling across the tarmac toward private jets. No surfboards. The only difference between LAX and LaGuardia was the lack of snow.

It was my first trip to the West Coast and I should have been excited. Instead I slumped in my window seat back in steerage and contemplated my exhaustion. I had gotten up at three a.m. so I could brave a blizzard and reach LaGuardia by four thirty so I could catch a six a.m. flight to California. Six and a half hours in coach, and I didn't even get to sleep because I'd been pulled into this arbitration at the last minute by one of the partners at my law firm and I had to review the pleadings.

I hated playing last-minute catchup, but since David Sullivan had saved my life last August I figured I owed him, and seriously, the chance to meet Jeffery Montolbano made it a no-brainer.

I found myself remembering the scene in *Earth Defense Force* where Montolbano, as the heroic Commander Belmanor, had fought his way into the Council Chamber and then, instead of another shootout, had eloquently convinced the Alien Hegemony that Earth should not be destroyed and that humanity was worth saving. The space marine armor left little to the imagination, and sweat had his black hair plastered across his forehead. The negligent way his hands held the large pulse rifle had made more than a few women wish he would caress them just that way. The gossip columns and entertainment shows were filled with rumors about a possible rift with his beautiful actress wife. His charity work got less attention, but such was the world. I wondered if they really were having problems. Then I felt guilty daydreaming about an actor when John O'Shea, the man who had traded his freedom for mine, was trapped in Fey. Then I imagined what John would say and realized I was being stupid. Fantasizing about an actor wasn't some kind of emotional betrayal. I pushed away thoughts of the private investigator who had entered my life for a brief few days last summer. I didn't yet have a solution for breaking him free from the grasp of his Álfar mother, and right now I had a job that required me to focus.

Montolbano was the current president of the Screen Actors Guild, and he was trying to keep the organization from tearing itself to pieces as one set of actors sued another set of actors, the studios, the networks, and the producers, charging that Álfar actors had an unfair advantage over mere humans. As the entire mess crept toward litigation, Montolbano had used a clause in the SAG agreement to force the parties into arbitration.

Various law firms were floated to serve as the impartial arbitrator, and my firm, Ishmael, McGillary and Gold, had been selected. It made sense. We had an office in Los Angeles, but we tended to represent the aerospace industry, and Japanese and Chinese business interests, with limited forays into the entertainment industry, and we weren't strongly affiliated with any one side. Neither talent, as it was euphemistically called, nor the studios and networks. The consensus was that we would be fair, since we didn't really have a dog in this fight.

There was a *ding* as the seat-belt sign went off. People jumped to their feet and began hauling bags out of the overhead compartments. I was way back in the tail section and saw no point in joining the bump and wiggle in the narrow aisle of the airplane. We were trapped until the people up front made it off the plane.

The people two rows in front of me began to move, so I tugged my laptop bag from beneath the seat and stood up. I only had one item in the overhead: my ankle-length, fur-lined, leather coat with a dramatic Anna Karenina hood. I dragged it down and joined the shuffling conga line to freedom. To my exhausted imagination it seemed like I was being slowly extruded from a metal canister.

Passing through the now empty first-class section, I gazed longingly at the wide seats and imagined the champagne that had flowed, the meal that had been served, the in-flight movies. David Sullivan, my boss and the senior attorney, had been seated in first class. He hadn't waited for me; I hadn't really expected him to. He was a vampire and, while courtesy was important, there were limits.

If I had been in a high-powered all-human law firm I would have been flying on the firm's private executive jet, and I wouldn't have had to get up at ugh o'clock to catch a commercial flight. But I was with a white-fang, vampire-owned firm, so we flew commercial.

The reason? Because of all the Powers—vampires, werewolves, and Álfar—that had gone public back in the 1960s the vampires had decided they needed to try the hardest to integrate with the human population. Maybe they were right. They were definitely the scariest of the Powers. Werewolves looked like regular people until they changed, and the Álfar were just gorgeous. I knew from personal experience that that was deceptive, but most people loved the pretty elves. But vampires—the whole dead thing, drinking the blood of living people—gave our little inner monkeys a big shiver. All the Powers were predators; humans just sensed it more viscerally with the vampires.

Running counter to that argument was the fact that it would

make much more sense, given a vampire's aversion to the sun, to fly at night on private jets. So maybe this noblesse oblige argument was just a bogus corporate justification for being cheap.

The focus of all this thought and analysis was waiting just outside the gate. David was tall, slim, pale, with taffy-colored hair and dark brown eyes. Four thick scars gouged his right cheek where a were-wolf's claws had ripped his face. Apparently the windows at the LAX terminals hadn't been treated with UV-reducing glass because he was frowning while he opened his umbrella. I wasn't sure if the frown was meant for me or the windows, and I rushed into speech.

"Sorry, sorry," I said as I juggled purse, coat, and computer bag.

"What are you apologizing for?" he asked in that brusque way he had when dealing with people being codependent.

"You're right. Sorry." I cringed.

"Oh, for God's sake!"

"I mean, not sorry. It's a habit."

"Well, break it."

"I couldn't get off any faster."

I was talking to his back because he'd already started moving toward the escalators and the baggage claim. I yanked up the handle on my rolling computer bag, hurried after him, and wished I hadn't taken off my shoes during the flight because my feet had swelled and now the black pumps were pinching.

At the foot of the escalator there was a scrum of limo drivers in dark suits holding little signs with names on them. SULLIVAN was among them. A tall, ebony-skinned man studied the umbrella that shaded David and stepped forward, smiling, and introduced himself as our driver, Kobe.

We followed him through a pair of sliding glass doors and stood by the slowly revolving luggage carousel. There were a lot of hard-sided golf bags, tennis rackets, and even some scuba gear salted in among the suitcases. David's was already on the carousel. In a continuation of the-universe-makes-Linnet–the-big-holdup, it was thirty minutes before my suitcase came sliding down the ramp.

Kobe collected the bags and we followed him out of the terminal. The dampness beneath my cashmere sweater became full-blown sweat. It was one thirty in the afternoon. The temperature had to be in the low eighties and here I was dressed in a white wool skirt, beige cashmere sweater, and knee-high brown boots lugging a leather and fur-lined overcoat.

As we trailed Kobe across the street toward a parking structure I watched limos in various colors and designs with darkly tinted windows pull up and sweep away people wearing wide hats and large sunglasses. Interesting how celebrities and vampires were almost indistinguishable in this town. Since we were heading to a garage I figured we didn't rate a limo. I was right. A Lincoln town car was our ride. With the luggage stowed and David and me in the backseat, we headed out into Los Angeles.

I live in New York City. I'm used to traffic, but there was something about Los Angeles traffic that was overwhelming. Maybe it was just the sheer size of the city. New York was crazy, but it was contained. When we hit the ramp onto the 405 Freeway, Kobe glanced back and asked us, "Do you want to go to your hotel first or to the office?"

Hotel, I wanted to shriek, but the question was directed at David, and he gave the expected answer.

"Office."

I wanted to punch him, and as I sulked I reflected on how much it sucked to be the human paired with a vampire. They were always perfectly dressed and pressed. They didn't need sleep, so why should you? Dirt seemed to slide off them as if they were made of Teflon. I could only think of one time when David had been anything but perfectly groomed. It was when he'd rescued me (literally) from the jaws of death when an out-of-control werewolf had tried to kill me and my clients. During that fight he'd torn his suit and had the skin on one cheek nearly ripped off.

He still bore the scars from that battle because vampires didn't heal all that well. Scientists and medical researchers who studied vampirism still had no idea why dead men could function and survive anything but fire or decapitation. One thing they did know: The vampire infection led to a tendency to form keloids— overgrown, exuberant scar tissue. You could actually judge the age of a vampire by the number of scars. I had a feeling modern vampires weren't going to bear the scars of existence the way ancient vamps did. We lived in a far less violent time, and people didn't generally carry bladed weapons. But car wrecks were still going to leave their mark, I thought.

Muffled by the car windows, but still distinct, I heard the beat of propellers. Kobe indicated the cover on the sunroof. "May I?" he asked David. The vampire nodded and huddled in a corner of the backseat.

Once the cover was pulled back we saw a police helicopter and three press helicopters churning past overhead.

"Must be a really bad wreck up ahead," Kobe remarked.

"Perhaps that explains our snail-like progress," David said.

Kobe hit the turn signal, and slowly worked his way through the traffic to an exit marked SANTA MONICA BLVD/CENTURY CITY. I knew the address for the Los Angeles office was Avenue of the Stars, Century City. I saw a collection of skyscrapers ahead and to the right and assumed that's where we were headed. They weren't all that tall by New York standards, but in this city of low sprawl they stood out. They were also aggressively modern and very black.

We passed a gigantic Mormon temple on our left. On the right were shabby strip malls filled with nail salons and small ethnic restaurants. Then we turned down the broad avenue and shabby went away. There was a large shopping mall with digital billboards alternating between expensive electronics and chic women with pouty expressions. The street was clogged with luxury cars—in the space of a block I saw multiple BMWs, Mercedes, Lexuses, and even a Ferrari. Men in tailored suits and equally well dressed women hurried through crosswalks. Kobe turned into an underground parking lot beneath a black and glass tower and stopped at the valet parking area.

He unloaded David's briefcase and my computer bag. "I'll be waiting here to take you to your hotel," he said.

We rode the elevator to the lobby, and then another elevator to the twenty-third floor. "Is this office managed by a vampire partner?" I asked as the floors flashed past.

"Naturally," David said. "But Jackson is in Singapore negotiating a trade agreement. Our liaison will be Hank Pizer. He handles the small amount of entertainment law we do."

"And he's a vampire?"

"Yes."

We stepped out and made our way to the end of the hall and the tall steel and glass double doors. ISHMAEL, MCGILLARY & GOLD was emblazoned in stainless steel script across the pediment. David held the door for me, and I stepped into a beehive of activity. Phones were ringing, young lawyers were hurrying past reading off iPads or sheaves of paper, and there was the click of computer keyboards like technological rain. The windows were UV-tinted and looked out at some hills that I guess passed for mountains in southern California. The floor underfoot was glossy bamboo, and the furniture was extremely modern. It didn't look like a place a vampire would find comfortable.

A tall and lushly built woman with deep red hair piled high on her head left her desk and crossed to us. Her sky blue sundress displayed her every curve and deep décolletage.

"May I help you?" she asked, her voice low and husky.

Of course it was, I thought bitterly, as I stared up at her and felt the uncomfortable wetness beneath my arms. I should have had Kobe pull out my suitcase and changed into California clothes in the bathroom instead of continuing to swelter in my New York winter outfit.

"David Sullivan and Linnet Ellery in from New York," David answered.

"I'll tell Mr. Pizer you're here. I'm Elaine Gowdry, Mr. Pizer's personal assistant. Junie," Elaine called over her shoulder, "please put Ms. Ellery and Mr. Sullivan in the corner conference room."

Junie, who turned out to be a tall, gorgeous, willowy black woman, led us to the conference room. There was a giant stack of file folders already on the oval table. As I unlimbered my laptop and David snapped open his briefcase, Junie asked,

"Something to drink? Coffee?"

"Something cold," I said, plucking my sweater away from my damp skin.

"Water? Soft drink?"

"Coke, please," I said, deciding I needed a blast of sugar and caffeine if I was going to stay on my feet.

"And you, sir. We have a good choice of types."

"Something rich," David said.

So, I thought, he's tired.

Junie returned with a cut crystal glass filled with ice and an ice-cold can of Coke. Another assistant, a young man with carefully styled "casual" hair, carried a goblet of blood. He made eye contact with David and smoldered. When that didn't work he tried a twinkle. Neither one elicited a response. Looking disconsolate, the young man followed Junie out of the room.

"Do you ever get tired of it?" I asked

"What?"

"Having young straight men flirt with you?

David made a face and frowned down into his glass. "Puppy," he growled. For a moment I thought that was his final word on the subject, but he surprised me and continued. "Why do these children think we'd find them useful additions to the community? They know nothing, have done nothing. They're just pretty."

"And who vets potential candidates? Do you have to run it past the Council or can an individual just Make a vampire?" I asked. "Because, seriously, who thought Ryan was a good choice? A vampire who was seducing female associates and risking everybody's lives."

"It's a personal choice." David gave the tight, closed-lip vampire smile. "To question another's actions is tantamount to a challenge."

The way he said *challenge* made it seem like a piece of vampire etiquette, one that I had never heard of, despite being fostered in a vampire household.

I was getting answers from one of the notoriously close-mouthed members of the Powers. I decided to see how long it would last. "Given your strictures against turning women, does that mean there are a lot of gay vampires . . . or at least gay men who became vampires?"

"Are you asking about my sexuality?" David asked.

I shook my head. "No. It's me blurting out whatever is in my head. It's also about me adding to my store of vampire lore and understanding. But now that you mention it, are you . . . were you gay?"

David laughed. It wasn't the reaction I expected. "Linnet, Linnet, you are the oddest human I know. Perhaps it's because you were fostered, but you seem to be completely fearless about us."

"Let's just say unimpressed," I said.

"But still curious."

"Very."

"Your liege never discussed these matters?"

"Mr. Bainbridge wasn't your typical vampire, and even he would never discuss sex with a young woman in his care."

"And neither will I," David said.

"Because you consider me in your care? Because I'm a woman? Or because you're uncomfortable talking about it?"

David leaned back in his chair and took another long drink of blood. "You're a good lawyer, Linnet. No matter which part of that question I answer, and no matter how I answer it, I'm fucked."

I smiled at him, and he gave me a smile in return. At that moment the door to the conference room flew open, and a slim vampire of middle height blew in. Hank Pizer had a narrow, sharp-featured face with bright blue eyes and slicked-back black hair. Unlike every other vampire I'd ever met he had a deep tan. I looked closer and realized he had used a self-tanning spray. That was startling. More startling was the broad smile that he bestowed on us, revealing his long, pointed canines.

"Hey, Davy . . . Linnie. Welcome to LaLa Land."

I didn't mind the diminutive, having been called that for much of my childhood, but it was surprising to hear it from someone I hadn't even technically met, especially given the formality of the New York office. I glanced at David, expecting an explosion. Again, he surprised me. He just sighed and shook his head.

"Hank, strive to recall that you're a vampire now. You can get away with it around me, but don't try it with the senior partners."

"Yes, Daddy," Pizer said. Startled, I looked to David, but he studiously avoided my gaze.

Pizer flung himself into a chair. "So, here we are. In the center of a legal shit storm." His expression said how much he loved it.

"Let's discuss the case," David said.

Pizer shrugged. "You got the papers."

"I'd like your take on it," David said. "Right now it looks like one set of pretty, vapid, and narcissistic people is mad at another group of even prettier, more vapid, and far more narcissistic people."

"With that attitude toward actors you'd make a great producer,"

Pizer said. "Okay. Short version. The Powers come out. By the mid-1970s a few Álfar are starting to join the Screen Actors Guild and auditioning for parts, and getting them too, but it's just a trickle, so no big whoop. But then a lot of bankable human stars start to age and die, and more Álfar show up, and new, young execs take control of the studios and the networks. They're comfortable around the Powers, so they cast more Álfar, and then more Álfar come to Hollywood and join SAG. Now the Guild is half-human and half-Álfar, but guess who's getting most of the juicy roles?"

"The Álfar," I said.

Pizer made a gun with his forefinger and pretended to shoot me. "Right in one. They are awesome in the room."

"What does that mean?" I asked.

"That's Hollywood speak. You don't have a meeting, you *get in a room together.*"

"Well, that's obnoxious," David said.

"Point is, they're prettier than humans."

"Their charisma doesn't translate to the screen," I said. "They are gorgeous, but I know—knew—an Álfar. It's just not the same." John's perfect features swam briefly before my mind's eye.

"Yeah, but it doesn't matter. It works in the audition, and like you said, they are gorgeous," Pizer said.

"All of which proves my point. This is unworthy of serious legal action," David huffed.

"So what? You want me to tell them to forget it? Get a different firm? It's taken months to get the human actors, the Álfar actors, the studios, the networks, and all their lawyers to agree on Ishmael, and it's a big payday for the firm."

"Of course I'm not saying that." David shook his head like a bull bedeviled by flies. "I'm just complaining. It's too sunny here, and I can already tell I hate both sides, and this actor Montolbano who drew us into this."

"There's something I don't understand," I said. "The parties picked IMG to arbitrate. Why not use you? You're here. You do entertainment law. Why bring us in from New York?"

"Because I'm a *player*," Hank said.

"And Hank can always be found at a Hollywood party," David said somewhat sourly. "Not exactly impartial. Or so the argument would go."

Pizer did the gun/finger thing again. Hank was rather charming for a vampire, but I decided this 1970s habit could get real old real fast. "Exactly. They know we've got the moxie—as you would say—to handle this issue," he grinned at David. "But folks on the West Coast figured you cold, proper Yankees wouldn't be appropriately impressed with Hollywood glitz and glamour."

"Well, they'd be wrong," I said.

David slewed around in his chair and stared at me. "Oh, don't tell me you're a fan."

"There isn't a woman breathing who doesn't think Montolbano is hot, hot, hot," I said. Pizer gave a wild laugh.

"For an actor he's also whip smart," Pizer said. "It was genius to propose an arbitration before his guild tore itself apart."

I stood and crossed to the stack of folders, laid my hand on top. "We got the Cliff Notes version of this. I'm assuming that witnesses have been approved and most depositions have been taken?"

"Yeah, we're ready to rock and roll," Pizer said.

"I don't suppose you have copies of all this so we can read in our hotel rooms?" I asked.

"Of course I do. I'm Mr. Organization. Copies are already in each of your rooms and a second set in your offices. And no offense, but you look whipped."

I forced a smile and counted to ten. Vampires are all about the courtesy except when they're unbelievably rude, because humans just don't rate.

"I am pretty tired."

"Have the driver take you to the hotel," David said. "I'll stay here. The windows are UV-protected, and the blood is fresh."

I gathered up my belongings and started for the door. "Hey," Pizer said to David as I was leaving, "I didn't know that place in Cabo was just a front for the mob. I'm making up for it this time. You're staying at the Beverly fucking Hills Hotel. Just one of the premier hotels in LA. Why are you always such a—"

I shut the door behind me, cutting off the bickering, rolled my eyes, and headed for the elevators.

2

Kobe didn't return to the freeway. Instead we drove up a curving, tree-shaded street lined with giant houses that ranged from mission style to bloated Tudors. The lawns were manicured swathes of green, and crews of gardeners wielded lawn mowers, leaf blowers, and clippers against various vegetation.

"This is Beverly Hills," Kobe said from the front seat.

"Oh," I said.

"Rodeo Drive is a couple of blocks east of your office."

"Oh," I said again, and wondered if every limo driver played tour guide? Of course this was the town where they sold maps to movie stars' homes. Most people probably wanted to hear about these world-famous locations. I decided maybe I ought to offer more to the conversation, so I added, "That's the big shopping area, right?"

"Oh, yeah. You can drop twenty grand fast on Rodeo Drive."

"Guess I won't be shopping there."

Kobe laughed. "I hear you."

I leaned forward a bit, and studied the passing houses. They seemed to alternate between multistoried French châteaux, and sprawling Spanish-style haciendas. "So this is where the movie stars live?"

"Some of them. A lot of them live in Bel Air and on Mount Olympus."

"You're kidding, right? That can't really be the name of a subdivision."

He laid a hand over his heart. "Scout's honor. It's a real place. We won't be anywhere near Olympus, but we'll be driving right past the entrance to Bel Air. You'll see the guard gates."

The town car made a turn onto Sunset Boulevard, and a few blocks later Kobe pointed out the entrance to Bel Air. There wasn't much to see. Just a very steep driveway and a guardhouse manned by two men in private security uniforms. The houses were all screened by bushes and trees. A Jaguar was waiting while the guards inspected the driver's license. I wondered if a Jag was too déclassé for Bel Air? The traffic was really moving on this wide boulevard, and with all the trees and grass I could forget I was in a giant city. Kobe made a turn toward the hills and we wound up a narrow road. A discreet sign indicated the Beverly Hills Hotel. We turned up the driveway and the hotel came into view.

It was very . . . pink. It had three Mission-style towers that marked the main building and the entrance. Kobe pulled up to the front entrance and hopped out to open my door. A cute, young, redheaded bellman hurried down the red-carpeted steps to gather up my luggage. Kobe also gave him David's garment bag and told him it should be placed in Mr. Sullivan's room. I tipped Kobe and thanked him for the tour, then followed the redhead into the lobby.

A sleek, dark-haired bellhop took David's bag and disappeared out the back door. The redhead led me to the elevators. "My room isn't near Mr. Sullivan?"

"No, he's booked into a bungalow. You have a deluxe guest room. They're still nice, just not *as* nice."

"Okay."

"So what brings you here? Audition?" he asked. The smile he gave me had enough teeth to qualify for a toothpaste commercial. As he held the door and allowed me to precede him into the elevator.

"I'm not an actress. I'm a lawyer."

"No way. You're way too pretty to be a lawyer."

I knew it was absolutely insincere, that I looked like something the cat had dragged in, but it felt nice anyway. We went down a hall, and he opened the door for me. The room was very well appointed in tones of gold and cream. I was really glad they hadn't continued with the pink theme. There was only so much pink I could stand. I tipped the redheaded schmooze king and studiously ignored the giant stack of folders on the desk. Instead I opened my suitcase and arranged my toiletries in the bathroom. I looked at the big tub and contemplated a long soak in hot water. I walked back into the main room and studied the bed. Next I looked at the files. Sleep? Bathe? Eat? Work? My stomach won out. It might be three o'clock in New York, but it was just past noon in LA. I could have lunch.

Grabbing a room service menu, I studied the options and decided on a fruit and yogurt salad. While I waited I unpacked and wondered why on earth I had brought so many clothes? *Because you might be in LA for a number of weeks, if not months,* was the answer. I tucked my English riding boots into the closet and decided I would call around for stables and tack shops tomorrow. I could always rent a slug at a riding stable, but if you have skills and training, there is always a rank horse that somebody will let you ride if you're willing to be a crash dummy, or a horse who needs exercising because the owner has gotten pregnant or is too busy to ride. I had cadged rides my whole life, I figured it would be no different in California.

My salad arrived. It was good, but the price tag was rather staggering. I sat at the desk and wondered if the home office would get me an apartment? It would be less expensive than a hotel room, and in an apartment I could cook, which would reduce the chance of weight gain. Eating out all the time was hell on a body

I thought about working, but instead I turned on the flat-screen TV for company. As I was clicking through the channels I noticed that many of the broadcast channels had a breaking news bulletin. I finally found a local news channel, which was running multiple screens. On one screen there was a helicopter view of a deep blue Ferrari heading down one of the freeways followed by five police cruisers. Stuck behind the phalanx of cops was all the rest of the freeway traffic. Another screen showed a video from an amateur photographer standing on an overpass. Still another showed the newsroom with a pretty, blond female news anchor, her pretty male counterpart, and a former cop discussing the unfolding chase. It didn't look like much of a chase, since, according to the commentary, the Ferrari was moving at a very discreet thirty miles an hour. I wondered if this was the source of the traffic jam from earlier in the day. If so the cops were certainly not in any hurry to resolve the situation.

"Do you think they'll use spikes?" the male anchor asked.

"Those can be risky, and Kerrinan Ta Shena is famous," the woman said.

And I had my explanation. Kerrinan was an Álfar heart throb. Had starred in a boatload of movies. I'd seen a number of them. He was also the primary spokesman for the Android smartphone.

"Not when you're moving that slow, and no one is above the law," said the ex-cop piously.

So what had happened that he was driving on a freeway with a phalanx of cops? I remembered his wife had died—no, been killed: it had been in the news a few weeks ago. But if they were talking road spikes to deflate the tires, it looked like the authorities had begun to suspect the spouse.

"I wonder why they don't just move in," the female anchor asked.

"Well, there's a problem with that, Trina," the male anchor said in a tone that made it sound like she was retarded. "The Álfar have this ability to move in and out of our reality. Makes it tough to make an arrest."

"So why hasn't he done it? Why hasn't he left our world? Why spend hours in this glacial chase?"

"You'll have to ask him that, Trina, once he's apprehended."

They were joined by a Hollywood reporter, and the group began to discuss Kerrinan's films. He specialized in frothy romantic comedies where a human woman wins out over all the Álfar hotties for the heart of an elf lord. It had happened in real life too; Kerrinan had married a human actress, Michelle Balley. They had been Hollywood's "it couple." Until she fetched up dead.

There was something riveting about the chase, or maybe that was because I was so tired. I ate, watched the images on the tube, and listened to the never-ending babble. In an effort to fill the slowly passing minutes the reporters and experts in the studio, and their compatriots in the helicopter, in cars, and on bridges, rehashed the events that had led to this chase.

Three weeks ago Kerrinan had called the police to his Bel Air mansion. They found Michelle brutally murdered, and Kerrinan covered in blood and claiming no memory of the events. His defense attorneys claimed he'd gotten the blood on himself from holding his murdered wife, and that grief and shock had affected his memory. But forensics told a different story. DNA evidence proved that Kerrinan had wielded the knife that killed his wife. The police had been going to his house to arrest him when Kerrinan had fled into the garage, jumped in the Ferrari, and hit the highway. There was more speculation from the blow-dried news readers that the actor had been tipped off by a fan in the police department.

"Or maybe he just saw the flashing cherries and realized it wasn't a parade," the ex-cop said with a look of pity and contempt for the news anchors.

Forty minutes later I realized nothing had changed or was going to change. I reached for the remote to turn off the TV, when the male model newsreader suddenly shouted, "Whoa!" as the car shimmered, pulsed in and out of view as it phased in and out of our reality, and then vanished.

So, that's what it looks like from outside, I thought, and remembered John's and my mad flight from Virginia to New York City last summer as we were pursued by Securitech and killer werewolves. I also remembered how it ended: in the Álfar equivalent of the Dakota as John's real mother had forced him to choose between me and my clients—a terrified mother and daughter—and his own freedom. Of course John had done the noble thing.

The male anchor was gabbling, almost hyperventilating. Even though he had corrected his female counterpart in a particularly snotty way, he had clearly never seen the effect and maybe didn't believe the Álfar could actually do it.

And suddenly the incongruity of the whole thing struck me. As the retired cop had said, if Kerrinan had spotted the cops, why not just step out of his house and into the Fey? Why get into a car and spend hours in a slow-motion chase down the LA freeways when you had the power to be gone in an instant? It didn't make any sense.

I waited a few more minutes, but the Ferrari didn't reappear and the chatter became an endless loop. So Kerrinan had fled to the Fey. I wondered how the DA's office in LA was going to cope with that? There were so many Álfar in Los Angeles, maybe California had some kind of extradition treaty with the Álfar? Maybe it would have application in New York? The federal kidnapping statutes should have applied to John. I'd raised that with the FBI, and then with a Department of Justice lawyer in the Manhattan office, who'd looked at me like I'd been on crack.

I decided I'd talk to the California DA. I turned off the television. Thinking about John and my, so far, ineffectual attempts to free him made me depressed. I realized I hadn't called John's parents in Philadelphia with an update in over a month. I had met Big Red, the retired policeman, and his wife Meg shortly after John had been trapped and told them exactly what had happened. I owed them that much. They were lovely people, neither college-educated nor wealthy, but good, solid middle-class Americans who had raised four human kids and one changeling, all of them growing up to serve their communities as a firefighter, a nurse, a fisherman, a Marine, and John, who had followed his father into the police force. I shouldn't be dodging them just because I hadn't made any progress on freeing their son. *Who's trapped because of you*, whispered a nasty voice.

I tried to drown the depression with a hot bath. When that didn't work I settled for a nap.

A shrilling ring brought me awake. It was dark in the room, and I fumbled for the phone, knocked it onto the floor, cursed, kicked away the covers, and finally ended up kneeling naked on the carpet pressing the receiver to my ear.

"What? Yes? Hello? Hello?"

"Good Lord, what are you doing in there? Wrestling crocodiles?" David's cool baritone filled my ear.

"You woke me up." I scraped the hair off my face.

"Sorry."

"No, it's okay." Outside the wind set the fronds on the palm trees to rattling like castanets, whistled around the railing of the balcony, and rain exploded against the sliding glass doors. "What time is it?"

"Ten past seven."

"Oh, shit."

"Yes, we're meeting Montolbano at seven thirty."

"Why didn't you get me up?" I said, scrambling to my feet.

"I just did," came the snotty reply.

"In time to get dressed and put on my makeup!"

"You'll look fine."

"I guess being dead has made you forget everything you ever knew about women," I said. I forced myself to unclench my teeth, lunged at the closet, and started tossing outfits on the bed.

"Look, we were going to meet in the bar. I'll have him come to my bungalow instead. That should buy you a few more minutes."

"Great! Thanks."

Jeffery Montolbano. Holy shit. I raced into the bathroom, pulled out my makeup, washed and then made up my face. I went with the more dramatic yellow and brown eye shadow rather than the paler daywear. Eyeliner, lip liner, lipstick. Hair dryer to fluff my bed-head hair. Ready.

Back into the bedroom to pick an outfit. *Jeffery Montolbano.* I sat on the bed and pulled on my panty hose. *Movie star.*

Client. The sensible part of myself was standing off to the side waving her hand for attention as I got my bra hooked.

I selected a pale gold watered-silk sleeveless dress, the skirt of which came to rest a couple of inches above my knee. It had a square neck that worked well, given my height. I added a multistrand necklace of gray pearls and a gold bracelet. I threw on the matching thigh-length jacket and slid on a pair of very high-heeled black pumps. I paused to dither over the rolling briefcase but decided to leave it behind. This was dinner, not a formal meeting, and the case was dorky—practical but dorky.

The cute redheaded bellhop was in the lobby, and he pulled out a large golf umbrella to escort me down the pathways to David's bungalow. Flowering bushes shivered and shed water as we passed, and I felt the cold spray against my legs. The bungalow was tucked discreetly away behind bushes and trees. A winding walkway led to the front door. We reached the door, but before I could knock the bellhop thrust a thick card into my hand.

"My friend Nu says he drove Jeffery Montolbano out here in the golf cart. Montolbano's starting to produce now. May even start directing. I'm so going to drive the cart when you guys leave, even if I have to wrestle Nu." Then in an abrupt change of topic he added, "Maybe you could give this to him?" It was a business card, but one of the new kind that was a flash card and could be read on a computer. It showed the smiling face of the redhead and the words "Toby Wilson, Actor."

"Who? Nu?" I asked, confused.

Impatient. "No, Montolbano. Thanks."

"I don't know if I—"

But he knocked and David answered before I could finish my demurrers.

"Just call when your party is ready to leave, and we'll send the golf cart so you can stay dry," Toby said brightly. David gave him five dollars and I used the cover of the tip to stuff the card in my pocket as I stepped over the threshold.

Being a partner clearly rated. There was a sitting room with a gas fireplace. The blue-tinged flames flickered cozily. Sofas, armchairs, and a coffee table surrounded the fireplace, and I saw a cheese platter and a tray with a wine glass and an open bottle of merlot. There was a small garden patio off the sitting room, the plants and potted flowers drooping from the rain, and a separate bedroom. A brief glance through the door showed a four-poster bed adorned with floating draperies.

A man was seated on the sofa, one arm outstretched along the back and a glass of wine in his other hand. I noticed how the light reflected off his perfectly manicured nails. He had glossy black hair flecked lightly with gray. It was long enough to brush the top of his cashmere and silk turtleneck sweater. He stood and turned to face me. It was Jeffery Montolbano. He was gorgeous . . . and short. I'm no giant, but he was only a few inches taller than me. He came around the sofa, giving me plenty of time to appreciate his chiseled cheekbones, square jaw, lush lower lip, and trim, narrow-hipped body. He held out a hand.

His brown eyes, warm and humorous, were locked on mine, and I found myself unable to look away. His handshake was firm and lasted longer than was strictly necessary. "How do you do? I'm Jeff. You must be Linnet." He had a basic midwestern American accent that was totally devoid of his famous, faintly European on-screen cadence.

"Ye-yes," I stammered. I thought I caught a glimpse of David rolling his eyes.

"Wine?"

"Uh . . . yes . . . please."

We all moved to the fireplace. David settled into a large armchair, which left me on the sofa with the actor. Montolbano filled the glass and handed it to me. His fingers brushed mine. I wondered if it was deliberate? It was certainly electric. Then he said to David, "You're sure we can't get you anything?"

"No, thanks, I'd rather wait for dinner than drink decanted."

There was the briefest flicker of discomfort, then Montolbano's expression went completely blank as he covered. I glanced toward David, but he had caught it. In the forty or so years since the Powers went public, vampires had gotten very good at catching human cues.

"Or maybe I'll just nip over to the hotel restaurant now and grab a bite." The words hung in the air, and David looked like someone who had just swallowed a particularly large and disgusting fly as the irony hit.

Now it was my turn to roll my eyes. We all sat in frozen silence for a moment, then the actor started laughing. "Wow, phrases like that just have all kinds of meaning now."

"Yes, yes, they do," David said. "But seriously, that sounds like a good idea. I work among humans who are accustomed to vampires, and Linnet, in addition to working at the firm, was fostered in a vampire household. I forget that others might not be as comfortable with our . . . dietary needs."

He started for the door, picking up an umbrella on his way. "I shouldn't be gone above half an hour, and then I'll keep you company while you two eat."

A new concern intruded, prompted by the empty hole I felt in the pit of my stomach. "We'll be really late for our reservation. Should we call? Or will they hold it?"

Montolbano spoke up. "I made it. They'll hold it."

"Excellent," David said, and he left.

I took a sip of wine and tried to think of some innocuous social prattle. I considered saying something about his charity work with the Special Olympics, the restraining order he'd had to get against a woman who thought she was going to marry him even though he was already happily married. As usual that didn't happen. My penchant for saying whatever I thought took hold. "I know you're famous and all, but why would they hold it if we're really late?"

"Because someone on the staff has informed the paparazzi, and they'll get a kickback from any pictures sold. They will not be happy if I go someplace else."

"People do that?"

"Oh, yes. Morgue attendants, nurses, cops, gardeners, pool boys, waiters, limo drivers." He ticked off the list on his fingers and seemed amused. "Am I missing anybody?"

"That's . . . that's horrible."

He smiled at me. "Welcome to Tinsel Town. Where the only coin is fame, and fame is fleeting." He shrugged. "It's a lucrative business, and I don't begrudge them. This is a tough town if you don't have money. Everybody else feeds off the famous, so why not them?"

We both fell silent. Being female, and knowing that most women (and probably more than a few men) in America would kill to be in my position, I searched around for a new topic of conversation. Something safer. "So," I said brightly, "I thought it never rained in California?"

"Only in January and February. Then the vegetation goes crazy on the hills and in the canyons. Next, the summer drought hits and it all becomes a tinder box. Somewhere in August and September the fires start and burn down some houses. Then the winter rains come and cause the mudslides that take out a few more houses. And then the whole cycle repeats. With the occasional earthquake thrown in so things don't get boring." He tried to keep it light, but I heard a cry of despair beneath the bantering delivery.

"Really love this place, don't you?" I said sarcastically.

He gave me a sad, weary smile. "Caught that, did you? Yeah, I'm sick to death of it all. The traffic, the smog, the constant hustle from everybody." I slipped a hand into my pocket and touched the bell-hop's video card. "Running as fast as you can to stay in one spot."

I hadn't expected the *Through the Looking-Glass* allusion. It made me look past the handsome face and wonder about the man inside the public figure. He took a long drink of wine.

"And now this fucking lawsuit."

"But you're the one who forced it into arbitration," I said.

"Yeah, because actors have enough problems without fighting each other like a bunch of caged badgers. There are two hundred thousand members in SAG worldwide. At any given moment only a handful are working. Add to that the avatar technology where you can create a computer-generated actor, and you wonder how long before we all become voice talent. And now Álfar versus human." He sighed. "The studios must be fucking loving this. A house divided and all that."

David returned. His color was high, cheeks fuller. He had fed, and well, it seemed. Jeff stood.

"Okay, shall we go?"

At that moment a gust of wind sent a palm frond sailing into the patio, and the pelting rain plastered against the sliding glass doors. It flopped like an alien creature. "Maybe we should call for the golf cart," I said, and picked up the phone.

Apparently Toby won the arm wrestling contest with Nu because he was driving the cart. We all ducked from the door into the uncertain cover of the golf cart, and Toby kept up an unending stream of artless prattle while we made the two-minute drive to the doors of the lobby. Maybe he thought he was being charming, but he came across like a desperate court jester, flinging out bad jokes and flop sweat. David stared at the young man in bemusement, while Montolbano looked like a stone effigy. I writhed with embarrassment for the kid.

Montolbano gave his valet ticket to the bell captain, and a few minutes later the large model BMW convertible, top prudently up, arrived. We hurried down the red carpet beneath the awning. The doorman, umbrella at the ready, opened the doors for us. I expected to end up in the backseat while the men sat up front and talked, but David surprised me by sliding into the back. I climbed in, the door was shut, and Montolbano pulled away

"No driver?" David asked.

"I get driven whenever I'm on a shoot, but I like cars, and I like to drive." Montolbano gave a shrug. "And sometimes I just like the privacy of a car and my own head."

3

Montolbano took us back to Sunset Boulevard and headed east. The parklike scenery gave way to tall office buildings and more upscale strip malls. Some of the tall buildings sported giant billboards with movie posters. One of them was a thirty-foot-tall image of the man seated next to me. It was advertising his latest movie, *Steel Pinnacle,* which didn't tell me much. There was a big skyscraper; Montolbano, looking grim, grimy, and gritty, was dressed in Ninja black and holding a big gun.

I must have made some sound because Jeff gave me a look out of the corner of his eye and said, "Go ahead—you can laugh. It's a gobbler."

"But will it make money?" David asked from the backseat.

"I have no doubt."

"But you just said it was terrible," I objected.

He looked over and smiled that ten-thousand-watt smile. "Linnet, there's no connection between quality and the box office. You saw *Transformers,* right?" Jeff drove in silence for a moment. I watched the headlights and the light from neon signs play across the chiseled cheekbones and square jaw. "I'm getting a little long in the tooth for these action films. I don't want to end up like Harrison

Ford or Stallone, embarrassing myself. I'm in that awkward stage. Too old for action hero. Too young for eccentric geezer roles. That's why I'm moving more into producing and directing."

"Must be hard when everything revolves around how you look," I said.

"Yeah, it's a tough business and every rejection is very personal." He added in an nasal singsong. "You're too short. Too tall. Too ethnic-looking. Your tits are too small, too big. Your voice is too high. Too low. Not pretty enough. Not young enough. All stuff you can't change. Really personal and really hurtful. I got lucky, became famous. Now I get asked. I don't audition anymore. But I ache for the kids. I see what it does to them. I try to be kind and encouraging, but now that I'm making movies I'm the one making those kind of judgments."

"So why do it?" David again.

Jeff glanced back and shot him a smile. "If I could answer that question I'd have saved myself a fortune in couch time, and I'd be making a fortune counseling other actors. I don't know. . . . Why do I act? I'm insecure? I crave attention? Truth is, I love making movies from both sides of the camera. On the first day of principal photography, when you hear an actor deliver that first line of dialog . . . well, it's a total high." As if embarrassed by his own enthusiasm he added in a blasé tone, "And the pay ain't bad either."

He took us into a turning bay and made a U-turn. A red umbrella marked a valet parking service in front of a two-story white building with lots of windows, and the word KETCHUP in bright red letters on the wall. The rain was still pissing down, but there was a gaggle of men in raincoats or windbreakers trying to protect their cameras. Not ordinary cameras either. These had lenses that looked like you could sight in on Saturn, they were so long and the apertures were so wide.

David had spotted them too, and he had the vampire's usual reaction to most things human. "Idiots," he muttered as we pulled to a stop.

A couple of men in short red jackets rushed forward to open the car doors for us. One of them, an elderly man with a weather-seamed face and iron gray hair, offered his hand to assist me out of the car. His palm was rough and callused, his thin black pants and jacket were soaked through, and rain ran down his face.

Then I had other things to worry about because the minute my leg emerged from the car the frantic whir and click of digital cameras began. I had a flashback to that awful picture of me in the *New York Post* last year, and I wished my skirt was longer. The maître d' came rushing out the front door of the restaurant armed with a giant golf umbrella; behind him was a hostess with another large umbrella. David, Jeff, and I were now protected from the elements. Jeff took my arm, pulled me close to his side, and paused to smile and wave at the throng of photographers.

"Who's the babe?" somebody yelled from the crowd. Jeff just gave an enigmatic smile. I opened my mouth to call "Lawyer, I'm a lawyer," but then we were hustled into the interior of Ketchup.

"Well, that was unbelievably humiliating," David said.

"Bread and circuses, my friend, bread and circuses. You've got to give the public what it wants." Then he added in a lower tone, "Or they'll eat you alive."

"Yeah, but does that include staking me in front of them like a gazelle at a tiger hunt?" I asked. Jeff realized I was annoyed and looked contrite.

"I'm sorry," he said with absolute sincerity, and I liked him again.

It didn't seem to mollify David, however. He said rather acidly, "You do that very well. Do you rehearse it in front of a mirror?"

Which had me then wondering if it really had been sincere or if I had just fallen victim to a masterful performance?

We were turned over to a beautiful young hostess, who took us up in the elevator to the second floor and the main body of the restaurant. Her demeanor was obsequious and flirtatious as she led us to our table, the only open table in the place. It was definitely a happening place. Some of the other customers pointedly pretended a famous movie star was not walking past, but others stared and whispered. The waitstaff was mostly female, all very pretty and dressed in strappy mini bandage dresses that barely covered their rear ends. I suddenly felt like a dowdy librarian in my dress and jacket.

The decor was very sleek, very modern, and very red. The lights looked like suspended red balloons; then I thought about the name and realized they were meant to represent tomatoes. The upholstery on the chairs and booths was white leather, and my heels clicked on the hard shiny white floor. Large pieces of modern art adorned the walls; many were pictures of ketchup bottles.

One little girl ran up with a napkin clutched in her hand.

"Please, may I have an autograph?"

Montolbano knelt in front of her. "Of course, honey, what's your name?

"Samantha."

Pulling a pen out of his pocket he wrote, "For Samantha, reach for the stars, best, Jeffery Montolbano." The little girl looked stunned, and her father was snapping pictures with his phone. Montolbano didn't hurry, he posed for quite some time with the child. In that moment he became Jeff for me.

Just before her father led her away Jeff asked, "Would you like a Space Command pin?"

The child was speechless with joy. She could only nod vigorously. Jeff pulled an enamel pin from his pocket and pressed it into her plump little hand.

We were led to a plush booth that could easily have accommodated another three people. I leaned back to rest and realized my feet were kicking in the air as if I were a five-year-old. On the table in place of flowers or a candle was a juicy red tomato in a glass box. I wondered how many tomatoes got wasted every night, maybe even twice a day if you added in lunch. Or did they get served in the next meal's salad? I tried to make a quick count of the number of tables but gave up.

The menu was eccentric. Lots of things with ketchup and very all-American. Jeff went with the Barking Dogs appetizer, which was two mini Kobe beef hotdogs, chili, melted cheddar, and homemade ketchup. The idea of making hotdogs out of Kobe beef sort of hurt my head. I went with the Californication appetizer which was Dungeness crab cakes with chili lime aioli. In an effort to keep down the calories I went with a cup of the lobster bisque for my main course, while Jeff ordered this giant twelve-ounce Kobe burger with bacon and blue cheese. He also added the Threesome appetizer, which was garlic parmesan, sweet potato, and Cajun fries with all five varieties of the restaurant's homemade ketchup. I wished I'd gone with just a salad for dinner because I was never going to be able to resist.

While we were ordering the waiter kept up a nonstop conversation that consisted of not very funny quips and schmoozing compliments. Jeff kept his easy smile and quipped back. It was a repeat of Toby and the golf cart. David stared at the young man with the frozen expression of an offended vampire. The kid didn't notice because he was totally focused on Jeff, which made sense, and on me—which made no sense.

"How appalling. I could never live here," David stated. "Is everyone auditioning all the time?"

Jeff shrugged. "Pretty much. You make a point of being friendly and charming because you never know who might be seated at your table, whose car you might be parking, whose pool you're cleaning."

"But he wasn't charming," David complained.

"He's a puppy. I wasn't any different when I moved out here. You learn to be a little tolerant."

I spoke up. "Look, I get why you'd get the full court press, but why include me? I'm nobody?"

"You might be a casting director or my new squeeze, so he doesn't want to offend me by ignoring you."

"An impression you fostered outside," David said, then added, "And why leave me out?" David asked.

"You're piqued by that," I said and choked on a laugh.

David glared at me. "I am not. I'm just trying to understand the dynamics at work in this insane town."

"Vampires have never been big players in this town," Jeff said. "Maybe most of them have your attitude," but he smiled to pull the sting out of the words. "The major players in town from the Powers are, of course, the Álfar, and there are a couple of powerful werewolf agents. My guy, Scott, is a hound—nobody drives a harder deal. But vampires, not so much." He grinned and looked like a mischievous ten-year-old. "We're too déclassé for you guys."

After that we engaged in social chitchat until the appetizers arrived. Then I raised a point. "Look, David is the AAA-approved arbitrator. I'm here to assist him, but are any of the parties likely to raise an objection because you're meeting alone with him? And me?" I added as an afterthought.

"As I understand it, SAG isn't a party to the arbitration," Jeff said.

David shook his head. "Not quite correct. You are designated as an *interested* party, so I think there can be no objection."

Jeff shrugged, his expression rueful. "Yeah, and since both sides hate me probably more than they hate each other, I don't think anyone's going to kick up a fuss."

"Hate you, why?" I asked, and found myself adding, "I think it would be very hard to dislike you."

He gave me a suggestive smile. "I work very hard at it . . . being charming." He leaned in close.

He was clearly overplaying it, and I picked up on the game. "Be careful you don't sprain something," I shot back. Montolbano laughed and leaned back. I tried a bite of crab cake. It was very good, and the chili didn't send me diving for my water glass.

"I didn't want this in the courts, and I didn't want the organization I love to tear itself apart over this fight. I went back to the constitution and the bylaws of the Screen Actors Guild and found a clause about arbitration. Our lawyers said the wording was vague, but I decided to interpret it *my* way."

"That being?" David asked.

"That I can force everybody into an arbitration when it's an in-house dispute. The human actors screamed and the Álfar actors screamed, but I don't give a crap. I want this settled peacefully. The studios and networks and producers fuck us over all the time. Weakening ourselves by fighting each other is just stupid."

"So, what are you looking for?" David asked.

"Everybody to stop fighting," Jeff said. He reacted to David's expression. "I know, I'm being naive. Look, the human actors have real grievances. I know. Hell, I've started to lose roles to Álfar, but there has to be a solution."

"Quotas?" I suggested.

"Which have had less than stellar outcomes," David said.

"And have, at times, been absolutely necessary," I countered.

"I kind of hate that," Jeff said. "It's like getting a part out of pity."

"So, every part is won on pure merit?" I couldn't hide the sarcasm. "Guess the casting couch is just a myth." For some reason I was feeling argumentative.

"No, it's real, and of course people get parts for reasons aside from merit. It happens because of family connections, because they're owed, or because someone wants to get in their pants. But to force a set quota on the industry—" He shook his head.

"And the Powers wouldn't much like it either," David said in his dry way. "We're a very small percentage of the population. We don't want the perception that we wield disproportionate power."

"Worried about peasants with pitchforks," I said.

"Always," David said, then added, "Well, tomorrow we'll start hearing evidence and see if we can find that solution."

Our main courses and the stack of exotic french fries arrived, carried by a young, very pretty waitress. I wondered if she'd bribed the waiter to get to bring the food or if there was an unwritten rule about giving every aspiring actor a shot at the famous actor-producer-director?

"Who are you planning to have eat with you?" David asked. "I've watched Linnet eat. Birds consume more." It was spoken in that way men have when they are trying to prove they know more about you than the other male in the room, which meant I couldn't let it pass.

"First off, birds actually eat a lot considering their size, and you know I'm always hungry . . . especially when I get nervous or stressed."

"Are you nervous now?" Jeff asked with a teasing grin.

"Well, duh. I'm having dinner with a famous movie star and heartthrob."

"Well, good, then you'll help me with the fries."

For a few moments Jeff was busy doctoring his gigantic hamburger while our waitress hovered; she kept leaning across the table to offer both David and Jeff an unrestricted view of her décolletage. She seemed to focus more on David—there is something so alluring to women about a man who seems unattainable. I wanted to take her aside, and tell her it was probably hopeless. Some vampires and werewolves would skate dangerously close to the edge of the ban on turning women by forming relationships with them—I'd had a client who was married to an abusive werewolf, and of course there was my own stupid and disastrous one-night-stand with a vampire lawyer in our office—but many followed an almost monastic rule and just didn't get involved. David struck me as that sort. The waitress seemed to get my telepathic message because she moved away from the table.

I took a sip of my lobster bisque, and nibbled on a Cajun fry. Then a sweet potato fry. Then a garlic parmesan fry. Add to that the crème fraîche in my soup, and I mentally added another twenty minutes to the time I would spend in the gym tomorrow.

"So, Linnet, I checked you out. Both of you," he added with a nod to David. He turned back to me. "But you're way more interesting," Jeff said. I was once again treated to that total focus that locked his eyes on mine. "But I'm nosy, so I've got to ask: You were fostered in a vampire household—what does that mean, exactly?"

"That when I was eight years old my parents sent me off to live with a vampire in his household." I wasn't surprised at the question. Most human families never meet a vampire, much less send a child to one, and the whole custom must seem strange.

"Why would they do that?" Jeff asked. "It seems sort of cruel." He laid his hand lightly on mine.

"For access," David said in a too loud voice. I slipped my hand from beneath Jeff's, and David seemed to relax. "We tend to be rich and successful. Easily accomplished when we live for centuries. Humans are attracted by power and money." He shrugged. "We have both."

"You used to be human," Jeff said. David just stared at him. It's hard to meet a vampire's direct gaze, and David was giving it a little more punch than normal. Jeff proved to be no different than any other human. The actor cleared his throat and asked, "Okay, maybe not so much, but what's in it for the vampire?" Jeff asked. "Why raise a human kid? Looking for a steady supply of food? Kidding," he added after David stiffened.

I shook my head. "We're considered *súbito* or *súbita de casa*—a servant of the house. To feed on us would be a gross violation of honor and virtue."

"Also, she's female," David added. "We don't feed on women."

Jeff turned his thousand-watt smile on me and leaned in a little closer. "Their loss, my . . . er our gain, huh?"

David stiffened, but I didn't even blush because it sounded so trite and canned. Not that I would have bought it anyway. I had a feeling an actor's flirtation was about as real as an Álfar's glamour. Not that Montolbano wasn't handsome as hell, and very charming, and he seemed bright, but he was married, which was a nonstarter for me. Even if I was interested in Montolbano, spending time with him wouldn't look all that good. While not an actual party in the arbitration, he had forced the parties to the table. Caesar's wife and all that.

And I was still hurting over the loss of John. I'd never actually been on a date with John. We'd gone straight to making love, sharing fear and deadly danger, and finally he had sacrificed himself and stayed in Fey (a place he hated) so his bat-shit crazy Álfar mother would release me and my clients, but I didn't actually know him all that well. I knew he was a changeling who had been switched for a human infant. That he had followed in his human foster father's footsteps and joined the police force. That after twenty years with the Philly police force he'd retired and turned private investigator doing a lot of work for my firm, IMG. John described himself as a blue-collar elf, and it fit.

And I was, by God, going to free him, though I had no expectations about what our relationship might be or become after he returned.

David's voice pulled me out of my navel gazing. "I was surprised when I heard you speak in person," the vampire said to Montolbano. "You don't sound like you do on screen."

"Wow. You go to those newfangled talkies?" The response to my teasing was a glare.

"We do move with and adapt to the times."

"Just very slowly," I added sotto voce.

"I heard that. I apologize," he added with a nod to the actor. Montolbano was laughing.

"You two, you're like . . ."

"What?" asked David, his tone a bit dangerous.

Montolbano shook his head. "I can't really figure it out. But to answer your question, no, I don't sound the same on screen. Given my looks, I affect a touch of a Central European Eurotrash accent, but I'm a kid who grew up in Omaha, Nebraska."

"Get out of here!" I said.

"Yeah, really. I keep my background pretty quiet, all part of that privacy mystique, but I'm fifth generation in the States. My great-great-grandfather came over and opened a restaurant in Brooklyn. Then Granddad decided the rest of the country deserved real Italian food, so he moved the family to Nebraska."

"Wow. I understand that actors put on roles, but that makes you seem like a complete chiseler."

"Not content to follow in the family business, I take it?" David said, and he made it sound like Jeff was some kind of sellout.

I wondered why he was being so snotty. Maybe because he'd been forced to eat hotel food because of Jeff's squeamishness?

"Nope, got the bug early, hammed it up in every school play, went to school at CAST in Minneapolis. Quit before I graduated and drifted west."

"No legitimate theater for you, I take it." David really was sneering. I shot him a questioning look, but he refused to meet my eye.

For an instant Montolbano stiffened then relaxed, and the lazy smile was back in place. "Nope. I knew I was prettier than I was talented. I figured I had a better chance in Hollywood." A shrug. "I was right."

Desperately, I shifted the conversation, bringing up the past November's presidential election. We found common ground in approving of the new occupant in the White House, and we brushed through the rest of dinner without any further tension between the two men.

Montolbano dropped us off at the hotel. I walked up the red carpet and wondered what it would be like to walk a real red carpet—at a movie premier or the Academy Awards. David was stalking along behind me. He paused at the front desk to check for messages.

"Well, see you in the morning," I said and turned to head for the elevators. "Do we know how we're getting to the arbitration in the morning?"

"I assume Kobe will pick us up."

"Look, if we're going to be here for weeks, I'd like to have my own car. Can we rent something?" I asked.

"I'm sure that can be arranged," David said.

"Okay. Well, good night."

He surprised me by saying, "Let me walk you to your room." Vampires were all about the old-world courtesy, but this was a bit extreme. Something was up. I decided to try for a joke.

"I don't think I'm going to get mugged in the Beverly Hills Hotel, but thanks."

We rode the elevator in silence. Even with the nap I was pretty tired, and looking forward to sinking into the pillow-top mattress. At the door to my room I swiped the key card and, trying to forestall whatever was going on, said, "Good night."

"I want to talk to you privately."

"Yeah, I kind of got that. What's going on?"

"Not in a public hallway, if you please."

We went into the room and I was horribly aware of the unmade bed, strewn with various rejected outfits. "Looks like you put a lot of thought into what to wear tonight," David said,

I didn't like the implication. "I wanted to make a good professional impression. This is the guy who brought us in."

"Really? That's all it was? How hard can it be to pick an appropriate outfit?"

"For men? Not hard at all. You put on a suit. Your only choice is what color shirt and tie. Women have to think about so many other issues. Where's the hem? What kind of neckline? Jewelry, how much and what kind? What shoes—" I broke off. "And why, exactly, are we talking about this?"

"You were clearly trying to make an impression," David said.

"Yes, I said that."

"There's a certain standard of professional behavior that Ishmael, McGillary and Gold expects from its associates."

"Why are you sounding like the prudish school teacher in a Merchant Ivory movie?" I was starting to get mad. "Are you saying my behavior wasn't professional? In what way? What did I do?"

"You allowed him to take liberties with you!"

"What?" Shock had my voice spiraling into dolphin sonic mode. I regained control and decided to turn it into a joke. "Wow, rethinking that gay thing. Did you ever actually go out with a girl before you died? He was flirting, and he didn't mean a bit of it."

"I'm not joking. You were all over him."

"And I was joking, and so was he. I think you should leave now." I drew myself up to my full height and tried to look down my nose at him. It wasn't entirely successful since he was six feet tall.

David did start for the door, but as he left he added, "I want you to keep an appropriate distance from Mr. Montolbano."

The door closed behind him. I stared at the blank expanse of wood, emitted an enraged squeak, snatched a pillow off the rumpled bed, and threw it at the door. I then resolved to spend as much time as possible with Jeffery Montolbano.

4

Since I was still on New York time I woke up at 4:20 a.m. Lying perfectly still, and squeezing my eyes shut did not return me to dreamland. After fifteen minutes I gave up and got up. Since I had a lot of time before the car arrived I hied myself down to the health club and did a hard workout on the stationary bike and the balance ball. I can never remember if I have fast or slow twitch muscles, but the result was that I bulk up quickly. Which is why I don't run or use the elliptical machines. The muscles in my calves get huge, and my handmade König dressage riding boots don't fit. And since they cost twelve hundred dollars and take several months between order and delivery, I wasn't about to run the risk.

Thinking about my boots had me thinking about the horse I rode back in New York. Vento was a sparkling white, young Lusitano stallion. I had done legal work for his owner, and in addition to paying my fee he loaned me his horse to ride. Jolyon Bryce had been crippled in a car accident and couldn't ride any longer, but wasn't willing to part with his horse. I could see why: Vento was great. And now I was going to be away from him for weeks and possibly months on end. It made me sad thinking about it, and I resolved to look for a stable. Maybe there was someplace I could rent a horse to ride in this vast megalopolis.

The sun was coming up when I returned, panting and sweaty, to my room, and the clouds seemed to be breaking up. I took a hot bath, did my hair, put on my makeup and picked an appropriate powerful professional woman outfit—black pencil skirt, deep purple blouse, and high black heels. After checking through my briefcase to make sure I had everything I needed, I headed down to the restaurant for breakfast.

Despite the wide window the room felt dark because of the carpet and paisley upholstery. I noticed one end had been screened off, granting privacy to the vampires and comfort to the humans. I caught the faintest whiff of blood. Somebody had been feeding. I wondered if it had been David?

An attentive waiter seated me and flipped the napkin across my lap with practiced ease within seconds of my arriving. I studied the menu. There was the Polo Lounge Famous French Toast, made with sun-dried cranberry bread, banana cream, and sugar-toasted pecans. (*Eight billion calories!*) There was the So-Cal omelette made with avocado, chorizo, cheese, cilantro, and tomato (*Bleh!*) There was a Japanese breakfast listed, which told me a lot about high-end hotels in Los Angeles. I decided I needed protein to face the day, so I went with the American breakfast with a side of bacon.

I had a couple of text messages. One was from Caroline, a friend and fellow associate in the New York office. She reported that Gadzooks, John's cat that I'd adopted, had handled the move to her apartment with an aplomb rarely seen in felines. The other was from Cecelia, another associate who was known for her sharp mind and smutty mouth. *Have you met Montolbano? How hot is he?* Smiling I texted back. *Yes, and very.*

My meal arrived. I ate, and read through my bookmarked, online newspapers. I had added the *LA Times* to the mix when I knew I was getting pulled into this case. The headline was about the president's decision to commit troops in a stan I'd never heard of. The next largest headline concerned Kerrinan's arrest on murder charges. Apparently the human authorities had gotten him back out of Fey.

There were photos from the Beverly Hills police station, a sort of Disneyesque vision of a white Spanish mission, and there were a lot of angry people gathered on either side of the steps holding up signs. The picture quality wasn't good enough to read most of them, but the one I could make out read, MARRIAGE IS BETWEEN TWO HUMANS.

After I finished I went back to my room to brush my teeth and take one final look through the legal papers, and then I headed down to the lobby to wait for Kobe. I was pleased to see that David hadn't arrived yet. Having been reamed out for not behaving in a professional manner, I felt that being ready before him was a small victory.

He showed up a few minutes later looking flush and plump. Yep, he'd stoked up on blood. He held his briefcase in one hand and a broadbrimmed Panama hat in the other. Not a minute later Kobe came in the front door. David put on his hat, and we headed to the car.

The rush hour traffic was intense, but we stayed on city streets and arrived at the IMG forty-five minutes before the arbitration was set to begin.

Junie took us in hand the minute we entered. "Coffee? Blood?" she asked.

"Coffee," I said, and David waved her off.

"I've dined."

It was an interesting word choice. The older vampires of my acquaintance, like my foster liege Meredith Bainbridge and Shade, said *fed*. The younger ones tended to say *eaten* or *dined*. I suppose it did make the human hosts sound less like cattle when you phrased it that way. It was also evidence of how even the most conservative and hidebound society can change, albeit slowly.

Junie led us to the other end of the office and threw open silver-chased double doors to reveal a gigantic conference room with heavily treated glass that made the sunlight look like it was being filtered through layers of seawater. Pizer was waiting for us, wearing a suit of coppery brown.

He gave me a grin that exposed his fangs. "You're in the news."

David made a face. "I'm not surprised. There must be thousands of other businesses in this city, but people only seem to care about the damn movie business." A new thought intruded, and he gave Pizer a thunderous frown. "I sincerely hope no one in this office leaked. We can't function if the parties don't have confidence in our discretion and impartiality."

Pizer, still smiling, waited for David to finish his rather pompous speech, then he said, "Oh, *you're* not in the news. *She* is."

"What?" I pulled my voice back down. "Me? Why?"

A newspaper appeared from behind Pizer's back. There was a big photo spread of me on Montolbano's arm entering Ketchup. It was an improvement over the last time I'd been the picture above the fold. Then I'd been flashing my breast in the *New York Post* and leaving the scene of a grisly murder.

The headline screamed: "Illegal Affair?" I scanned the opening lines of the story: "There have been rumors of problems between Kate Billingham and Jeff Montolbano. Now there may be fire to add to that smoke. Last night Montolbano was seen at one of LA's hot spots with a beautiful mystery woman who turned out to be Linnet Ellery, superstar lawyer at Ishmael, McGillary and Gold."

I liked the beautiful part. Usually I got described as cute. I even kind of liked the mystery part, but I didn't like getting cast in the role of home wrecker. "No stranger to controversy, Ellery was associated with a series of grisly murders . . ." Before I could read further David snatched the paper out of my hands.

"Oh, dear God." The words emerged like a groan. "Just what we need. Linnet, how do you manage to end up in these . . . these . . . situations?"

"Me? How is this my fault? You're the one who agreed to have dinner with Montolbano. We could have done room service in your cabana."

Pizer took back the paper. I snatched at it, but they were passing it well over my head. I stepped back, fuming.

Pizer shrugged. "I don't see the problem. More ink for IMG is never a bad thing."

The paper went back to David.

"And that is precisely the problem, Hank . . . that you don't see a problem. I think you've been in this environment for too long."

I watched the newsprint float by as it went back to Pizer.

"The reason I'm on the West Coast is because I'm not a fossil," Pizer replied.

"The senior partners are not going to like having an associate involved in a media circus, and it creates the appearance of bias."

Especially this associate, I thought. I comforted myself that this time nobody had died.

Pizer wasn't backing down. "If they don't want press, then they shouldn't have opened an office in Los Angeles and taken on a high-profile industry case." I thought Pizer had a point, and I nodded in agreement. That had David rounding on me.

"Linnet, you need to stay in the background. Okay?"

"I just went out to dinner," I said. "Short of wearing a burqua or never leaving my room, I'm not sure what more I can do."

"Well, just . . ." David looked frustrated. "Just let me take point in this opening session."

"Fine," I snapped.

"And don't talk to Montolbano. Now, could we please get back to the case," David said, and he sounded really exasperated.

Pizer was still grinning. Clearly he loved to tweak David. "Sure. I assumed you want to start with a general meeting, so I had all the parties come in."

David nodded. "Good, yes, excellent."

"Do you want them brought in one at a time or in a big scrum?" I asked.

David considered, then said, "Bring them all in together. How they interact with each other should be interesting, and it may help us start to get a fix on these people."

"Remember, they are actors," Pizer warned. "They'll show you what they think you want to see."

The idea that a bunch of actors could fool him had David assuming the full-on vampire. "They can try," he said. "I've had some experience with human subterfuge."

Pizer shook his head, but said nothing. He went away to summon the various parties. While he was gone, assistants hurried in with coffee, tea, soft drinks, and a platter of donuts. Yellow legal pads and pens were arranged on the big oval table.

"Can you be charmed, bedazzled, whatever you want to call it by the Álfar?" I asked. "My foster father warned me about them, but I thought that had to do more with my being female."

"You'd be correct. Magic or whatever the Álfar use isn't effective against vampires. It seems to only work on humans and other Álfar."

"But you were human once," I argued.

"But we're not any longer," came the short answer. It did rather say it all.

Jeff Montolbano ambled in and gave me one of the famous lopsided smiles that had devastated audiences for ten years. He was dressed casually in khaki slacks, a polo shirt, and a sports jacket.

I sidled over to him. "Well, you fed the beast, but I really don't appreciate being made a prop."

He looked contrite. "That really wasn't my intention. I thought they'd be more interested in your colleague."

"Bullshit," I said. "And are you and your wife really having marital difficulties?"

"No," he said. "We're just trying to get some ink. This weekend you'll hear about her being seen with Mark Wiley on the set of her movie in Italy."

"Under the theory that there's no such thing as bad publicity?" It came out more acerbic than I'd intended.

"That'd be it."

We had to break it off because people began entering the room. Up until now these people had just been names in the documents, so I was interested to meet them.

The human actors were represented by Sheila LeBlanc. She was midfifties, fit and tan, with flint gray eyes, too black hair, and designer glasses that sported bling and harkened back to the batwings of the 1950s. I recognized her because every time there was a high-profile case in California she ended up on CNN or some other cable station, either representing some side in the issue or commenting on the case.

The client of record on the human side was Missy (short for Melissa) Able. She was on the shady side of forty; her eyes seemed odd, and then I realized part of her face wasn't moving. The wonders of Botox. She didn't look much like the younger ditzy sister she had played on a twenty-year-old sitcom that I had caught in reruns on *Nick at Night* during my college years. All the Botox in the world couldn't hide the downturned mouth and angry expression. Especially when she looked over at Jeff.

Even if there were no Álfar, I'm betting you wouldn't be getting parts, I thought, then tried to forget I'd ever had the nasty little thought because we were the arbitrators and we were supposed to be impartial.

Representing the studios and networks was an enormously fat man with luxuriant light gray hair that set a sharp contrast with his black skin, a lazy smile, and a southern accent that poured honey over you. This was Gordon McPhee, and when he enfolded my hand in his own pillow-soft hand I took note of an antique signet ring and the suit vest crossed with an elaborate watch chain and fob. I looked up and meet his basset hound eyes, and caught the sharp glint of calculation beneath the sleepy demeanor. *Yeah, cunning as a fox,* I thought. *He's the one to watch.*

His clients were a gaggle of sharp men in expensive suits, the heads of various studios and networks, and two women. One was young and self-effacing, Valerie Frank, who was the newly appointed head of Paramount Pictures, and the other woman made Sheila Le-Blanc look like Mother Theresa. Ginjer Balkin was the head of the NBC network and all its cable subsidiaries. She was sharp-featured, with perfectly coiffed, highlighted hair, super-high-heeled Christian Louboutin shoes, a pencil skirt, and an inhuman coldness in her eyes that made me wonder if she was a vampire even though I knew that to be impossible.

The various talent agencies—William Morris, CAA, etc.—had hired Stan Brubaker. Midforties, gray-blond hair, a megawatt smile, surfer's tan, and a hard-charging werewolf litigator. I didn't want to be a bigot, even in the privacy of my own head, but after what had happened last year when a dispute over ownership of a powerful werewolf company had led to no fewer than six werewolves trying to kill me, it didn't matter that they had all ended up dead and I was fine: I wasn't real comfortable being around them.

And there were three more hounds among his clients. Like the studio executives the agents tended to be male and intense but with readier smiles, and their attire was more casual than the network and studio executives.

Representing the Álfar was Barbara Gabaldon, a very pretty woman in her thirties with tawny skin, liquid dark eyes, and black hair that showed what natural black hair should look like. She was very stylishly dressed, with lots of gold jewelry that looked great with her Latin looks. The Álfar actor who was the client of record for that side was Palendar, who had made a career out of turning Japanese anime into live action movies. There was no question that the look of anime characters had been affected by the advent of the Álfar into our world, and Palendar looked like he could have modeled for those early comics and movies. Like many Álfar he had multicolored hair; his tended toward an unusual lavender mixed with white and silver. He had narrow features with upturned eyes and a pointed chin, and he was so thin I wanted to offer him a donut. Like his human counterpart, Palendar glared at Jeff and ignored the human's outstretched hand.

I had about reached the conclusion that actors tended to act like bratty kids when they weren't inhabiting a role. Then another Álfar entered, accompanied by Pizer, and he stopped me in my tracks because he actually looked *old*. I knew from John that the Álfar aged very slowly, so I couldn't begin to guess his age. He was dressed in a bespoke suit of silver gray with blue highlights that picked up the color of his eyes. His hair, which hung to the middle of his back, was nearly pure white with a few dramatic streaks of black and red.

He was handsome in the way of all Álfar, but wrinkles lay like cobwebs across his skin.

"Qwendar," he said softly, and shook hands with the various principles.

David was frowning at the elderly Álfar, and he turned to Gabaldon and asked, "May I inquire as to why Mr. Qwendar is present?"

Qwendar didn't give her the opportunity to answer. "I am here on behalf of the Álfar Council. To assure ourselves that these proceedings are conducted fairly, and that it doesn't become an opportunity to demean and degrade our people. There's been quite enough of that in this state recently."

David and I exchanged a glance. Was this about Kerrinan's arrest, or was something else going on? Pizer stepped in close, put a finger to his lips, and said softly, "I'll fill you in later."

"That would be nice," David replied, and the muscles in his jaw were clenched. Like most vampires, he hated surprises.

Pizer leaned in to David and me. "Look, this all happened at ugh o'clock this morning and just got resolved. I got the call literally moments ago."

"It should have been cleared with us."

"Yeah, well, it came down ex cathedra from people with a way higher pay grade than yours or mine," Pizer said tensely.

There was the buzz of conversation punctuated occasionally by quick bursts of laughter like lightning against the dark of a rising storm. People fortified themselves with beverages. I noticed that only McPhee touched the donuts and he took three. Of the beverages only water, coffee, and the diet drinks were touched. I gave one final longing glance at a glazed, raised, chocolate donut, but the peer pressure was too much. I poured myself a black coffee and took a seat at the end of the conference table where I could see all the parties. David took the seat at the other end. People took the cue and settled into the remaining chairs.

"Thank you all for coming," David began. "This is an arbitration and the hope is that we can reach some agreement and consensus without resorting to the courts. This process does share certain similarities with a judicial proceeding. We will take evidence and interview witnesses. Such testimony can be under oath at the discretion of the arbitrator, and it's my intention to require that an oath be administered. I find it tends to focus the mind." He paused and gave them all a thin, closed-lip vampire smile.

"My associate"—he nodded at me—"and I will question the witnesses, and your representatives will be allowed to question the witnesses. We will begin with the claimant"— David indicated Missy Able—"who will go first, and make the claim for the human actors. After their arguments have been presented, the other parties will present their defense." He pinned the gaggle of studio people, the agents, and the Álfar with a glance.

"I expect this to be handled civilly and discreetly. I don't want to read about these proceedings in the press." Here he paused to glare at Jeff. "Or hear about it on *Access Hollywood*."

That amazed me. The idea of David sitting in front of a television, watching the entertainment news show with its breathless hosts, had me hiding a smile. Once again I wondered when he had been made? You didn't expect vampires to keep up with current events or cutting-edge technology. In contrast Palendar, who wasn't listening to a word David was saying, was unpacking his man purse setting out an iPhone and an iPad.

David continued. "This is a judicial proceeding though it is taking place outside the confines of a court. I expect decorum to be observed."

It was a very vampirelike statement. Everyone nodded somberly. Then McPhee drawled out, "Will we begin presenting testimony today, or was this just a little mill and swill?"

Everyone looked to Sheila. I had to hand it to her—she was

unperturbed. She rose to her feet in one smooth motion and gave McPhee an ironic nod. "I'm quite prepared to make an opening statement. I indicated that we were going to begin with an expert witness. In the interest of not wasting my client's money I did not have him standing by because I wasn't certain if you would actually begin hearing testimony today. But as I said, I can make my opening remarks."

"Then please do," David said. "And we will hold off on starting testimony until tomorrow."

Sheila walked behind her chair and gripped the high back. She had long nails painted a deep crimson that matched her lipstick. I wondered if they were artificial or if she grew them herself? She did sort of give off that whole dragon lady vibe. They were probably hers.

"People are losing their livelihoods. I'm sure . . ." Here she paused to look at Gabaldon and her clients, Brubaker and McPhee and their clients. "I'm sure that some in this room will argue it's happened before. When talkies replaced silent films. When computers replaced the need for extras in crowd scenes. But this is different. This isn't the march of technology. This is an invasion."

Qwendar stiffened and stared at LeBlanc. His pale eyes held both heat and ice, and I wouldn't have liked to have that look directed at me. "Invasion? Really? That implies the outsider. I would argue my people have been resident on this planet as sentient beings far longer than *you*."

David's response was swift and summary. "Mr. Qwendar. You will keep quiet or I will ask that you leave."

Sheila gave David a smile. "Thank you, Mr. Sullivan. But to continue. Are the Álfar more talented than humans? We're going to present evidence that will show it's quite the opposite. No, they're getting more and more of the parts because they are using inhuman powers at the very start of the process, during their auditions, to deny human actors their chance. This is an issue of basic fairness. We're talking about people here, not buggy whips or Moviolas or eight-tracks." I briefly wondered what a Moviola might be. "People who can't pay their mortgages or support their families, and maybe more importantly, can't fulfill themselves and pursue their passion because the Álfar are taking unfair advantage." She sat down.

Qwendar took to his feet. "Mr. Sullivan, I must protest these kinds of racist and hyperbolic statements. If such defamatory remarks are leaked to the press I will respond most strongly."

"Mr. Qwendar," David said wearily. "This was an opening statement. Ms. LeBlanc will have to prove her assertions. Just as your side will." David turned to Barbara. "Ms. Gabaldon, do you wish to make a statement at this time?"

"No, I'll wait until Ms. LeBlanc has made her arguments."

"Very good. Mr. McPhee?"

The big man hooked his thumbs in his vest pockets and leaned back in his chair until it squeaked in protest. "I'll bide."

"Mr. Brubaker?"

"We'll wait."

"Fine, then, if there is nothing more we will reconvene day after tomorrow and hear the first of Ms. LeBlanc's witnesses."

"Why the delay?" Brubaker asked.

"Because I want to do my own statistical research."

I gave a mental groan because David's *I* meant *me*.

5

Pizer had said there were offices for David and me. There were. David had been given an office next door to Pizer, a large, elegant space as befitted a full partner and vampire. Which meant the occupant of that office was kicked into a different office, which set off a chain reaction. Which meant that I was going to share space with the guy who had been left standing when the music stopped. It was the smallest private office, and it looked like a converted coat closet.

"Way to win friends and influence people," I muttered at the desk as I unloaded my briefcase and set up my computer. I was crawling under the desk to plug in the power cord when the door opened and my office mate entered.

"Hi," came a chipper voice.

I quickly tried to turn around to get my butt on the floor, but instead gave myself a painful bump on the head. There is no graceful way to handle the situation when you're on hands and knees with your ass pointed at the door.

"Wow, that sounded like it hurt," the chipper voice continued.

I scooted out from beneath the desk struggling to keep my skirt from hiking up around my waist and losing a shoe in the process. I finally emerged with one hand clutching a shoe, the other clutching my skirt to meet the amused gaze of a very short man with a head of red-gold curls that resembled those of a Botticelli angel. He was grinning at me, and it was clear from the expression in his dancing blue eyes that he was loving the situation.

"It did," I said. "Hi, I'm Linnet Ellery. Who are you?"

"Merlin Ambinder. The man with no office."

As usual my internal editor was asleep on the job. "Merlin? Really?" I asked before I could control myself

His cupid's-bow lips quirked in a rueful smile. "Yes, I am a man with a really silly name. Blame my parents. They were hippies long after it was time for any sensible people to be hippies."

I stood up and indicated the tiny space with my outstretched arms. "And as for no office, we have all this." We shared a laugh, and he set down a stack of files on the second desk, then fell into his chair.

"How long is this likely to continue?"

I took my chair and we faced each other across our kissing desks. "If we're lucky—a month. I don't think we're going to be lucky. And meanwhile I get to live in a hotel room."

"You should rent an Oakwood. Well, rent an apartment at the Oakwood. Corporate housing—studio, one, two, and three bedrooms. No lease and everything is included. Even maid service if you want to add that in."

"It's got to be cheaper than the Beverly Hills Hotel." I fired up my laptop and started a Google search.

"Yeah, no kidding."

"I could get a one-bedroom. Actually cook some meals." Chrome loaded the Google search page. There were a number of Oakwoods in the greater LA area. I swung the computer around so Ambinder could see the screen. "Which would be the best choice?"

"Well, the one in Santa Monica near the beach would be great, but they hike the rates because you're on the water. The one down on Washington is a pit. I'd go with the Barham Oakwood. Easy access to the Valley or the Basin. Close to Universal and the City Walk, Warner Bros., and Griffith Park."

"How do you know so much about Oakwoods?" I asked.

"My folks got a divorce when I was eight. My dad moved into an Oakwood."

"Oh, great, it's a divorcee's paradise."

Merlin shrugged. "Look at the upside. You can get a lot of dates."

I ignored that and asked, "So why isn't the firm using them? Lot cheaper than a hotel."

"It's usually the partners who commute between offices, and while getting a pizza or takeout Chinese delivered to an Oakwood is no big deal, I think delivering a host would be tricky. The better hotels are set up for that. And you know vampires. They like to be catered to."

"Is that ever the truth. So, what's your specialty?"

"I'm the research monkey. I would be totally petrified to go into court, but I love digging through minutia."

"Glad somebody does." I cupped my chin in my hands, elbows resting on the desk. "Hollywood has a lot to answer for with their portrayal of lawyers. I thought this profession was going to be exciting," I said.

"You're in Hollywood now."

"And it's still not exciting." I laid my hand on my stack of folders. "I get to read and summarize a statistical analysis of casting patterns over the past ten years for my boss."

"We also serve who only burn our eyes out," Merlin said, mangling the Milton quote to suit our situation.

Having bonded, we settled in to work. Merlin was a good office companion. We started off wearing headphones so our music didn't bug the other, but it turned out we had similar tastes so we just let his IPod and Pandora play for us. We took turns on the coffee run to refill our cups. He even made sure the sandwich lady didn't over-look us in our cave.

A few hours later I had a gross overview of the piles of statistical analysis. I knew David would want my initial impression, so I wrote up a short report. While statistics is the discipline where you lie with numbers, it was still pretty clear that the human actors were getting screwed. I hit Print on my computer and stood up, ready to head out to the network center to pull my report off the printer.

Merlin's ruddy eyebrows climbed up into his bangs. "You can't just email him your report?"

"Are you kidding? He's a vampire. He wants the feel of paper."

"Wow, Mr. Pizer isn't that way."

"Then he must be a very young vampire," I said and left.

As I walked to the network center I thought about the calcifica-tion that eventually overtook all vampires. They claimed it was a good thing, but I wondered if it hid an underlying concern. The world was moving so fast today, and it was important to keep up. They would never admit that, however; they presented their hide-bound habits as a way to revere and honor the past, which was why you found them most often in the law or curating at museums—in fact, the newest head of the Metropolitan Museum of Art in New York was a vampire. Once they'd gone public they tried to broaden their involvement in the world. There had been a few efforts to have them teach history, but these hadn't worked out so well. The bustle of a campus and the manic desperation of undergraduates—*But I just have to pass this class, Professor!*—did not suit a vampire's person-ality.

But did that bode ill for the future of the country, and maybe even the planet, when you had people with such hidebound and conservative outlooks assuming open positions of power? Not that the Powers hadn't pulled the strings of politicians, kings, and poten-tates long before they went public, but their interest had been in staying protected and hidden. Now that they were giving interviews on Fox and CNN, would that increased visibility have an impact on society's attitudes? Make humans more cautious and conservative? Some problems required nimbleness and risk taking to solve, and neither of those were a vampire's strong suit.

I pulled my summation out of the printer and headed into David's office. It was very sleek and modern, with a wallpaper that looked like beige silk and abstract art on the walls. David was making notes on a yellow legal pad. I took note of the pen he was using. It was a ballpoint. Both Shade and Meredith used fountain pens. Guess it was too hard to get quills these days. The errant little thought gave me a quick chuckle.

David looked up. "What?"

"Nothing." I laid the report on his desk. "And the human actors are definitely getting the short end of this particular stick."

"But should they be offered redress?" David asked.

"Affirmative action has a long and . . ."

"Checkered career?" David asked. "It was necessary to ease the injustice of Jim Crow, but can it, should it, be applied in this situation?"

"And if we rule that way, are we suggesting that all humans are a protected class," I said.

He indicated a chair, a modern affair that looked more like art than furniture, with about the same comfort level. I sat and we contemplated each other in silence for a few minutes.

"It's early days. We haven't heard enough to make any kind of judgment, much less suggest a remedy," I said.

"Agreed."

"Look, David, can we talk to the New York office and see about my renting an apartment? I gotta be honest, I hate living in hotels, even one as nice as the Beverly Hills Hotel."

"I don't want to leave the hotel," he said, his expression mulish.

"And I'm not suggesting you should. *I* want to leave the hotel. Look, I get why you would want to stay. Room service and all that. Then you're not having to drive all over town looking for restaurants that have hosts and cater to vampires." I paused, Merlin's comment about takeout had raised an interesting question. "Is there takeout for vampires?"

"There was one in New York, but the attorney general's office figured out it was actually a cover for a high-priced prostitution ring. They got busted." I chuckled. "It's not funny," he said. "It's actually an interesting business idea, but now it will be years before anyone tries it again." He looked out the heavily tinted windows where the rays of the setting sun looked like physical spikes. "Los Angeles is a big city, but inside it's a small town. Even after forty years we're not well accepted here. Maybe not anywhere."

"A million years of evolution tells us humans that you're predators and we're prey," I said quietly. "We can intellectualize all we want, but the fear is still there, living down deep. And there's fault on both sides. You guys have this distant, disengaged attitude when you deal with humans. Which adds to the feeling that you don't actually see us as anything but prey."

"Are you afraid of me?" he asked, and there was something behind the words that I couldn't quite interpret.

"No, of course not. I—" I broke off. I owed him honesty rather than platitudes. "Yes, sometimes I'm afraid. When one of you walks up on me and I don't hear you coming. It helps if I have time to prepare."

"Even with me?"

"Yes."

"Even after being fostered."

I held out one hand. "A million years of evolution." I held out the other. "Ten years living in a vampire household." I made a balancing gesture. "Which do you think wins?"

He slapped his hands onto the desk and stood up. "I think it's quitting time." It was an abrupt end to an odd conversation that had clearly discomfited him. "And yes."

"Yes what?"

"Go get an apartment. I'll clear it with New York."

"Thanks." I also stood. "It will be cheaper."

While I arranged for a rental car, and investigated the Barham Oakwood, I also snagged an appointment with the district attorney. Henry Jacobs was an older African American man who towered over me. I couldn't help it. I gaped up at him.

He laughed and guided me to a chair. "Yes, I really am six-foot-ten. I played basketball for the Lakers, blew out my knee, and decided I didn't really want to be a coach. So law school, and . . . ," he looked around the office, "and this."

The space had the usual accoutrements of a DA's office—diplomas and pictures of Jacobs shaking hands with various nationally known politicians—but the desk and several chairs were also piled high with files. This was a DA who was clearly hands-on, and not just a blow-dried politician pretending to be a lawyer.

"Sorry, I should have heard of you," I said.

"Unless you're a basketball fanatic and a lot older than you look I don't know why you should." Jacobs perched on the front of his desk and smiled at me. "So, what can I do for you?"

"I was wondering how you got Kerrinan out of Fey? I'm trying to do something similar. Well, not exactly, the man I'm trying to extricate isn't a criminal, but he is trapped." I gave him the rundown on John's situation.

He heard me out, then gave a slow shake of his head. "Well, I wish I could claim some insight, or brilliant legal trick, but the truth is there's some kind of powerful Álfar Council in charge over there, and they forced Kerrinan to return. It was a smart decision. If human folks got the idea the Álfar are above the law . . . well, it wouldn't sit well, and there's growing tension about the Álfar out here, and not just inside SAG."

"Damn. That was what I got from the Justice Department and the DA in New York. There should be some kind of extradition agreement," I said.

"Yeah, but then a human who harms an Álfar on this side could potentially get hauled to Fey to stand trial, and I'm not sure how many constitutional protections they would have. Also, do they get an Álfar attorney? Haven't heard of any. The whole thing on that side seems fairly medieval to me," Jacobs said.

"Yeah, John's mother is referred to as a queen. I have no idea what that actually means."

"And the Álfar aren't real forthcoming about their customs and institutions."

"Gee, how is that any different from the other Powers?" I asked, and we shared a laugh, though mine was rather hollow.

"I'm afraid this is a problem for politicians and diplomats," Jacobs said. "Clearly something needs to be done as more and more Álfar get involved in our world. Some kind of conflict of law has to apply."

"Yeah, well, politicians aren't known for their burning desire to take on tough problems," I said with a sigh. I stood and held out my hand. "Thank you for your time."

"Not a problem. I just wish I had a solution to offer. Seems to me that high-powered law firm ought to be doing more."

"I agree, but even vampires are wary of the Álfar."

"Not a comforting thought," Jacobs concluded.

Merlin hadn't steered me wrong. The Barham Oakwood was built on a series of hills that separated the San Fernando Valley from the

LA Basin and it was quite pretty. Feeling paranoid about earthquakes I had requested a one-bedroom apartment on the third floor. I had seen the pictures from the Northridge quake. Things fell down, and if you were in an underground parking garage or on the bottom floor in a building you got squashed. I also figured that, along with the on-site gym, walking up the stairs would be good exercise. The cool, rainy weather made the outdoor pools less attractive.

I stood on my balcony and looked out at the iconic water tower on the Warner Bros. lot. Even though I'd been in the apartment for three days it still gave me a shiver and a giggle. Hollywood really was the domain of American royalty. Even the most cynical were starstruck, and I was no cynic.

Behind the studio hills climbed toward a cloud-drenched sky bare of those unique LA structures—houses on stilts. That was because the hills were part of Griffith Park, donated to the city by Colonel Griffith J. Griffith back in the 1890s. There was a theater on the property, the famous Griffith Observatory, a merry-go-round, and a riding stable. I hadn't checked it out yet because I didn't love riding stable horses. They were usually old, tired, and sour. Or once people figured out I knew how to ride I got assigned the angry, young problem horse to "fix," and because I was small I often got stuck with fixing cranky ponies.

The phone rang. I went back inside to answer it. There was a long silence. This had been happening with increasing regularity over the past few days. In the beginning I did the hello, hello, hello? thing in ever-increasing tones of testiness. Now I just answered and stayed silent, waiting to see if anyone would speak. I was just about to hang up when a harsh voice whispered,

"Elf whore." There was the click of a disconnected line and I stared in shock at the handset.

Elf whore? What the hell did that mean? Because I was an arbitrator in this human-Álfar case? But I wasn't representing the

Álfar—I stood in the position of a judge. Had someone found out that John and I had been intimate? It wasn't a secret, but who the hell would care? And that was just too creepy for words. A shiver ran through me. I hurried over to the white brick gas fireplace and turned it on. Blue and yellow flames played like coy children around the artificial logs. I sat down on the floor, rubbed my arms, and contemplated the fire.

John. Last summer I'd had what I thought was contact with him. I'd dreamed he was in my bedroom with me, and when I'd awakened there had been a flowering branch at the foot of the bed. Even now I could recall the perfume from those flowers. Since then—nothing. Had he been punished for that incursion into our reality? Or had he just moved on and forgotten about me? Come to accept his life in Fey? That I didn't buy. He seemed to have an active dislike, if not downright hatred, for the Álfar and a deep love for his human family and human institutions. My mind returned to that hateful phone call. Why not vampire whore? I worked for a white-fang law firm. I couldn't find any rational explanation.

Giving myself a shake I stood up and went into the tiny kitchen area. I opened the fridge, contemplated the contents, and decided to settle for a Trader Joe's prepackaged seafood salad. After dressing it, and dumping it out onto a plate I wandered through the apartment, nibbling. The call had really disturbed me. It had left me shaky and very sad. Was this any less depressing than a hotel room? I missed my female colleagues back at the New York firm. Suddenly the city seemed very large and I seemed very small, lost in a vast, sprawling web of lights, roads, houses, and people.

The phone rang. I studied it with apprehension, forced my feet to move, and picked up the handset.

"Hello?" came Jeff Montolbano's voice. "Linnet? Are you there?"

"Yeah, I'm here. Hi, Jeff, what's up?"

"I just got word that there's only going to be a morning session tomorrow because of some of the participants' shooting schedules. That made me think, hey, I bet Linnet has never been on a movie set."

"You'd be right."

"Want to change that? I'm an executive producer on a new spy thriller starring Jondin. I was going by the set tomorrow afternoon. I could take you along."

Jondin was the female version of Kerrinan, who was now occupying a cell in county lockup. "This isn't going to be a repeat of Ketchup, right? Not using me for a prop."

"No. This is me trying to make up for that."

"In that case, I would love to go with you. Where are they filming?"

"On a soundstage at Warner's," he said.

"Well, it just so happens I was looking at the water tower at Warner's from my balcony this evening."

"Perfect. How about we just go from the office tomorrow. We can grab lunch in Toluca Lake."

"I rented a car and it will be at the office."

He dismissed the problem. "I can take you back there after we're done."

"Sounds like a plan. "

"Good. See you tomorrow."

This was going to be my first day driving myself to the IMG office, so I left absurdly early. And found myself in a long line of cars inching their way up Barham Boulevard. Apparently everybody had the same idea. I had rented a portable GPS system when I rented the car, and I had the address to the office entered into the Garmin. I selected a male voice as the guide because the default woman reminded me of a first-grade teacher I had really hated. The softly accented Brit voice, which I had dubbed Nigel, suggested I take a right in five hundred feet onto Highway 101.

Nigel guided me onto the I-405 freeway heading south. Now it was easy. Just ride this to the Santa Monica exit. I listened to the radio as I drove, flipping back and forth between a contemporary pop and a classical station. My average speed seemed to hover around five miles an hour. Getting to shoot up to fifteen miles an hour was exciting, but this was quickly dispelled when the traffic would inexplicably stop. After twenty minutes I gave up stressing about it, and cultivated a Zen attitude. It would take as long as it took.

Eventually I reached the office and pulled into a space reserved for IMG employees. I dumped my computer and the files I'd been reading at home and headed into the break room for a cup of coffee. It was a more utilitarian space then the opulent kitchen on the partner's floor in New York. White refrigerator and microwave, no china plates or cups. A toaster but no stove.

Merlin, Junie, and a few other people were present, toasting bagels, doctoring coffee, brewing tea. Merlin was drinking a Coke and eating a cupcake. He grinned at my expression.

"Breakfast of champions," he said.

"Ugh," was my articulate response. I poured out a cup of coffee and the rich smell was like a hug. I wasn't really hungry, but I opened up the full-size refrigerator just to see what might be lurking and found myself staring at a carton of nonfat half-and-half surrounded by premade salads and lots of diet drinks.

I took out the container of half-and-half and held it out to the room. "What is the point?"

"Calories," said Junie. "But if you want real half-and-half just put it on the shopping list. She indicated a small notebook.

"No, thanks. I take mine black," I said.

"Like your heart?" Merlin asked.

"No, like my mood."

"You do look frazzled," Junie remarked.

"I am. I drove for the first time. How do you people stand it?"

"How did you come?" a young male PA asked.

"The 101 to the 405."

"Well, there's your problem," Merlin said. "Where do you live?"

"I took your advice. I'm in the Barham Oakwood."

"Okay." He took a big swig of Coke. "You've got to use surface streets to get over the hill and into the Basin. You want to get on Riverside and go down to Laurel Canyon and over."

Junie was shaking her head. "No, Laurel Canyon's a nightmare at rush hour. Coldwater Canyon is better."

"No, too many curves and too many accidents," said the PA. "One wreck and the road is shut down for hours."

"What if she went down Cahuenga past the Rose Bowl, caught Santa Monica, and headed west?"

The others considered Merlin's suggestion. "Yeah, that makes sense," Junie said. "Then she'd have the option to bail out onto Sunset or Melrose depending on what she's hearing on the radio."

I just stared at them. I hadn't seen this much focus since the New York office wrote an amicus brief for the Supreme Court. They correctly interpreted my expression.

Merlin was grinning again. "You have just experienced the most common LA conversation. It breaks the ice, it can be used as a pickup method, and it covers all social gaffs."

"Yeah, well, we've got the same thing in New York. Except we discuss apartments. I would submit that our discussions are ultimately more useful," I said.

Merlin grinned at me, enjoying the sparring. "Big-city rivalry. We're more exciting."

"We're more sophisticated."

"We've got movie stars."

"We've got skyscrapers."

He threw up a hand. "Okay, I call it a draw."

"You do know to tune your radio to 1070 am for traffic updates?" asked the PA. She clearly hadn't gotten the memo that we were teasing now.

"No, but I guess I do now. Okay, all you California dreamers, this hard-charging New Yorker is going to work." I gave them a finger wave and went back to my office to prepare for the day's testimony.

6

David had called for a fifteen-minute recess while we waited for the next witness to arrive. This was going to be the big enchilada, the world-famous director George Campos, who was going to talk about human versus Álfar actors. The previous three hours had been taken up with a statistician, and my brain felt as numb as my butt. Barbara Gabaldon hadn't even bothered to question the man because she could sense he wasn't having that much impact. My three days of burrowing into the reports had only intensified the sense that humans were getting the short end of the stick. But what to do about it?

As I bolted for the bathroom I reflected that this was another problem with vampires: they tended to forget that humans had bodily functions. The ladies room was outside the office proper, down the hall past the elevators. Missy had already beaten me to the facility. While I was in the stall I heard her washing her hands, but I didn't hear the door close. Sure enough, she was waiting for me when I emerged. She leaned against the wall by the towel dispenser and glared at me. I let the warm water roll across my hands and tried to think of something to say. The soap offered a conversational opening, and I seized it like a drowning woman.

"You know, this new foam soap makes me think of shaving

cream." The inanity made me cringe, but the angry silence had just been too much.

"We're checking into you," Missy said. She was so stiff I thought her jaw would crack.

"Okay. What else did you say?"

"You're a whore for the Spooks."

Spook was an incredibly pejorative term for the vampires, werewolves, and Álfar who made up the Powers, and it offended me. She'd gotten under my skin.

"Okay, I'm not going to take you up on this," I said. "First, you shouldn't be approaching me without the other parties being present, and do you really think this is a winning strategy—to be nasty to one of the people judging this case?"

"That's the problem. There's only one *person* judging, and you're questionable."

To get a towel I had to stand right next to her, and she didn't budge. We were inches apart. "I'm going to do you a favor," I said. "I'm not going to mention this conversation to Mr. Sullivan, but don't you ever approach me again. Understand?"

"I'm not afraid of you. Once we finish with the Álfar we'll take care of the others, and people like you, too." Missy slammed out of the bathroom.

There was a quivering in the pit of my stomach. I waved, the dispenser burped out a towel, and I clutched the material so tightly that my nails broke through the rough paper. We'll take care of the others? Who was the we? My mind jumped to the threatening phone call from last night. Maybe I should say something to David, but I didn't want to prejudice the proceedings for all the human actors because Missy was a bitch.

I left and found myself walking with a whip-thin older man whose deep-set dark eyes seemed even blacker when contrasted with his shock of silver hair. He seemed familiar, but I couldn't place him. He was also heading for the doors leading to IMG. He held open the door and indicated for me to go ahead, displaying the kind of manners you only saw in vampires and the elderly.

Inside it seemed like the entire firm was milling around in the reception area. Everyone was staring at us. No, correction, they were staring at the old man. He paused for an instant. The young PA from earlier edged closer and said in a breathless voice, "Mr. Campos, it's an honor to meet you. I think *No Miracle* was the best movie ever made."

So, this was the expert witness, the world-famous director whose films had influenced Spielberg, Lucas, and Coppola. I knew from our documents that he was eighty-two years old, and hadn't worked much in the past twenty years.

"Well, then, you'd be an idiot. *Citizen Kane* was the best movie ever made," the man said in a rumbling, gravel bass that could have doubled for the voice of God.

The kid didn't seem embarrassed; he just seemed dazed that he had spoken to his idol.

"Mr. Campos, I'm Linnet Ellery, one of the arbitrators in this case. I'm heading back to the conference room if you'd like to ac-company me," I said.

"Certainly."

"Can we get you anything? Coffee? Water? Soda?"

"Water, please."

There was a scramble as the PA and several others went lunging for the break room. We walked in silence. Then just before the door to the conference room he said, "Nothing's like it used to be, not the town or the industry. This is just part of the change." And he once again held the door for me.

"They've been a disaster." Campos's words were flat and uncompro-mising.

"But they are beautiful," Sheila LeBlanc said. It was more of a statement than a question.

"Oh, yeah, they're gorgeous, but looks aren't what makes an actor. Look at Bogart, Astaire, Tracy, Orson Welles, Hepburn—who was, frankly, funny looking. Those were *actors*. These Álfar, they're like pretty dolls with just about as much animation."

There was a stir from Qwendar, and Palendar looked outraged.

"I won't use them in my movies, and most directors feel the same way if you get them in private."

I looked down at the statistics I'd compiled and stepped in before LeBlanc could pose another question. "I don't understand, Mr. Campos. If we extrapolate from your statement, then the Álfar shouldn't be getting cast. But they are. A lot. The statistics are here." I held up the papers.

David pinned Sheila with a look. "Is there going to be a long line of directors who support Mr. Campos's view? Because if so you seem to be making Ms. Gabaldon's case that the Álfar don't have an advantage."

"We're getting to how this is relevant," she said. "Mr. Campos, if you would, please."

Campos jumped in. "They get cast because they whammy the humans when they audition. They're not winning these parts on merit. They're cheating. Using their magic."

Qwendar took to his feet. "That is gross slander, and I object." It was declaimed more than spoken. I remembered John telling me that the Álfar all lived as if they were in an opera. Qwendar seemed to bear that out.

David gave the ancient elf a weary look—and a vampire could pack a lot of ennui into a look. "Mr. Qwendar, this is not a courtroom, and you aren't representing the other party, so you really can't object to anything. Now sit down."

"I will report your attitude to the Council," Qwendar said.

"That is your prerogative," David answered. "Though I don't see how they have any relevance to this case."

Barbara Gabaldon stood up. "If I may, Mr. Sullivan?" David nodded in assent. She turned to the director. "Mr. Campos, you state this as if it's a fact, but by your own testimony you say you've never cast an Álfar. So how could you have experienced this reputed magic power?"

"No, I haven't felt it because I don't read them. But everyone knows it exists. It's the only thing that explains what's been happening."

Gabaldon looked at us. "Forgive me, but belief isn't evidence. I don't think it's appropriate for you to consider this witness's testimony."

David and I exchanged a glance. She had made a good point, and LeBlanc had walked right into it. "We'll keep that in mind, Ms. Gabaldon."

Both Missy and Palendar were looking confused and pissed. They could sense something had happened, but seemed not to understand the ramifications. Jeff, watching quietly from a seat against the back wall, gave a sad, slow headshake.

McPhee was next. It was like watching a breaching whale as he levered himself out of his chair. "Well, Mr. Sullivan, this has been most interesting testimony. Most interesting indeed. And if it's true that these Álfar actors have put the whammy on people, then my clients"—he indicated all the studio and network suits—"can't be held liable in any way. They were under the influence, so to speak. It seems to me that this fight is between the human actors and the Álfar actors, and all the rest of us are just innocent bystanders."

One corner of David's mouth quirked up in a barely suppressed smile. "Nice try, Mr. McPhee, but no. And now you can sit down, too." He looked back at Sheila. "Are you finished with this witness, Ms. LeBlanc." She nodded. "Well, as Mr. Palendar has an afternoon call and Ms. Gabaldon has a court appearance on another case this afternoon, we will adjourn for the day. See you all tomorrow."

People stood and milled, random movements like spooked fish in a tank. I slipped along the wall to where Qwendar was packing up his briefcase.

"Sir," I said.

He looked down at me. "Yes . . . Ms. Ellery, isn't it?"

"Yes. I was wondering if humans ever got to address the Álfar Council, and if there was a mechanism for making such a request?"

"Is this a question on your behalf, or are you asking for your firm?"

"Maybe a little of both. IMG had an Álfar on retainer. He was . . . assisting me on a case." I firmly pushed aside the memory of the night John and I had spent together. "When he . . . we were forcibly pulled into your realm, and John was forced to stay."

"His mother would dispute your characterization," he said dryly.

My mouth had gone dry. I swallowed hard. "Oh, so you know her."

"Yes. She's a very powerful figure in our world."

"Maybe so, but she used threats to get John to agree, and then she did something to him."

Qwendar looked at me intently. "You care for him."

"He's my . . . friend," I hedged. "And I want to be sure that he's remaining in Fey because he wants to, and not because he was coerced."

"Then you are not sympathetic to these nativist humanist hate groups?"

"You know I can't answer that. And there's a plethora of these nut jobs. Which group in particular are you talking about?"

"Check out the Human First movement, then maybe you will have a better understanding of my role here and why it's so vitally important."

Jeff came up at that moment. "Hey, Linnie, ready to go?"

"Yep, just let me put my things in my office. Meet you at the door?"

"Sounds good."

"Thank you," I said to Qwendar.

"I'll consider your request," he called after me.

I returned to my office floating on hope.

The Mercedes seemed to dance through the traffic with Jeff driving. Watching him made me realize I needed to embrace my inner formula-one driver if I was going to get anywhere in LA. He took the Barham exit and we went sailing past the Oakwood. I should have driven home and met Jeff out front so he wouldn't have had to drive me back to Century City. I said as much, and he shrugged.

"Not a problem. I live in Newport Beach. I have to go right past Century City to get home."

We continued down the hill where Barham turned into Pass Avenue. On our left loomed the walls of massive buildings. They ended up forming a walled-city effect on the edge of the Warner Bros. lot. The walls had been painted with pictures of Batman, Superman, and Sherlock Holmes. Interspersed between the massive pictures of characters were publicity photos of the human cast members of several television sitcoms. We turned in the front gate. Jeff took us around the line of cars inching toward the guard shack to a lane with a card reader. He had the card tucked into the car's sunshade. A brief wave at the reader, the gate lifted, and we drove through. I was on a movie lot.

On our left were low buildings with tile roofs, and a very Spanish feel. Jeff saw me looking and said, "Those are some of the original buildings from the 1920s. When you get an office in there it means you really rate." He indicated the big buildings on our right. "Sound-stages."

There were a lot of people walking or biking down the palm tree–lined street while golf carts with candy cane–colored tops wove through them. There were narrow side streets between the soundstages and trucks were parked there, many loaded with equipment. The only thing I recognized were stage lights, and only because I'd been the stage manager on a high school production of *Mame*. I saw people carrying takeout food containers and beverage cups. It reminded me that I hadn't eaten lunch. Jeff seemed to read my mind.

"The set's on lunch break right now, so we can grab a bite. There's a cafeteria where below-the-line people, day players, and writers tend to eat. Then there's the restaurant where the studio suits and big-name actors eat."

"You're a big-name actor. Where do you eat?" I asked, throwing it back on him.

"In my trailer after sending some gopher out for food, but since I'm a producer and not an actor on this film I can mingle with the hoi polloi."

"Would I see famous people in the restaurant?" I asked in a small voice.

"Probably." He gave me a smile. "Restaurant it is."

We wove down a few more streets, and Jeff went to park. The tire stop was painted with his name. I gave him a look. This time there was a rueful grin. "It's how we count coup around here. Part of the perks my agent and manager negotiate—a parking space with my name, an office, an assistant."

"So, is your office in the old buildings?" I asked.

"Well, yes."

"So, you rate."

"For now." His demeanor became sober. "I really need this movie to be a box-office success if I'm going to make the transition from heartthrob and action figure to producer and director."

"I'm sure it will."

He recovered the usual grin. "Well, I've sure as hell done everything to ensure that happens. I got Boucher to direct, and Jondin to star and Michael Cassutt to write the script. It's a fucking trifecta."

He led me across a small park with a small city street on one side. There was a movie theater, and a store that had been decorated to look like a bookstore. There was a famous actor in the center of the park staring in consternation at a giant white pig. I tried to keep from goggling. As we walked past, the man holding the pig on its leash was saying,

"You don't have to worry. She's just as friendly as all get-out."

Once we were out of earshot I gripped Jeff's arm. "Was that really . . . ?"

"Yep."

"Oh, wow," I breathed. "Why is he meeting a pig?"

"I couldn't say. But I'm sure we can find out."

The restaurant on the lot was an elegant affair with brushed-glass doors, blue carpeting, and subdued lighting. The hostess started to lead us to a secluded table, but Jeff whispered something to her, and she changed direction, steering us to a table that offered a view of the entire restaurant and the front door. For a moment I felt embarrassed, then I decided to hell with it. This was all totally new and very exciting for me, and I wasn't going to pretend bored sophistication. It was just too cool.

I settled on a seafood salad and a glass of white wine, and people-watched and eavesdropped on conversations. They ranged from "The second act just doesn't work" to "Yeah, she's an idiot, but if we keep her shirt off no one will notice." A beautiful English actress whose work I'd admired came in with a pair of men in expensive suits and open collars. I saw a couple of people whose faces I recognized from movie posters, if not from the films themselves.

Then, surprisingly, Qwendar entered. He was with a tall, broad-shouldered man with curling black hair liberally streaked with gray. Conversations stuttered and died. Everyone was looking at the Álfar and his companion.

"They act like they've never seen an Álfar, but—"

Jeff interrupted me. "It's not that," he said. "It's who he's *with*. That's Chip Diggins, head of the studio. Believe me, everybody in the industry knows about the lawsuit. When they see an Álfar with the studio head there's going to be talk. And doesn't this violate the rules David set?"

"It's skirting the edge, but Qwendar isn't actually a party to the dispute; he's an observer. But I will tell David." I had an uncomfortable moment sensing that I was skirting the edge too, but like Qwendar, Jeff wasn't actually a party to the arbitration. And I did so want to go on a movie set. Also, I had a feeling that David's order to stay away from the actor had less to do with the case and more with marking territory

"So answer another question for me. Why so many recesses or half-days of testimony? On TV, trials just move right along," Jeff said.

"That's because TV lawyers only seem to have one case at a time. It's not that way in real life. The parties to this arbitration have other court dates, hearings, depositions, appointments. We're working around a lot of schedules. Also, this is a civil case and an arbitration to boot. The Sixth Amendment guarantees the right to a speedy trial but that applies to criminal cases. Bottom line, the law grinds slowly, but it grinds exceedingly fine."

"Okay, that makes sense," Jeff said,

Our lunches arrived. After a few bites I set aside my fork. "Okay, I've got to ask. Why in *Earth Defense Force* did they not have the commander marry Tabitha at the end?"

Jeff threw back his head and laughed. He had a good laugh, full-throated and uninhibited. "Oh, God love you, you're a romantic."

"No, I'm not. It was all set up in the scene where you . . . they were trapped in the ship that was about to burn up in the atmosphere."

"Why do you think?

"I don't know, which is why I'm asking you."

"Because we thought there was going to be a sequel, and the producers thought a staid and married Commander Belmanor wasn't going to pull in the female audience. It also didn't help that Miranda got pregnant. That, together with somewhat disappointing overseas box office, meant the commander's adventures were over. There is going to be a video game set in that universe."

"Okay, I said, that makes it a little better. Can I play Tabitha if I buy the game?" I asked.

"I think they're going with new characters, since I haven't been asked in to voice the commander."

"Well, now I'm less interested."

"Looking to romance me?" Jeff teased.

"I've got a crush on the commander, not on you."

"Ouch."

We finished and walked outside into bright California sun. I threw my head back and let it beat on my face.

"More like what you were expecting?" he asked and his usual smile was back.

"It is a nice change after February in New York and all the rain since I got here."

Jeff led me down one of the narrow streets between soundstages. Many of the streets had large white travel trailers with blue and pink piping parked against the walls and the words STAR WAGGON in bold blue letters emblazoned across the outside. I pointed mutely.

"Private trailers for the actors. Also makeup, wardrobe, some are even set up as schoolrooms when you're shooting with kids. You've arrived as an actor when you get a private one. And trust me, size matters. Your costar's better not be bigger than yours."

"Wow, is everything out here about perception?" I asked.

"Pretty much, yeah."

Outside several of the buildings were whirling red lights mounted on tripods. There would be the harsh ring of a bell, and the light would start spinning. "I'm guessing that's some kind of warning?" I suggested.

"Yeah, it tells people that they're shooting so no one blunders in from outside." Jeff was whispering, and I guiltily put a hand over my mouth. "You're fine. You weren't exactly shouting."

We reached a building, and Jeff led me up the steps and through a heavy metal door. I took a step and stumbled. Jeff caught me under the arm. "You have to look down on a stage," he said. I followed his advice, and saw massive cables snaking across the wood floor. There were voices calling from overhead. I stood still so I could look up. Men were on catwalks probably thirty feet above the floor, adjusting lights and placing gels.

Three men began pushing a flat across the floor with a howl of wood on wood. Set dressers scurried through setting up a vase of flowers on an end table, plumping up pillows on a sofa. In another area a man was pushing squibs into holes in a flat, and covering them with wood putty. In the center of it all was the director with a device hanging around his neck that looked like a light meter. As the light changed he would pick it up on its lanyard and look through it.

You didn't have to be a movie geek to have heard of Boucher. Though young, the director had burst onto the scene three years before with a celluloid ghost story that had terrified audiences around the world. Now his name was heard in conjunction with Spielberg, Scorsese, and Nolan. He was the new face of movies.

Standing on his right was a young woman with a walkie-talkie;

on his left was a big man with a shock of curly black hair and his own light meter. He and Boucher would occasionally lean in close and exchange a few words.

"Okay, who are the two people with Boucher?" I asked.

"The girl is Debbie, his assistant. She's taking notes on everything that's discussed. The other man is Christian Alter, the DP."

"What's a DP?" I asked

"Director of photography. It's his job to light each scene. He does that in consultation with the director, but he brings a lot of his own ideas to the table. If you're an actor you want to be very, very nice to the DP. They're the ones who make you look good."

"I thought makeup did that," I said.

Jeff flashed me a grin. "That helps too, but in a pinch I can do my own makeup. I can't go reset all the lights, and the DP and the gaffers can do something subtle. Light you from below so you look like you've got a double chin. Little tricks, and you, as the actor, won't know until the movie's released. And then you're wishing you'd been nicer."

"Be nice to people on the way up because you'll meet them on your way down," I said, quoting my human father.

"Exactly. Words to live by in Hollywood."

"Anywhere, really," I countered.

"Yeah, good point."

The meeting broke up and Jeff led me over to Boucher. The lights overhead flashed off the sweat on his forehead.

"Tom, I'd like you to meet Linnet Ellery," Jeff said.

He held out a shovel-like hand and gave me a startlingly shy smile. "Hi. Welcome."

"Thank you," I said. "This is very exciting."

"First time?" Boucher asked. I nodded.

"It's thrilling for the first hour. Then it gets really boring when you are just watching. But enjoy it before the disillusionment sets in."

"Thank you, I will."

Boucher waved a hand off to the side. "The craft table's over on the left. Help yourself to anything."

The girl friday was suddenly back at Boucher's elbow. "Would you like something, Tom?"

"Yeah, an apple juice."

Debbie gestured. "Follow me, I'll take you over."

Jeff held back. "I'll catch up with you. Got something to discuss with Tom."

I nearly tripped again because in addition to the tangle of big cables there was a metal track, and a tall metal column topped by a camera and mounted on wheels resting on the track. The contraption looked like an anorexic, cyclopian robot.

Then we were off the set, behind the flats, and up against the wall of the soundstage. There was a long table loaded down with bowls of apples, bananas, and oranges. Giant jars of peanut butter and jelly, loaves of bread. A bowl of M&M's. Some bags of chips. There was a coffee maker and powdered creamer and artificial sweeteners.

My cell phone chirped. Debbie whirled at the sound emerging from my purse. "You need to turn that off. The mikes are incredibly sensitive, and I don't want you forgetting before we start shooting."

"Sorry, sorry," I mumbled. I pulled out my phone and turned it off.

We reached the food-laden table just as a young man in a policeman's uniform furtively grabbed an apple. "Hey!" Debbie said. "Extras aren't allowed. Stay in your own area." She did schoolmarm really well. I had probably looked as guilty as the young extra.

"All we've got is bottled water," he said. "And you won't let us go over to the commissary."

"We're about to start shooting."

"You said that three hours ago." The young man's Adam's apple bobbed up and down, propelled by both nerves and outrage.

"Yeah, well, you're a fucking extra and I can replace you in three minutes flat, so if you want to keep your job, scat!"

He scooted away, but I noticed he kept the apple.

"Locusts," Debbie muttered.

"Don't you feed them?"

"Only when we have to," she said. "If we hit Golden Time."

"Which is?" I asked.

"Over sixteen hours." She glanced at her watch. "And the way we're going, that may happen. Jondin needs to get her skinny Álfar ass over here. Look, I need to head over to her trailer and see what's up. You can look after yourself?"

I nodded. "Sure. Of course. Don't worry about me. I don't want to be a bother." I had been talking to air after the third word.

A young woman knelt on the floor in a corner and snapped open a case. As she lifted the lid I spotted the red cross indicating it was a first-aid kit. I walked over, and she looked up at me with a smile and blew a fringe of curly black bangs out of her eyes. "Hi. Need something?"

"Just curious. I've never been on a movie set before. I didn't know they had medics."

"Yep. Required by law." She gave me that bright grin again. "Good for EMTs like me, and we're kept busy, too."

"That's sort of scary."

"It's mostly just small stuff. Some grip takes a header off a scaffold. Somebody sprains an ankle tripping on a cable. Today, because they're messing around with explosives, I double-check my supplies. Everything usually works great, but once in a while somebody gets burned. And sometimes you can get a bad one. I was on a the set for a TV show once, and the guest star had a heart attack." She patted the case. "But I'm ready for almost anything. I even have a separate case for Jondin."

"Why's that?" I asked.

"Álfar physiology is really different from ours. A human-to-Álfar blood transfusion would kill the Álfar—as we discovered the hard way back in the day. That's why all the Álfar actors donate blood. When you've got an Álfar in the cast we send down to Cedars, and they send over a few pints. I've got a little fridge where I keep it." She pointed and I saw the small mini-fridge humming away in a corner.

"This is really cool. I had no idea that a set was like a little city. I mean you've got food, and medics, and—"

"And drivers and contractors and our very own tyrant." The EMT nodded at Boucher, but her smile removed the sting.

I held out my hand. "I'm Linnet, by the way."

She stood and shook my hand. "Consuela, Connie. My pleasure. Enjoy. It's fun for a while, but then you're going to get really bored."

I got a cup of coffee, and took a blue M&M, and wandered back toward the edge of the set. I watched the color and intensity of the light play across the set. Over the calls from the crew and the whine of dollies and scissor lifts carrying cameras into position there were a series of dull popping sounds from outside. A man wearing head-phones, carrying a clipboard, and sporting a harried expression came through calling, "Stand-ins. Stand-ins. We're ready for you."

A man and a woman walked onto the set. They studied the floor, and I realized they were looking at multicolored duct tape that had been placed there. The woman was human, but she wore a long silver wig with touches of green and gold mingled in. With the wild hair she was clearly the stand-in for Jondin. The man was shorter than I expected, but his hair color and overall features resembled Michael Tennant. Tennant was a serious heartthrob, and he had wowed me when he stared as Mr. Darcy in a remake of *Pride and Prejudice*. I sidled over to Jeff.

"Is Michael Tennant starring in this movie?"

Jeff gave me a smile. "Yes, he is." He correctly read my expression and added, "I'll be sure to introduce you."

"Okay." The word seemed to get stuck in a throat that suddenly seemed too small.

He's just an actor. Don't make a fool of yourself, Linnet. Wow! Michael Tennant and Jeff Montolbano. How did I get this lucky?

I was dying to text this news back to my friends in the New York office, but I had turned off my phone. Then Michael Tennant walked in, and I forgot all about texting anybody. He was gorgeous: tousled blond hair and deep brown eyes and a trim, elegant body. I knew he was twenty-eight. I was twenty-seven. He looked to be five-feet-six or seven. A good height for a boyfriend when you're only five feet tall. I indulged in a few moments of make-believe and built a few castles in the air.

Boucher looked around. A thunderous frown gouged canyons into his sunburned forehead. "Where the hell is Debbie? And where the hell is Jondin?"

The outer door crashed open. Everyone looked around. The sunlight formed jagged streaks around the woman framed in the door.

"So glad you could join us," Boucher said, the snark dripping off each word.

Then Jondin started shooting.

7

Boucher's chest blossomed with blood, and chunks of bloody flesh, mingled with scraps of material blew out his back. He didn't make a sound, just looked surprised before his body tumbled to the floor to lie in an ever widening pool of blood.

People were screaming, and Jondin wasn't holding back. She raked the gun back and forth across the set while holding down the trigger, the buck and kick of the Uzi sending the barrel climbing toward the ceiling. Bullets skipped and whined off cameras, lights, and microphones. A lighting guy fell screaming from a catwalk high above. His body hit the floor with a meaty thud.

She got control of the gun, and brought it back down only to start shooting again. Bullets ripped through sets and knocked wood chips out of the walls. My body responded faster than my brain, sending me in a dive toward a stack of film boxes. I heard bullets singing and ricocheting as they hit the metal boxes. I wasn't sure where Jeff had gone. He had been right beside me. He must have gone a different direction to find cover. Or maybe he was dead. I bit my lip and whimpered.

A lot of lead found human targets. Shrieks of pain joined cries of terror as metal slugs tore through flesh and shattered bone. The sound of bullets erupting from the barrel of the machine gun was like a giant's teeth chattering. A cameraman went down, clutching at his gut. Blood welled around his fingers. The two stunt doubles were down—hurt, maybe dead.

Silence. Which made me all the more aware that my ears were ringing from the percussive force of the shooting. I heard the muffled but unmistakable sound of a clip being dropped and another one being rammed into place.

Between the cracks between the boxes I saw pointy-toed, high-heeled lavender boots approaching my hiding place. Inside I was whimpering. *Oh God, I'm gonna die! Oh Daddy. Help me. Somebody please help me.*

Another part of me, less limp and terrified, was shouting *MOVE, MOVE, MOVE.* I looked left and right. To my right was a big, plush leather couch. I slipped off my high heels. My stomach felt loose, and my knees were shaking so hard that my muscles were aching. Somehow I managed to balance on my fingertips and toes like a runner in a starting block and pushed off hard, running for the sofa. Bullets snapped and whined at my heels until I was safely behind it.

A quavering voice shouted out, "Drop the gun!"

I peeked over the back of the sofa to see a security guard confronting Jondin. Both hands gripped his pistol, and he had it thrust out at her. Unfortunately the barrel was shaking like a branch in a strong wind. I wanted to shriek at him, *Shoot her! Just fucking shoot her!* but I couldn't force air through my constricted throat, and then it was too late because Jondin brought the Uzi up to her hip, and fired off a burst. She was definitely getting better at controlling the gun. The security guard was slammed backward by the force of the bullets. I choked back a cry, dropped down, and looked across the set in search of an exit. I saw Jeff huddled behind an armchair. He was hunkered down, arms wrapped protectively around his head. I felt a flare of disappointment.

Not an action hero. Just an actor. A terrified human, just like me. The room reeked of cordite and blood, and tendrils of smoke from the Uzi drifted like witch's hair.

In the center of the set various crew members and Michael Tennant were down on the floor bleeding. Consuela, clutching her first-aid kit, came scrabbling out from behind the set to reach them. Even though her back was to her, somehow Jondin was aware of the EMT. Her head swung around and she studied the woman. From my hiding place I could see her face framed by the long white, green, and gold hair and utterly devoid of expression. A few wisps of hair were caught in her lips. She casually brushed them away.

Connie struggled to open the first-aid kit, but her hands were shaking so badly that it took her three tries before she succeeded. She slapped a pressure bandage over the wound in Tennant's chest. I couldn't believe she had done this incredibly brave thing.

Jondin dropped the Uzi so it hung on its neck strap, reached into the waistband of her trousers, and pulled out a pistol. She began walking toward the EMT with slow, deliberate steps. It looked like the actress intended to shoot the girl from point-blank range. I couldn't stand it. I couldn't just stand by and let this girl be killed.

I looked around for any kind of weapon, but there was nothing. All I had was me. And she had a gun. Actually more than one.

A flash of memory etched itself against my mind. Mr. Bainbridge, my vampire foster liege, taking me out and teaching me how to shoot when I was twelve years old. His usually genially smiling round face was unaccustomedly serious.

"You're almost a young woman, Linnet, and your greatest predator will be men. They're stronger than you, and more violent, so I'm going to teach you how to even the odds." He had then smiled and added, "In the words of the old adage, 'God didn't make men and women equal. Colonel Colt did.'"

Then he taught me how to shoot. How to break down a gun.

How to clean it. How not to treat it as a toy. He had taught me one other thing. That most people missed, even at close range. If I could distract Jondin, maybe the little EMT would run, and maybe we would both survive.

I jumped up and ran around the sofa, cutting across the set on an angle designed to take me between Jondin and Connie. The actress watched me, eyes following, and I felt like one of the little rabbit figures in the shooting gallery of a midway carnival. Soon Jondin would knock me down and win a stuffed toy. The image of the Álfar woman standing over my bleeding body while holding a giant panda bear made me giggle. A hysterical reaction if ever there was one.

The barrel of Jondin's gun swiveled away from Connie and sighted on me. Every muscle in my body tensed as I prepared for the coming bullet. Instead there was the sound of tortured metal from overhead. I looked up just as a giant light hurtled down, clipping Jondin's wrist and hand as it passed. The pistol fell from her hand. Whimpering, she gripped her clearly broken wrist. The light hit the ground with a horrendous crash, and the lens exploded, sending glass in all directions. One chip gouged my shoulder, but the bulk of the shards hit Jondin in the face. She transferred her hands to her face and the whimpers became screams.

The pistol lay on the floor just in front of her. I wondered if I could reach it before her. I decided to try. I changed course and ran straight at her. Behind the set a huge electrical panel spat sparks like a roman candle. As I passed Consuela I screamed out, "Run!"

She did and then I stumbled on the metal track that was laid across the floor. Arms windmilling I tried to keep on my feet, but gravity won. I went down. The edges of the track dug painfully into my neck and back. I faintly heard the whining of a motor. Jondin strode over and only stopped once she stood directly over me. Blood pumped from the myriad cuts on her face and stained the front of her shirt. She was standing between the rails of the track.

She raised the Uzi on its strap. The barrel lifted, sighted down at me. Because of her broken wrist she had the gun balanced on her forearm. It would affect her aim, but not enough: the Uzi fired a lot of rounds—there was no way they were all going to miss. I considered just closing my eyes so I wouldn't see death coming, but I couldn't. I struggled to regain my feet. A shadow loomed against the wall of the set. I looked past Jondin: the remote camera was running down the track at an alarming clip.

Jondin's finger tightened on the trigger just as the protruding lens on the camera slammed into the back of her head. The shots went wide. Then the body of the camera hit her heels and back and knocked her flat. The camera tried to roll over her body, but lost balance and crashed onto its side.

Jeff came running past me, yanked the Uzi out of Jondin's hands, and flung it aside. He then landed hard on her back, and searched her for more guns. He found two—both pistols, one a tiny lady's-handbag derringer. Then Connie rushed back out and began treating people. Outside sirens were wailing, drawing ever closer. The electrical panel gave one final massive spark and every light on the soundstage went out.

People screamed again. Then the stage door slammed open allowing in the sunlight, and I saw the silhouette of a fireman. Within moments the stage was filled with EMTs, firefighters, and security guards. Eventually the real police arrived. That's when I allowed myself to start crying.

Being present at the scene of a hideous mass murder with a world-famous actor means you don't get dragged down to the police station to give your statement and you get treated with kid gloves. Which is how I found myself seated in a large, deep armchair in the office of Chip Diggins, current head of Warner Bros. Plush carpet underfoot, an acre-wide desk that looked like it had been tiled with pink message slips, and a pile of scripts walling off one side. More scripts, and a selection of current bestsellers filled a bookcase. The office was on the top floor of one of the historic buildings, and the windows looked out toward the back lot and the park.

Lights were beginning to flick on across the studio as night slunk in. Out in the park Christmas lights twinkled in the trees. They were either filming some kind of Christmas movie or really lazy about taking down decorations.

Diggins himself was on the phone talking in hushed tones. If I had to bet, I'd say it was the studio lawyers or PR people. Either group was going to have their hands full dealing with the situation.

I shivered and took a sip of tea. The mug was warm comfort against my palms, but even the hot liquid couldn't ease the cold terror that still gripped me. I had come so close to dying. Again. If that light hadn't fallen . . . if a power surge hadn't sent the camera careening along the track . . . if, if, if.

My shoulder had been cleaned and bandaged by a sympathetic EMT, but my blouse was a complete loss. To keep me decent Diggins had sent his assistant over to the company store. I guess she'd just grabbed the first thing she found, because what I was now wearing was a large T-shirt sporting a picture of the Road Runner and Wile E. Coyote.

The door to the office opened and Jeff came back in. He had gone into the hall to call his wife and assure her that he was all right. The news of the studio massacre had begun to leak out. He checked when he spotted the T-shirt.

"Yeah, that's certainly appropriate," he said.

"Huh?" was my snappy response.

"You did definite Road Runner-fu on Jondin"

"I didn't do anything. I ran around and then I fell down. You're the one who disarmed her," I said.

Diggins hung up the phone and looked at Jeff. "Not to sound like a total Hollywood asshole, but what the hell are we going to do? We've got twenty-three days of film in the can, our director is dead, and our leading man is in the hospital, shot by our leading lady, who is now in jail. And I don't see how we get her out."

I goggled at him. "Are you nuts? Why would you *want* her out? She killed eleven people and wounded fifteen others. Sixteen if you count me, though I guess it was technically the light . . ." I firmly shut my mouth so I would stop babbling. "Anyway, you can't."

Jeff looked at Diggins. "Then we've got to recast and reshoot."

"I'm not sure the studio will support that," Diggins said.

Jeff looked sick. "I've sunk a lot of my own money into this film. We can't just fold it."

"We've got to consider how it looks. The young lady's right. People are dead."

"So, we go to Romania or Latvia and shoot there. Away from the press. Do it quiet." Jeff was pleading, but Diggins just shook his head. "So, what you're saying is, 'Forget it, Jake. It's Chinatown,'" Jeff said bitterly. He correctly read my expression as one of complete confusion. "Not a movie buff, huh?" Then he gave a sharp laugh that turned into a choking sob. He turned away and drew his sleeve across his eyes.

I looked away, wanting to excuse myself. "Pardon me, where's the restroom?"

Diggins pointed at a door on the left side of his office. "There's one in here you can use."

It wasn't exactly what I was looking for. I wanted to go into the bathroom and bawl like a little kid for a minute, but I was stuck. I stood up and the office door opened. Diggins's assistant escorted in David, who was looking thunderous.

He crossed to my side in three long strides and took hold of my shoulders. I winced, and he released me like I was hot. "Are you all right?" he asked.

It was one of those reflexive, stupid statements that make you want to scream at the person, *No, I'm not all right. I just saw eleven people killed right in front of me.* But I didn't say that, since he did seem honestly concerned. I settled for a nod.

"What?" Diggins said. I looked around, confused by the question, but it had been directed to the assistant.

"Sorry, Chip, but the lead detective is really insistent about talking with Mr. Montolbano and Ms. Ellery."

David stepped in. "Tell him we'll have both of them available tomorrow morning." He quirked an eyebrow at Jeff. "I assume you won't object if we involve Ishmael, McGillary and Gold?"

"Why would I need a lawyer?" Jeff asked.

"It's a good idea to always have representation when you're dealing with the police," I said.

"Why? I didn't do anything wrong. And I didn't have a lawyer when my house got robbed last year. I just told the cops what happened, they took a statement, and then nothing happened. Never got back a single item." He seemed to realize he was babbling because he abruptly shut up.

"Burglary is one thing. You witnessed murder today," I said.

"And you were the victim when your house was robbed," David added.

"Well, I can tell you I found today's events pretty damn victimizing," Jeff said.

David twitched a shoulder impatiently. "Not the same."

I stepped in. "Look, Jeff, I'm going to be taking someone—"

"That would be me," David interrupted.

"Thanks." I hoped I'd successfully hid my surprise. I then added, "Point is, I'm a lawyer and I'm going to take a lawyer." I was also remembering the long hours in a police station in Bayonne, New Jersey, after werewolves had attacked and killed an old man and damned near killed me. Hours in which I'd had no help, and for a time it looked like I was going to be charged with murder. That time John had come and taken me home. I blinked hard at the fresh rush of tears.

David pushed his argument. "If you go now, Jeff, you won't get home until three or four in the morning. You've all been through a shocking experience. You'll be fresher in the morning."

"And they'll argue that memories will fade," Montolbano said. He gave a sick little smile. "I played a cop in four Knight Shield movies, did some ride-alongs. Makes me an expert, right?" He paused and shivered. "Truthfully, I don't think the memory will ever fade. Never seen anything like that."

"Who's going to tell the cops?" Diggins asked. "I'm sure as hell not making Cindi." The assistant looked grateful. "And I'm not real keen on doing it myself."

"I'll handle it," David said. He turned to Jeff. "Go home. We'll call you in the morning with the details."

"That's another issue," Cindi said. "The press is seven deep at every gate. How do we get him out?"

Diggins considered, then said, "Call one of the limo companies. Have them send a big white stretch to the main gate. Have somebody leak that it's for Montolbano. That should pull most of them off the other gates."

"My car's pretty recognizable," Jeff said.

"Would you be willing to let Cindi take you home?" Diggins asked. Cindi tried to look blasé, but I saw the excitement beneath the weary industry sophisticate.

Jeff gave her that patented smile, though it seemed a little rough around the edges. "Sure. That would be fine."

"It's just a Prius," she said apologetically.

Diggins looked at David. David took my hand. The icy touch removed any warmth supplied by the tea. "I'll handle getting us out. Just tell me which of these other gates to use."

8

"We need to go get my car. It's still at the office," I said, as David led me across a parking lot.

Overhead the sky was lit by city glow and not a star was visible. Bushes with heavy palmlike branches rattled in a sharp breeze that carried the smell of exhaust and, maybe very faintly, the smell of the ocean.

"It can wait. Right now I'm going to get you back to your apartment." He pulled out keys, and hit the unlock button. The headlights flashed on a blue Sebring, and the interior lights came on.

"You drove yourself," I said rather stupidly. It wasn't all that common with vampires. Servants were part of a vampire's life. Even the awful Ryan had a driver. It was also another clue to the mystery that was David. Either he'd learned to drive before he was turned, which meant he wasn't that old by vampire standards, or he'd learned afterward, which indicated that he wanted very badly to integrate into human society.

"I can drive. Also, it's the middle of the night. I didn't want to roust Kobe this late."

"That was nice of you," I said as David opened the passenger door for me.

"Meaning surprising and unexpected?" he asked.

"Well, yes. You're polite, but you're not considerate." I immediately cursed my too ready and blunt tongue.

He leaned into the car. "Meaning me in particular or vampires in general?"

Well, may as well be hung for a sheep as a lamb. "Both," I said.

He gave a short laugh and shook his head. He came around the car, got in, and started the engine. "Well, it wasn't total altruism. I wanted a chance to talk to you alone."

A cold knot settled in my already aching stomach. "Are you mad because I came to the set with Jeff?"

"No . . . yes . . . well, maybe a little. It's the situation." He put the car in gear and we headed toward a side gate. "I'm going to do a little—in the words of Mr. Campos—whammy here. You won't tell on me, will you?"

"Depends on how much of a whammy it is, and on who," was my cautious reply. Stoker wasn't completely off base on some of the powers he gave vampires, but vamps were careful not to use them too often on humans. To do otherwise sort of undercut that whole assimilation effort.

"Not on you. On the guards at the gate and the press vultures."

As we approached the gate David's eyes narrowed with concentration, and his hands tightened on the steering wheel. A gray fog rose up around the vehicle. As we came level with the guard shack David muttered beneath his breath. The guard's expression turned vague and dreamy and he raised the gate pole.

David shot me a quick glance. "These aren't the droids you're looking for." I gaped at him. We drove through and past a couple of people standing on the sidewalk just outside the gate. In addition to the pedestrians, there were three parked cars. The doors flew open, people stepped out then stopped and looked confused. Some of the watchers looked at us, or whatever we appeared to be. One raised his camera. I wasn't sure if he snapped a photo or not, and then we were past and turning onto Riverside Drive. From there it was a close hop up the hill to my apartment.

"Why did you tell Jeff to wait until tomorrow to go to the police?" I asked.

"So I could keep *you* away from the police," came the answer that gave me a bit of a chill.

"Why? I can't possibly be blamed for this."

"No, but all that unpleasantness back in New York and Virginia is going to come up, and that will be . . . awkward. I wanted a chance to talk with you first and find out exactly what happened before I allowed a bunch of unimaginative cops to grill you."

I remembered a conversation with John about the police. He'd been an officer in Philly, and while he liked and respected the people in his former profession, he was also blunt about the drawbacks. "Cops like simple stories," he'd said. "The simpler the better. You start messing with the story, and they're not going to like you. When cops don't like you, your life gets complicated."

I repeated this aloud to David as we headed up the hill toward the Oakwood. "Right now they have a story. Crazy elf actress goes nuts and shoots up set," I said.

"And you're the one discordant note in this song."

"Gee, thanks," I said.

"Think about it, Linnet. You're the woman who was present when nine people got killed last year too."

"Not all at the same time or in the same place," I protested. "Three at one place and six at the other . . ." My voice trailed away.

"And you don't think that makes it look even worse?"

I had no answer to that. I just slumped into sullen silence. David started to pull in the main gate at the Oakwood but suddenly swerved back into the traffic streaming up the hill, occasioning more than a few blaring horns, and Anglo-Saxon gestures of disapproval aimed in our general direction. What had spooked him was a TV truck and a gaggle of reporters besieging the gates.

"Well, damn. Back to the hotel?" David suggested.

"I have no clothes, not even a toothbrush. They may get bored, and I can always slip in the pedestrian gate on the side."

"So, what do we do in the meantime?" David asked.

It was embarrassing to admit. Societal norms said I should be more like a nineteenth-century heroine, shattered by what I'd seen, but awful as it was it wasn't as horrible as watching a werewolf literally tear a fellow associate to pieces right in front of me. Bottom line, I was hungry. A lot of hours had passed since that lunch in the Warner's restaurant. Shamefaced, I confessed as much to David.

"Start looking for something that looks good and is open at this hour."

We were on Ventura Boulevard and despite the late hour there were still a lot of cars. The small strip malls held a lot of sushi restaurants, but they were all closed. Which was good: I didn't want sushi.

"I want comfort food," I said, and then I saw a large building on our left that looked like a 1950s diner. A large sign read DUPAR'S— OPEN TWENTY-FOUR HOURS. "There," I said and pointed.

"You're kidding, right?"

"No. And don't be a snob."

He forced extra air through his lungs so he could produce a gusting sigh and turned into the parking lot. Behind the restaurant were other stores, a Trader Joe's, a beauty supply house, and a Mc-Donald's.

"I guess I should be grateful you didn't want to eat there," he said with a jerk of his head toward the golden arches.

We walked into the smell of french fries and coffee. There were booths, and linoleum underfoot. It really was a blast from the past. David requested a booth near the back of the restaurant from the hostess, an older woman whose face looked like five miles of bad road and whose voice was a husky smoker's rasp. She didn't move from her position behind the cash register. Instead she waved over a young woman in a starched white uniform complete with the little cap perched in her hair like a nesting bird. The young woman took two menus from the older woman.

David held up a hand. "I don't need a menu." But the girl ignored it and led us to the booth, where she tried to give David a menu.

"No, thank you," he said.

"So, you know what you want already?" she asked.

"I'm not having anything."

"If you look at the menu you might change your mind. We make our own pies. They're real good."

"I'm sure they are, but I'm not having anything." He was fast losing patience. I could hear it in his voice.

While the argument continued I perused the big menu, and decided on a hot roast beef sandwich and a Coke. "Well, I'll leave the menu just in case you change your mind," she chirped.

"I'm. Not. Having. Anything."

I snapped shut my menu. "Well, I am." I placed my order, and she went away. David was almost growling.

"Does she not get that I'm a vampire?"

"I don't think she even noticed," I said.

"That kind of inattention can get you killed," David said.

"What? You're planning on going rogue?"

"I don't mean with vampires. In general. You've got to be aware of your surroundings. Especially women."

That hit a little too close to home. "Look, she came in the door and started shooting. There wasn't a lot of opportunity for me to assess the situation."

"I'm not blaming you."

"Oh. Okay. It just sounded like you were."

The girl returned with my Coke and a cup of coffee. She smiled brightly at David and set it down in front of him. "Here. It's on the house. It just looks so lonely with you sitting there with nothing in front of you." Another smile and she went away.

David looked like he'd been pole-axed. I stifled a giggle. "She's flirting with you," I said.

"Does she know nothing?"

"Apparently not."

He gave an irritated shrug of a shoulder. "Enough of this. Tell me what happened."

So I did. I summarized the end. "The camera knocked her down. Jeff jumped on her. Then security, ambulances, and police arrived." My dinner arrived just as I was finishing.

Slices of roast beef on two pieces of white bread smothered with brown gravy. Mashed potatoes, also swimming in gravy, were on one side, and green beans on the other. They were the nod toward healthy eating. I picked up my knife and fork and tucked in.

"Even with your history there is no way the police can make you into anything other than a witness and a victim."

I nodded because my mouth was full. I swallowed, took a sip of Coke, and gathered the strands of thoughts that had been niggling at me and had finally begun to crystallize.

"David, I think something is going on." At his expression I hastened to add, "Beyond the obvious."

"I'm listening." The response was shorthand for "I'm really dubious, but I'll humor you."

I set aside my utensils and held up my index finger. "First, this high-profile lawsuit gets filed—human actors versus Álfar actors. It gets moved out of the courts, but it's still a hot news item because it involves our version of royalty. Everybody reads *People* and *Us*. And think about all the entertainment news shows that are on television—*Entertainment Tonight, Extra, Access Hollywood*. Everybody wants to know about the lives of the beautiful, glamorous, rich and famous people—"

"Okay, okay, I get all that. What's your point?"

"Everybody's watching this arbitration. Millions of ordinary Americans. Three weeks ago a heartthrob Álfar actor allegedly hacks his beautiful human actress wife to pieces with a kitchen knife. Then today an Álfar actress, who has starred in numerous blockbuster movies and who's been on the cover of *People* about a zillion times, goes nuts on the set. She kills a world-famous human director whose name is known to all those ordinary Americans, and she nearly kills a popular human actor who has millions of fans on Facebook and Twitter and an international fan club. You starting to see a pattern here?"

David had been leaning farther and farther forward as I talked. Now he leaned back in the booth, stretched out his arms and studied me. A frown furrowed his brow. "So, you're suggesting one of the human actors may be putting a thumb on the scale . . . but how would they do that? How would they make someone murderous?"

"I'm not suggesting anything, and I don't know the answer to your question. I don't even know if this is real or just too much adrenalin in my veins, but it sure looks like someone is trying to make the Álfar look bad, and they're succeeding. I can just picture the headlines in tomorrow's . . ." I glanced at my watch. "Er, make that today's papers. I think this arbitration is the tip of an iceberg. This isn't about who gets a part. There's something much darker at work here."

"Let's assume you're right. What do we do? We're the arbitrators."

"You're senior, and the person everyone is looking to. Why don't you let me make some inquiries?"

"Like what?"

"Talk to Kerrinan for starters. And probably to Jondin too."

"That's never going to happen. You're a witness. You'll probably be called to testify. If I were her defense attorney I wouldn't let you anywhere near her, and I'd get a judge to back me up."

"Yeah, you're probably right." I drew channels in the mashed potatoes and let the gravy flow through them like superfund rivers of sludge. "But Kerrinan's a different matter. Do we know who's representing him?"

David shook his head. "For all I know, it's us. If I were a Power being accused of murdering a human, I'd want a Power defending me."

"Bad choice. I'd pick a human and a woman."

He stared at me for a long moment. "Which is why I don't do much litigation unless it involves contracts. Do you have any interest in the courtroom, Linnet? I think you might be good at it."

A faint glow of pleasure ran through me. "Thank you, that's a really nice thing to say."

He reverted back to being a vampire. "It wasn't meant as a compliment. It's purely calculation. What you can do for the firm."

The waitress returned with a fresh glass of Coke. I took a sip, feeling the carbonation fizz against the roof of my mouth. For an instant I wished the bubbles were champagne. John had said we would pop a cork once we got back to New York with the will. That hadn't happened, and maybe never would now.

It began a new avenue of thought. "I wish John were here. To talk to us about the Álfar."

"Not sure how helpful he would be since he never lived among them until, uh—" He broke off abruptly realizing this was maybe just a tad painful. "Well, until recently," he concluded quietly.

I blinked hard, and resolved to prove how tough and focused I was. "Well, there's Qwendar," I said, and was pleased to hear that my voice sounded normal. No huskiness at all.

David shook his head. "Let's hold off on that. He's at least peripherally involved in the arbitration and I don't want to do any-thing to get us in trouble."

"We've got a dodge," I argued. "He said he might help me re-garding John. I can talk to him, and truthfully say that's what we were discussing."

"A sin of omission then?" David said dryly.

"Yeah. I think he's worried about how volatile the situation has become. He did mention a group he wanted me to check out. I can do that once I'm at my computer."

David nodded. "Okay, call him and set up a meeting. Just keep it well away from the office, and keep it on the QT, okay?" He glanced down at my messy plate. "Done? Or do you want a piece of Dupar's fine pie? Maybe a little à la mode?"

"And put a little ice cream on that?" I added.

David gave a short laugh. "I had an acquaintance who used to say that. We'd go out to eat, and he would always order apple pie à la mode, and then add, *and put a little ice cream on that* . . . I wanted to kill him."

I wondered when that had been, and who that had been, but knew not to ask. I wouldn't get an answer. Instead I said, "No, thanks. I've done enough damage to my arteries already."

He paid for my dinner. I tried to remonstrate and got a curt, "Don't be silly, Linnet."

The press was still huddled at the main gate of the Oakwood, so David dropped me off on Forest Lawn Drive. A footpath wound up the hill to a keyed gate. The famous cemetery that gave the road its name was just around the curve from the apartment complex. As I trudged up the hill I considered how close I'd come to being a resi-dent. It wasn't pleasant to contemplate.

Xenophobia has been part of American culture almost since the founding of the country, beginning with the Order of the Star

Spangled Banner, founded way back in 1849 to resist waves of Irish and German immigrants, to the late nineteenth and early twentieth century that brought us the Immigration Resistance League, formed by a bunch of Harvard graduates, and the Tea Party movement, with their resentment of Latinos. And now the Human First movement was another entry in that sorry history, reacting to a new kind of Outsider and Other.

The Firsters were pushing a ballot initiative in California that would ban marriage between an Álfar and a human. Would criminalize sexual contact between an Álfar and a human. John and I would have been in the slammer. Would bar adoption of human children by any Álfar. Since the Álfar had a history of stealing human children and leaving one of their own in its place (evidence John and his brother) this seemed sort of pointless, but throwing in the kitchen sink seemed to be par for the course with these groups. The Firsters had been founded by a minister in some small, fundamentalist Christian sect. Interviews with Reverend Bob Trager produced such lovely comments as: "We have no idea what god or gods they worship, or if they have any god at all. One thing's for certain, they don't worship the one true God, and they are damned to Hell." Another charmer read, "They're not human. You let this stand, and you could have a man marrying his dog."

Which raised an interesting question. Were the Álfar a strain of humans that had branched off way back in the evolutionary tree, or were we a less magical strain of Álfar? Or, final choice, were they a different species altogether? The Firsters movement was now led by a savvy lobbyist by the name of Belinda Cartwright, and Reverend Trager had been pushed to the background, which was probably why the initiative was starting to gain traction. I found a few man on the street interviews that had been uploaded onto YouTube. A few people defended the Álfar, but most talked about mesmerizing powers that drew in unsuspecting girls. I found the whole thing incredibly depressing.

I dug a bit deeper into Ms. Cartwright and found she and her advocacy group, Liberty Front, had been behind several anti-immigrant statutes passed in various states and now making their way up to the Supreme Court. They also made commercials that were in favor of carbon dioxide and said the melting of the permafrost was a *good* thing. If you warm up Siberia it could be a new breadbasket.

"Which we're going to fucking need, since Iowa, Kansas, and Nebraska are going to be deserts!" I muttered aloud.

Grit seemed to have invaded my eyes. I rubbed them, and realized that it was not just my eyes, but the tops of my thighs were burning from the heat of the laptop. I sat it on the couch next to me and went into the kitchen area for a glass of water. It was three thirty a.m., and I had been at this for hours. I should have gone to bed, especially since I had to talk to the police in the morning—*this* morning—but I was damn sure I wasn't going to be able to sleep, and not sure what I'd dream about if I did manage to.

Tomorrow, or rather later today, I would try to find out who was representing Kerrinan. I took my phone from my purse to charge it and realized I had turned it off when we went onto the movie set hours and another lifetime ago. I turned it on and found a number of messages that was depressingly reminiscent of when Chip had been killed and lots and lots of media outlets had called—*LA Times, Entertainment Weekly, Variety,* the *Hollywood Reporter.* Among them was a message from my father.

"I'm at the airport. I'll be there as soon as I can. I love you, honey."

I snuffled and wiped away a sudden surge of tears. Last time I had been in trouble he had been inexplicably absent. I knew it was crazy for him to fly across the country, but I was so glad he was.

The earliest message was from Joylon. It was the call I had missed when Debbie had told me to turn off my phone. The woman's face swam into focus. I remembered her intensity and obvious love of her job. I sank down on the couch. As the police had hustled us away from the soundstage I had seen her body at the bottom of the stairs leading into Jondin's Star Waggon. She had been the first victim of the actress's murderous rage. I blinked back tears and keyed back the message. This one I would listen to; maybe it would make me feel better.

The rich baritone made even more velvety by a BBC British accent filled the room. "Hallo, Linnet, first, not to worry, Vento is fine. He misses you. Which got me to thinking; if you're going to be stuck on the Left Coast for weeks and perhaps months it might make it more tolerable if you had your horse. So, Vento is on a van heading to the LA Equestrian Center. He should arrive day after tomorrow. Everything in terms of board has been arranged, and I have a dressage instructor friend who will keep an eye on him, and she can both coach you and ride Vento if you are just too busy. Cheers."

I stared at the phone. It wasn't all that uncommon in horse circles. Vans crisscrossed the country carrying race horses and top show horses from coast to coast each week, but I wasn't a professional rider, and Vento wasn't really my horse; he was Jolly's. He was clearly a madman, but if the Englishman had been closer I would have kissed him. I was good about using the health club at the Oakwood, but the surroundings were so sterile. How much better to be outside with a horse.

I went to bed, feeling marginally better because I had good news and a plan of action. Something strange was happening, and I wanted to get to the bottom of it.

9

In addition to the pools, the heath club, and the clubhouse complete with Ping-Pong and pool tables, the Oakwood had a dry cleaner and a small grocery store on site. At six thirty, after three hours of sleep, I staggered into the kitchen. An examination of my fridge revealed a deficit of orange juice, so I decided to make use of the market. As I walked down paths and stairs to the little market to pick up a carton of orange juice and the *LA Times,* I wished David had called to tell me the time of my appointment at police headquarters. Stressing that it might be at eight a.m. was what had me get up at so damn early.

As if in answer to my thoughts my cell phone rang, but it wasn't David, it was Caroline calling from New York. My first paranoid thought was for the cat.

"Oh, God, is Gadzooks okay?"

"He's fine," she said with that faint tone of impatience that she always had when she talked to me.

"Then why are you calling?" I asked.

"Don't be dense! To check on *you*, of course."

"Oh, no. How did you find out? Is it in the New York papers. Tell me it's not in the New York papers."

"The shooting is, but you're not singled out. David called the senior partners, and the word got out."

"Wow, the vamps must be slipping. They're usually better about keeping things quiet. Wonder—"

"Would you stop nattering! Linnet, how are you? Are you okay? Did you get hurt? All we heard was that you were there, the partners did fine about keeping quiet about the stuff that really mattered. Like if you were okay. And why didn't you call any of us?"

Even through the forced impatience I could hear the honest concern, and it warmed the cold place that I hadn't realized had settled into my chest. I sat down on a convenient (if damp) bench and blinked away the sudden moisture that filled my eyes.

"I didn't think about it. There's something—" I broke off realizing how easy it was to hack cell phones. "I was checking out a few things, and then I tried to get a little sleep."

Caroline wasn't stupid. Nobody was who worked at Ishmael, McGillary and Gold. "Call me back when you feel like it's appropriate."

"Will do. Tell everybody hi."

"I will. They'll be glad to know you're okay."

Tears threatened once again as I stuck the phone back in my pants pocket and considered the women that I worked with. All of them brilliant and dedicated, graduates of the finest law schools, and most of them would never make partner as long as they stayed at a vampire-owned law firm. Maybe we were all crazy, and what we really needed to do was set up our own firm. I continued to the market, stepped through the doors, and headed to the cold case. There was an elderly man with a great smile pulling out a yogurt.

"What do you need, young lady?" he asked.

"Orange juice."

"Good healthy thing. That's how you stay so beautiful." I blushed, as he handed me a carton. "Did you get up early to watch the announcement?"

"Announcement?" I repeated stupidly.

"For the Academy Awards. I'm still interested even though I've been retired for almost twenty years."

"Uh, no. I didn't know it was happening," I replied.

He chuckled. "You must not be from around here or in the industry."

"Both. Anything interesting in the nominations?" I asked as we walked toward the checkout counter together.

"One of those Álfar fellahs got nominated. Best Supporting Actor."

We reached the counter. There was a stack of newspapers next to the register, and I nearly dropped the juice because on the front page was a picture of David and me driving off the Warner Bros. lot. It looked like the old vampire whammy could cloud men's minds but not digital cameras. I bought the paper along with my juice, and rushed out of the store. My elderly admirer gave me a wink as I raced past.

Back in the apartment I scanned the article. It was basic just-the-facts-ma'am reporting, including the statements by the reporters and paparazzi that all they saw was fog. But deep in the paper the editorial knives came out. It was all about the similarities between the industry and the Powers in terms of believing they were above the law, and that the rules that applied to ordinary people didn't apply to them. They reflected that Jondin would probably get off by going into rehab and issuing a tearful apology on *The Tonight Show*. Especially since "supposed" officers of the court seemed determined to impede the investigation by refusing to talk to the police. From there it segued into musing about the first Álfar Academy Award nomination.

Information about the nominations was on page two. I had managed to knock a bunch of actors off the front page of the *Los Angeles Times* in friggin' Hollywood. There were pictures of the nominees for Best Actor and Best Actress, and the first Álfar nomination was felt to be worthy of a photograph too. I studied the picture of a smiling Álfar with a slightly beaky nose, and a lump that suggested it had been broken sometime in the distant past, a pointed chin, and up-tilted eyes. Since the photo was a black-and-white there was no sense of the colors of his hair, but the different shades of gray suggested he was a piebald like so many of them. I didn't think I'd ever seen a film with Jujuran Ne Seran, but apparently he had turned in a stunning performance as the gay lover of a politician torn between love and a run at the White House.

My phone rang as I was wallowing in Hollywood news and trying to forget I was once more on the front page of a major newspaper. It was David.

"Did you see . . . ," we said in concert.

"You first," I said.

"Montolbano is going in at eleven a.m. with Hank. I think you and I need to get in there as quickly as possible."

"I agree. I don't have a car."

"I'll pick you up. Can you be ready in twenty minutes?"

"Yes, but you won't be here in twenty minutes. I'll call the front gate to get you on the drive-on list."

He hung up and I tossed an English muffin in the toaster and ran for the shower. I had just gotten lather all over me when I heard the phone ringing. Usually I would have just let it go to voice mail, but the photo and the implications being drawn from it had me rattled. I bolted out of the shower, ran into the living room, and grabbed the phone on the kitchen counter.

"Hello?"

"Bitch. Too good to defend decent human people. You'll burn in hell!" It was the same voice that had called me a whore a few nights before.

The naked hatred in the voice shook me, then my initial shock and fear passed, and rage buzzed in my head.

"Fuck you!" I screamed into the phone, but they had already hung up.

The smell of burning muffin assailed my nose. I popped the charred muffin out of the toaster, turned down the setting and put in another one, then headed back to my interrupted shower. Somehow I had become the focus for the anti-Álfar fury. The vitriol had shaken me, but also made me angry. Yeah, I was so going to talk to the people at Human First.

I ate with one hand while I dried my hair and applied makeup with the other, and I was ready in thirty minutes. I then sat down to watch the local news. It was all about the shooting at Warner Bros. and the nominations. The picture of David and me kept making an appearance with much tsk-tsking and editorializing from the anchors about the secrecy of the Powers. David put in a literal appearance forty minutes after his call. His expression was sour, and his face was pinched and hollow. Clearly he hadn't had time for breakfast.

"Told you," I said. He made a growly sound, settled his broad-brimmed hat back on his head, and opened his umbrella. "That's bad luck, you know."

The growl resolved into words. "Why are you irritating me this morning?"

"Low impulse control due to lack of sleep?" I suggested.

"You always have low impulse control," he said.

"Gee, thanks."

"Let's go."

I followed him down the hall to the stairs. The metal and concrete rang hollowly beneath our feet as we hurried down. I considered telling him about the phone calls, but decided to wait until he'd eaten. It would just make him angrier, and I could imagine what he would say: "And just what am I supposed to do about it?" Which would be a fair question. No, I'd hold off until I'd done a bit more investigating.

Downtown Los Angeles was easy to spot. The skyscrapers seemed more like steel-and-glass spikes that had been driven in the heart of a tangle of single-story buildings rather than an actual city center.

LAPD headquarters was in a multistory, glass monolith in the center of downtown. The old headquarters was known as Parker Center, after a police chief who'd run the LAPD through all of the 1950s and into the 1960s. Some people wanted the new building to bear the same name, but since William Parker had a somewhat checkered history when it came to minority relations—the Watts riot had occurred during his tenure—bestowing his name on the new building was proving to be a political hot potato.

We parked, walked through the lobby, which was so long it seemed more like a runway than a lobby, and were taken up to a conference room to Detective Ernesto Rodriquez. He stood up at our entrance and studied me while I studied him. He sported a conquistador's spade beard, which didn't really suit his round face, but he had gentle eyes and a nice smile, with curved full lips beneath the mustache.

"Ms. Ellery, thanks for coming in."

"My pleasure."

"Get you anything?" he asked.

"Coffee would be great. I didn't have time for a cup this morning."

"Take anything?"

"No, straight."

"A woman after my own heart." He disappeared out the door.

I leaned in to David. "He didn't offer you anything."

"Somehow I think the police would be uncomfortable with having beakers of blood in their fridge," he whispered back.

"Bet they do in New York," I said.

"Let's not find out, shall we?"

Rodriquez returned with two cups and settled into a chair across from me. "Mind if I tape this?" I glanced at David, who gave an almost imperceptible nod. My nod was bigger. "Great." Rodriquez set a small recorder on the table between us and turned it on. "Just tell me in your own words what happened."

So I did. By the end he had the strangest expression on his face. I had seen the same expression on the face of the detective in New York when I told him how a werewolf had taken a header down an elevator shaft while trying to rend me limb from limb. I'd seen it again on the face of the detective in Bayonne when I'd told him about the werewolf attack on an old retired lawyer that had ended up with five dead werewolves and a dead lawyer, and me escaping unharmed. Now here it was again.

There was a long silence, then Rodriquez said, sort of hesitantly, "You must be the luckiest person alive."

"Yeah, I guess. I mean . . . I'm alive."

"I know it seems incredible—" David began, but Rodriquez cut him off.

"Yeah, it does, but it also pretty much matches what Ms. Morales told us."

"Ms. Morales?" I asked.

"The EMT."

"Oh, Consuela . . . Connie."

"Well, she says you saved her life when you ran between her and the shooter."

David turned and gave me a look. I hadn't exactly mentioned that part, figuring I would get just this reaction. I gave him an apologetic shrug. "I had to do something."

"Let me make the argument that hiding also constitutes doing something," he said.

"She was going to shoot that girl."

The detective jumped back in, sensing a squabble coming. "How did Jondin seem to you? During the events?" Rodriquez asked.

I sat and thought about that. Tried to picture that cold, beautiful face. Then it struck me. "Expressionless. She seemed . . . detached."

"Not angry?"

"No."

"Did she say anything?" he asked.

"No. She didn't make a sound until she got hurt and then she just screamed." The detective gave a gusting sigh and leaned back in his chair. "What?" I asked and gave him an encouraging smile.

"Jondin claims she has no memory of the events. None. Says she has no idea even where she got the guns," the detective said.

"She had a freaking arsenal. That's not something you buy in an afternoon," I said.

"Have you been able to trace them?" David asked.

"It's only been a day. Once we have that information, hopefully, it will give us some more to go on."

David stood. "Well, it seems you've exhausted your questions for Ms. Ellery."

Rodriquez scrambled to his feet. "Yeah, yeah, that's it for now. Thanks again for coming in."

We shook hands all around though I noticed that the policeman thrust his hand into his pants pocket after the cold clasp of David's hand.

"If you should think of anything else." He handed me his card.

As David and I walked to the elevator I said, "Well, that was painless. You probably didn't need to come with me."

"I was not going to leave you alone." He then suddenly added. "You tend to get into trouble when left alone."

"That is so totally unfair," I said. The elevator arrived with an anemic ding.

"Oh really? Three werewolf assaults, and now this." We stepped onto the elevator, and David punched the lobby button.

"I wasn't the target of this. I was just in the wrong place at the wrong time," I countered.

"You could say that's how all the trouble started back in New York. You were just in the wrong place at the wrong time when Chip got killed, and then things . . . escalated." He gazed down at me. And now you're digging into these events here. I worry, Linnet.

"I'll be okay," I said, and hoped it wasn't famous last words.

10

Even though I had a million questions buzzing around in my head and things I needed to do, by the time we finished at LAPD headquarters I was a zombie. I would think I had grasped a thought thread only to have it turn to smoke or grind to a halt as my brain tried to shut down. Since the day's hearing had been canceled, I collected my car from the office parking garage and very carefully drove myself back to the Oakwood.

There was a takeout menu from a nearby Chinese place hanging on the doorknob. That looked good to me. I ordered in kung pao chicken with fried rice, sat down to wait for the food, and tried not to fall asleep. Didn't work. I was jerked awake by a knock at the door.

"Just a minute," I called, stumbled over to my purse and grabbed out some cash.

After some fumbling I got the chain off the door, threw the deadbolt, and opened the door. Instead of the usual pimple-faced delivery teenager there was my father. Fatigue had painted dark circles beneath his gray eyes, which were filled with worry. I gave a half sob, half moan of relief and fell into his embrace.

"Oh, Linnie, honey." One hand was patting all over my back as if reassuring himself that I was there and intact.

"Oh, Daddy, I'm so glad you're here, but it's such a long way—"

"Shhh."

"Come in." I noticed there was an overnight case at his feet. He gathered up his small bag and followed me into the apartment.

We settled onto the couch and I nestled against him. "How did you find out?"

"It was all over the news."

"About me?"

"No, about the shootings, but then Shade let me know you had been there. Now, tell me what happened."

So, I did. After I finished we sat in silence for a few minutes. Then I hesitantly asked, "Daddy, do you think there's something weird about me?"

The arm around my shoulder stiffened. "What do you mean?"

"Everybody talks about how lucky I am, but I don't feel lucky because these awful things keep happening to me or around me." I sighed. "Eventually I'm going to be afraid to leave home."

"Well, speaking of home . . . why don't you come back to Rhode Island with me? Catch your breath. Decide what you want to do."

"Is Mom away on a trip?"

"No."

"Then you know how relaxing it's going to be. We drive each other crazy. I want to see it through out here, and David needs my help." I didn't mention my belief that some other force was at work or my determination to figure out what it was. That would only have worried him.

A memory came jostling and pushing its way to the fore. Last time I'd been in terrible danger during the werewolf attacks my dad had been adamant that I not leave IMG. In fact he had made damn sure my job was secure even before he came to see me. Now suddenly it was all "Why don't you come home?" I pointed this out to him.

He spread his hands apologetically. "This is the fourth time you've been in terrible danger. I guess I'm worried that if it happened again you wouldn't be so lucky."

"Hey, I made it past the third time. Isn't that the key? Should be smooth sailing from here on out." I suggested with gallows humor.

There was a knock. My dad looked at the door, concern pulling his brows into a sharp frown. "I ordered takeout," I explained as I once again gathered up cash and went to answer. This time it was the pimple-faced adolescent. I handed over cash, told him to keep the change. There were delicious smells emanating from the depths of the bag.

"Dinner?" I said, and held up the sack.

"Why don't I take you out, and you can save the leftovers for another night?" he suggested.

"I like the way you think," I said. I stowed the little white cartons in the fridge and ran into the bedroom for a jacket.

He was holding his phone when I emerged, and I saw he was on Google. "There's a steak place just down from here. Damn good reviews too. Supposedly their garlic bread isn't to be missed." he added.

The Smokehouse was totally my dad's kind of place. Red leather booths, wood paneling, dark carpet, and unlike the more modern concrete-and-chrome restaurants, it was very quiet. The bar was a dark mahogany horseshoe, and I kept thinking I would see Sam Spade in a trench coat with a fedora pulled low over his eyes slouched there. I told my dad what I was thinking, and he gave me a smile.

"Except no man in that era would ever have worn a hat indoors," he said.

"Oh, right," I said as the maitre d' led us to our table. "Is it true that men stopped wearing hats because President Kennedy didn't wear a hat at his inauguration?"

"That's the legend, but now they're coming back because vampires all wear them."

"Well, if they're using them as sunshades they'd be better off with a sombrero," I said as I slid into the booth.

My dad chuckled. "Yes, but that wouldn't look very dignified, and they're all about the dignity."

"Well, those umbrellas they all carry look pretty silly too."

A young waiter approached our booth, and we ordered.

I went with a small piece of rare prime rib with a side of crab legs. Dad had his usual, a New York strip steak, medium.

He leaned back and stretched his arms along the back of the booth. "You're the only one in the family who eats their meat rare," he said. "Sometimes I wonder if it's from being fostered with a vampire," he added with a smile.

The garlic bread arrived and it was completely delicious, oozing butter, topped with melted parmesan cheese and paprika. Moments later the waiter returned with a rolling cart topped with a large wooden bowl and various smaller bowls filled with coddled egg, parmesan cheese, anchovies, half a lemon, cloves of garlic, lettuce, croutons and two carafes, for oil and vinegar, and a bottle of Worcestershire. The waiter made an appropriate production of preparing the Caesar salad. As I watched him rub the sides of the bowl with garlic, I said,

"Probably not the best choice for a date."

"Not unless both of you ate it," Dad said.

Plates heaped with romaine lettuce were placed in front of us. "Speaking of dating . . . are you seeing anyone?" Dad asked. I shook my head. "Anyone look promising?"

"There was a guy I liked, but things have gotten . . . complicated." Given his expression I felt like I needed to say more. "He's Álfar. You don't . . . wouldn't mind, would you?"

"Well, I'd like grandkids. And sometimes these mixed marriages don't work out all that well."

My father applied himself to his salad. Then he said, "And in some ways the Álfar are the least human of all the Powers."

"Really? How do you figure?"

"Different species. With vampires and werewolves they at least began life as humans."

I leaned back and considered that. He had a point, but I still felt I had to defend John. "John was a changeling. His mother exchanged him for a human baby and he was raised by humans."

"Okay. And when am I going to meet this paragon?"

I played with my fork, beat out a tattoo on the edge of my plate. "Well, that's what's complicated." I paused, considering how to sum up all the craziness from last summer. "For a lot of really complicated reasons we had to travel in Fey, and John's mom decided he needed to stay with her, and . . . well, he had to agree so she would let me go."

My dad's expression was serious. "I was being facetious about paragon, but it sounds like he just might be."

"He's brave and chivalrous and smart." I swallowed, trying to force down the sudden obstruction in my throat. My father's hand was warm as he clasped mine. "Look, can we talk about something else?"

"Sure. What do you want to talk about?"

"Did you always want me to be a lawyer?" I asked.

"I hoped one of my children would follow in Granddad's footsteps. Did I push too hard?"

"Charlie kind of implied that," I said referring to my younger brother. "I never thought so."

"Well, I'm really the aberration, being a businessman. Law and revolution have been the hallmarks of the Ellerys from the very beginning," Dad said.

I knew he was referring to the illustrious founder of our family, William Ellery, who signed the Declaration of Independence, was a judge on the supreme court of Rhode Island, the first customs collector under the Constitution, and an early abolitionist. I thought about that for a moment then said, "I wonder how he'd feel about his umpty-umpth great-granddaughter working for a bunch of vampires?"

An expression I couldn't identify swept across my father's face. "I think he'd understand," he said softly.

Our main course arrived, distracting us, and Daddy turned the conversation to Charlie, his interest in architecture, and the ongoing arguments over where he was going to go to college. By the time we'd finished our dinner I was almost asleep.

"Can you stay awake for dessert?" Dad asked. I shook my head. "Okay. Let me take you home."

The following day I returned to the office. David had wisely canceled hearings for the next two days. Anyone even remotely associated with the movie business was in a state of shock over the shootings, and a lot of them were going to be attending funerals. I asked Elaine if Mr. Pizer was available.

"I'm sure he is for you," she said. I wondered if the knowing smile was meant to convey something, but then decided that was just the way she smiled. She left her desk and went into the corner office, closing the door behind her. A moment later the door opened and she beckoned me inside.

Pizer was practicing putting in the center of the big office. I just stared at him. He gave me a rueful look and cocked the putter over his shoulder like a rifle. "Okay, I'm a cliché, what can I say?"

"I didn't know they had night golf," I said.

"The courses that want to cater to a better class of player have installed lights." He stopped. "I didn't mean to say better class. I meant to say *different* class of player."

I had a feeling he wouldn't have made that adjustment if he'd been talking to another vampire. I let it go. They thought they were superior because in so many ways they were. It was also clear that Pizer played human better than many others of his kind I had met. It was an odd dynamic. They wanted to do business with humans, which meant they had to play human power games or else redefine the game. Thus far they'd elected to play, mostly, on human terms.

"So, what can I do you for?" Pizer asked, pulling me back.

"I want to talk to Kerrinan. Do we know who's representing him?"

"Christine Valada at Wein, Ellison and Martin." He pulled out his BlackBerry. "I'll send it over to you." I pulled out my iPhone, and he made the transfer.

"Thanks."

Pizer sat down on the edge of his desk and swung a foot in a monotonous rhythm. "So, what's up?"

"Something's not adding up," I said.

"David said you were niftic."

"Meaning . . . ?"

"Not sure. Sounds like one of those 1940s things, but good . . . I think. Ask him."

"I'm almost scared to. Thanks for the information. I'll give her a call." I paused at the door. "So the firm is okay with me asking some questions?"

"Yes. I've discussed it with David."

"Okay, thanks."

I went back to my broom closet office and met Merlin's wide-eyed gaze. "Wow. You nearly got killed."

"Gosh, really? I hadn't noticed." I was immediately ashamed of myself. "Sorry, Merlin, I'm not usually a bitch. I'm running on too little sleep."

"Hey, I'm sorry. That was gauche." The grin was back. "But true."

I settled at my desk. Rested my chin in my hands, and contemplated Christine Valada's telephone number. My mind skipped away to Jondin. How had she gotten the guns?

"Hey." I looked up at Merlin's call. "You look sort of fried. Can I help?"

"I wish. I want to make some inquiries, but I don't really know where to start. I'm way off my home turf out here, and I'm a lawyer, not a policeman or a PI. I mean, I know how to research case law and case files, but . . ." I made a hopeless and frustrated gesture.

"If you don't mind I've got a suggestion for you."

"Why would I mind? Your last suggestion turned out really well."

"What was that?"

"The Oakwood."

"Oh, yeah, well, glad it worked out." He sucked in a quick breath. "I've got a twin brother."

He stared at me expectantly. I just blinked at him. "Okay," I said slowly.

"We were the Blue Fairy ice-cream kids." I was starting to wonder if I needed to move slowly for the door, then run like hell and call for security and men in white coats. "Commercials?" Merlin prodded. "We'd sit in wading pools and bathtubs and eat ice cream and end up with it all over our faces."

A vague memory from childhood surfaced. Of naked cherubic children with red-gold curls and ice cream smeared all over their chubby cheeks while I watched cartoons on Saturday morning. "Oh God, you were *those* kids?"

"Yep. But then we hit five and we weren't so cute any longer." He looked pensive for a brief moment. "It's tough to be told you're all washed up at five."

"That's . . . terrible." I remembered him mentioning his parents' divorce, and I wondered if the loss of the career had something to do with it, but for once I kept my mouth shut.

He shrugged. "Hey, our parents made a boat load of money, invested it well, and didn't rob us, so we ended up all right. I went to Harvard, and Maslin went to Columbia, so don't cry for us, Argentina."

I had to admit I was getting really tired of people in LA talking in pop-culture quotes. I released my irritation and asked, "Does Maslin work at the *LA Times*?"

"No, he's a freelancer. Travels to shitholes in the third world and covers bush wars. Goes undercover in corporations to reveal dangerous working conditions and dangerous products. Exposes corrupt politicians. Then he sells his articles to magazines and major papers. Since he doesn't give a crap about access and doesn't think it's the job of a journalist to be a stenographer, he wins Pulitzers. Don't expect to ever see him at a cocktail party in D.C. He's in town right now, taking a break after his last trip to the latest shithole. I'm sure he'd love to help you."

I sat with the idea for a few minutes and started to like it more and more. "Since David gave his blessing to my making inquiries, I'll bet we can squeeze some bucks out of the firm to pay him," I offered.

"I'm sure he won't say no."

"So, how do we arrange this?"

"How about we all have dinner tonight?"

"Let's make it tomorrow. I'm going to try and see Kerrinan today."

"You got it."

Merlin turned away to call his brother, and I put in a call to Christine Valada.

11

The rendezvous took place in the lobby of the main police station. At first Christine Valada had been suspicious to the point of hostile, but finally I convinced her that I wasn't working for the DA and frankly thought something really strange was going on. She agreed to meet me at two thiry and take me in to see Kerrinan.

I hadn't thought to ask what she looked like, or describe myself, or look her up on Facebook and see if she had posted a photo. As I drove I thought, how hard can it be? Two female lawyers. Turned out to be really hard. The lobby was filled with women in chic suits carrying slim briefcases, with faces set in serious frowns. (I once again felt inferior, with my bulky rolling bag, but how the hell did you carry anything with you in those tiny leather folders?) Statistics stated that women were a majority in the nation's law firms. Here was the empirical evidence.

I was staring in consternation at the flood of women when someone touched my arm and a voice said, "Linnet Ellery, right?"

I turned and found myself facing a woman a few inches taller than me and probably twenty years older. She had thick, dark brown hair touched lightly with silver. It flowed over her shoulders in a tumble of crisp curls and made her creamy golden skin all the more striking. Deep brown eyes studied me critically.

"Yes. Ms. Valada?"

"Chris, please."

"Call me Linnet. Sorry, I forgot to tell you what I looked like or ask for a description. How did you—"

"You've been in the papers a lot, and while the photo from last night was fuzzy, the one with Jeffery Montolbano wasn't."

"Shall we go up?" She shifted a large and bulky purse briefcase higher onto her shoulder, and I pulled up the handle on my rolling bag. For an instant we glanced at each other's giant bags, shared a quick smile, but said nothing. Chris continued. "We'll be interviewing him in his cell, and it won't be easy,"

"And why is that?" I asked. I followed Valada as she headed toward an elevator.

"I take it you've never visited an Álfar in jail?"

"No."

"It takes a special facility to hold one."

I felt really stupid. "I should have thought of that. How do you hold an Álfar when they can just walk out of our world?"

"They've found a way."

The elevator arrived and we rode up to the jail level. The female guard at the desk searched our briefcases and treated us to a hostile stare, which took me aback. Chris leaned over the high-tech desk. I peered over her shoulder and saw that the entire back of the horseshoe-shaped desk was lined with screens displaying pictures of prisoners in their cells. One of the screens had multiple windows offering different views of the cell. Occasionally one picture would be blocked, though I couldn't tell why.

"Hey! Back off!" The female guard had come out of her chair, and she and Chris were almost nose to nose.

"And you guys better back off. I'm forced to interview my client in his cell where he is under constant surveillance rather than in an interview room where I'm assured confidentiality. You better not have microphones in that cell, because if you do and if anything turns up in the DA's evidence I'm going to sue a lot of people naked and put some others in jail. And I want the cameras turned off until I'm finished. Got that?"

"I can't do that. He might—" the guard began.

"The cameras aren't what's keeping him there. The walls keep him there. Now turn the cameras off or I call the DA and a judge." Valada pulled her cell phone out of her purse and brandished it like a small, blunt sword.

"Let me check with my boss." She made a call and had a quick, hushed conversation. "He says okay." She jabbed at a button and the screen went dark. "Go on through." She buzzed us through the heavy bulletproof glass that separated the outer lobby from the jail proper.

"What's with her?" I said in a low voice to Chris.

"Never done criminal law, I take it?"

"A few weeks in the summer during my clinical work."

"Cops do not like defense attorneys. They think we put scumbags back on the streets and play gotcha with good cops. I try to explain to them I only play gotcha with bad cops. And it's bad cops doing bad work that gets scumbags released. Defense attorneys just take advantage of their failings."

A guard approached us. "Come with me. He's in the special cell at the end of the block."

He led us down a long hallway lined with cells. Men hung on the bars staring, hooting, and catcalling. "Hey chickie, chickie, chickie. See what I got. Big man over here." I forced myself to meet the gazes of the men haranguing me. They were dressed in orange prison jumpsuits; several had pulled down the top to reveal either bare chests, or wife-beater T-shirts. Where skin was exposed it was almost always heavily decorated with tattoos: barbed wire, swastikas, dragons, swords, and Chinese and Japanese ideograms. The harsh scent of cigarette smoke caught in the back of my throat and tickled the nose, and the wild male odor of sweat mingled with a less than inefficient sewer system. And somewhere in the building dinner was being prepared. It smelled as if cabbage was on the menu.

I hadn't been in a jail since my senior year in law school when they had taken us for a tour of several prisons and given us an up-close look at the execution chamber. Intellect told me to oppose the death penalty after so many people on death row had been exonerated by DNA evidence. But there were some cases where my gut took over, and the angry, frightened, and far more emotional side screamed for blood and vengeance. My only other brush with criminal law had been a six-week course at the public defender's office that I had mentioned to Chris. The students got the small fry cases—drunk driving, marijuana busts, bar fights that didn't leave anybody dead or maimed. I never represented anyone I thought was innocent, but I found myself deeply involved in every case because my clients seemed so helpless and confused at being enmeshed in the American justice system.

The one certain thing I had learned during that summer was that the likelihood of prosecution and jail time was a direct function of class and race. I never met any affluent whites at the morning arraignments where the shuffling men stank of stale booze, sweat, and vomit after a night in the drunk tank. The white guys from Temple or Crowne got escorted home, or if they did get arrested they got bailed out in a hurry because they could afford the bond. Which was why I was uncomfortable with the death penalty.

I had found the entire experience unsettling, and had rejected job offers from both the Public Defender's Office and the District Attorney. Partly because my vampire foster father and Shade, one of the senior partners, had pretty much prepared a place for me at

IMG, but also because I wanted the dry, unemotional aspect of corporate law well away from these uncomfortable thoughts about social inequity. It was hard to face that about myself, and I was grateful when the guard spoke up, pulling me out of my naval gazing.

"Do not approach within two feet of the prisoner, and no physical contact. Got it?"

"Well, that's going to be a little tough, given the cell," Chris said and her tone was pure acid. "The only static place is the bunk and the john, and I don't think all of us are going to fit on the john."

The guard looked confused. "Uh . . . yeah, right. Guess that's true. Well, do what you need to do."

He led us to the final cell at the end. This one didn't offer a view through bars. There was an actual steel door with a small, mesh-reinforced window set into the metal. He inserted the key and swung open the door.

I found myself staring at a blank metal wall that was sliding past. It moved in a track with a high-pitched whine that was almost painful to the ears. It seemed like we waited for a long time before we saw an opening. Then Chris darted through. I was rooted to the spot, trying to understand what I was seeing. The guard put a hand between my shoulder blades, and gave me a small push.

"Move! While you've got the chance."

I rushed in to find Chris seated next to Kerrinan on the bunk. "Sit down. Quick!" she ordered.

I realized another wall was moving and it was going to intersect with my position. I leaped to the bunk and sat down on the other side of the Álfar actor. He looked haggard. Álfar are like Teflon. It seems like no dirt ever sticks to them. Their features are so regular that some modeling agencies described them as walking manne-quins, but there is something in the eyes that is tremendously allur-ing to humans. That ability seemed beyond Kerrinan this day. Despite the unusual color of his eyes, pale gray flecked with purple, they had the flat, uncomprehending stare of the eyes in a stuffed animal head.

I could tell that concentrating with the constant mechanical whine of the moving walls was not going to be easy. Another one was cutting on a diagonal across the cell. That's when I figured out the purpose of the moving walls.

I didn't understand the physics behind it—nobody did—but apparently Fey was sort of overlaid on top or maybe beneath our world. Geography was the same, but somehow buildings changed or vanished, Álfar vehicles both motorized and horse-drawn didn't intersect with our vehicles, and humans and Álfar in the same building didn't see each other. John's mother and now John lived in the Dakota.

For a moment I reflected that it must be torture for John to know he was a shadow veil away from the human world he loved. Or maybe not. Maybe when she'd driven that sliver of ice deep into his eye it had somehow broken his connection to the world where he'd grown up. Whatever she had done, it was Álfar magic, and it had worked.

Well, the same thing was now being applied to Kerrinan, but in the other direction. Humans couldn't use some kind of magical whammy to keep him in our reality. So we had fallen back on science, which was something humans did pretty well. I had a feeling the constant changing geometry of the room made it impossible for Kerrinan to get a fix on the Álfar world and thus kept him trapped in his cell. I wondered how they avoided having a pattern emerge that would enable a determined prisoner to escape? I concluded it was probably computer-controlled and the movement was being randomized. I couldn't imagine how much that was costing the county of Los Angeles.

"Kerrinan, this is Linnet Ellery," Chris said. "She wanted to ask you some questions."

"Is she part of my defense team?" the Álfar asked. "Because if she's not, perhaps I shouldn't be talking with her." The mellifluous voice that had set a generation of women to swooning in movie theaters around the world was now ragged and harsh. He gave a cough. "Sorry, not sleeping. When I'm fatigued it always shows up in my voice first."

Chris and I exchanged a glance. We had already discussed this earlier and found a solution. I was just surprised that Kerrinan had been this astute. According to John, the Álfar weren't known for their logic and caution. He had described them as a species of raging ids.

"Chris has hired me as a researcher, which means the same rules of client confidentiality apply to me as to her," I said.

"I take it this is a dodge from the way she introduced you."

"A little bit. Look, I think something strange is happening with regard to the Álfar, and I need more information than I can get from the newspapers," I said. "I'll understand if you're not comfortable with this, and I'll leave, but I think your people are being . . ." I hesitated, not wanting to put voice to it because it did sound kind of crazy.

"What?" Kerrinan prodded.

"Okay, this is going to sound really melodramatic, but I think you're being targeted."

"Me?"

"Well, not you specifically. The Álfar."

He was frowning, marring the smooth perfection of that handsome face. "Has something else happened?"

I closed my eyes briefly. "Yeah, you could say that."

I gave him an abbreviated version of what had happened the day before on the Warner lot.

Kerrinan was shaking his head. "This is crazy. I know Jondin. She's a ditz but never a diva," Kerrinan said.

"I'd say this goes a little past diva, Kerrinan, and straight to crazy mass murderer," Chris Valada said in her usual dry way.

"Will you tell me what happened? The day your wife died," I asked. The actor looked at me in confusion. "Look, bear with me. I want to see if there are any similarities to what Jondin is telling the authorities."

"Like what?" Kerrinan asked.

I shook my head. "No, I don't want to lead you or suggest anything. Just tell me about the day."

The eyes that met mine were shadowed, haunted by doubt and fear. "I want you to know, I loved Michelle. More than anything. More than life. I would have done anything for her, and I would never have hurt her. But . . ." Kerrinan's voice trailed away. The question hung in the silence. *But what if I did?* Chris gave his arm a quick squeeze.

"Let's start at the beginning. Walk me through the whole day. Try to remember everything. Even if it seems trivial it might be important," I said.

He closed his eyes briefly, gathering his thoughts. "We got up early, and we worked out together."

"Did you go to a gym?" I asked, looking up from the pad where I was taking notes.

"No, we have a full gym at the house."

"Okay, go on."

"We went out for breakfast at Mary's Lamb. Michelle liked the orange-pecan muffins . . ." His voice broke. If this was an act, I thought, he should win an Oscar. "I dropped her off back at the house around eleven and went to a photo shoot for *GQ*"

"Anything unusual happen there?" I asked.

"No."

"Who was there?"

"Guillermo, he's the photographer, and a couple of assistants to set the lights. I don't know their names."

"All of them human?" He nodded. "Okay, go on."

"That lasted until around one thirty. I was hungry so I took myself to lunch at Terra Sushi."

"By yourself?" Chris asked.

"Yeah, sometimes it's nice to just be alone."

"I can't believe you got to sit and eat and nobody approached you," Chris said. "Terra Sushi's in Studio City along Sushi Row. Very trendy."

"I signed an autograph for my waitress, but there weren't a lot of ordinary people there . . . fans, I mean."

"Why is that?" I asked.

"Most of the tables were industry people. A bunch of agents."

"You didn't tell me that. You just told me where you had lunch. Was it an office party?" Chris asked.

"No, they were from a lot of different agencies. It was sort of like a little mini-conference. There was another Álfar there, a really old guy who is on the Council."

"Did you speak to him?" I asked.

"Yeah, briefly. He just introduced himself and said he liked my work. After that I left."

"After lunch?" Chris prompted.

"Oh, I went over to that little driving range just down Ventura from the restaurant and hit a bucket of balls. One of the employees must have called the press because there were a few cameras when I came out, and my fan club got the Tweet so there were maybe fourteen, fifteen fans looking for autographs. Oh, and a couple of crazy people."

"Crazy people?" Chris and I said in concert.

"Well, maybe that's a little harsh, but the guy really was nutso.

He waved a Bible in my face and said I was an abomination, or something. The woman, this skinny old broad with a tan so dark she looked like jerky was shouting at me about how I was just an empty suit and a no-talent. There were some others, just yelling. I couldn't really make out what they were saying. My fans chased them off. I have great fans." A smile flickered briefly.

"And then?"

"Haircut in Beverly Hills. I got out of there around six."

"Nothing unusual happened at the barbershop?" Both Chris and Kerrinan were giving me strangest looks. "What?" I asked.

Chris shook her head. "Yeah, you are not from around here. Actors like Kerrinan don't go to barbershops. They go to a salon and have a designer. The only way they'd go to a barbershop is if it was some kind of new place that was so retro it was hip and therefore trendy, and George Clooney decided to go there first."

"Okay, even New York isn't that bad."

"Welcome to Tinsel Town," Kerrinan said, then sighed and continued. "And what do you mean . . . unusual?"

"Nobody took some of your hair or something." I was groping and it showed.

He shook his head. "No."

"Okay, go on."

"Michelle and I didn't have plans that night. We were going to eat at home. Watch a little TV." He fell silent and started to shake. So hard that I could feel it through a bunk bolted to a cinderblock wall.

My muscles were tight with tension, and a headache was starting to climb up over my head to lodge just over my brows. I realized it was because of that constant, horrible *screeeee* as the metal walls slid in their tracks. Kerrinan had to listen to it 24/7, and if he was convicted of murdering his wife he would be listening to it for the rest of his very long Álfar life.

I realized we had all been silent for a long time. It was Chris who prodded this time. "Go on, Kerrinan, finish it."

He gulped down a sob, a harsh, guttural sound, and said, "We were watching a DVD of *Moulin Rouge*. Michelle got up and went into the kitchen to make us some popcorn. I love popcorn when I watch a movie. Then blackness. I don't remember anything else until I could see again and I was in the kitchen, and my hand was all sticky, and I was holding . . . holding . . ."

"Michelle?" Chris asked.

There was a confused moment where he first shook his head, then nodded and said, "I was holding her in my left arm, but there was a . . . knife in my right hand."

"You didn't tell me that before!" Chris said. "You just said you were holding her."

"I . . . I was scared to. Afraid you wouldn't defend me." Tears rolled down his face. He drew an arm across his eyes and pulled in a shuddering breath.

Chris was staring at him in frustration, but she was clearly worried. I stepped in. "If he had a traumatic blackout from the shock of finding her body he could have knelt down, gathered up Michelle, and then picked up the knife."

"Yeah, and the DA is going to say he came out of a blinding, killing rage and that's why he was holding a knife. Also, why didn't he hear her screaming if he blacked out when he found the body? She didn't die from the first stab wound, and she had defensive cuts all over her hands." Kerrinan moaned and leaned forward, holding his gut. "I know you haven't done a lot of courtroom work, I can tell you that juries believe the theory that's the easiest to understand. In this case that's the one that has Kerrinan butchering Michelle."

That did it. Kerrinan hurled, vomit spewing across the bare concrete floor.

12

I found Qwendar just where he'd said he would be, in the interior courtyard of the Getty Museum. The elderly Álfar had suggested the venue. I had done a quick Google search and discovered that the Getty was a completely and perfectly reconstructed Roman villa built by J. Paul Getty to house his collection of antiquities. Another oddity in the enigma that was California.

The building, gleaming white in the sunshine, sat on a hill overlooking the Pacific Coast Highway and the majesty of the Pacific beyond the asphalt and passing cars. My research revealed that entrance to the Getty was free, but you had to reserve a time and pay for parking. It was also on the outskirts of Malibu, and I hoped I'd have time to drive through that famous locale before meeting Merlin and his brother for dinner. Then I walked through the museum in search of the courtyard, saw the quality of the collection, and decided I really needed to tour the museum instead. Malibu could wait.

A friendly docent had directed me toward the courtyard. I stepped out of the shady interior, blinked in the sudden glare and spotted Qwendar seated on a marble bench, surrounded by lush vegetation and contemplating a long, narrow marble pool filled with very blue water. Bronze statues stood on the edge of the pool, also seeming to contemplate the water. "Thank you for agreeing to meet me," I said as I walked up.

Qwendar looked up. "I was intrigued by your phone call."

I looked around at the white pillars supporting an overhanging porch on all four sides and the bright red tile roof, listened to the distant pound and whoosh of waves, and felt tension melting out of my back and shoulders. "And thank you for suggesting we meet here. I would never have found it, and it's . . . remarkable."

"Yes, humans did have a great capacity for beauty."

"But no longer?" I asked.

His arms swept out in an encompassing wave. "Consider the rest of Los Angeles."

"That's a little unfair. Comparing a city to a garden at a museum."

"Perhaps you are right. But there are profound differences between Álfar and human tastes." He stood and straightened his suit coat. "There is a place in the gardens that offers a lovely view of the ocean and is fairly private. Madam, will you walk?" He gave a funny little half bow and offered his arm.

Touched and faintly amused by the old-fashioned courtesy, I laid the tips of my fingers on his forearm, and we moved away in stately dignity.

"You're amused," he said, with uncanny perspicacity.

"I'm sorry, I don't mean to be insulting. I just thought it was mostly vampires who went in for the whole manners as—" I broke off realizing I was about to sound insulting again.

"As what?" Qwendar asked.

I threw caution to the winds and decided to give it straight. "As a form of one-upmanship. A way to do interpersonal warfare."

"You are a most perceptive young woman."

"Not really. I just grew up with them." I paused, then added, "So how do the Álfar use manners?"

"Without any agenda beyond our desire to play the leading role in our own personal drama."

"Okay, that fits with what John told me," I said.

"Ah, yes, John."

We had reached a stone-paved veranda edged with a stone wall. I leaned my elbows on the wall and let my eyes trail across the expanse of lawn and the windswept California pines. Across the highway the Pacific rolled and rumbled. Gulls and pelicans swooped and spun like white kites over the water.

"Your phone call implied this was about more than one changeling brought back to the fold."

"I'll dispute your characterization of what happened to John in a minute. What I wanted to discuss was what's been happening with your people."

Qwendar became very still, his body almost rigid. "I'm listening."

"I interviewed Kerrinan yesterday."

"Ah."

"Kerrinan said there was an older Álfar at the restaurant where he had lunch. Was that you?"

"Yes."

"So you saw him on the day of the killing."

"I suppose I did. I hadn't really put that together."

"How did he seem to you?" I asked.

"Fine. He was dining alone, so I took the liberty of speaking to him," Qwendar added.

"What did you talk about?"

"I complimented him on his movies. Then I returned to my luncheon party." I sat silent for a few moments, flicking at a few loose chips of rock with my forefinger. "Is this going someplace?" Qwendar finally prodded.

"I don't want you to think I'm some kind of conspiracy nut." Drawing in a steadying breath I turned to face him straight on. "I think there's something strange going on. I think Kerrinan killed his wife, but I also don't think he wanted to kill his wife. I also don't think Jondin was in her right mind, though I haven't been able to talk to her. I also think the narrative of Álfar as dangerous killers of humans is certainly happening at a most convenient time for Human First."

"Ah, so you checked them out."

"I did some research. Next step is to actually talk to them."

"So what do you need from me?" Qwendar asked.

"Information on the Álfar. Any insights on how one might be . . . controlled or . . . something." I met his impassive gaze. "You think I'm a nut."

"No, I think you are an unusual human, and I think you might be the face of the future. A human who accepts and is comfortable with the Powers. A thing that some view with great disapprobation." I basked in the approval for a moment. Qwendar continued. "I will provide you with what information I can. And since you are willing to help us, I will return the favor and arrange a meeting with John."

There was a sudden tightness in my throat matched only by the feeling that my heart wanted to jump out of my chest.

I cleared the obstruction out of my throat. "Thank you."

"No. Thank *you*." He held out his hand. "Pact?"

"Partners, definitely." We shook on it.

"Now, may I suggest that we stroll through the exhibits. They are quite impressive. And there is a very nice café. We can have tea afterward."

I did notice that he didn't actually say we would talk about the Álfar.

Thank God they dress differently.

It was the thought foremost in my mind as I faced the brothers across a table at Sompun, a Thai restaurant just off Ventura. The decor was upscale, with a blue vaulted ceiling and plants in the windows and mirrors along one wall that made the space seem larger. Scents of lemongrass, mint, and chili were so thick that they seemed visible in the air.

The journalist twin stared at me with frank interest that bordered on rude. Maslin was dressed in blue jeans, a cotton turtleneck sweater, and sturdy hiking boots. A backpack was slung over the corner of his chair. Merlin was still in his suit from work. The difference in attire was the only way I was ever going to tell them apart. Then, as I looked closer, I realized that Maslin's skin carried a ruddier tinge, the redhead's version of a tan, and he had the first hint of squint wrinkles around his blue eyes.

"Merl tells me you've got an investigation you need to run," Maslin said.

"Well, I think so," was my cautious response, and for the second time that day I launched into my explanation of why I thought someone was targeting the Álfar.

Unlike Qwendar whose expression had been one of sympathetic interest, Maslin's expression was so neutral that I began to stammer, losing the thread of my narrative occasionally. I ended plaintively, "And now you probably think I'm bat-shit crazy."

He didn't answer right away. Instead he opened the backpack and pulled out a laptop computer.

"Qwendar didn't," I added rather desperately.

"Who's Qwendar?" Maslin asked while the computer powered up.

"Old Álfar dude," Merlin said.

"Old Álfar dude with major clout," I amended. "He's been sent by some kind of Álfar Council to observe the arbitration." I cocked a brow at Maslin. "I can't really fill in details about the arbitration."

He shook his head. "Merl filled me in." The computer was up and running, and the journalist started typing, fingers flying across the keyboard. "The first question is always, who profits? Well, obviously the folks who brought this lawsuit would profit. If the industry starts to believe that every Álfar is a potential time bomb likely to go off and kill people at any moment and without any warning, then they'll stop hiring them. Human actors win. We need to take a look at every one of the humans involved."

"I can't do that. I'm an arbitrator in this case. I'm just focused on the killings."

"Yes, you've been a good little lawyer. You haven't violated any of your ethical—such as they are—standards."

"Hey!" Merlin interjected.

Maslin grinned at his brother and then at me. "I give him shit all the time about being a shyster."

"Muckraker," Merlin said affectionately to his brother.

"Why, thank you. A title of honor." They had turned to face each other, and with their identical grins it was like looking at mirror images.

I waved a hand between them. "Look, back on the subject. I've got to maintain neutrality. If anyone discovered I was investigating the human actors—"

"Which is why you won't. I'll dig into the background of the various parties."

"I think this Human First movement is a more likely candidate," Merlin said. "Those people really are bat-shit crazy. And hateful," he added.

"Maybe you can answer a question for me," I said. "Is this a home-grown group, because I thought California was the Left Coast, a liberal enclave, the epicenter of degeneracy that undermines American values."

"We are," the twins said in chorus.

"All of those things," Merlin continued. "But we're also the state with the screwiest political system in the entire country."

"Which is?"

"The ballot proposition." Again in stereo.

Merlin continued. "Get enough signatures on a petition using the initiative system, and any crazy-ass idea can end up on the ballot at the next election."

Now it was Maslin's turn. "It grew out of a good impulse back in the early days of the Progressive Movement. The idea that the citizenry should and could have an impact on legislation. A way to counter the influence of powerful, entrenched interests. It's direct democracy by citizen lawmaking."

"Unfortunately the citizens are often idiots or bigots," Merlin said. "The only check on the ballot proposition is the Constitution. And since the Álfar haven't been declared a protected class under the U.S. Constitution if this proposition passes this ban will apply in California until somebody takes it up with the Supreme Court. Until then the state can violate the Fourteenth Amendment's Equal Protection clause with impunity."

I leaned back in my chair and considered. "They might not have to be declared a protected class." I quoted Section one of the amendment. "All persons born or naturalized in the United States, and subject to the jurisdiction thereof, are citizens of the United States and of the state wherein they reside. No state shall make or enforce any law which shall abridge the privileges or immunities of citizens of the United States; nor shall any state deprive any person of life, liberty, or property, without due process of law; nor deny to any person within its jurisdiction the equal protection of the laws."

"Well, there's a question," Maslin said. "Are the Álfar citizens? Were they born in this country?"

"The due process and equal protection clauses use the word person rather than citizen," I pointed out. "And courts have ruled that marriage is a fundamental right. It would certainly fall under the rubric of privileges. Bottom line: you can't just single out a group of people, be they African-Americans or gays or women, and arbitrarily deny them their rights. Civil rights should never be subject to the ballot box."

Merlin laid the tip of his right index finger on the end of his nose and pointed at me with the left. A young waiter and an older woman (I was betting she was his mother because of their body language) came to the table with our appetizers. We sat silent for a few minutes, munching on rice paper–wrapped spring rolls, pork satay, and mee krob.

I played with my fork, tapping it against the edge of my plate, and said, "I've been getting a lot of weird hang-up phone calls. Then it progressed to a couple of nasty phone calls. I think the Human First movement, or at least some member of the group, is behind the calls, though I can't prove it."

Identical pairs of blue eyes focused on me. "That's kind of scary," Merlin said.

I shrugged. "As long as it doesn't escalate beyond phone calls I'm not worried."

"Good woman," Maslin said, and then punched his brother on the shoulder. "You are such a wimp."

"Better than being a macho asshole."

I jabbed my fork at them. "Hey! No sibling rivalry bullshit. I have enough of that with my own brother." I pinned Maslin with a look, and drawled, "And aren't you a little short to be a macho asshole?" I wanted to kick myself. I'd been complaining about the constant movie quotes, and here I was doing it. I decided the habit must be catching. Something in the water of California.

"Precisely why I have to be a macho asshole. And you should talk, shorty," he said with a grin.

"But back on the subject, guys. Kerrinan said Human First protestors were on the sidewalk in front of the driving range, and they were certainly outside the studio after Jondin's . . . episode."

Maslin typed on his netbook. "Okay, so we have possible suspects. The real question is, how? How in the hell do you drive an Álfar to murder?"

"Well, that's why I went to talk to Qwendar."

"And what insights did he have to offer?" Maslin asked.

I opened my mouth and realized that while we'd talked for a number of hours, and I enjoyed the conversation I didn't have a lot of specifics. "He said Álfar physiology differs from human in terms of blood types and blood chemistry. He told me a lot about their pride and love of beauty." I frowned.

"Not very helpful," Maslin said.

At that moment our food arrived. I had ordered the pad thai, but the aroma of Merlin's garlic beef and Maslin's mint noodles with chicken was seductive. I saw them eyeing my noodles.

"Family style?" I suggested. Smiles broke out all around, and we quickly passed the plates.

We ate for a few minutes, then Maslin pulled his Apple Air back in front of him and started typing. "Okay, following up on what we do know. Different physiology . . . maybe drugs? Something like angel dust that can cause a murderous rage but in Álfar."

"Hypnosis. Manchurian candidate stuff," Merlin suggested.

"You watch too many movies," Maslin said. "Blackmail. They were forced to do these things."

"Because somebody can threaten them with something worse than a first-degree murder charge and life imprisonment?" Merlin asked. Once again the snark was on the rise between the twins.

They fell silent. I gathered my courage and said, "There's a reason the Powers are called the Powers, and it's not just because they've had their hands on the levers of power in the world for millennia."

"What are you saying?" Merlin asked.

"Well, for lack of a better word—magic. That's what I really wanted Qwendar to talk about, but he stayed pretty mum." They both stared at me. "Look, I know it's the twenty-first century, and we're all about science and being rational, but let's get real." I pinned Merlin with a look. "We work for a bunch of immortal dead guys. I was raised in a vampire household, and I don't have a full understanding of their abilities. They're careful about what they show humans." I turned my attention to Maslin. "You wrote a piece for *Time* last month. That means a werewolf authorized your paycheck. Hounds are stronger than normal people, heal faster, live longer, and they can turn into a wild animal at will, and that's what we know. What other powers and abilities might they have? We know the Álfar live in a slightly skewed reality. Legend has it that they are irresistible to normal people. My vampire foster father was always warning me about the Álfar. Once again, we have no idea the range of their powers and abilities. And it's not like they share this information with each other. Despite what people . . . real people . . . human people think, the Powers aren't united in their interests or their methods. They're just united when it comes to dealing with us."

The men seated across from me sat silent, but their expressions betrayed their discomfort.

"Okay," Merlin said. "That gave me a shiver."

"So if they're secretive with each other, how the hell do *we* find out about these powers?" Maslin asked.

"We hope our ally proves to be more forthcoming," I said brightly.

Merlin pulled his brother's laptop over, and his fingers flew across the keyboard, the click of the keys like bird pecks on glass. "Looking for authorities on the Powers. Wow, lot of cranks out there . . . a few university papers. I'm going to have to do some research."

"That's right, you're the research guru," I said. I looked at Maslin. "Is there anything we can do?"

"Back to the basics. Meet people, ask them questions. We'll talk to the Human First people and retrace Kerrinan's steps on the day of the murder."

"Won't that alert Human First?"

"Yeah, but when people get nervous they make mistakes," Maslin said breezily.

"You know, last summer I said almost the same exact thing to a friend—about how desperate people make mistakes." For an instant John's face was before me, and I was back in his apartment. The sudden memory brought a heavy lump into the back of my throat. "He said sometimes they made mistakes and sometimes they didn't, and if they didn't you ended up dead. He was right—I damn near got killed."

"So, you think we shouldn't talk to them?"

"No. I just think we should be careful."

I had started sleeping with my cell phone under my pillow. That way if there was an earthquake, and the roof fell in I could call out to the rescuers digging for me. Of course that was predicated on the assumption I wouldn't be thrown from the bed, and lose track of said cell phone. But I wasn't much paranoid about earthquakes . . . oh, no.

So when my ear started vibrating and the theme from *Star Wars* came muffled through the pillow, it levitated me right off the mattress. I jammed my hand under the pillow with enough force to send the phone skittering to the other side of the bed. The music was now below me. It must have slid right off the bed. I flung myself in a belly flop across the mattress, and groped for the faint glow of the phone.

"Hello? Hello!"

"Linnet Ellery?"

"Speaking."

"This is Sam with Equine Transporters. I just wanted to let you know that I'm about thirty minutes out from the Equestrian Center. I've informed the trainer, but the shipper thought you might like to be on hand to help unload the horse."

"Right. Yes. Absolutely. I'll be there."

Sam hung up. I scraped the hair off my face, and peered at the time. Four a.m. It was a law of nature that haulers either picked up or dropped off a horse at ugh o'clock. I snapped on a light and realized that water was washing down the outside of windows. And it was raining. Perfect.

I scrambled into jeans, boots, and a hoodie and headed out to the car. Horrifyingly, there were already a few people getting into their vehicles, and judging by the clothes and briefcases they were heading to work. They had to have the commute from hell. I got into the car and headed down rain-slick streets toward the Equestrian Center. I hadn't actually gotten to the facility since Jolly's call had come, but a Google map gave me what I needed.

What I hadn't expected was to drive past the Disney Studio on my left and a weirdly shaped building on my right. It was all glass and wood like the gondola of a dirigible. Above the entrance to the building was a giant blue wizard's hat covered with stars and a moon. I recognized it as the hat Mickey Mouse wore when he was the sorcerer's apprentice in *Fantasia*. A sign informed me that this was the Animation Building. I tried to imagine having enough money and cultural relevance that architecture matched your dreams.

Then I was a few blocks past the studio. I entered into a pretty residential neighborhood. A street sign showed the outline of a horse and rider, which I thought was encouraging. The road curved lazily along and then on my right the large white gate of the LA Equestrian Center appeared. Turning in I drove past a grass jump arena on my left, then what looked like retail space and a clubhouse. Behind the low buildings the darker shadow of an indoor arena showed against pale clouds. On my right was more grass, a little house, a dressage arena, and then three barns with parking out front.

There weren't a lot of cars. There was the familiar shape of a vet's truck parked near one barn, and I knew someone was having a stressful night. I shivered with sympathy. There was nothing worse than needing a vet in the wee small hours for your horse. The only other vehicle was an SUV. The interior light was on, and I saw someone inside. She appeared to be texting. I pulled up next to her and cut the headlights. We eyed each other through rain-washed car windows.

What I saw was a young woman around my age with a mane of thick black hair. We both stepped out of our cars and pulled up our hoods against the persistent rain. She was taller than me (of course), with really long legs. No matter how you sliced it I was short, and short is hard when you ride dressage.

"Why don't we wait in the breezeway?" she suggested and pointed at the wide doorway into the first barn.

"Sounds like a plan."

We ran inside. There were the sounds of shifting hooves in sawdust, a soft *chussing* sound. Down the line of stalls a horse coughed, and another blew out air in a gentle *whuff*. The air warmer than the damp chill outside, thanks to forty or so hay burners. The air was rich with the scents of dust, stall shavings, leather, hay, manure, and horse, a smell that for me was the embodiment of love and comfort.

"Hi, I'm Natalie Ogden. You must be Linnet."

"Yep." We smiled at each other.

"Well, at least he didn't arrive at two a.m.," Natalie said. "I'd be getting up at five anyway, so this wasn't too bad."

"Wow, you're hard-core. I get up at six," I said

"I'm at the gym by five thirty because my first lesson is at seven."

"So, what is the plan? What did Jolly . . . Mr. Bryce arrange?"

"I'll work the horse when you can't, and if you want coaching that's included," she said.

"Oh, that would be great. Eyes on the ground."

"What level do you ride?" Natalie asked.

"I've ridden the Grand Prix, but then I lost my horse and just haven't had much heart for it. Vento is a joy. He's third level right now, but he'll go up the levels really quickly. But you'll see."

Small talk, punctuated by more than a few yawns filled the minutes until we heard the deep-throated rumble of a diesel engine. We stepped to the door of the barn as a giant semi pulled down the road. It went past us and into a large dirt area where it carefully turned around. We braved the rain as the haulers jumped out of the cab and began pulling down the ramp on the side of the truck and putting safety rails in place. There were plaintive whinnies from inside the giant rig, which set off a chorus of neighs, whinnies, bugles, and whickers from across the Equestrian Center. I realized there were more barns on the other side of the facility, and in front of me was a galloping track and another big jump arena. It was an impressive setup.

I moved up to the edge of the ramp. In the front end of the truck were four yearling Clydesdales looking nervous and alarmed. Across from them was a box stall. One of the haulers pulled open the gate, and Vento stepped out. The baby Clydesdales were as large as my boy, but it didn't matter. He was perfect in my eyes. His expression was curious but soft. No sign of alarm or nerves. The man brought him down the ramp, and put the lead rope in my hand. While the driver got Natalie to sign the shipping order indicating we'd received the horse, the hauler said to me, "Nicest horse I've ever hauled. Nothing bothers him. I swear I kept expecting him to talk."

I patted Vento's neck. "He is great, isn't he."

"Oh, there's a blanket for him." He ran back up the ramp and emerged with a bulging black plastic garbage sack.

Natalie led us to his stall. Vento paced around, inspecting his surroundings, pawed the shavings, lay down, and had a good roll. He then stood and shook, sending shavings flying. It made him look like a fantasy horse figure in the center of a shaken snow globe. He then paced to the front of the stall and studied me carefully.

I went off and prepared a bran mash mixed with carrots and apples and moistened with corn oil and hot water. Natalie and I watched as he ate, though he paused after every couple of bites to gaze at me.

"I can see why you're so crazy about him. It's like he thinks that you're his rather than the other way around, and he's making sure you're all right," Natalie said.

"Yep. He's special. Look, how about if we meet tomorrow and get him out for a ride." I dug into my purse for my card case. I was still carrying the one that had been dented by a killer's bullet. It was a good reminder. Of what I wasn't exactly sure, but I just felt I needed to keep it, and not replace the case. I gave Natalie my card. "My cell phone number and email address are on there. We'll coordinate a time."

"Good." She checked her watch. "Well, off to the club."

"Well, back to bed," I said and we exchanged smiles.

I wasn't meeting Maslin until ten a.m. Plenty of time to catch another few hours of sleep. Back in the car I checked the time. Five thirty. Which put it at—I did sleep-deprived calculation—eight thirty in New York. Jolly would want to know his horse had arrived safely. I dug out my phone and called. He answered on the first ring.

"Hi, Jolly, the boy arrived. Looking calm and collected and fresh as a daisy. I fixed him up with a bran mash, and I'll give him today to rest."

"Excellent. I've been following the news reports about this shooting. Bound to make your situation more complicated." He had one of those teeth-aching, upper-class English accents that made you think of PBS and *Masterpiece Theater*. Politicians with that accent seem intrinsically more trustworthy, and men more attractive.

"Yes, you can definitely say that . . . especially since I was there for the gunfest."

Joylon audibly gasped. "Were you hurt?"

"No. Well, I got cut by a piece of broken glass, but I avoided being a bullet magnet." My hand was slick with sweat and I realized I was shaking. "It was really scary."

"Do you want to talk about it?"

"Not really, no."

But he didn't back off. Instead he asked, "Did you hide? Is that how you avoided getting shot?"

"No. I . . . was an idiot. She was about to shoot this girl and I ran . . . look, I really don't want to talk about it."

"Right. Sorry. "

"Look, Jolyon, it's five thirty, and I got the call at four. I want to try and catch a few more winks of sleep before I have to go to work."

"Oh, right. Yes. Sorry. Check in with me now and then. Let me know how you and Vento are doing."

"Will do."

With all the obligations met, I headed back to the apartment through a watery dawn.

13

The knock on the door came twenty minutes late. Maslin had said he would pick me up at ten, and I'd begun twitching once we hit ten after. I have a quirk about being late—I hate it, and I didn't like it in others. Probably something I had learned from my vampire foster father. Meredith had a thing about being on time, and he often quoted King Louis XVIII of France: Punctuality is the courtesy of kings.

As I snatched up my tweed jacket—the rains had decided to stay and it was quite chilly—a flip folder with pad and pen, and hurried to the door, I wondered if Maslin might have traded in his Indiana Jones look, but he was dressed the same as the evening before— jeans, turtleneck, hiking boots. The only addition was a black leather bomber jacket.

"Sorry I'm late."

"Okay, just don't make a habit of it," I said and then blushed at his startled expression. "Sorry. Internal editor didn't get enough sleep last night. I have this thing about being on time."

"It's okay, I deserved the hit, I'm bad about it. Merl gets on me all the time."

We hurried down the stairs and ran through the rain to an old-

model canvas-topped jeep, which seemed in character with a cru-
sading journalist in hiking boots.

"So, where do we start?" I asked loudly over the drumming of the
rain as a rivulet of water found its way through a thin place in
the canvas.

"I thought we'd retrace Kerrinan's steps that day."

"Sounds good." I flipped open my case and checked my notes.
"The day started at a restaurant—Mary's Lamb."

"Okay, here we go." He put the jeep in gear and we headed out.

He opted to avoid the freeways, so I had plenty of time to stifle
yawns and watch the storefronts roll past. Tanning salons, sushi,
nail salons, Chinese food, hair salons, Thai food, waxing salons,
Mexican food, twenty-four-hour gyms, vegetarian cuisine. I wasn't
feeling terribly generous this day, and it seemed like a metaphor for
Los Angeles. It was all about what you put in the body, and then
how you maintained and pampered the body.

Mary's Lamb was on a shaded street nestled among single-story
Spanish-style houses, and in fact it was located in a converted house.
We found a place to park, fed the meter, and walked back to the
restaurant. Maslin held the door for me, and we walked into the
rich, yeasty smell of freshly baked bread and muffins, topped off by
the aroma of brewing coffee. The odors wove around me like dancing food dervishes, and my bowl of Cheerios suddenly seemed inad-
equate. The room was painted a bright yellow with one accent wall
in Tuscan red. There were flowers on every table, and the furnish-
ings were rustic wood.

A bright-faced and very pretty girl hurried over. "Table for you?"

"I may get a muffin to go," Maslin said. "But actually I wondered
if there was anybody working today who was here when Kerrinan
and his wife came in. It would have been about a month ago."

"Why?" the girl asked, and her faced closed down with suspicion.

I played a hunch and quickly said, "We're working with his attorney to try and help him."

Her face cleared. "Oh. Well. Okay. Actually, I was. They come . . . came in a lot. In fact, I waited on them that morning. I assume you want to know about the day of the murder, right?"

"Yeah." Maslin sucked in a deep breath. "Would you tell us what you remember about that morning?"

"You're really working for his attorney?"

I held out my cell phone. "We can call her, and you can check."

That seemed to convince her. She gave an emphatic nod and began. "They came in early, a few minutes after we opened."

"What time would that have been?" Maslin asked.

"Ten, maybe fifteen minutes after seven."

"And how long did they stay?" I asked.

"We weren't very busy that early, so they were done by eight or a little after."

A stone seemed to settle with a thud into the pit of my stomach. "Really, you're sure about that?" Maslin seemed to hear the hollow note in my voice because he cast me a quick, questioning glance.

"Yeah. Pretty sure. I know it was before eight thirty because I got a call from my roommate that the plumbing had started leaking, but she had an audition, so I had to go home to take care of it."

"Okay, thanks," I said, and headed for the door.

Maslin hurried after me. "Hey, what about my muffin?" he asked once we were on the sidewalk.

"Kerrinan told me he dropped off Michelle at home around eleven a.m., and went straight to the *GQ* shoot."

I had a feeling Maslin's face reflected mine—wan and worried. He shook his head. "That's not credible. They live not that far from here. Even if they walked they'd have been home by nine at the latest."

"And he said 'dropped off.' Which implies car." We stared at each other for a few minutes, then Maslin pulled out his phone, and made a call.

"The photography studio says he arrived at the shoot at eleven thirty."

I gave voice to the question. "So where the hell was he between eight thirty and eleven thirty that morning?"

We headed for the county jail. As Maslin negotiated the traffic he asked, "I don't get it. How come his lawyer didn't find out about this?"

"Defense attorneys don't ask questions beyond the ones necessary to build their defense. They don't want to know. The one question you never ask your client is: Did you do it? Valada's looking for some other explanation for what happened at nine that night other than Kerrinan butchered his wife. She could care less what happened at eight a.m."

"Okay, I can see that, but what about the DA and the police?"

"How many crimes do you think are being prosecuted in LA right now?" I asked.

"Oh, God, thousands probably."

"Exactly. The police and the prosecutors have a case that hangs together. Hell, it's stronger that that—it's almost cut and dried. There's no reason for them to investigate where Kerrinan and Michelle ate breakfast. It's not relevant. They have an explanation, and they have limited time and resources."

"So nobody has done what we've done," Maslin said thoughtfully.

"Exactly."

The more I thought about the time discrepancy, the angrier I got, so I was spitting nails by the time I reached the jail. Christine had left instructions that I could see Kerrinan whenever I wanted. Since

Maslin wasn't on that list I left him in the lobby browsing through old *Guns and Ammo* and *People* magazines. I ended up landing on the bunk with more haste than grace because of a fast-advancing wall. Kerrinan smiled, but it curled up and died when he got a look at my expression. He cleared his throat,

"Ah, it's good to see you."

"Trust me, that feeling's not going to last. Where were you between breakfast at Mary's Lamb and the *GQ* shoot?"

"I don't know what—"

"Cut the crap!"

My words and tone hit him like a whip. He jumped up, took two agitated steps, then had to go dancing over to the toilet to avoid an oncoming wall. For the next few minutes I couldn't see him for the moving walls. I could hear an indistinct mumble, but I couldn't make out any words over the squealing of metal on metal.

A wall cleared and we could see each other. "Get over here. Now." He did. "Where were you? Opium den? Massage parlor? Knife shop?" He flinched. "Where?"

"Balling my mistress! Okay?"

That took all the outraged wind out of my sails, but only for a moment. A new gust shook me. "God, you are so disgusting." In a mocking sing-song I chanted, " 'Oh, I loved Michelle. More than life. I would have done anything for her. I would never have hurt her.' What a crock."

"No! I did love Michelle. It was just sex with Rachel." His eyes pleaded with me. "It's like a smorgasbord. They fling themselves at you. All long limbs and young bodies and soft skin. I'm a male!" He stood up, sat down, knotted his fingers together. "They tell you what you want to hear, stroke your vanity, but they're not real. They're just bodies. I always went home to *her*. She was what mattered. And I never lied to her. I always told her about them."

"Convenient we can't ask her."

It wasn't like I had known this woman, but I had seen her in films with her bright, crooked smile and perfect comedic timing. Then I pictured her dead on the floor of her kitchen. Granted, I hadn't seen the crime scene photos, but I had a pretty good imagination, and I had seen just how much blood a human body contains the night Chip had been murdered. This woman had been in her own home with her husband, the man she believed loved her. Then terror. If he had killed her, what had she felt when the man she loved and trusted had come after her with a knife? I swallowed hard, trying to force down the rage.

Kerrinan hung his head, defeat lying across his shoulders. "Fine, nothing I can say will make you believe me."

"Who is she and where can I find her?"

"Are you going to tell the police?"

"No. You are technically my client."

"Some court won't force you to talk? I mean, you're doing that other Álfar case. Isn't that a conflict?"

"There is no relationship between the two cases, and I was brought in by your attorney as an investigator. I can't be forced to violate confidentiality. That doesn't mean, however, that I can't and won't walk away if you keep on neglecting to tell me things."

"The temptation is ubiquitous and constant," Maslin said when we were back in the car.

"So that makes it okay?"

"No, but it makes it understandable. Kerrinan may not be human, but he is male."

"That's pretty much what he said."

"Doesn't make it less true. We think about sex all the time. We just put up a front to fool you that we have an occasional intellectual thought." He put the jeep into gear. "So, shall we go see Ms. Steele?"

Rachel Steele lived in Pacific Palisades, but far enough from the beach to be affordable. I studied the face of the young woman who was Kerrinan's mistress. She was tall and slender with prominent collarbones, and hollow cheeks. A bag lay in one corner of the room overflowing with dance skirts, leg warmers, and toe shoes. Long red hair hung like a curtain to her hips, and she couldn't have been more than twenty. The smell of patchouli incense filled the room. There was a yoga mat rolled up in one corner, and lots and lots of candles.

Her head jerked back and forth. Looking at me. Looking at Maslin. Back to me. Her expression was two-thirds guilt, one-third defiance, as she said, "Kerri loves me. He was going to leave Michelle."

I managed to keep control of my features—barely. Maslin, not so much. He let out a snort.

Rachel bounced to her feet, fists clenched at her sides. "Don't you laugh. Don't you dare laugh. It's true. At least it was for us."

"Damn, wish I had a nickel for every woman who's ever said that," Maslin said. I kicked him on the ankle. "Ow."

"Look, we're actually trying to help . . . Kerri," I said trying to sooth the ruffled feathers. She sank back down on the sofa.

"Just tell us what happened that morning," Maslin said.

She gave him a look. "Well, what do you think?"

I felt myself blushing. Maslin was undeterred. "So, just the horizontal hula, huh? He didn't say anything about getting a haircut, hitting a few balls—golf balls this time, killing the missus?"

"No, of course not!" Rachel's voice throbbed with outrage.

I stepped in and tried a more diplomatic approach. "Was there *anything* different about his demeanor that morning?" I asked.

The hair swung like sunset clouds blown by the wind. "No, he was a little preoccupied because he had to get to the *GQ* shoot. But very loving," she hastened to add.

"Did you do drugs? Anything that could explain a killing rage?" Maslin asked. I gave him an admiring look. Even though we'd discussed drugs at dinner, I wouldn't have thought to ask that question.

"No. It was early, and we only do pot in the afternoon." Alarm creased her face. "You won't tell anybody, will you? I don't want to get arrested."

Maslin gave a snort. "It's not a news flash to the cops that starlets smoke dope. And they'd never handle real crimes if they chased down every starlet with a joint."

"I am *not* a starlet. I am a serious dancer."

"Yeah, right, sorry. And LA is so the bright center of the universe for classical ballet."

I was beginning to wonder if Maslin's techniques for getting a story was being rude and annoying until people just blurted out damning or revealing stuff.

I jumped in again. "So there was nothing that morning that might explain what happened that night?"

"No."

I glanced over at Maslin, and he gave a tiny head shake. "Well, thank you, Rachel, for your time." I gave her my card. "If you think of anything, no matter how trivial, please call me."

The apartment complex was built in a square around a central courtyard containing a swimming pool, a few permanent barbecues, and some lawn furniture. Maslin and I walked down the stairs toward the courtyard.

"This establishes motive in a big way," I said.

"Not that they need any more evidence then they already have," Maslin said.

"Yeah, but this would really put the nail in his coffin, so to speak."

"So, where to now?" Maslin asked.

I checked the notes on my phone. "Terra Sushi."

"Well, that works. It's time for lunch anyway."

Maslin hadn't been kidding about this stretch of Ventura Boulevard in Studio City being Sushi Row. We must have passed five Japanese restaurants within a four-block range before reaching Terra Sushi, and that didn't include the unfortunately named Todai. Maslin swung the jeep into the minuscule parking lot, and a valet popped out from beneath the awning in front of the door. Nobody came rushing up with an umbrella—Maslin and I didn't rate like Jeff.

We made a dash through the rain; my boots and pants were soaked by the time we got to the door. Then we were into the wood-paneled, soft-lit interior of the restaurant. The pungent scent of wasabi hit the back of my nose, and beneath it was the salty promise of the sea. The sushi chefs behind the bar grinned when they saw Maslin.

"Hey, cowboy, how are you?" the older one called. He was short and round and had a sweatband around his bald head just above his eyebrows.

A lovely Japanese hostess led us to a table behind little wooden walls that separated the walkway from the sushi bar but didn't impede anyone's view. She seemed to glide rather than walk, and I was fascinated with the way she had twisted up her black hair and secured it with a pair of jade sticks. I wondered if I could do that with my hair and almost immediately rejected the idea. My hair was baby fine and so straight it looked like it had been ironed. I'd be shedding jade sticks like a tree sheds leaves in the autumn.

"You want your usual?

"Yeah, and bring my friend a chilled pear saki."

"Oh, no, I don't drink at—"

"Are you a cop?" Maslin asked me.

"No."

"Are you in a courtroom?"

"No, but I'm still technically working," I said.

"But not as a lawyer." His eyes gleamed as he worked up his Hollywood scenario. "You're the spunky girl reporter working with the hard-bitten case who leads you into trouble."

The journalist then leered at me, and I burst out laughing because it was like being propositioned by a cherub. He looked hurt. I stifled my giggles and gave in. "Okay, I'll have a saki, and since you're obviously a regular why don't you order for us."

The gleam in his eye was speculative as he studied me. "And your firm is footing the bill?"

"Absolutely."

"All right, then."

And he proceeded to order a massive amount of sushi. I requested extra ginger, and we happily ate our way through the famous Terra sushi roll (tempura on the outside, all yum on the inside), a California roll, several kinds of tuna, and salmon, eel and octopus. It was delicious. I gave up long before Maslin.

Once we were down to the green tea ice cream he called over the hostess whose name was Kiyumi and asked her about the day Kerrinan had come in for lunch. I didn't figure we'd get lucky twice in a day, but Kiyumi was the owner's daughter—the owner was the rotund man behind the bar—so with an eye roll toward her father she said, "Oh, no, I was here. I. Work. All. The. Time." Her father just gave her an indulgent smile and a jaunty little wave with a wicked sharp little knife.

"Anything unusual happen?" I asked.

She shook her head. "We had that gang of agents in. They weren't their usual rowdy selves. It was a pretty serious conversation."

"With an Álfar, right?" I pressed.

"Yes. He seemed very old and stately."

"And he and Kerrinan spoke." It felt strange to be asking such leading questions, but the girl wasn't terribly forthcoming. Probably an asset when you ran a popular restaurant frequented by famous people who value their privacy. She scrunched her face up, and Maslin jumped in.

"Look, Kiyumi, she's a lawyer trying to help Kerrinan. And I'm not on a story right now. I've been hired to help her investigate."

"But you will write something," the Japanese girl said.

"Yes. Eventually, but right now I give you my word you aren't going to see it on the front page."

"Okay, well, it really wasn't all that much. There was just a little accident after the old . . . man said he liked Kerrinan's work. I think the old one was a little unsteady on his feet. He bumped into the table, and the teapot and cup fell off and broke. They were both scrambling to pick up the pieces—I told them to leave it, I would get it—but they didn't listen and Kerrinan cut his palm on a shard of china"

It wasn't much. "And Kerrinan didn't seem agitated or upset, or like he was on anything?" Maslin asked.

"No. He read a book while he ate."

"What book?" Maslin asked.

"Why? How is that important to what happened later?" Kiyumi asked.

"It's not. It's just interesting," he answered. "What does an Álfar read? Potboilers? Dickens? Austin? A mystery?"

"It had a spaceship on the cover," Kiyumi offered. "If there is nothing else . . . ?"

Maslin looked at me. I shrugged. "No, just the check," he said.

She went off to get our bill. Maslin shook his head. "Science fiction. That's just a head trip. Ellllves in Spaaaaace," he intoned in a takeoff on the old Muppet riff of Pigs in Space.

"I guess everybody needs their fantasy," I said as I looked at the bill and blanched a bit. I dug out my corporate credit card, and a few minutes later we were paying the valet and heading to the next stop.

It was a short drive down Ventura Boulevard to the driving range on Whitsett. The range backed up against the LA River, which was a giant concrete ditch filled with roaring, muddy water heading toward the Pacific. As Maslin and I watched, a hapless bicycle went bobbing past; it was sucked under by the raging water and disappeared. Maslin reacted to my expression.

"Eleven months of the year it's basically bone-dry. There's a tiny six-inch channel down at the very bottom that most of the year has a small amount of water trickling through it. Film crews shoot in the ditch all the time. Remember *Terminator 2*?"

I nodded and we went through the gate and into the confines of Weddington Golf and Tennis. The entire property was lined with extremely tall green netting designed to keep errant balls from braining runners, walkers, or bikers who might be using the path along the river's edge or the occasional pedestrian out on Whitsett. Despite the rain there was the sharp swish-*crack* of golf clubs connecting with golf balls. I did notice that nobody was on the tennis courts. The concrete was probably too slippery.

We headed into the office. The man behind the counter was a fit and handsome fifty-something with a deep tan, smile wrinkles around his eyes, and a mane of silver-streaked hair. Introductions were made, and this time Maslin gave me a tiny nod and then hung back. I smiled and got back a blazingly white smile. It looked like Mr. Jim Dann had been taking advantage of all the tooth-whitening salons along Ventura.

"I'm working with the defense team for Kerrinan Ta Shena. We understand he was here on the day of the murder. I was wondering, hoping you might talk to us about that day."

Dann shrugged. "Sure. Can't hurt. I mean the guy's in a world of hurt right now, isn't he? So what do you want to know?"

"How was his demeanor that day?" I asked.

"Fine. Well, he was a little pissed off."

"Why?"

"His play was definitely off. He's a really good golfer, but he was slicing like mad. Makes a guy . . . well, mad."

"Any reason for the problem?" Maslin asked.

"He had cut his hand at lunch. It affected his grip."

"Ah," I said stupidly. The three of us stood and contemplated each other for a few seconds. Then I said, "I understand there was an altercation as he was leaving."

"Yeah, those dickheads from Human First. I called the cops. I wanted 'em run off, but the cops told me they had a right to be there as long as they stayed on the sidewalk. Public property, they said. Your tax dollars at work." The concluding snort gave me all the information I needed about how much Dann thought of that idea.

"Why all the animosity?" Maslin asked.

"Are you from around here?" Dann asked.

"Born and raised," Maslin said.

"Then you know. California used to be the land of milk and honey, California dreamin', everybody wants to be a California girl. Then we went broke and became a banana republic."

"The confrontation. What, exactly, happened?" I stepped in before the conversation could become solely about the deficiencies of life in California between two lifetime residents.

"This guy literally got in Kerrinan's face and slammed a Bible into his chest. I call that assault. He was ranting about abominations and being contrary to God's law. I got to hand it to Kerrinan;

he kept his cool. He just stepped back out of range—they're so quick those elves. He even smiled at the man and thanked him for his comments. There were seven or eight of these nut jobs, and they were all yelling about God and the Bible. That's when Kerrinan's groupies got in on the act. They formed a flying wedge between Kerrinan and the crazies and escorted him to his car. One of the girls, Liesl, got a kiss for her trouble. Then he drove away."

Maslin asked a few more follow-up questions, but we learned nothing more. Then, after a bit more conversation between the two residents about how California had become unlivable, we tied it up and headed back out to the car. The rain had slowed to a mere mizzle.

Maslin rested his elbows on the bottom of the steering wheel and shot me a glance. "So, what have you learned?"

"I don't think you kill your wife because you sliced your drive," I said.

"I agree. So what's left?"

"The photo shoot."

"Onward and upward," he said.

But that didn't happen because the photographer had gone to Big Bear for a photo shoot of a hot new rock star who, despite her grunge look and reputation, wanted to be photographed against a backdrop of nature. We tried to track down the ancillary crew who had worked the day of the Kerrinan shoot, but the *GQ* offices in New York had closed. We admitted defeat.

"So, you want to have dinner?" Maslin asked with forced casualness.

"Actually, may I have a rain check? We're resuming the arbitration tomorrow, and I need to go over the files."

"Sure. Look, I may just boom on up to Big Bear and find the guy tonight. I'm feeling restless," Maslin said.

I looked at him with admiration, since I felt like a limp rag. "That would be great."

14

Pizer gave me the less then happy news when I arrived at the office: David wasn't going to be in today, so I got to preside. Which raised the question: why? It wasn't like vampires took sick days.

"Is he in LA?" I asked Pizer.

"I believe not," was the cautious response.

I didn't have to be a rocket scientist to figure out what that meant. David had been called back to the New York office to report. Since we were maybe halfway through the arbitration, that could only mean one thing. He was reporting about me and my latest adventure. Which meant I was once more under scrutiny from the senior partners. *So you better do a kick ass job today,* came the unwelcome thought.

Since I had to do David's job, I figured I could use David's office. This was nothing against Merlin, but if I was going to play judge for the first time in my life and the partners were turning their attention to me, I wanted time to gather my wits and confidence, and that was a process better done in private.

Two cups of coffee later, and Junie let me know the parties had assembled. I gathered up the files, a legal pad, and several pens and headed to the conference room. Jeff was in his usual position, seated in a chair against the wall. There were shadows under his eyes, and he seemed smaller and thinner, as if the events on the Warner lot had diminished him physically as well as emotionally. We didn't speak, and he even looked away as I passed. Trying to avoid any hint of impropriety? Or was I just a painful reminder. I know how seeing him affected me. I shook off the memories of that day and settled at the head of the table. Sheila LeBlanc stood and gave a small tug to straighten her gray jacket. There was a large, somewhat abstract pin of a jaguar pinned to her lapel. The way it was placed made it appear it was about to savage her left breast.

"Before we start with evidence I want to bring to your attention a disturbing discovery." Her eyes shifted to where Jeff sat in his usual position against the wall.

"Very well," I said.

"We have learned that Mrs. Montolbano—Kate Billingham— is a member of a cult religion known as the Phase Change Center, based on Álfar beliefs. We wish to determine if Mr. Montolbano is also a member of this cult. If so, it might explain his sudden and unwarranted intervention, some could even say intrusion, into this case. These are important issues, and they should have been heard before a court of law, not in an arbitration."

Jeff's spine stiffed as if he'd been hit with a cattle prod. The reaction did not make me happy. Generally that meant something had hit a nerve. I noticed that Qwendar on the other side of the room shot Jeff a look that was hard to interpret.

"It seems an odd time to be raising this issue, Ms. LeBlanc," I said.

"This information just came to our attention," was the smooth reply.

I looked over at the attorney for the Álfar. "Well, Ms. Gabaldon, have you anything to add?"

"This has taken me as much by surprise as it has you, Your Honor."

My stomach gave an odd little flip as I heard those words. It wasn't correct. I wasn't a judge. I was an arbitrator. A baby arbitrator who actually hadn't arbitrated yet, and I had a nasty problem staring me in the face.

Stalling for time I picked up one of my pens, balanced it between two fingers, and beat out a tattoo on the table. *"When in doubt punt or bunt, depending on which sport you favor."* My vampire foster father's nasal tones and merry smile floated up out of my chaotic, whirling thoughts.

"Given the suddenness of this objection, I think it only fair that we recess until two this afternoon to give all the parties time to gather evidence and testimony."

LeBlanc looked sour, Gabaldon looked relieved, Brubaker looked inscrutable, and Gordon McPhee gave a purse-lipped smile and a tiny nod. I clung to what I perceived as approval like a shipwreck victim to a floating spar. Gathering up my materials I swept out of the room. Well, as much as I could sweep given my height.

This time I did head to the broom closet. Merlin looked up as I blew through the door. "My brother thinks you're cute," he said, then he stammered to a stop at my expression. "I take it my brother didn't impress—"

"Nothing to do with Maslin." And I outlined the problem. "So you're supposed to be the research monkey. Get researching."

"Aren't they supposed to bring you supporting or exculpatory evidence?" he asked.

"Yeah, but I want to know who's playing hide the football. LeBlanc is definitely playing games, and Jeff certainly reacted."

"Good point," and he turned to his computer.

I squeezed past him to sit at my desk and started typing. I checked my watch: 9:23. Four and a half hours to take this beyond the superficiality of a Google search. If LeBlanc's assertions were true it was going to call into question Jeff's reasons for forcing the case into arbitration. If it went back to court I would get to go home to New York, but I wanted to find out what was going on. The next few hours would determine if that happened or not.

In the intervening months since John had been trapped in Fey I had made it a point to learn everything I could about the Álfar. In terms of being closemouthed the Álfar made the vampires look like let-it-all-hang-out guests on a Jerry Springer show. The practical result of that secrecy meant that I had read a lot of bat-shit crazy stuff about Álfar powers. Their secret goal to rule the world. The nature of Fey—depending on who you read, it was either an alternate reality, the past, or another planet. Which meant they were really aliens. There were essays about their government structure—libertarian, communist, green, utopian. (Since I'd met Qwendar I now knew they had a council.) There were the people who believed the Álfar were the *real* humans and we were evil Morlock conquerors. Others postulated they were the gnomes of Zurich and they manipulated world finance. That they had no gods. That they worshiped many gods. No, actually they *were* gods. In short nobody knew nothin'. Serious, credible information was hard to come by, and what there was could fill a thimble.

What I'd been able to glean was that the basis of Álfar religion was mutability. The idea of something being unchanging was anathema to them, so they had one god, but he/she/it changed form, name, and function constantly. It made the Trinity look simple.

Naturally humans had tried to join this bandwagon. In my reading I discovered that the Álfar did not proselytize, and they were horrified that humans were adopting their practices. Since the Álfar were so tight-lipped we didn't actually know what they called their faith. Nellie Winston, the first convert and founder of the first center, took a page from science, awkwardly bolted it onto the concept of change and transformation, and called it *Phase Change*. Water is an example of things that go through Phase Change. Water can be a solid—ice. It can be a liquid—water. And it can be a gas—steam. But at its core it's all the same substance—H_2O. I guess what was worshiped in a Phase Change Center was God_2O.

Point was that, fairly or unfairly, when I ever bothered to think about Phase Change, I'd filed it under "loony cult" or "elfology," which probably wasn't fair since it was practiced by an entire race who had as much right to their respective looniness as the rest of us.

There weren't a lot of phase centers because it was at heart an alien religion and it was confusing. The centers also seemed to be more prevalent where there was a lot of interaction between humans and Álfar. Which mean they tended to cluster in big cosmopolitan areas and in countries where religion wasn't taken too seriously.

Naturally the first and by far the largest center was located in Los Angeles. Which made sense because this was a place where Álfar and humans had been living in fairly close proximity since the late 1960s. It was also a place that was in a constant state of flux. Don't like your boobs, your lips, your hair, your name, your character? Change 'em! The Álfar worship of mutability made complete sense in Hollywood.

So the issue wasn't understanding Phase Change. The issue was whether Kate Billingham's embrace of this faith had influenced her husband. Merlin was a whiz. I was always links and pages behind him as we tore through everything we could find about Billingham, Montolbano, and Phase Change.

This temple to the Álfar gods resided in an old mansion just off Hollywood Boulevard. Kate Billingham, Jeff's wife, was on the board of directors and had helped purchase the building. She wasn't just a casual convert. She was deeply involved. Which would have made LeBlanc's objection credible if the articles about Kate's conversion hadn't gone back *seven years*. The whole idea that this had just come to their attention was crap, and LeBlanc knew it.

I made them wait. Because I was really annoyed. Actually pissed was closer to how I felt, but pissed didn't sound very professional. I knew how I was going to rule, and I had a feeling I was going to be hearing about it on *Entertainment Tonight* or reading about it on a blog somewhere.

I walked back into the conference room and surveyed the terrain. Everyone was keeping to their individual tribes. It wasn't surprising that the human and Álfar actors weren't mingling, but even the agents and the studios and networks who should have had common cause were keeping to themselves. It disturbed me because for the first time I was getting an inkling of how most humans viewed the Powers. I had an admittedly skewed view. My father had business interests with them. I had been fostered by them. I worked for them.

Most humans never really interacted with them. They just knew the Powers were richer and far more powerful than themselves. Of course this was nothing new. Before they'd gone public the Powers had still wielded enormous power, both financial and political, but from behind the scenes. They had pulled the strings. The difference now was that humans could see the strings being pulled. Groups like Human First were manipulating people, convincing them that they were being denied rights, wealth, power. Right now they were just going after the Álfar, but how long before they broadened the attack to the entire triad of inhuman powers? And a steady diet of resentment and hatred could only have one result—violence.

I feared this case was the first salvo.

But the broader societal implications weren't my problem right now. This arbitration was my problem. I walked back up to the head of the conference room table. There was a rattling of china as coffee cups and plates were set aside, the chattering as chair wheels rolled across bamboo flooring, the whisper of shuffled paper, a few coughs, then silence. Everyone was now seated and regarding me. I met LeBlanc's lizard stare and wondered if she would have raised this if David had been present? I decided she wouldn't have, and the fact that she obviously viewed me with disdain got me mad all over again and stiffened my spine.

Gabaldon got to her feet. "Ms. Ellery, if I might have the opportunity to rebut Ms. LeBlanc's assertions."

For an instant I considered allowing her to take point. It lowered my visibility, defused any accusation of bias, but I could read the other woman's expression. She wasn't as overtly dismissive as Le-Blanc, but it was there. Some of it was age. I was a baby lawyer, not even a year out of law school, but some of it was also because women still have a tendency to give greater credence to men. I suspected that if David had been present Gabaldon wouldn't have been so quick to rise to her feet. I understood the impulse, I did it too, but I wasn't going to let it stand. And it was time I tested myself. Maybe past time.

"Thank you, Ms. Gabaldon, but I will address this myself." I shifted to look at LeBlanc. "Ms. LeBlanc. I've researched your claim." I picked up the three-inch-thick stack of papers I'd carried in with me and dropped them with a dull *thwack* back onto the table. "And I find it unpersuasive. In the words of the late Senator Moynihan, you are entitled to your own opinion but you are not entitled to your own facts. There was nothing covert about Ms. Bill-ingham's involvement in Phase Change. It's been widely known for years. Which then begs the question, why did you bring it up now? Unless you think your client's position and assertions are unsupported and unpersuasive, and you're grasping at straws. The statistics you provided indicate support for your position. Why undermine that with a, frankly, personal attack against Mr. Montolbano? Your objection is overruled."

I leaned back in my chair and realized I hadn't taken a breath the entire time I'd been talking. I sucked in a lungful of air and felt the pain in my chest and the fluttering in my stomach recede. I snuck a glance at my watch: 2:20 p.m.

"Ms. LeBlanc, do you intend to present evidence in the time remaining to us?"

"I had a casting director lined up, but when you called the recess she had to get back to work."

"Can you get her back?"

"No, ma'am."

"Will you have her first thing tomorrow morning?" I asked.

"Yes."

"Fine, then, we are recessed until tomorrow morning at nine a.m." I stood.

"Will Mr. Sullivan be back tomorrow?" Brubaker asked.

"I have no idea. You may just have to deal with me." I was startled when he ducked his head and looked down.

I gathered up my papers and headed for the door. Jeff touched me on the elbow before I could exit.

"Thank you," he said and then his expression darkened. "They can go after me all they want, but when they start in on my wife . . ."

I touched his arm gently. "I know. You don't have to say anything more."

I headed back to my office cave reflecting on love. Conclusion: it was a good thing, and I wished I had somebody as protective of me as Jeff was of his Kate.

Qwendar was at the water cooler filling a paper cup. He gave me his wintery smile. "You are a most interesting young lady."

"Interesting in the Chinese proverb sense?" I asked, a bit suspicious.

He chuckled, a sound like a breeze whispering through fallen leaves. "No, interesting as in intelligent, passionate, determined. In short, you were rather impressive."

"Tiny but mighty, that's me . . . okay, maybe not so much."

"You should not doubt yourself."

I slumped. "Thanks, but I was really nervous."

"It didn't show."

"If it didn't I can thank Mr. Bainbridge and my father. I channeled them."

"Well, it worked." He paused for a sip. "Though it is a bit disconcerting to have humans trying to worship in our manner when they cannot possibly understand our faith."

"What do you mean?"

"You cannot walk the worlds, so you can't see the face of . . ." He paused. "Well, let's call it God since you really don't have a word for it." He correctly interpreted my expression. "You don't agree."

"I think there's a constant tension between inclusion and superiority in religions. The "chosen people" strain versus the "do unto others" Golden Rule thread."

"That can be said for people as well," Qwendar said.

"Meaning what?"

"That it's in the nature of all creatures to think that their particular kind is superior to all others."

"And that's part of why we have law—to try to counter those tribal instincts."

"You place law above religion," Qwendar said.

I considered that for a moment. "Yeah, I do."

"Why?"

"Because law adjudicates outcomes based on facts, evidence. While faith is important, it shouldn't have a place in law."

"But sometimes your facts are flawed," Qwendar argued.

"Yes, and we have in place a system to try and counter that. It's not perfect and mistakes are made, but it's there. There's no recourse with faith."

"So, you're saying you cannot question faith?"

"Oh, you can question it. What you can't do is examine it. It's not subject to analysis or investigation."

"But at the end of the day don't you have . . . er . . . faith," his lips quirked in that thin smile. "That justice will be done?"

I threw up a hand. "Okay, touché. Remind me never to debate you in public."

He surprised me by taking my hand and brushing his lips across the back of it. "I think you would be a worthy opponent."

15

Given Maslin's less than diplomatic approach to interviews I thought it was better that I visited the Human First headquarters on my own. That afternoon when I presented my reasoning, he disputed my conclusion—vociferously.

"They will want to talk to me. I promise you. They will want ink . . . well, phosphers, since magazines are pretty much all online now, on this."

We were having the dispute in the center of reception. Not my choice of venue. Interested faces were peeping over the office dividers.

I planted my hands on my hips. "A two-second Google search and they're going to know you're not going to be sympathetic."

"And that's fine. I'll make it clear that I'm giving them the chance to present themselves rather than letting their opponents define them." He flashed a grin at me. "That almost always works."

"They can't be that stupid. You're going to do a hatchet job on them."

"And Cartwright won't care. She's savvy about playing the political game. Having the lame-stream media"—he rolled his eyes—"take out after the group will put them in hog heaven. It'll fire up their supporters. And she knows there is no such thing as bad press.

Most people are too busy living their lives to pay attention to this kind of thing. The more press the more likely it is that people will look up and notice. She'll want to talk to me," he repeated.

I threw my hands up and surrendered. "I'll drive," I said over my shoulder. "I'm not dressed for the jeep today."

Turned out that Human First didn't have an actual headquarters. They shared space with Cartwright's lobbying group, Liberty Front, and were located in a strip mall in Van Nuys. I could tell from the curl of Maslin's lip that Van Nuys was not up to his standards. I asked him about his reaction, and he answered cryptically, "It's the Valley."

I figured I'd follow up on that later. Right now I wanted to stay focused. We got out of the car and I studied the storefront. There were a lot of American flags in evidence, both the real variety and on posters. The latter tended to be eagles superimposed over American flags depicted in way too saturated colors. Another poster divided into three sections showing the Marines raising the flag on Iwo Jima, firefighters at Ground Zero raising a flag, and American astronauts on the moon with the flag. Then there were scary posters showing Álfar men lurking near angelic-looking human children and young, Madonna-like human women. Just inside the door there was another poster showing a demur young woman in a wedding gown standing at the altar with a giant lizard dressed in a tuxedo.

"Wow, that's subtle," Maslin said loudly.

The people seated behind desks and phone banks looked at us. They didn't look friendly. I noticed they were all mostly white, mostly female, and mostly older. There were a few exceptions. There was a skinny old duffer whose bow tie just accentuated his neck's resemblance to a turkey's. There was a plump young woman with five little towheaded girls playing on the floor around her desk. Then I realized the plumpness was due to pregnancy. The room was filled with the sounds of ringing phones, hushed conversations, and the patter and click of keyboards. It had all the earmarks of a campaign headquarters.

I approached the desk that looked sort of receptiony. The woman eyed me. "I'd like to see Ms. Cartwright," I said.

"Do you have an appointment?"

"No."

"Who are you?"

"Linnet Ellery and Maslin Ambinder."

There was a flicker deep in her eyes at my name. No reaction to Maslin's. "I'll see if she's available." She picked up the phone, then indicated with a jerk of her chin a leather sofa against the wall near the front door. "If you'll wait over there."

Maslin and I moved away. The receptionist kept a hand cupped over the mouthpiece on the phone and kept shooting glances at us as she whispered into the phone. She nodded, hung up, and came over to us. "Ms. Cartwright is finishing up a conference call. She can be with you in fifteen minutes if you want to wait."

"We'll wait," Maslin said, and he leaned back, folded his arms across his chest and grinned up at her.

There were printed materials on a small table next to the sofa. The bold heading read "Voter Information Guide." Beneath it were listed all the reasons why a person should support Proposition 9.

1. Contact between different species has always been banned by biblical law. Such prohibitions are even found in secular law.

"Yeah, you got to force those commie, pinko, socialist lawmakers to ban bestiality," Maslin murmured as he read along with me.

The Álfar have been proved by modern science to be a different species from humans.

"Funny how science can't be trusted when it's talking about climate change or evolution, but it's cool when it can be used to support bigotry," Maslin added. Maslin's constant kibitzing had me struggling not to giggle.

2. The rise of a relativistic attitude toward cultural and moral norms will lead to public schools teaching our children that a mixing of species is okay.

"Yeah, it's up to parents to decide whether Johnny can diddle the Labrador."

"Stop it!" I gasped nearly choking on a hastily swallowed laugh. We returned to reading.

3. The purpose of marriage is procreation and responsible child rearing. Unions between Álfar and humans are always sterile, thus undermining the purpose of marriage in a civil society.

"Wow, my grandfather, ninety-three, is romancing a woman, eighty-six, in his nursing home. Guess we better tell him to stop.

But I wasn't laughing any longer. I hadn't realized that Álfar and humans couldn't reproduce. Now my father's remark about how he wanted grandchildren came into focus. I wanted children. Or at least one. If John and I— I cut off the thought. We were hardly at that point. We might never reach that point. Especially since John was a prisoner in Fey.

4. All currently existing marriages between Álfar and humans must be annulled.

The receptionist called over that Mrs. Cartwright would see us now. Maslin plucked the page out of my hand and carried it as we wended our way through the desks accompanied by the trilling of phones. And now that we were among them I could hear more than a murmur; I could hear actual words. The volunteers were busy sending the arguments listed on the voter guide into receivers and presumably from there into the credulous ears of California voters.

Belinda Cartwright was waiting in the door of her office. She was a pretty, perky brunette, taller than me with a very curvaceous figure. She was dressed in a red suit set with gold buttons on the coat, a skirt at a demur mid-knee length, and red, open-toed, high-heeled shoes. A pen thrust into her chignon, and a pair of designer glasses gave her the look of a naughty librarian. She smiled at both of us and offered her hand.

"Miss Ellery, Mr. Ambinder. Pleased to meet you. Mr. Ambinder, I enjoyed your series of articles on female circumcision in sub-Saharan Africa. Very enlightening and offered a stark comparison of religious ideas."

Maslin shot me an I-told-you-so look, then turned back to Cartwright and said, "It wasn't intended as a moral comparison. I was looking at the medical effects of the procedure on women."

"Of course you were maintaining your journalistic integrity, but I could see what lay beneath the words," she said.

"Wow, that's quite an extraordinary power you have," Maslin said.

The smile didn't slip. "Mock me if you want, but I really have an ability to know what's in a person's heart."

I wasn't sure what happened, but suddenly I found myself channeling Maslin. "Ms. Cartwright, please. I've done my research. You're a graduate of Cornell, you worked for Congressman Rankin from Mississippi as his chief of staff, you worked for the Senate Finance Committee, you've written articles for the Cato Institute, and you were a lobbyist before you founded Liberty Front. Remember who you're talking to."

She gave me a look that revealed the woman behind the mask. What I saw was smart, sharp, and calculating. "That's fair, and allow me to remind you that I also do my research. Linnet Ellery— graduate of Yale Law School, summa cum laude. Did Law Review. Clerked for a Supreme Court justice one summer. Joined Ishmael, McGillary and Gold last year and won a major case regarding the ownership of a multimillion-dollar company."

There was a moment of silence, then I said, "I guess we're even."

She gave me a predator's smile. "Do come in," and she waved us into her office.

There was the usual assortment of framed photos on the walls. Cartwright with various presidents and religious leaders. There was a gavel on the desk with a brass plaque from a former congressman who gave out "civic awards" to people in exchange for a five-thousand-dollar "donation." The furniture was nice and tastefully arranged. She waved us to a sofa and took a seat in an armchair across a coffee table from us.

"So how much of this manure do you actually believe?" Maslin asked and tossed the voter guide onto the coffee table between us. "Or are you just using the energy of the angry and ignorant to push your agenda?"

There wasn't the reaction I expected. Cartwright kept her cool and just studied Maslin as if he were an interesting new specimen of bacteria. She then swept up the voter guide, crumpled it, and tossed it aside.

"Yes, it's simplistic, and you would probably call it blatant fear mongering, but I'm working this issue because I am actually very concerned. We have inhuman creatures—for God's sake, some of them are dead—taking greater and greater control of our institutions and industries. The position of humans in this brave new world is in question. I'm damned worried, and you should be too."

You hate to admit an opponent might have a point, but she had a point. Vampires were scary, and I could attest to how frightening a ravening werewolf could be, but then I saw the flaw in her logic.

"But why target the Álfar?" I asked. "They're probably the least involved in human affairs in any significant way, and unlike vampires they don't have to prey on humans to survive."

"Not true. Their conquest of Hollywood is deeply troubling. The more they fill our television and movie screens, the more accepted the Powers become. We'll be conquered, and we won't have seen it happening."

"So why aren't you involved in this lawsuit?" Maslin asked, and I wanted to kick him.

Cartwright read my dismay and gave me an edged smile. "Already in the works. Our attorneys are preparing papers and will be petitioning Mr. Sullivan to be joined in the same fashion as Jeff Montolbano and that Álfar. Getting the Álfar off our televisions and out of our movies would go a long way to neutralizing their influence on our children."

"Let's get back to Proposition 9. Why marriage?" Maslin asked.

"Because it's visceral. No daddy thinks any man is good enough for his little princess. If we can make all those daddies—and mommies for that matter—think a monster is after their daughters, it'll be the first step. If we can convince people that the Álfar aren't human—which they aren't—we're a step closer to having humans take a look at all the Powers and realizing how dangerous they are."

"You're giving me whiplash here," Maslin complained. "So which is it? Are the Powers secret masters of the universe controlling every human institution and our very lives, or are they undeserving minorities looking for special treatment?"

"Both. And any other argument that's going to work and rally the humans."

"Wow, cynical much?"

I jumped in. "So you must be very pleased about these killings."

"Naturally we're always deeply saddened when someone loses their life, but this did shine a bright light on the issues we are raising." It was a politician's answer, smooth and noncommittal.

"Kind of convenient how the murders started happening right when you're flogging this proposition," Maslin said.

"Are you implying we had something to do with them? You people on the left always ascribe nefarious plots to conservatives. I suppose we should thank you for believing we're so powerful, but it's utter nonsense. And our members aren't violent."

"Well, I certainly hope not, because I've been getting threatening phone calls, and I think they're from someone in your group."

"Do they identify themselves?"

"No. It's a threatening phone call. They don't usually introduce themselves," I said, more tartly than I intended.

"Then you have absolutely no proof. It might be some Álfar making the calls to make us look bad."

Maslin let out a snort. "I think you manage that pretty much all on your own."

I shot him a shut up look and got us back on track. "But back to these murders: you will take advantage of them," I said.

"Why wouldn't we? It's the Álfar finally showing their true colors."

"Okay, now, that's utter nonsense," Maslin broke in again. "If the Álfar are a bunch of murdering whack jobs, why hasn't it happened before now? Why didn't it happen forty years ago, or thirty years ago, or twenty years ago? What's so different about now?" Maslin asked.

"I have no idea. Maybe you should ask an Álfar." Despite Cartwright's best efforts, Maslin was starting to get under her skin so she focused back on me. "Miss Ellery, I understand that you work for a white-fang law firm, that you were fostered by vampires, but you're a human, and a very intelligent one. Put aside some of our more colorful claims and look at the underlying facts. The Powers have been manipulating us for generations, but suddenly they have come into the open." She looked back at Maslin. "You might want to consider that question too, Mr. Ambinder. Why have they gone public? What are they planning? And what do they want?"

Human First is high on my list of suspects, but how in the hell could they have gotten the two Álfar to go rogue?

Those had been Maslin's final words when I dropped him off at his car. He had gone off to research. I had gone back to work, but a day spent banging my head had me no closer to an answer. I realized I needed to get out of my head and out of a chair, so I'd headed to the Equestrian Center. It was a foggy night. The white planks of the fencing formed ghostly lines, and the lights around the riding arena couldn't really penetrate the mist. They just made it more pearlescent and reflective. Vento gave a disgusted snort as I brought him down from a flowing canter to a walk. It was clear he missed the pasture back at his barn in Brooklyn, and he was eager to stretch his legs and run.

I had hoped that doing something physical would jump-start some ideas, but so far it hadn't worked. All I could remember was Kerrinan's bitter grief over the loss of his wife. Maybe it was just an Álfar trick, or maybe he was a great actor, but he seemed to genuinely have loved Michelle.

I pulled back the edge of my glove and checked my watch. It was seven thirty p.m. and it was clear that neither Vento nor I had the patience for detailed dressage work. I nudged him forward off my leg and walked across the parking lot and over to the breezing track. I found the electrical box and flipped on the lights around the track. They didn't help much, but it gave us a clearer sense of the edges of the track. Here, near the back of the Equestrian Center the hum from the cars on the 134 freeway was like droning deep in my chest.

We reached the center of the track and I turned Vento to face the expanse of dragged dirt. His muscles vibrated beneath me, and he began to piaffe. I wrapped my hands in his flowing mane, sent my hips forward slightly, and backed it up with a touch of my calf. He rocketed into a canter, and within three strides we were at a full gallop. He didn't have the bounding stride or the speed of the thoroughbreds I had breezed one summer when I was looking for extra cash, but he was still going plenty fast enough for a foggy February night. And what he lacked in speed he made up for in stamina. We had circled the quarter-mile track three times before I began to feel his hindquarters losing push.

I began to reel him in. Then Vento leaped sideways, and I fought to maintain my seat. My intestinal tract seemed to be somewhere in the vicinity of my throat as I looked around wildly for what had spooked him. I spotted a dark figure vaulting over the rail and rushing toward me, hand outstretched toward the bridle. Vento took umbrage at that and went hopping backward.

The figure was now close enough that I could recognize David. "You're not helping!" I yelled, and he put on the brakes. A second later Vento was standing quietly, though I could feel his sides heaving against my legs, and his breath sounded like a bellows. He swung his head back toward me then looked at David with what I could only interpret as disapprobation.

"Sorry, I guess I spooked him," said the vampire.

"Do you think?"

"Sorry," he repeated.

"Why did you run at us?"

"I thought you were in trouble . . . I was trying . . . it was stupid."

"Agreed. Don't you know anything about horses?"

"Not really."

Which was another clue to the cypher that was David. He clearly wasn't as old as many of the vampires of my acquaintance since he wasn't conversant with horses. I turned to a more pressing question.

"What are you doing out here? And more to the point, where the hell were you yesterday?" The fog was condensing on the brim of his fedora, threatening to become actual droplets of water. His face was a pale oval in the darkness.

"I wanted to check in with you. I heard what happened in the arbitration yesterday." I tensed waiting for a reprimand. "You did good."

It wasn't what I expected. "Thank you."

"You sound surprised."

"You guys tend to be a little stingy on the compliment front."

"You proved yourself. It's why I decided to help you with the Securitech case," he said.

"Okay, I call bullshit. You started helping me as a way to get back at Ryan." I said, laughing.

David stiffened. Vampires hate to be laughed at, but he again surprised me. "All right, that's true, but once I started to work with you I saw your quality."

"What exactly does quality mean?"

He gave me a quick smile. "I'm not going to pander to your vanity, and I need to keep you striving to impress me." There was the echo of laughter in his voice

"And I need to head back to the barn." I jerked my head behind me. "Want a ride?"

He stepped in close and put his hand on the pommel of the saddle. His arm rested against my hip. I kicked my foot out of the stirrup so he could use it. He looked up at me. I looked down at him. Then he abruptly stepped back and shook his head. "I'll walk." We started back toward the barns. "Your horse doesn't seem very alarmed."

"Not now. You're no longer a scary, shadowy figure in the darkness."

"Most animals object to my kind."

"They sense you're a predator and . . ." I tried to think of a more tactful way to say dead.

"Not alive," David supplied.

"Yeah."

"The staff reports you weren't in the office today," David said as we walked across the Equestrian Center.

"I was off interviewing the Human First people, and while I don't like them I just can't see them engineering something like this. Really wish I could talk to Jondin so I could compare her statement to Kerrinan's."

"Linnet, I want you to be careful with this."

"It won't have any effect on the arbitration."

"That's not what I meant. People have been killed."

We reached the barn, I kicked loose my stirrups and jumped down, and found David's arm closing around me to help lower me gently to the ground. "He's not that tall," I said, indicating the horse. "But thank you. And thanks for the concern, but our two murderous Álfar are locked up."

"There are a lot of Álfar in Hollywood."

"Now you sound like you're channeling Human First."

It felt cozy inside the barn and out of the fog and the dark. I put Vento in the tack-up area, pulled off his saddle, and began brushing him down. The smell of hay, dust, and horse was calming, and he was warm beneath my hand.

David leaned his shoulders against the tall wood divider and said, "I'll see what I can do about seeing Jondin, but don't expect it to work. It might be easier to get your gnome in to see her."

I looked over my shoulder at David. "Gnome? Really? I call

that tall-man bias. And I think Maslin's a good height for a shrimp like me."

"You make up for the lack of inches in attitude."

I returned the dandy brush to the tack box and said carefully, "Okay, now you really are starting to freak me out with all the compliments."

"You're showing live-person bias."

It wasn't all that funny, but it still made me chuckle. "Okay, now I know you're sick. Humor is not your strong suit."

"Vampires in general or me in particular?"

"You in particular. You must have supped from a drunk."

"Well, if you're going to be insulting, I'll leave you. See you tomorrow."

For an instant the tall, broad-shouldered figure was silhouetted against the doorway of the barn, and then he was gone. Then I realized he never had answered the second question. So where had he been?

16

Even though intellectually I didn't agree with Cartwright's final words, they stayed with me. Maybe that's what makes demagoguery work. Why had the Powers gone public? Historians argued that it was the times—the 1960s was a time of social and cultural turmoil. I wasn't sure that held together. Sure, groups had been looking for a place—African Americans, women, gays, young people—but they were, for the most part, the disenfranchised. The Powers had a place—they were in charge. The vampires and the hounds had been pulling the strings from behind the scenes for hundreds, if not thousands, of years, and it had worked really well for them. Why reveal themselves?

I sat on the sofa in my apartment, elbows on knees, chin in hand. The winter night had crept in while I sat staring morosely into the fireplace, and I hadn't really noticed. The only light was provided by the gas flames licking fitfully around the fake logs.

I forced my thoughts back to the Álfar. They hadn't been deeply involved in human affairs prior to 1963. Oh, they occasionally stole a human child or led an unwary human away into the Fey, but after the Powers went public they began spending more and more time on our side of the reality divide. So far their deep involvement had been just in the entertainment industry, but what if they decided to move into the political arena? If they could use their preternatural charisma to win parts, why not to win a seat in Congress? Or the White House?

There was something in my last thought that had me straightening and considering, but before I could quite grasp it there was a knock on my door. I jumped because I wasn't expecting anyone. I stood, hesitated, staring at the door. The knock came again. I stood on tiptoes and looked through the peep hole. It was Qwendar. I removed the chain and opened the door.

"Pardon me for calling so late. I was hesitant to disturb you, but I wondered how your inquiries were proceeding?" He stood, holding his hat.

For a moment I just stood and blinked at him. How had he gotten my home address? And even though he wasn't an actual party to the arbitration, this was pretty irregular. Then the slump in his shoulders and the deepened lines in his face penetrated. He looked exhausted, and I felt bad for my suspicions and rudeness. I stepped back and opened the door wider.

"Please come in. And you're not disturbing me. I won't go to bed for hours yet. Can I get you anything?"

"If you are going to have something."

"I thought I'd make hot chocolate."

"That sounds lovely." I busied myself in the kitchen with a box of cocoa, sugar, and milk.

"You don't use a mix?" he asked, taking a seat at the small bar that divided the kitchen area from the rest of the apartment.

"No, they're too sweet."

"That would never be a problem for my kind. We love all manner of confection."

"The Álfar have a sweet tooth. Who knew?" I began to stir the milk to keep it from scorching. "I visited Human First."

"And?"

"And . . . nothing. I don't think they're behind it. Oh, they'll make hay over what happened with Kerrinan and Jondin, but I can't see how they could have caused it." I frowned.

"You seem perturbed."

"I thought I had a train of thought that was going someplace, but . . ." I shrugged and mixed the chocolate and sugar paste into the milk.

"And then I disturbed you, and you lost it," he said rather ruefully.

"It was probably just smoke."

"Why don't you talk about it. It might help you pursue it to a conclusion." I started to shake my head. "Linnet, our goals are the same. We joined this arbitration so I could try to protect my people. You think my people are being targeted and you're trying to help them. Wouldn't it make more sense if we pooled our information? Worked together?"

I blew out a breath, pushed back my hair with my forearm. "Okay. I was just reflecting how the other Powers—vampires and werewolves—had been affecting human events from behind the scenes, and now that they're public they're still doing it, just making no bones about it." I filled two mugs with the bubbling chocolate. "But the Álfar haven't really done that, and when you did decide to enter human society your people ended up in entertainment."

"Meaning?" he probed.

"That's the problem, I don't really see where this is taking me. Other than the fact that vampires and werewolves have enormous influence over law and commerce, and the Álfar are actors or singers, and yeah, art and culture have a powerful impact on society, but it takes time. Vampires and werewolves are having a lot more immediate impact. So why target you guys?" I shrugged and sipped my hot chocolate. "And werewolves marry human woman too, and

Human First isn't going ape-shit about that. Wish I'd thought to say that to Belinda Cartwright." I shook my head. "See, I'm just nattering, and it's going nowhere."

Qwendar drained his mug and set it aside. "Perhaps we are both simply, what do you humans say . . . paranoid? Perhaps there's nothing more here than simple jealousy."

"Doesn't feel right. What makes two people go suddenly nuts within weeks of each other? Can you do the Álfar whammy on each other?"

"The glamour works much better on humans. And we use it to make people like us . . . or love us." He slid off the bar stool. "And vampires can mesmerize too, and blood is certainly an essential component in their existence."

"Interesting. I just can't see why they'd want to make the Álfar look bad."

"It's puzzling, yes. Well, thank you for the chocolate. I'll leave you to your evening now."

I walked him to the door. He took my hand. "There is something here, I just can't quite bring it into focus." I gave his hand a squeeze. "We'll figure this out."

"I believe you will."

The arbitration resumed the next day. LeBlanc, realizing that Campos, the director, hadn't actually helped her all that much, had a new expert witness. Unfortunately he was in New York City, which meant an AV expert had joined us in the conference room to handle the linkup. Computers had been placed strategically to create the illusion that Ashley Schultz was seated at the front of the room near to David and me, and our seats had been moved since we couldn't look sideways at a computer screen. LeBlanc moved along the table handing out a sheaf of papers. They were emblazoned with a heading that read "Q Squared" in a logo that had overtones of an Escher drawing.

The big thirty-six-inch screen went from black to gray, then stabilized, and I saw a man in his thirties with slicked-back black hair, a pair of coolly appraising gray eyes, and an understated but very good suit. He was fiddling with a tiny microphone, trying to clip it onto his shirt collar. One of the assistants in our Park Avenue office in New York was trying to help him. I recognized one of the conference rooms.

Chuck, our AV guy, said, "Mr. Schultz, can you hear me?"

"Yes, I can hear, but I can't see you."

Chuck made grumbling noises that almost became words and fiddled with the console. "Yes, that's got it," Schultz called. Like many people using a video link he seemed to think he had to speak louder than normal and enunciate very carefully.

I looked down and referred to the witness profile that LeBlanc had provided. Ashley Schultz owned Q Squared, a marketing and research company that specialized in taking the temperature of the public about everything from television shows to computers.

"Are we ready to begin," David asked, his tone huffy. I wondered if it was because of the intrusion of the computer equipment, never a vampire's favorite thing. Chuck gave him a thumbs-up and adjusted his headphones. David nodded at LeBlanc. "You may begin."

"The pages I've just handed out are last month's Q scores for every Álfar actor currently working. The second section is the Q score for every human actor currently working. If you'll take a moment to glance over the figures, my point will become immediately apparent."

David and I looked at each other and started flipping through the pages. From the corner of my eye I could see Gabaldon doing the same. I didn't need to be a statistician or a marketing analyst. The numbers were boldly clear. The human actors consistently scored twice as high as the Álfar actors. I remembered Campos's words: *they're just pretty dolls.*

After having allowed us all to fully digest the numbers, LeBlanc turned back to Schultz's image on the screen. "I hired you to run a Q rating for me, didn't I?"

"Yes, ma'am."

"And whom did you test?"

"Casting directors, producers, and directors, but only those who have actually used Álfar actors," the marketing man answered.

"And what did you find?"

"That the Álfar scores—"

There was a sudden screaming burst of feedback from the speakers on the computer in our conference room. People jerked, clapped hands over their ears, and erupted into a few exclamations and curses.

"New York, it's on your end!" Chuck was yelling into his microphone. We saw the technician come scurrying into range of the cameras in New York and rip off the microphone. Chuck was frantically dialing down the volume. The awful sound ended, and people pulled their hands away from their ears.

"What the devil is happening? Have you no control over this damn stuff," David huffed.

"Sorry, sorry," Chuck panted as his hands played across the console. A few minutes later and the New York technician gave us a thumbs-up.

"Is it safe for us to resume?" David asked, each word dripping ice.

"Yeah, go ahead," Chuck said.

"Ms. LeBlanc, please continue," David said.

"Let's go back a little, Mr. Schultz. So you tested casting directors, producers, and directors who had worked with Álfar actors?"

"Yes."

"And you found?"

"That the Álfar scores were almost off the charts among that group. A complete reversal of the numbers we saw when we polled only viewers," Schultz answered.

"And do you have a conclusion, Mr. Schultz?" LeBlanc's voice was a husky purr.

"I can only speak to what the numbers tell us, and they tell us that humans who have had direct, personal interaction with the Álfar have a much higher regard for them than people who merely view them on the screen."

"So, in other words, whatever it is that the Álfar project, it doesn't cross the barrier of the screen. Physically they are beautiful, but the something that makes a Julia Roberts or a Leonardo DiCaprio a star is lacking."

Before LeBlanc had finished Gabaldon was on her feet. "Objection. This witness hasn't been established as an expert at anything aside from taking polls."

David looked at LeBlanc. "It's a fair point. Please establish Mr. Schultz's expertise in this area, aside from the company he owns."

Schultz gave David a long, level look, clearly not intimidated by the vampire. "I have a PhD in psychology from USC and a PhD in mathematics and statistics from CalTech." LeBlanc handed over the man's vita and we looked at it together.

"I'm inclined to agree that Mr. Schultz is, in fact, an expert," David said. He cocked a brow at me.

I nodded, but then a question occurred to me. I directed it toward McPhee and the studio executives. "How is this not a self-correcting problem? If the Álfar actors aren't appealing to audiences, then the movies fail to make money. Wouldn't the bottom line ultimately win out?"

One of the executives tugged at McPhee's sleeve and whispered to him. The old lawyer answered me. "A movie is a collaborative effort, Ms. Ellery. Many things go into making a hit. Yes, the stars are important, but there's thematic material and special effects. The real bottom line is that no one knows what makes a hit. For years Tom Cruise got twenty million dollars a movie because it was believed he could open a film. Sometimes it was true." He shrugged. "Sometimes it wasn't."

David glanced at me. "Finished?" I nodded. "Please continue, Ms. LeBlanc."

She returned to her place at the conference table, picked up another sheaf of papers, and handed them out. "These are the ratings from people who actually interacted with both human and Álfar actors."

I studied the pages. The scores for the Álfar were stratospheric. Four times as high as the reactions to the human actors.

"Are there any other conclusions you can draw from these statistics, Mr. Schultz?" LeBlanc asked.

"These numbers make no sense statistically. Putting aside the fact that people respond more favorably toward people they actually meet, these numbers are out of line with the norm."

LeBlanc looked pleased. "It's known that the Álfar have the ability to fascinate and attract. Could that power account for these numbers?"

"I don't know how to test for unknown powers. I will go this far: something is skewing these numbers, and the only data point we have is physical proximity."

"Thank you, Mr. Schultz."

Gabaldon was shuffling rapidly through her papers. Gordon McPhee leaned over and whispered something to her. She gave a sharp nod. David cleared his throat. "Ms. Gabaldon, Mr. Brubaker, Mr. McPhee. Have you questions for this witness?"

McPhee rose to his feet. "Mr. Schultz, let me see if I understand in plain English what you appear to be saying. You seem to be saying that when people meet each other in person they tend to like each other, correct?" Schultz gave a cautious assent. "And since the object of these meetings was to get hired for work, one assumes that the parties in question were putting their best foot forward, so to speak."

"I'm not sure I follow," Schultz said.

"Meaning the Álfar weren't going to be rude or unpleasant."

"Yes, that is true."

"And people when they go to job interviews they tend to dress well, and look their best—"

"Is there a question in this, or is Mr. McPhee simply offering us pointers for our next interview?" LeBlanc asked.

The older attorney inclined his head toward LeBlanc with courtly dignity. "I'm always happy to be of service, Ms LeBlanc."

"Is there a point to this?" David asked.

"Yes, sir. Indeed there is. The conclusion Ms. LeBlanc seems to be wishing the arbitrators to reach is that the Álfar are using their god-given natural talents to achieve their ends, namely, a job. Is that correct, Ms. LeBlanc?"

"Yes, they're using unnatural abilities."

"Mr. Sullivan, I should like to call Missy Able as a rebuttal witnesses to Mr. Schultz."

That got a big reaction from the room. Missy came half out of her chair, face reddening. LeBlanc hurried over to talk with her. Despite being the person who had brought the lawsuit initially, the actress seemed deeply shaken at being singled out.

"Mr. Sullivan, Ms Able is a plaintiff in this action," LeBlanc argued.

"I see no reason why she can't be questioned, assuming the same right is extended to the defendants. Ms. Gabaldon?"

"We have no objection if counsel wishes to question Palendar or any other Álfar actor."

"Very well," David said. "Mr. McPhee, you may question Ms. Able."

"I don't want to!" Missy said.

"And bluntly, Ms. Able, that's too bad. You brought this lawsuit. Presumably you feel strongly enough to defend your position. Now, you can either submit to questioning or I may be forced to decide this case right now in favor of the defendants."

There was more hurried conversation between Missy and Le-Blanc, then Missy reluctantly took the chair indicated by McPhee.

"Now, Ms. Able, or may I call you Missy? My boys and I just loved you in *Rednecks*. My eldest son had your poster in his bedroom." He beamed down at the woman and got a reluctant smile.

"Yeah, okay."

"Now, Missy, what is your profession?"

"You know that."

"I know, but humor me."

"I'm an actress."

"An actress. That's a tough job, isn't it?"

"Tougher now," she snapped back.

"Yes, well, putting that aside for right now—it's a tough job because so much of it hinges on things like how you look, your height, and so forth, things you really can't change"

"Yeah."

"So I presume that when you go in to read for a part or audition for a director you try to find out everything about the role and try to bring yourself in line with that character. Dress like that character. Or put on extra-high high heels. Maybe even dye your hair. You ever been known to do that?"

"A few times."

"And sometimes people are inclined to take more permanent measures, aren't they?"

"I'm not sure I know what you mean."

"Well, you had breast augmentation when you were nineteen years old, didn't you?"

"That's . . . that's . . . none of your business."

McPhee lifted up a Xeroxed page. "You talk about it in this article you gave to *Rolling Stone* about how you credited those . . ." He perched reading glasses on his nose and read, his voice supplying the quote marks. " 'Those tits really did the trick for me. I'm sure they're why I got the part of Crissy on *Rednecks*.' "

"Okay, maybe I did say that, but I was twenty, and you say stupid things when you're twenty."

"But you did have breast augmentation surgery, yes?"

"Okay, yes!"

"And seven years ago, according to sources, you had a face lift."

I didn't like Missy Able and she had overtly threatened me, but McPhee's pointed questions were flaying her in front of us, and I found myself writhing in sympathy for the woman.

"What if I did?"

"You're fortunate that you were able to have the financial wherewithal to afford these procedures."

"I suppose I was."

"But I'm sure there were many actresses who didn't have your resources and were unable to afford similar procedures."

"I guess."

"Do they have a right to sue you because you had an advantage over them in auditions?"

Missy goggled at him. McPhee turned his back on her and addressed David and me. "I have nothing further."

"I, however, have a question for you, Mr. McPhee," David said, stopping the lawyer before he could resume his seat.

"Of course."

"So your contention is that it is completely fair for the Álfar to use abilities that might surpass those of humans in an effort to win parts?"

"Yes, sir, that is exactly what I am saying."

"It's an interesting argument."

We were in David's office. The parties to the arbitration had left, and we were indulging in a postmortem. David sat at his desk, buffing his nails, an oddly dandyish behavior and a side of him I hadn't seen before. I stood at the UV-treated window watching the traffic in the street below. I was listening, but with only half my attention. There was something about the day's testimony that was teasing at the back of my mind and refusing to come into focus.

I turned my back on the view and faced him. "It's the old meritocracy versus affirmative action argument. " I said.

"It going to be a constant tension in a society that has any desire to be fair." He reacted to my expression. "What?"

"That is a very curious attitude for a vampire. You guys are all about the rule of the elites."

"Maybe Roosevelt affected me more than I knew."

"Which one?" I couldn't resist asking.

"Both," was the bland response. Which was a new data point but didn't really take me any closer to knowing when David had been turned. "Truth is, you have to be careful. Elites can ossify. It's not that much of a problem among my kind. We don't hand down power to children."

"When you turn someone, they're like your child."

"True, but we pick them based on merit, not on the luck of the genetic draw."

"Bringing us back to that whole meritocracy thing," I said. "The truth is that affirmative action is an imperfect solution to the problem. We can't make everybody equal. We can make sure there aren't artificial obstacles placed in the way of people, but genetics are a bitch. I can't carry a tune in a bucket, but I love music. Doesn't mean I should get to sing at the Met."

"And it's human, and probably Álfar, nature to try and use every advantage."

"And launch a thousand industries—hair dye, face cream, diet books."

"So, where is the line? When does an advantage become an unfair advantage?" David asked. He threw aside the nail buffer and ran a hand across his face, his fingers seeming to linger on the scars. "Everyone screams about drug use in professional sports and seems to think the modern home run stats have been ruined by steroids. 'The Babe didn't take no stinkin' steroids.' But players in the modern era receive vaccinations, have a better diet, take vitamins. They're stronger, taller, faster than players back in the day. Does that mean that every modern statistic is suspect?"

"A baseball neep?" I asked. "I'm learning all kinds of things about you today."

He gave me a quick, closed-lip vampire smile. "Well, I better fix that. Back to our case. The Álfar are more beautiful than humans, and stardom is often based on beauty."

"Where does it stop? The Álfar could argue that they're being treated unfairly because until this year no Álfar has ever been nominated for an Academy Award, much less won one."

"Really?"

"Yeah, I looked it up after Campos testified about how the Álfar are such shitty actors. Now, either they're being discriminated against by the Academy members, or they really are shitty actors."

"They do tend to star in these action or fantasy pieces. I don't see them doing the remake of *Who's Afraid of Virginia Wolf*," David said.

"You've seen a lot of Palendar's and Jondin's films?"

"I like to go to the pictures."

"Okay." I threw myself down on the sofa and frowned at him. "Look, if it's just beauty that's at work, then the human actors don't really have a case, and that's how we should rule. But anecdotal evidence suggests that the Álfar can cast a . . . ." I waved my hand in the air. "What should I call it? A . . . a glamour whammy?"

"No, don't call it that, but I take your meaning, and those statistics today suggest it's more than anecdotal," David said.

"So, beauty is okay, but whammy's not?"

"McPhee thinks both should be allowed," David said.

"Because he's trying to get the studios off the hook so they don't have to potentially pay settlements to human actors. The human actors want the Álfar banned from using their special abilities. The Álfar are arguing they don't have any special abilities."

"And the agents and managers don't care so long as their clients are landing roles and bringing in money," David said.

"Which means there's probably a rift inside their ranks too. The agents with Álfar clients think this is great, and those with human actors in the stable, not so much." I sank down in a chair.

"We are trying to thread a really tiny needle here." We both chewed on that for a moment, then I added, "It all comes back to Álfar magic. Is it real? If it is, how does it work. What are their abilities?"

"Let me know what you discover," David said. He was looking down at the papers on his desk. I had clearly been dismissed.

I was surprised to find Jeff waiting in the lobby. He looked tired and very woebegone. "Hey, what's up?" I asked.

"Correct me if I'm wrong, but it seems to me that McPhee just won the case for the human actors. I mean, don't you have to decide for Missy now?"

I led him back into the conference room where we could talk in private. "Jeff, there are four different parties with four different agendas in this arbitration. Gabaldon is trying to win for the Álfar and prove they have a right to the parts they're getting. LeBlanc is trying to prove they don't. McPhee and Brubaker just want to get their clients off the hook for damages, so they'll make any argument that will accomplish that."

"Are you like that?"

I thought about it. "Yeah, I am. I can argue both sides of an issue, and if I'm really good, I can find a side nobody ever thought of before and argue that one too."

"But what's the truth? Isn't that why we're here?"

I patted him on the shoulder. "Oh, Jeff, you have a very romantic view of the law. We're not trying to find truth. We're trying to find an acceptable solution within the framework of our laws."

17

I went to the only Álfar source I had at hand. Qwendar studied me over the top of his wine glass as I said, "Look, you said you wanted to help me. That we could pool information. So now's the time. I need you to tell me about Álfar magic."

"That is very difficult. I can't make that decision on my own. I must talk to the Council first." We were seated in a small French bistro with well-padded white leather booths, lots of greenery, and arbors creating the illusion that we were outside, not seated in a bay window looking out at the traffic streaming past on Melrose Boulevard.

"But you'll do that, right?"

He smiled at me. "I don't see how I can be less tenacious than you. I will ask. I can't promise they will agree. Such things are intensely private to us and tied up in our religion, of which humans have only the most imperfect understanding."

My hand clenched on the stem of my wine glass. "I am going to find the answers."

"But do you even know the questions, dear Linnet?"

I couldn't help it. I smiled at the tendentious tone. "Oh, don't go all Mr. Miyagi on me."

"I have no idea what that means."

"*The Karate Kid.*" He looked blank. Then I stopped myself. "Oh, God, now *I'm* doing it."

"What?" Qwendar was smiling now, and the stiffness had retreated from his shoulders.

"Making movie references like everybody else in this crazy town." I dropped my forehead onto the table. "I'm doomed."

"Drink your wine, child, and tell me why you want this information."

"I'm just trying to understand your abilities and powers. Both for the arbitration and for Kerrinan's and Jondin's sakes. Do you cast glamours that humans can't resist? Is it even reasonable to think that something could affect one of you enough to make you commit murder? The truth is, all the Powers are way more powerful than us." I gave him a small smile. "It's why we call you the Powers."

We sipped wine in silence for a moment, then he said gently, "I may have some good news regarding your friend John."

"She's going to let him go?"

"Not that good, but I believe I will be able to arrange for a meeting between the two of you. I'll let you know once all is in place."

"Thank you. I can't tell you how much this means to me."

"Shall we dine?" he asked.

"Actually, I've got a lot of work to do, so I'm just going to eat at the apartment. Thank you for meeting with me on such short notice."

He rose, as I stood to leave. "It was my pleasure. I'll let you know as soon as I have an answer from the Council."

The next day I went to see Kerrinan, who was pathetically pleased to see me. We sat side by side on the bunk while the squealing walls moved around us.

He sat staring down at his hands. "I'm actually thinking about pleading guilty."

"What? Why?"

"Because as more evidence comes to light and the more Christine and I talk, the more I come to believe I *did* kill Michelle. Even though I have no memory of doing so."

"Please, don't do that." I laid a hand on his arm. "That's not a bell we can unring," I said. "And there may be mitigating circumstances."

"But it doesn't seem like you're getting anywhere."

"Please, just give me a little more time. You can always have Christine go to the DA any time before trial and offer a guilty plea. Actually even during the trial. Please, just wait."

He sighed. "All right."

"And actually I had some questions that I was hoping you will answer."

"You know I'll do anything," he said.

"Some of the testimony we've been hearing suggests that the effects you have on humans can only really happen when you're in close proximity. Is that also true between Álfar?"

"So this is about our magic?"

"Yeah, it is."

He blew out a breath and shook his head. "So my defense may come down to this."

"Are you hedging because you think I'm crazy or because it's all a big secret and you can't say anythi—"

"No, no. I'm not like the hoary old guard, always protecting our ancestral secrets. I don't give a crap about all this secret *woo woo* shit, and I don't know much about it. The really big stuff takes years of study, and frankly, why would you bother in the modern era? So you can light a candle with magic. Big fucking deal. Why not snap on a light switch? The easy stuff we can all do. The whole throwing a glamour is easy. We can do that practically without thinking."

"Well, all rightee, then. Looks like that question is answered." He gave me a blank look. I explained. "You'd make a hell of a witness for LeBlanc if you weren't an accused murderer."

"Oh, the lawsuit." He shook his head. "Not really my biggest worry right now."

I spent another moment thinking how Gabaldon would refute the charge. Swear that the Álfar didn't do that? But the statistical evidence proved otherwise. I pulled myself back to Kerrinan and the current problem.

"So what . . . magic can you do?" I asked.

"We all learn how to move between Fey and Dirt. That's harder than the glamour and the tricks, and I think even that's breaking down. My feeling is, pick a spot to live. I made my choice twenty years ago. LA is my home. I haven't been back to Fey in—"

"Not true. When you were on the run you went into Fey."

"Yeah," he said slowly and sadly. He gave me a sidewise glance. "Except I don't remember doing that either."

"Okay," I said, drawing out the word. "What part of it?"

"Any of it. Making the decision. Driving. I was at my house and then I was in Fey."

"Just like you don't remember the events the night of the murder."

Fear and despair left the muscles in his face sagging. "Am I crazy?" His voice was a thread of sound.

"I don't know, Kerrinan." A new question came floating up. "So why did you come back? You were completely out of reach of human justice."

"The Council. They thought it would inflame the humans against us if I could just duck out. And I didn't want to stay. I wanted justice for Michelle. I wanted to know what had happened. There were a few people on the Council who thought it was wrong for humans to judge an Álfar, but they lost the vote."

I considered Human First's campaign to vilify the Álfar and decided that the Council had shown a lot of wisdom.

"Is Qwendar on the Council?"

"No. He was, but a long time ago. Now he's more of a gray eminence."

I stood. "So you can't tell me if there's anything about Álfar magic that could make you . . . well, kill?"

"Not that I know of." He stared at me with growing horror. "And who would do something like that?"

"I don't know. I may just be grasping at straws here."

"A gray beard might know."

"And he's working to get an answer." I stood. "Hang in there."

He stared down at his clasped hands. "I hope they reinstate the death penalty."

"God, Kerri, why?"

"Because if I killed her I don't deserve to live." He watched a wall sliding past. "And I couldn't take decades living in this. I'd find a way to end it."

"We'll figure this out."

"That's the problem. There isn't a we; there's just *you*."

"And my crazy ideas," I finished the unspoken thought. "Do you think I'm crazy?" I asked turning the question back on him.

I got a wan smile in return. "No more than me."

Headlights wove patterns, electric plaid, all around me. Nerves and anticipation had left my hands slick with sweat. I took a firmer grip on the steering wheel. *I'm going to see John. I'm going to see John.* He was not going to love these sweaty palms. I removed first one hand, then the other, and wiped them on my jeans.

The call from Qwendar had come at ten p.m. the day after my conversation with Kerrinan. I had just settled down to watch a movie on Stars, wrapped up in a bathrobe and with a pint of Cherry Garcia for company when the shrilling phone had me bolting off the sofa.

"If you can be at the Chateau Marmont by eleven I'll have John there. Room 323."

"Okay. Yes. I'll be there. Wait. What's the Chateau Marmont? Wait, it's probably a hotel 'cause you gave me a room number. Okay, where is it?" I stammered and yammered.

"I don't know the location in this world."

"Right, I'll get directions," but I was talking to a broken connection.

So, now I was making my way down Cahuenga Boulevard, which suddenly turned into North Highland Avenue. I nearly panicked but managed to glance at my MapQuest printout by the glare from the headlights of a farting truck that rumbled past. The gates of the Hollywood Bowl bulked on my right. The traffic slowed to a crawl, and I wondered why all these people didn't go the hell home? Up ahead was a stop light. Mercifully it turned red. Franklin Avenue. I rolled to a stop, switched on the interior light, and checked my MapQuest printout. The next light would be Hollywood Boulevard, where I would turn right. Then a few more twists and turns until I was on West Sunset Boulevard.

I realized I should have called Big Red and Meg to tell them I was going to see their son. No, I shouldn't. It was nearly two a.m. on the East Coast, and a call this late would just panic them. I'd give them a report in the morning.

The hotel should be on my right. It shouldn't be hard to spot. From the pictures on my computer it looked like a French castle. I checked the clock on the dash. 10:43. Oh God, why didn't this traffic move? I checked my watch, hoping it showed a more favorable time. It didn't. In fact it read 10:47. I decided to trust the car. I feared what would happen if I was late. Finally the car in front of me moved.

I made the turn onto Sunset and said aloud, "All right, Mr. DeMille, I'm ready for my close-up," then decided that talking to myself didn't say much for my stability, and damn if it wasn't a movie reference again. I had to get out of this town. I switched on the radio, flicked through the dial, but the music felt like it was etching my skin. I switched it off.

An extremely garish orange, red, pink, and blue neon sign shaped like a shield with an arrow through it glared against the fronds of a palm tree. ENTRANCE CHATEAU MARMONT, it read. This was the place. I turned into the almost hidden driveway. Even at 10:55 a valet was on duty. He leaped forward as I bolted out of the car. I felt bad, but I literally threw my keys at him.

"I'm going to be in room 323," I called back over my shoulder.

"Miss," he was frantically waving the claim check at me. I didn't slow down, but raced through the front doors. I had a brief impression of gray stone walls and cloister-walk-shaped windows.

There was an elegant staircase in front of me. Not wanting to wait for an elevator (I figured they would be slow in an old hotel like this), I bounded up the stairs, taking two steps at a time. I found the stairs at the end of the hall and continued up to the third floor. Room 323. I was there. I reflexively checked my watch. 11:02. Not bad. I gave a quick fluff to my hair, straightened my tweed jacket, and knocked. An instant later the door opened.

I quickly scanned the room. Mercifully John's terrifying mother wasn't present. Qwendar was there, and I was relieved to see his lined face. There were also a number of Álfar men in the room. I recognized some of them: they had been present in the Dakota when John's mother had taken him prisoner. Whether they were guards or advisers I really couldn't say, and I wondered why the hell they were here? I stood on tiptoe, craning to see, but John was hidden from me. Qwendar stepped forward and took my hand.

"Linnet, welcome. Please come in."

I did. Several of the Álfar men stepped aside. I looked up at them. "Am I that formidable? Or are you afraid John will stay?" They didn't answer, and I finally saw John. He was elaborately attired in tight pants, high boots, and a high-collared jacket like a Hussar's uniform or an extra in *The Student Prince*. Since he favored khaki slacks or blue jeans, polo shirts, sport coats, and tennis shoes when he had worked for IMG, this look was jarring. He stood at a window gazing down on the gardens and pool.

"John."

He turned when I spoke his name, and I fell back a step. His left eye was cloudy, an expanse of milk white, and the way he cocked his head told me that when his mother had driven what had looked to be a sliver of ice into his eye it had blinded him. I choked briefly on a sob.

"I got your flowers," I said softly, after I cleared the obstruction in my throat.

His good eye raked me, and the expression was so cold, so filled with ennui, that it was as if acid followed his gaze, etching my skin. I shivered, suddenly uncertain.

"I have no idea what she is talking about. Why, exactly, is she here?" The timbre of the voice was John, but it didn't sound like John. The question was addressed to one of the men standing next to him.

Uncertainty gave way to anger. I jumped in before the factotum could answer. "Why don't you ask me directly? I'm standing right here."

"She's rude," John remarked again to the man.

"What can you expect?" said the first man.

Another of his—guards? entourage?—joined in the pile-on. "She's a human," and he gave a shrug as if that said everything necessary.

John took a step toward me. The tap of his boot heels was loud on the parquet floor at the edge of the carpet. "You wanted to see me. Why?"

"To make sure you were all right." He stared at me as if I'd suddenly burst out speaking in Swahili. "You were forced to stay behind by your mother." Nothing. "Mommy Dearest said if you didn't stay behind she was going to force Charity and Destiny and me to stay. You sacrificed yourself for us." Silence. "This ringing any bells?" My tone was becoming increasingly belligerent.

"Yes. I remember that, but I disagree with your characterization. It was a chance to find my way home. I hadn't realized how superior life among my own kind was to life with you monkeys."

I stiffened at the slur. Just as it wasn't polite to call members of the Powers spooks it wasn't cool to call humans monkeys. "I'm sure your father, your human father, the one who raised you, Big Red, would just love to hear you talk like that." There was an instant when I thought that had gotten a reaction. Something flickered deep in his one good eye, but it was too fleeting for me to be sure, and then the ice mask was back in place.

"Ah, the large, sweating, red-faced man," one guard said.

"Perhaps that is how he got the nickname," another of the supercilious guards suggested. Laughter, like the whisper of water in a fountain, rippled around the room.

A pounding settled behind my eyes and the room felt hot. "John, this is your father. He loves you. And your mother, she's grieving for you. Missing you. Don't let them talk like that about them."

Given the hateful crap I was hearing in this room I was even more glad I hadn't called Big Red and Meg. John's voice pulled me from my reverie.

"We returned their human child. They have no cause to complain," John said.

"What?" This was news to me. I tried to imagine Big Red coping with an unknown man now in his midforties who had spent his entire life in Fey. It must be a nightmare for both of them. "Your mother threw out Parlan?"

"Why wouldn't she? She has me now."

"Yeah, and that's so great," I said. I wondered if this new pod person, John, would recognize sarcasm. It seemed he did.

"You are once again becoming rude."

"You don't even sound like yourself. Who are you? What's happened to you, John? Where is the man who was my friend and . . ." I choked a bit, and didn't say the word that hovered on my lips. *Lover.* I couldn't be that vulnerable to this arrogant stranger. "Protector?" I finished lamely.

John didn't answer. He looked over at Qwendar. "How long is this going to go on? I agreed to this meeting because of the position you hold, but this is tiresome in the extreme."

Qwendar looked over at me. I read pity in his eyes. "Well, Linnet? Are you satisfied? Have you ascertained what you wished?"

"No." The word was so explosive that one of the guards actually jumped a bit. "This isn't John. Putting aside whatever might have been between us, John would never talk about his father that way."

"Perhaps he has remembered who and what he is," Qwendar said.

John stepped closer to me. He was wearing a scent that was like sandalwood and honey, but beneath it I caught the tang of sweat, acrid and musky. "You may talk about the human that raised me, but this is really about you. Because I bedded you once, you imagine that I care for you."

Sometimes agony can emerge as laughter. I choked on a bitter chuckle. "Bedded? Really? What are we, in a Victorian romance novel? My John, and Big Red's son, would have said 'fucked.'"

"If you choose to be denigrated in that way—"

"Oh, you're doing a fine job of that all on your own."

"Look, I used you because you were there. Nothing more. So stop thinking there was ever anything between us, or that there will ever be. You are part of a life that no longer exists for me. Your presence in my life now bothers me. So. Go. Away."

He spun, balanced like a dancer on the heel of one boot, and walked toward the window. I thought he might return to his contemplation of the gardens, but instead there was the wavering of his outline and he and his entourage vanished into Fey. My rage faded, leaving me cold. I stood bereft and shivering. If a boot had been planted on my chest it wouldn't have hurt this much.

"I wish he'd just refused to see me." My voice sounded hollow and very far away. "He could have done that. He didn't have to be cruel. This can't be happening." I ran my fingers through my hair, clutched at it so hard it pulled and hurt.

"What will you do?" Qwendar asked.

"I don't know, but it can't end like this. It just can't!"

"Perhaps things are different with humans, but that seemed like a pretty solid rejection."

I shook my head. "He came to see me. He brought me the flowers. Something to tell me he still cared. He's being controlled. Maybe that thing she put in his eye. Maybe it can be removed." I broke off abruptly, arrested by a sudden thought. I turned and started for the door.

"What? What is it? I could see you thought of something."

"What's been done can be undone, and now I've got a source who grew up with the Álfar and may have some advice."

"The human exchanged for John."

I made a gun with my finger, pointed it at him. "You got it on one."

18

David came into the broom closet the next morning just as I was getting ready to dial the O'Shea household. He was carrying a copy of *Daily Variety*. I opened my mouth to tease him about going all Hollywood since he was now reading *Variety* instead of his beloved *Chicago Sun-Times*, but I never got the words out because he was peering at me so oddly. I put down the phone that I'd just picked up. "What?" I asked. "Why are you looking at me like that?"

"You don't look upset."

"I'm going to if you don't stop staring at me like I'm the corpse at a wake and tell me what's going on," I replied.

"Qwendar called me early this morning. He said you had a rough meeting with John, and he was concerned about you. Did you see John?"

"Yes. But this is bullshit. How dare Qwendar call you. As if you have anything to do with this at all. And how could he think I'd go into a decline because a man—" I shut up before I could reveal just how much I was hurt.

"Why did you do that without telling me?" David asked.

"Because Qwendar called me late last night, and I don't see how it's any of your business anyway."

"O'Shea was an employee of the firm. We have an interest."

"Okay, that's just hooey. He was an independent contractor. I know full well that the senior partners hired another private eye to handle investigations for the firm. They certainly weren't losing any sleep over John."

"But you were, and the firm does have an interest in you."

"And I'm fine. Actually I'm glad you're here. I was about to come see you. I talked with Kerrinan yesterday, and he just flat admitted that the Álfar throw glamours, almost without thinking about it was how he put it."

"Palendar will deny it," David said.

"And an accused murderer probably isn't the best witness to refute that claim, but when you look at Kerrinan's statement and the statistical evidence, it's pretty damn clear."

"So we need to find an Álfar who will come clean," David said. "Although it rather galls me to be doing LeBlanc's job."

"To be fair she probably hasn't been able to find an Álfar who would testify. No offense, but the Powers tend to stick together. We do want an equitable outcome, don't we? And it's pretty clear the humans can't fairly compete."

"So you've decided against McPhee's position?" he asked.

"I thought about it a lot, but ultimately his analogy breaks down. Yes, money can be an obstacle to people getting cosmetic surgery, but people can acquire money. They can't acquire Álfar magic." An idea began to blossom. "We have the right to call witnesses too," I said.

"Yes, so? We don't have an Álfar either."

"But we can get one. Well, he's sort of a half-assed Álfar, but I'm betting he might be willing to testify about Álfar magic since he just got kicked out of Fey on his ass. Assuming he knows about their magic, of course. I'd have to find out."

"What are you talking about?" David demanded.

"John's brother . . . well, I guess you'd call him a brother. The human child John was switched for. He's back with his human family. I found out last night."

David frowned and thought. "Before we go chasing off after this changeling, are you getting anywhere with Qwendar?"

"He's trying to get permission, but who knows how long that will take?"

David frowned some more, then gave an abrupt nod. "All right."

"I'll call him—"

"No, go. You need to evaluate him as a witness, and he might not be willing. You can exert more influence in person. You can also report back to the senior partners while you're on the East Coast."

"You know, they have phones too."

"They like the personal touch."

"What about the arbitration?"

"You can be present via video conference." He turned and left.

I called our assistant and asked her to get me booked on a flight to Philly. I also had her order a car to take me to the airport. I just didn't want to deal with the traffic around LAX. Then I gathered up my files, left a note for Merlin, and headed back to the Oakwood to pack.

"So you wish me to be a witness in a hearing that will discomfit the Álfar actors? I would be delighted. I don't feel particularly loyal right now. They threw me out of the only home I've ever known."

The final words of Parlan's harsh indictment were suddenly blurred by being forced past a lump in his throat. He coughed. I looked away. Men crying is the one thing that could truly slay me.

We were seated in the living room of the O'Shea house, and quite alone. Big Red and Meg had gone off to watch one of the grandsons play in a hockey game. It was a typical East Coast house. Narrow, three stories, siding, and steep steps leading up to the front door. There were identical houses to either side, the only difference being the color of the siding. The O'Shea house was blue, the ones on either side were gray and beige. Through the living room window I could see an array of snowmen illuminated by streetlights and standing like sentries in the front yards of the houses across the street.

The room had a comfortable, lived-in look. One arm on the big sofa had a kid's western saddle and an arrangement of rope on the end so a grandchild could play cowboy. The bookcase held an assortment of novels, books on criminology, and coloring books. There was a big flat screen TV, and a braided rug on the wood floor. There were a few paintings on the wall, watercolors that had been done by Meg O'Shea on summer vacations on the coast, but most of the walls were filled with photos of the children and grandchildren. John, proud in his PPD dress uniform, smiled out at me from the east wall. It was my turn to look away and swallow a few times.

Parlan and I looked back at each other at the same time. He was an attractive man. I knew he was forty-three because he and John had been switched as infants, but the lost expression made him seem younger. Parlan had his red-headed father's flamboyant coloring though silver now frosted the hair at his temples. It was long, held with a silver clip at the nape of his neck, and the tail hung over his shoulder. I wondered how long before Big Red got him in for a haircut? Parlan's eyes were a deep blue, almost aquamarine, with crow's feet etching the corners. He had a square jaw with a cleft in the chin, and a powerful, barrel-chested body. He was the antithesis of the delicate Álfar physique. He was dressed in blue jeans and an oatmeal-colored cable-knit sweater that suited him very well.

"But only if you can shed light on the case. What do you know about Álfar magic?"

"Quite a lot, actually. I can't do it, of course, but I did study with a court enchanter."

"I don't understand. If you couldn't do magic, why have you study it?"

"I had to learn how to resist the glamours. If I hadn't, I could have been tormented by any Álfars who weren't terribly keen about having me around."

"Okay, it sounds like glamours are little magic, something an Álfar does almost without thinking."

Parlan was nodding. "Yes, that's correct."

"So, are there big magics, the kind of magic that would put an Álfar into a killing rage and then not have any memory of it afterward?"

"Yes. I think so. Some of the powerful old ones can really get inside your head and essentially turn you into a meat puppet. But you need blood from the person that you're looking to control."

Outside the wind had started to kick, moaning around the eaves of the house and setting the limbs on a big beech tree scraping against the window like nails on a blackboard.

"So, does the glamour require blood?"

"Oh no, no, no, that's like breathing for them. They don't even have to think about it. They just do it."

"Wouldn't an Álfar know if another Álfar was trying to control them?"

"Not if the enchanter was powerful enough and had enough training."

"How much blood are we talking about?" I asked.

Parlan shrugged. "It would depend on the skill of the controller. If they were good—not a terribly large amount." He paused and cocked his head to the side. "So, do you think I can help you?"

"Definitely."

He gave a rather predatory smile. "Good."

I couldn't help it, I blurted out the question. "Did you really like living there?" I asked.

"Of course I did. I was the pampered son of a powerful queen. I was exotic. I got laid a lot. Of course, what I realized too late is that I wasn't really her son. I was a toy that she played with until she became tired of me."

I couldn't help but ask another question. "What's it like? Do you have modern conveniences? I know you have cars. I saw them when John and I . . ." Now it was my turn to clear the obstruction in my throat. "Well, I saw them."

"There wouldn't be a tree left in the world if we were still living like it was the Middle Ages. We've been stealing power off the human grid for decades. Electricity and gas heaters beat the hell out of fireplaces. The translation to Fey does seem to play all holy hell with computers and cell phones, so that hasn't happened."

"Were you educated?" I asked.

"Not in a way you'd recognize. I have a courtier's skills." He glanced up at me from beneath his lashes and this time the smile was bitter.

"I don't know what that means," I said.

"I can dance, hunt, dress well, make conversation. I also found that I liked studying their history and magical arts. They let me because I had something they lacked—focus."

"John said something like that. I think that's why he didn't like it after growing up here. So what are you going to do now that you're in this world?" I blurted because my internal editor had gone on strike.

"I have no idea. My . . . father." The hesitation didn't escape me. "Says I have to get my GED. Or perhaps I'll just ask if you want special sauce on that burger. Or deliver pizzas. I hear there's good money in delivering pizzas." He gave me a smile. "Of course, I'll have to learn to drive. Wonder if I could use a horse? Riding was one of my great joys." Again the smile, both brave and ironic.

"I love horses too," I said.

"I miss mine. He was spectacular." The brave front trembled a little, but Parlan recovered.

"She's just awful," I said.

"I can't disagree. All she had to do was wait another thirty or so years and the problem of the human changeling would have been resolved. Now I have to live what remains of my life in a world I don't know and don't understand."

The sadness touched me. I reached out and laid my hand lightly over his. "You'll be okay. You have good people around you. A family that can help you."

"But they don't love me."

"And she didn't love you either," I shot back. "If she did she wouldn't have treated you this way. Or John. You're both just objects to her. Things to possess until she gets tired of you."

His hand was jerked from beneath mine, and he held it up like a shield. "Don't! I can't bear to . . ." He broke off and coughed again.

"Would you like a drink?"

"Sure, but nothing alcoholic. I'm jet-lagged and booze would put me to sleep, and I have to get up to New York tonight."

"Come on," Parlan said, and gestured toward the door. I followed him down the hall and into the kitchen. It was another homey space redolent with the scent of recently baked cookies. "Hot chocolate?" Parlan asked.

"That sounds great," I replied. I settled down at the kitchen table and watched as he prepared a pan, milk, sugar, and cocoa. "I didn't think cooking was a princely skill," I said, and smiled to indicate it was a joke. He took it in the spirit it was offered and smiled back.

"We are permitted eccentric hobbies," he answered dryly.

A stunning idea struck me. "You should open a restaurant. Serve Álfar dishes. You really are the prince from a foreign land. You'd make a fortune."

He stood frowning at me, the wooden spoon hanging between his fingers. Then the lines in his forehead smoothed, and he slowly nodded and used a word I'd never heard. "*Hilial,* you may be right."

"What does that mean, *hilial*?"

He pursed his lips considering as he stirred the hot chocolate. For a long moment the only sound in the room was the hiss from the gas burner and the slow scrape of the spoon on the bottom of the pan. "None of these are exactly right, but morph, transfigure, transmute."

"So you follow the Álfar religion."

"Of course. It's how I was raised."

"How's that going over with Big Red?"

"As you can imagine, not great." He poured cocoa into a mug and handed it to me.

The ceramic sides were warm against the palms of my hands. I blew across the surface, and streamers of steam bowed and danced. Risking a sip, I managed not to burn my mouth, and I was pleasantly surprised. It wasn't too sweet.

A few more sips of chocolate gave me the courage I needed. "May I ask you something else?"

"Of course."

"It's about John, so it might be awkward, painful."

"I don't blame him. He's as much a victim as I am. I know he didn't want to stay in Fey," Parlan said.

"How do you know that?"

"I lived there forty-three years. I had friends, even among my mother's guards, and they're still my friends. Some of them slip over to visit me, and they told me the devil's bargain she offered."

Outside, snow had begun to swirl. I was jumpy enough that I kept expecting something to coalesce out of the whirling flakes. I drew in a breath. "I saw John, and he was so changed. And she blinded him in one eye. Why would she do that?"

"Control. Also part of Álfar magic. A sliver of ice that blunts all emotion toward anyone but herself."

"Well, he had contempt down pretty well," I said, trying to mask the hurt and pretty sure I hadn't succeeded.

"That's actually a good sign. It means he's fighting back."

"So she rejects the son who does love her and has to use magic to make the other one love her. Wow, that is really fucked up."

"Yes." Parlan dropped his head and stared down at his hands. "And you're right. I do love her, still."

His expression was so lost and despairing that I couldn't help it. I once again reached out, and this time I clasped his hand in mine. "It will get better."

There was again that smile that flickered like summer lightning. "You promise?"

My lawyer caution warred with a human reaction. I was proud to see that human won. "Yeah, I promise."

"So what happens now?"

"I tell my boss you can help us," I said.

19

The next morning I walked back into the main office at Ishmael, McGillary and Gold. The snow that had blanketed Philadelphia had also hit New York City. Central Park looked beautiful under a layer of white. Dogs and children romped in the snow, while a few parents and owners, and mostly nannies and dog walkers, looked on. Now I was glad I had lugged my heavy coat to Los Angeles. Otherwise, I would have been in New York without a coat. Though the thought of taking it back to LA was daunting.

The Legal Eagles Pop Brigade was on hand to greet me. It was what we young female associates in the firm had dubbed ourselves after we'd all issued an epic smackdown on a vampire partner who had been using and harassing female associates. Caroline, looking elegant as always, was in the lead and gave me a fierce hug.

"You don't have a tan," she accused.

"It's been raining in LA and cold. Well, cold for them."

"So no picking up hunky blond surfers on the beach and fucking their brains out, huh?" Cecelia asked, living up to her reputation as the bawdy broad.

"Afraid not."

"It seems like you've been gone forever," Juliette, a beautiful woman from Jamaica, said.

I thought about it. "It has been a month and a half. God help me."

"Any sign it's going to end soon?" Delia asked.

"Not really."

"Can we all go to lunch?" Nancy asked as my flying scrum of friends escorted me to my office.

"Sorry, no. I'm joining in the arbitration via video conference, and the time difference means I'm going to be sneaking bites of sandwich during the testimony."

My assistant, Norma, rose from behind her desk like an iceberg calving off a glacier and stared down at me. Her teased, silver-white hair was like a helmet. "Well, I'm surprised to see you."

From her tone it was clear it wasn't a pleasure, and as usual there was no evidence her computer had been turned on once since I had been gone. I had to assume she used it. Just never when I was watching. I had inherited Norma along with my office from my deceased boss, and I didn't have the nerve to suggest a change. The fact that she was tech-phobic wasn't that big of a drawback in a white-fang law firm; most of the vampire partners felt the same way, and she did defend me behind my back while insulting me to my face. It was a little like having my mother working for me.

"Hi, Norma, glad to see you, too. And I'm only in for the day."

"Hmmm!" She sniffed. "Lot of damn money to fly coast-to-coast for one day."

"Good thing it was the firm's money," I said brightly. Norma almost cracked a smile.

"We should all get back to work," Caroline said, asserting her control as the most charismatic among us. There were more hugs and everyone headed off to their offices.

Mine looked deserted. The desk was bare except for the

computer. My plants had been moved by the watering service. The waste can was empty. For an instant I felt like I had been erased from the firm. I shook off the feeling, dumped my briefcase and coat, and went in search of the AV tech to make sure everything was ready for the conference.

I found Ollie in his cluttered office filled with computers, headphones, cables, soundboards and other mysterious electronic items. Ollie was a plump, balding, twenty-something who wore a suit because this was Ishmael, McGillary and Gold, but somehow he always looked rumpled. Today a button was missing on his shirt and his tie was uneven.

"All set?" I asked.

He took another swallow of coffee before answering. "Totally. I'm gonna eat while this is happening. Okay?"

I sighed. "Sure. Just don't make it anything too delicious. Otherwise I won't be able to hear over my stomach growling."

"Check." His thumb thrust up. "I'll be sure to buy something shitty for lunch."

With a wave and a chuckle I left. When I returned to my office, Norma informed me that I was wanted on the seventy-third floor. "Why?" I asked with some trepidation.

"And you think I would know? The senior partners don't give reasons; they just say frog."

"Okay, I'm jumping." I headed to the elevators.

Those of us on the lower floors referred to the seventy-third floor as Teak Heaven. It was opulent in the way Versailles is opulent. The incredibly handsome and incredibly supercilious receptionist, Bruce, told me I was expected in Mr. Ishmael's office. Which gave me some relief. Since it was Shade who had summoned me, perhaps I wasn't in trouble. He was my mentor and champion at the firm.

Shade's secretary nodded at the door, indicating I could go in. Shade looked up as I entered, and the sharp blue eyes scanned me critically. He came around from behind his desk and gave me a gentle kiss on the forehead. His lips were very cold.

"Linnet, child. Thank God, you're all right. You have the most alarming tendency to find yourself in mortal danger."

"I think I'm a chaos magnet," I said, trying to keep it light. "Trouble always finds me."

Shade pushed back a lock of silver-gray hair that had fallen over his forehead. A smile flickered briefly on his lips. "Just so you don't cause it," he quipped in that ponderous way that passed for humor among vampires.

I held up two fingers in the Boy Scout salute. "I promise I won't. Is that all you wanted? I've really got to get ready for the hearing."

"Actually, I wanted to ask about Sullivan."

"Oh, God, did he come back and defend me to Gold and McGillary? Is that why he missed the hearing?"

"I have no idea what you're talking about. I haven't seen Sullivan since you left for California."

Cautious now, I took a step back. "So what was it about David that you wanted to talk about?"

"It was a two-to-one vote to reinstate him. I wanted to make sure my vote of support isn't going to come back to haunt me," the senior partner said.

"So, who blackballed him? Let me guess: Gold," I said.

"You'd be wrong. It was McGillary."

I couldn't picture the Mr. Milk Toast third partner whose name appeared on the letter head taking such a strong stand. "Good God, why? What did David do that it would upset McGillary that much?"

"It is not something that should be discussed with a human."

I looked up into that pale, aristocratic face and knew I had been put firmly in my place. "If you're asking about his performance as the chief arbitrator on this case, he's doing a great job. He's firmly in control, very fair, and the parties respect him."

"He did place us uncomfortably in the news—"

"No, I did that," I interrupted. "If you're talking about the press getting a picture of us leaving the studio." There was a slight nod from Shade. "Well, he was trying to protect me. And the firm," I added hurriedly.

"He used power and was detected."

"Look, Shade, it's not a big news flash that all of you Powers have, well . . . powers. He's a terrific lawyer, okay?"

"You like him."

I considered the stiff, opinionated, curt man that I knew and realized Shade was right. "Yes, I do. And it's not just because he saved my life," I added forestalling the words that I could almost see forming in Shade's head. "He has integrity and he hates injustice. Sometimes he seems almost human," I added, making a little joke of my own. If it had been any vampire but Shade I wouldn't have dared. Though I expected my foster liege would have been amused as well.

But it didn't get the expected response. Instead Shade looked worried. He clasped his hands behind his back and turned away. Almost inaudibly he said, "And that is what worries me." Then more loudly he added, "You may go, Linnet."

At 11:50 Ollie and I were in the smallest conference room. He had a muffaletta from a nearby deli, and the rich smell of olive mix, meats, and cheeses was driving me crazy. I sipped my Diet Coke and waited at the head of the table as the tech guru adjusted the computer screen so I was caught by the camera and would be able to be seen once the video link was in place.

"Ollie, may I have a potato chip?" I asked.

"Actually, why don't you take half of this. It's a monster." He came over and gave me half the sandwich and shook out some potato chips from the bag.

"Thank you."

"De nada."

I ate the sandwich while Ollie alternated between muttering into his headphones, an indistinct buzz that never quite rose to the level of understandable words, and munching on his lunch.

He flashed a thumbs-up in my direction. "Okay. We're going live." I quickly swiped a Kleenex across my mouth, hoping that there were no crumbs or olive paste in evidence and I hadn't totally wrecked my makeup. Ollie pointed a forefinger at me. "Now!"

The computer screen on the conference table switched from the start page to an image of the conference room in California. I couldn't see David because we were arranged as if I was sitting next to him, but I had an excellent view of the rest of the room. The crowd was still in settling-down mode, with clumps of people at the coffee carafe, others peering at the tray of pastries, still others filling a glass with water from the cut-glass pitcher.

David's voice, sounding aggrieved, came in loudly through the speakers on the computer on my end. "I can't see Lin—Ms. Ellery."

There was a barely heard apology from Chuck, the tech guy in LA, more mumbling from Ollie, but what really caught my attention was Qwendar. He stiffened, glanced at the computer screen, then looked over to where Palendar was filling a glass with water.

"Can you say something," Ollie said. "Let's see if we've at least got audio on their end."

"Testing. Hello, Los Angeles," I said, but distractedly because I was watching Qwendar walking swiftly toward Palendar.

"I got half of that, then the sound cut out." David's voice sounding even more exasperated.

"Ms. Ellery, can you hear us?" Chuck called.

"And how will we know since we can't hear her?" David again, with scathing sarcasm.

"Oh, yeah, right."

I started to send David a text telling him I could hear, but I nearly dropped my phone because while I watched, Qwendar seemed to lose his balance just as he reached Palendar and fell against him. The Álfar actor lost his grip on the cut-crystal glass, and it shattered on the bamboo floor. Qwendar, murmuring apologies, bent slowly and painfully as if to begin picking up the shards of glass.

It was like a lightening flash through the inside of my skull. I was back at Terra Sushi listening to Kiyumi describe the broken-teapot scene between Qwendar and Kerrinan: "They were both scrambling to pick up the pieces . . . and Kerrinan cut his palm on a shard of glass."

Palendar hesitated, looking down at the bent head of the old Álfar. Qwendar looked up at him and said something that I couldn't hear, but it had the blood rising into Palendar's cheeks. He didn't look happy, but he knelt down next to the old Álfar.

"David! David!" I yelled, coming half out of my chair.

"He can't hear you. We still haven't got the audio back," Ollie said.

"Can you get him on camera for me?" I asked as I dove for my purse and yanked out my BlackBerry. My fingers flew across the keyboard as I sent David a text.

Don't let Palendar touch the glass! Stop him from touching the glass!

I knew he usually kept his phone on vibrate. "Please look at it! Please look at it!" It was both a prayer and an order. The camera angle on my computer screen panned, and I could see David. I saw him glance down toward his belt. I sent another text.

Stop Palendar! Urgent! Danger!

David's frown deepened and this time he reached down and unclipped his phone. His frown turned to one of puzzlement as he read my incoherent messages.

I sent another text.

No questions. Just do it!

David stood and moved away from the table.

"Keep him on camera," I snapped at Ollie. He fiddled with the console, switching to a different camera on a different computer. The angle wasn't great, but I could see David moving to the two kneeling men. Palendar had a large piece of glass in his hand. I saw Qwendar reach out and close his hand over the other Álfar's and begin to squeeze. Then David was between them. Qwendar was forced to drop Palendar's hand. A brief flash of anger skittered across his face, then the smooth facade was back.

And at that moment there were duel cries of triumph from the bicoastal tech gurus. "Got her! She's connected now."

Qwendar glanced at the computer screen and reacted when he saw me. An emotion I couldn't identify twisted his face, then he moved quickly away from the detritus of broken glass.

My phone chimed. I had a text from David.

What the hell is going on???!

Explain later, I replied.

I threw myself back into my chair. Qwendar thought that because they couldn't see me, I couldn't see them. Thank God most of the Powers are clueless about technology.

But I was left with a bigger problem. What was I going to do? I had no proof. All I had was suspicion based on a conversation with a girl at a Japanese restaurant. But what if Qwendar and Jondin had contact? My God, he had been on the Warner lot that day. I had seen him in the restaurant having lunch with Diggins. My chest felt too small to hold air, and the half-muffaletta lay in my stomach like a stone.

I stood. "Mr. Sullivan, everyone. I'm sorry, but I'm suddenly not feeling well. If you'll excuse me." I fled from the conference room.

In the bathroom I splashed water on my face, not worrying about the effect on my makeup. I scraped back my hair and met my own gaze in the mirror. I wanted to run to the airport, and grab any flight heading west. But if I did that it would it tip off Qwendar that I was on to him. Had I already tipped him off with my precipitous flight from the conference? I needed to go back and sit through the morning's testimony. The time difference between LA and New York had already dictated that it would be a half-day session.

Now I just needed to get an earlier flight instead of the red-eye back to Los Angeles.

And make sure Palendar stayed away from Qwendar. Wasn't sure how I was going to do that.

And convince David I wasn't crazy. That should be fun.

I composed my features and returned to the conference room to listen to testimony while trying not to look at Qwendar the entire time. Turned out that was the hardest thing I did all day.

Testimony ended at three thirty New York time. Norma had actually leaped into action and changed my ticket for a flight out of LaGuardia at 6:10 p.m. It was going to be tight, but I could make it if the traffic gods were kind. Everything with Norma was fraught, and this time was no exception. She made it very clear that it had been a huge hassle and had cost the firm an additional four hundred dollars, but I was going to arrive in Los Angeles at midnight instead of early tomorrow morning. I was throwing papers into my briefcase when Norma loomed in the door.

"Mr. Bryce is here."

"What? Now? Why? Does he have an appointment? Of course not."

"Would you like me to answer any of those questions, or are you going to keep on talking to yourself?"

"Sorry. Look, tell him I can't see him right now. I've got a plane to catch."

"So, let me drive you," came a cultured British accent from the doorway. Jolyon Bryce, midforties with silver-touched brown hair, rolled his wheelchair the rest of the way into my office. He gave me a sweet smile that made his rather plain face handsome and lit up his blue eyes.

"Are you here in the capacity of client or as Vento's daddy?" I asked, returning his smile.

"Vento's daddy." Then he added gently, "And as a friend who wanted to see if you were all right after all your adventures in Hollywood." I hesitated. "Come on, Linnie, I'm cheaper than a cab and probably more comfortable, and I drive very fast."

Norma gave a sniff. "Well, that'd convince me to take a cab. Why do they let cripples drive anyway?" She left. In an agony of embarrassment I looked over at Jolly, who burst out laughing.

"Your assistant is an original."

"I guess that's one way to put it. Okay, you can drive me to the airport." I grabbed my overnight case, my rolling briefcase-computer bag, and my purse and followed him out of the office.

Jolly's car was parked just down the street in a handicapped space. It was a zippy little silver turbo-charged BMW sedan. "We'll put your luggage in the backseat. My chair has to go in the trunk," he explained as he hit the key to unlock the car. "Would you mind putting my chair away for me? Then we don't have to bother one of these nice doormen."

"Of course." As I watched, he deftly levered himself out of the chair and into the driver's seat. I folded up the wheelchair and put it in the trunk, then piled my crap into the backseat and slid into the passenger side.

I studied the hand controls that replaced the gas and brake pedal in the car as we pulled smoothly out into traffic. "So, tell me, how is my boy?" Jolly asked.

"Doing great. Lauren is a terrific trainer and teacher. I generally ride either early in the morning or at night."

"Not too cold, is it?"

"It's California. They think it's cold, but they're all pussies." We shared another smile. Then we talked dressage and Vento.

Jolly was as good as his word. The car seemed to dance through traffic, and before I knew it we were into the residential neighborhood that surrounded LaGuardia. He pulled up to the departure area. As I pulled out my luggage I said, "Thank you for not bringing up the thing at Warner Bros. It's nice not to always be treated as a curiosity."

"You have had some extraordinary experiences, my dear," he said.

"Just lucky, I guess." I smiled and was surprised when there was no answering smile.

"Be careful." Then he added an odd tag, "Be thoughtful."

"Thank you for the ride. I'll keep you posted on Vento, and when we're likely to get home. Soon, I hope," I said.

He waved and pulled away, leaving me on the sidewalk outside the American Airlines desk. It wasn't until his taillights were lost in all the other traffic that it suddenly hit me. How had he known I was even in New York?

20

I was still on my cell phone arguing with David as the line went shuffling past the airline employee who was scanning our tickets.

"Yes, of course it's a theory, but it makes sense given what Parlan told me about the use of blood in Álfar magic."

"And he may just be a very old man who is not too steady on his pins," David countered. "And what's the rest of your theory? He knocks into people and things so something gets broken, and then what?"

"It looked like he was about to squeeze Palendar's hand so the piece of glass would cut him."

"Okay, so. If blood is the key, how does that help? Presumably he has to take the blood away to do his evil spell."

"Now you're just being snotty. I bet he would have pocketed the glass. I bet he did that at the sushi restaurant."

"Do you have proof of that? Did they report there was a piece missing from the broken teapot?"

I was into the jetway now, and the temperature had dropped about thirty degrees. Outside I could hear the wind moaning around the metal tube, causing it to vibrate a bit. Since I had a connection in Denver I really, really hoped there wasn't another winter storm marching across the country right now.

"Of course not. They weren't going to try to glue it back together. They probably just swept it up and threw it away. And maybe he wouldn't have taken the glass. Maybe he would have offered Palendar a handkerchief to wrap up his hand and taken the handkerchief away. It doesn't matter as long as he got the blood."

"You probably should have let the situation play out to see if Qwendar actually took the piece of glass or found some other way to get Palendar's blood. That would have verified your theory."

"Yeah, but then he'd have Palendar's blood, and if I'm right, we'd have another Álfar-goes-crazy-and-murders-people incident. It might even have happened at the arbitration."

The line stalled at the door of the plane while people struggled to find compartments for their carry-on luggage. I finally made it on board, and, juggling my rolling briefcase and cell phone, I staggered back to my seat.

"Linnet, I'm just not buying it. Qwendar is here to protect Álfar interests. Why would he endanger that by having them commit murders? It doesn't make any sense. I think it was a bizarre coincidence, and you overreacted because you are overtired and stressed. You've had another horrific experience. You've seen John and his brother, which can't have been easy"

"Stop patronizing me! I'm tired, yes, and if being really, really pissed off qualifies as stressed, then I guess I'm stressed too, but I am not overreacting. Qwendar was *angry* when you intervened. I saw his face."

The plump-faced flight attendant was staring at me. "Miss, you need to turn off your phone now."

"Look, we're about to take off. I've got to hang up. We'll talk about this once I'm back in LA."

I turned off my phone, put it away in my purse, and closed my eyes. It was going to be a long night. I thought about Kerrinan in his prison cell, and Jondin, presumably in another just like it. What if I could prove Álfar magic was behind the killings? Would the courts accept that as a defense? Had John been under a spell when he treated me so shittily? Where did David go on that one day? And what was with him and McGillary? Why was Shade nervous about David? And how had Jolly known I was in New York?

At some time while wrestling with these thoughts I fell asleep and didn't wake until we landed in Denver. Then there was a mad dash to catch my next flight, only to discover it was delayed forty minutes. I turned aside into a sports bar, to get something to eat and treat myself to a margarita. I had eaten half my burger when there was an announcement that my flight was leaving in twenty minutes instead of the anticipated forty. I threw money onto the table and ran for the gate.

Sleep eluded me on this leg of the trip. I ended up watching the in-flight movie, which was a low-brow comedy filled with young men behaving badly and lots of fart jokes. It was terrible, but at least it kept me from endlessly chewing over the problem of the Álfar.

As I rode down the escalator toward the baggage carousels, I turned on my phone. There was a message from Maslin, and he sounded excited.

"I found something on Human First. Call me."

I reached the ground floor and looked for a familiar figure. Instead I was surprised to see a burly man in a dark suit holding a sign that said ELLERY. I had had a half notion that David might have picked me up but realized that was a bit too thoughtful for a vampire. But apparently he had sent a car to pick me up. I walked up to the man.

"Linnet Ellery?"

"Yep, that's me."

"Do you have luggage?"

"Yeah. Just a small bag. It was a quick trip. Just one night," I continued and I wondered why I always had this tendency to say more than was necessary.

Amazingly my bag was one of the first out of the chute. The driver grabbed it in one massive hand and we headed outside. It was a clear night, with a full moon fighting Los Angeles light pollution and mostly winning. We crossed the street and into the parking structure. He led me to a black Lincoln town car and put my luggage in the trunk. He opened the back door, but the dome light didn't illuminate.

"Hey? Where are you?" the driver asked incongruously.

Something in the tone more than the words erased my exhaustion. I tensed, my body wanting to flee, but I paused to look back at him to determine if the flight response was appropriate. My mind should have listened to my body. There was a shimmer in the air as someone moved out of Fey. Among the concrete pillars and the bulking shadows of the parked cars there was a disconcerting view of a meadow. It vanished and Qwendar walked toward us. My stomach was suddenly filled with a cold, aching lump, and my knees began to shake.

I was in trouble, big, bad, deep trouble. I tried to bolt, but the driver grabbed me by the hair before I took two steps. His hands, hot and rough, slid down my arms and gripped my wrists with bone-grinding force. He wrenched my hands behind my back, and I felt the bite as plastic cuffs were slapped onto my wrists. Then I was flung violently into the back of the car.

"Be careful, fool. There mustn't be a mark on her." Qwendar's voice came out of the darkness.

"Where the hell were you?" the driver grunted.

"Establishing my alibi," Qwendar snapped. "Get control of her!"

I tried to thrash and kick out, but the big thug was too quick. Glancing over my shoulder I saw him rip off his belt and wrap it around my ankles. Feeling like a trussed goose on its way to market I lay on the backseat, my cheek pressed against the cold metal of the seat belt. The seat next to me shifted as Qwendar got into the backseat. He patted me on the hip. I jerked trying to get away from him. I heard the driver's door slam, and then we were in motion.

At first my mind was awash with panic. There wasn't a coherent thought anywhere in sight. I drew in several deep breaths and forced myself to think. We were in a parking garage. There would be someone in the kiosk to take their money. I would scream. Police would come.

"He has an E-ZPass," Qwendar said, as if he'd read my thoughts. "He waves a card at a reader. No stopping. No paying. No rescue. I do so love technology."

"Except when it fucks you," I said. I managed to lever myself up to a sort of sitting position. My arms were already going numb. "You thought I couldn't see you."

"True. It was a mistake on my part."

"David knows everything. We've talked."

"But where's the proof, dear Linnet? And after you're dead, no one will believe the ravings of one obsessed girl forcing her attentions on a man who has clearly said he doesn't want her."

Fear has a taste like bile and rancid oil. Panic made my gut feel loose, and I found I couldn't draw a full breath. Qwendar turned to gaze out the window, indicating our conversation was over.

"Why, Qwendar? Why are you destroying your own people?"

"You humans had a saying from your Vietnam War: 'We had to destroy the village in order to save it.' That's what I'm doing. I'm saving my people from your kind. Your world and your kind have become seductive to the Álfar." I couldn't help it. I let out a sound of derision. "I know it seems absurd. To me, too. Humans are constantly warning their children against Álfar charms, but your world of gadgets and ease has its allure too. Add to that, all of you humans attract our younger people. You are so short-lived, and as a result you live with such intensity and verve. Instead of understanding that you are chattel and playthings and nothing more, our youth are marrying you, living by your rules and values."

"So you're trying to turn us against the Álfar."

"Yes. Once I can force a sufficiently violent and retaliatory incident against the Álfar, I will be able to convince the Council to order all of us back to our realm. That will give us a chance to recover our past glories and inculcate our youth in their true roles and nature."

I shook my head and gave a bitter laugh. "God, I bet if I dig deep enough I'll find out you're one of the major funders of Human First."

"Yes, you probably would. I have your measure, Linnet, and you are tenacious and very bright. I can't risk it, and so I'm sorry to say you must become a casualty." He sighed. "Sad, but such are the fortunes of war."

He settled back into the corner of the seat and closed his eyes. It was clear our conversation was at an end.

I studied the wide neck of the driver. Maybe I could appeal to our shared humanity. An obvious ploy, but God knew I had nothing to lose. "Why are you doing this? Working for an Álfar. You heard him. He's going to kill me. Are you really going to let that happen?"

"Yep." He glanced over his shoulder at me. "When the pay's this good, I don't care who dies."

"Wow, are you really this stupid?" Thug Boy took a one hand off the steering wheel and cuffed me across the ear. It was like a love tap from a rhino.

"I told you, don't leave any marks on her!" Qwendar was obviously paying attention even while pretending to be asleep.

Desperate, I tried again with the driver. "Look, do you honestly think he's going to let you live after you help him with this?"

"He's taking me back to Fey with him. I can't leave. Problem solved, and I avoid a few legal problems here."

The car accelerated onto the freeway. We were heading north. I wondered where they were taking me. My mind ran in frenzied ferret circles. I tested the cuffs. They didn't budge. My only hope was outside intervention. I needed CHiPS. So I needed Thug Boy to do something that would attract the attention of any passing cop or have a concerned citizen call the police.

I glanced over at Qwendar before I risked another remark. He was watching me and listening with an indulgent smile.

"Legal problems, huh? What kind?"

His laugh had all the humor of boulders rolling down hill. "Why you want to know? You gonna represent me, Counselor?" He laughed again at his own wit.

"Fine. Don't tell me. I can guess. Bet you played football in high school. Probably the highlight of your life. Dated a cheerleader. Probably did a little date rape action on prom night. Beat up the queers and the geeks. You weren't good enough to win an athletic scholarship, and then suddenly you had graduated and discovered you were too damn dumb to get into college."

"You lose. I was in school selling blow, so I didn't have to take out student loans. You think you know me. You don't know anything."

Illuminated by the glare of headlights I watched his knuckles whitened as he took a harder grip on the steering wheel when a merging car cut us off. The car swerved into another lane to pass a slower car, and Thug Boy didn't slow down once we were past. I had to get it right. I cast around desperately. Then I noticed the lighter skin on the fourth finger of his left hand. Wedding ring. Gone now.

"So, what happened to your wedding ring? Your wife get sick of carrying the family because you didn't graduate and couldn't get a job?"

"I always had to work for cunts like you. Having it in for me."

The car jackrabbited forward as he smashed his foot against the accelerator. I was thrown against the door and felt the handle dig into my back. I thought briefly about trying to lever it open, but being thrown out of a moving car onto the 405 freeway would kill me just as surely as Qwendar and his knuckle dragger.

"Yeah. I'm sure. Well, maybe if you had an IQ above 80 you wouldn't have lost out to all these smart women. How you doing on that child support? Behind? Of course you are, because people like you always are. Big man. You can ejaculate, but you sure can't follow through. Although men as fat as you usually have problems in that department. Your wife find somebody who could satisfy her—"

"SHUT UP! Shut the fuck up or I'll come back there and gag you."

"Don't be an idiot," Qwendar drawled, while not opening his eyes. "She's baiting you. Don't fall for it."

The back of Thug Boy's neck was brick red. He hunched his shoulders, his hands closing spasmodically on the steering wheel, but he started to slow down. "I'm not an idiot. I'm not stupid," he said.

I started to open my mouth to respond, but lightning quick Qwendar thrust his handkerchief into my mouth and tied it in place with his tie. I fought the sense that I was choking and forced down vomit. Aspirating on vomit was not going to make the night better. Eventually they would have to get me out of the car. That would be my only chance, and I had to be ready for any opportunity that might present itself.

From the 405 we changed onto the 101 freeway. Sometime during that drive my cell phone began playing "Puttin' on the Ritz," which was the customized ring tone I had for David. Great—now he calls. Not that calling earlier would have made any difference to my situation. During the drive I had time to consider my every contact with Qwendar, and a lot of his statements now took on a whole new meaning. *One changeling brought back to the fold. I think you might be the face of the future. A human who accepts and is comfortable with the Powers. A thing that some view with great disapprobation. Perhaps he has remembered who and what he is.*

Headlights flared on the green and white overhead sign for the 134 freeway, and I realized we were going to the Equestrian Center. That added a whole new terror. What if they were going to hurt Vento, too? Images from *The Godfather* played in my head. I managed to get a glimpse at the clock on the dashboard. It was 1:23. Maybe a horse would be sick, I thought hopefully. But no lights beyond the safety lights burned in the barn, and there were no vet trucks parked out front.

Thug Boy parked. Qwendar got out and pulled a briefcase from the trunk. They pulled open my door, and I nearly pitched backward out of the car since my back had been resting against that door. The human managed to catch me before my head bounced on the pavement. I was flung unceremoniously over his shoulder and carried into the barn. There was shifting in the stalls and a few experimental nickers that seemed to say, Is it morning yet? Is it time to eat? When no hay was forthcoming the horses settled. I was deposited in the breezeway in front of Vento's stall. The stallion's long head was thrust over the stall door. He gazed down at me and chuffed, his breath ruffling the hair on the top of my head. I started to cry because I was scared and because I'd never get to ride him again and because I was going to die, and there was nothing I could do to prevent it.

The briefcase landed on a nearby tack truck with a thud. Qwendar opened it and removed a pistol, a legal pad, and a pen.

He turned to face me. "And now, Linnet, you are going to write a suicide note." It was then the fact that he was wearing gloves really penetrated. "An angry, ranting note about how your boyfriend

rejected you, and how he'll be sorry now that you're dead. He'll realize how special you were. How you came out here to die with the
only thing that loves you."

Vento had begun to paw in the stall, his hoof hitting the door
with echoing thuds. "Yeah. Fat chance," was what I tried to say but
it emerged from behind the gag like a series of grunts and squeaks.

"Untie her hands," Qwendar ordered. The muscle complied. My
hands began to tingle and ache with returning circulation. "Chafe
them. It's fine if the handwriting is shaky. It adds to the sense that
she was distraught and furious."

Qwendar came over and grabbed one of my hands. He drove a
pin into the ball of my thumb. I yelped behind the gag. I tried to
pull free, but Thug Boy pressed his hands down on my shoulders
effectively nailing me in place. Qwendar carefully wiped the oozing
drop of blood onto a mirror. "Soon you won't have to hold her," he
said to the driver. He squatted down so his eyes were level with
mine. He then pricked his own finger and mixed his blood with mine
on the surface of the mirror. He gazed intently into my eyes. I
tensed, preparing for him to bust out with some kind of Álfar shit.
Nothing happened. I watched a frown begin between Qwendar's
white brows and slowly spread to encompass his entire forehead.
Minutes passed. A bead of sweat trickled down the old Álfar's temple and lodged in his sideburn.

"Is something supposed to happen?" the thug asked.

Qwendar slowly stood up. "It seems we are going to have to do
this with less finesse. You're a very strange human, Linnet. In all my
long years I've never met a human who could resist me." He continued to regard me, and he even stroked his chin with the air of Em-
peror Palpatine regarding Luke Skywalker. I had an insane desire to
giggle that I knew was born out of sheer, bowel-loosening terror. "It
does explain how you cheated death when Jondin was spraying bullets all about. Even a wretch as pathetic as that girl should have been

able to have hit you." He fell silent again. "But Charles was able to
truss you up without incident. Perhaps your lover gave you some
kind of protection against us. I wish we had more time to figure out
exactly how you are doing it. But alas, I don't. I think I will leave it
to Charles to finish the job. It's a shame about the note. I doubt we
could persuade you to write one without doing violence to your
person, which would undermine the theory I'm providing for the
police. Charles, do you have gloves?"

"Yeah, of course."

"Excellent. Then please see to it that Ms. Ellery shoots herself in
the head. Through the temple, I think. Women are known to be
squeamish about shooting themselves in the mouth."

"I could slit her wrists."

"True, but they tend to do it in warm baths with candles all
around them. And someone might find her before she bled to death.
No, I want to know she is dead. But wait until I am gone. My presence might lead to another unlikely escape on her part."

"But you'll come back for me and take me with you?" Charles
asked

"Absolutely." Qwendar packed up the pen and legal pad, handed
the pistol to Charles, and walked to the end of the breezeway. In the
doorway of the barn he vanished into Fey.

Charles pressed the gun into my hand. Some feeling had returned
to my hands, and I waited for the moment when he was studying the
side of my head, pushing the hair back behind my ear. Then I struck
out and hit him hard on the hinge of his jaw. He yelled and lost his
balance as he squatted in the dirt and sawdust of the breezeway. I
scrabbled at the dirt, pulling myself away from him. There was a
pitchfork resting against the side of a stall across the breezeway from
me. The glow from the lights glittered off the sharp tines. If I could
reach it . . . I pictured driving it into Charles pendulous belly.
Could I do that? Hell, yes, I could. But I didn't get even halfway.

The thug landed hard on my back. I felt a rib crack and cried out in pain, though it was muffled by the gag. He was a crushing weight, his breath hot and reeking of beer and garlic puffed against my ear. It was like being smothered.

"Fuckin' bitch!"

He jerked me up and dragged me back to Vento's stall. Dirt and sawdust from the breezeway filled my shoes, and my skirt was rucked up around my waist. He grabbed my left hand in a crushing grip, forcing the gun into my hand, and my forefinger through the trigger. His thick finger pressed mine painfully against the metal of the trigger. With his free hand he gripped my chin, keeping my head still. I fought him, but I was no match for his bulk or his strength. The barrel of the gun approached my temple. *At least he had picked my left hand*, I thought in what were my final seconds. John would have known instantly that it was murder since I was right-handed. Maybe someone else would make the connection. David?

I closed my eyes and felt the cold kiss of metal on my temple.

21

A *whuff* of warm air across that top of my head ruffled my hair. *Vento telling me good-bye.* I choked on a sob. From overhead there came the sharp *tink* of metal breaking under enormous pressure. My eyes flew open just as the stall door went sliding to the right. Without that support against my back I toppled backward into the stall with a strangled, startled cry. Charles struggled to hang onto me, but his weight also pushed me back.

There was the glitter of light on steel shoes as Vento's hooves struck out over my face. One hoof took Charles in the head, the other hit him hard in the chest. He gave a high-pitched scream as the gash across his forehead gushed blood, blinding him. He lost his grip on the pistol and went scrabbling away on all fours, trying to elude the maddened horse. Vento went sailing over my head in pursuit of my would-be killer, his belly a flash of white.

The man was yelling, but it was hard to hear beneath the fierce scream of an outraged stallion. Other horses, terrified by the noise, the smell of blood, and the rampaging stallion, began to spin in their stalls and whinny. I managed to sit up in time to see Charles clamber to his feet and stagger toward the door. But Vento wasn't going to let that happen. He pushed the man hard in the back with his head and sent the thug sprawling. *What the fuck,* I thought? The only other time I'd seen anything like this was on a vacation out west when I'd watched a mare crush a rattlesnake that had entered her pen. Not that Charles wasn't as dangerous as that rattler, but how could a horse know that? Vento reared, a terrifying sight, and came down onto the man's back with both front hooves. There was an audible crack. The stallion continued to strike out, battering the limp form beneath his feet.

I tore the gag away, ripped off the belt that secured my legs, and struggled to my feet. I ran to the horse, arms outstretched. "Whoa, whoa, boy. Easy." I kept my voice low and soothing. "What a good boy. Easy now." The long head swung back to look at me, and the wild light faded from the deep brown eyes.

The horse turned away from the limp form and minced gingerly over to me. His front hooves were stained with blood. I swallowed hard. I threw my arms around the powerful neck, and hung on for dear life. Vento turned his head so he had me wrapped in the curve of his neck, his version of a hug. His nostrils flared, blowing warm breath across my back as his sides heaved with his frantic breaths. He was wet with sweat, his skin was hot, and I pressed closer because I was suddenly shivering. A sob burst from my chest. Over the chorus of frightened whinnies I heard the sound of car engines, one very close and one more distant.

A dark figure loomed in the door of the barn and ran toward me. "David!" I ran toward him and collapsed, sobbing, against his chest. His arms closed around me, pulling me close. He pressed his lips against my temple. He was cold, but the embrace was comforting in ways I couldn't explain.

"Linnet. Dear God." He looked over at the still form lying in the breezeway. "What happened here?"

I gestured at Charles. "He was going to kill me. He and Qwendar. Make it look like suicide." I wiped an arm across my streaming eyes and my running nose. "But Vento saved me."

David's expression was a study in confusion. "Wait. I'm lost. That's not Qwendar."

"No, that's Charles, a guy he hired."

"How do you know his name?"

"Qwendar used it. Why are you asking me that?"

He pressed a hand against his forehead. "You're right, that was stupid. I'm just so . . ." He shook his head like a boxer shaking off a hard uppercut. "Why don't you put the horse away. Let me take a look at this fellow."

It made sense. I took Vento's halter off the hook by his stall, slipped it over his head, and started to lead him back to his stall. But the sight of the blood on his hooves was too disturbing. I took him into the wash rack, thinking I would clean his feet.

David knelt next to Charles and pressed the tips of his fingers against the man's throat feeling for a pulse. He looked up at me and shook his head.

"He's dead." I shivered, turned on the hose. "Don't!" David snapped. "We have to call the police and we have to preserve the evidence." I hesitated but turned off the water.

"You won't let them hurt Vento, will you? He saved my life."

At that moment a man dressed in jeans and a pajama top, his bare feet thrust into tennis shoes, came running into the barn. "Jesus Christ!" he swore when he spotted the body.

David stepped forward, all competence and control. "Are you the manager of this facility?"

"Yeah. My house is on the other side of the property. I heard the horses going crazy and drove over. Who are you? And who's he?" he gestured at the body. "And who's she?"

"We need to call the police," David said.

"Yeah, I guess we do." The barn manager pulled out a cell phone and dialed 911. I led Vento back to his stall. David joined me. We slid the stall door closed together. I automatically went to clip it shut, but couldn't find the clip. David bent and picked it up out of the dirt and sawdust. It was a metal clip, and the metal was twisted and broken at the hasp.

"It's like the horse twisted it until the metal fatigued and broke," the vampire mused.

"And then he pulled open the door," I said. "That's what saved me. That guy was about to pull the trigger when I fell backward."

David looked around and spotted the pistol, half obscured by sawdust. He put an arm around my shoulders, led me over to a tack trunk, and sat down with me beside him.

"I don't know a lot about horses, and no disrespect to this one, but doesn't that rather make him the Einstein of horses?"

"I don't know . . . yes. I think he just sensed that I was terrified."

"Before the police arrive, start at the beginning and tell me what happened."

"When I got off the plane there was a man—him," I pointed at the dead man. "Waiting at the baggage claim with my name on a card."

"And you just went with him?" David exploded. "A total stranger, and you—"

It was irrational and unfair, and I snapped, "Hey! When we arrived last month you just got in a car with Kobe, a total stranger. People do it all the time. And I thought you might have sent a car for me. Stupid to have expected that, I know."

He was offended. "I was coming to pick you up!"

"You were? Oh. Sorry. How did we miss each other?"

"The airline overestimated how late the plane would be. You were gone by the time I got there. But go on with your story."

So I did. When I got to the part about Qwendar trying to force me to write a suicide note using his magic, I stuttered and became reticent. I wanted time to process what Qwendar had said before I shared it with anyone else. Qwendar had only remarked on my seemingly miraculous escape from Jondin's bullet fest, but he hadn't known my entire history. He didn't know about my equally improbable escapes from maddened werewolves. Escapes that had three different policemen in three different venues shaking their heads over my incredible "luck." Now I had to wonder if it was luck, or if there was something about me?

I cleared my throat and said, "He . . . he tried to get me to write a suicide note, but I refused. They would have had to hurt me to make me comply, and Qwendar wanted it to look like a suicide. That's when he ordered the thug to stick the gun in my hand, and shoot me in the head. Then Vento happened, and then you arrived." I ended with a vague gesture.

After I finished David sat silent for a few minutes. "Clever. Devilishly clever," he said finally. "Qwendar comes to me and tells me how he's worried about you after the meeting with John, thus setting the stage for your suicide." He made air quotes around the last word.

"Would you have believed him?" I demanded. The idea that I could be seen as crazy and obsessed didn't sit well.

David gave an emphatic head shake. "No. Not a chance. You are sometimes—oftentimes—irritating as hell, Linnet, but you are indomitable. Nothing knocks you down for long. You're like one of those damn punching clowns. The harder you hit them, the faster they bounce back up."

"I guess that's a compliment," I said.

"It was." An ironic smile twisted David's mouth. "Not a very good one, I'll admit."

I was back to thinking about Qwendar, John, and David. "So if Qwendar was using the meeting with John to set up the cause for my suicide, that means he'd been planning this for a while. Maybe he was controlling John and that's why he said all those terrible things to me," I added with a flare of hope.

"I wouldn't pin too much hope on that," came the depressing answer. "The Álfar are notoriously inconstant."

"Look, I'm not in love with John or anything like that. I just feel responsible because he gave up his freedom for me and Destiny and Chastity . . ." I realized I was sounding defensive and I shut up and returned to a more pressing issue. "But how did you know something was wrong and how did you know to come here?"

"One of your clients called me. Jolyon Bryce."

It was as if a line of ice water had run down my spine. I slowly turned my head and studied the horse that stood with his head hanging over the stall door. "He owns Vento," I said softly.

"He said his phone rang. It was your cell number and he could hear voices but couldn't make out the words. There was something about the tone of the voices that alarmed him, and he heard horses in the background. He called the firm's answering service, they called me, and I called him back. He caught me just as I was getting back to the hotel. Which put me close to the freeway, and at this time of night . . ." He checked his watch. "Morning. It didn't take long to get here."

I stood up, went over to my purse, took out my phone, and studied it. "That doesn't make any sense." I checked the called numbers. The last call it registered was the one I'd made to David back in New York. "The phone doesn't show a call to Jolyon."

"So maybe if it's an accidental thing it doesn't register it?"

I shook my head. "They don't work that way. If it had purse-dialed Jolyon it would have registered."

"I would say that's the smallest mystery we have to solve tonight. However it happened it got me here," David said.

"I know, and I'm glad you came. I just don't understand." Vento nickered softly to me. I walked over and stroked his muzzle, and he pressed his head against my chest.

Then the police arrived and things got interesting.

Detective Turnbow of the Burbank Police was not as sympathetic as Detective Rodriquez had been. He was a sallow-faced, narrow-chested man who moved like he was on stilts. He listened to my story with a sour expression, and when I finished he said, "So you were rescued by your horsey?"

At this point it was five thirty in the morning. Adrenaline had given way to bone-crushing exhaustion, and diplomacy was just right out. David stirred in his chair, but I got there first.

"Look, I've been kidnapped, nearly killed, and before all that I flew across the whole damn country. I'm the victim here. Yeah, and my horse saved me. He's at least as smart as you and maybe even—"

David laid a hand on my arm as Turnbow's chest started to puff out and his face turned a blotchy red. "Are you trying to imply that Ms. Ellery was somehow complicit in this man's death? There is blood on the horse's hooves; it's clear what happened."

"Well, let's talk about this mysterious second kidnapper, this Álfar guy."

"Yes, he was the mastermind. He hired the driver," I said.

"Yeah, and he was at a pre-Oscar party in Bel Air. Which is miles away from the Equestrian Center. People saw him there."

"How many people were attending?" David asked.

"Hundreds."

David's lip curled with derision. "So, a mill-and-swill. People moving from room to room, even outside. Easy enough to establish you were there and then slip away."

"The people on the door checking invites said he never left, and the valet guys say he asked for his car at two thirty a.m.," Turnbow said triumphantly.

I jumped back in. "Are you just being deliberately obtuse or are you really this stupid?" I practically snarled. "Everyone knows that Álfar can move through Fey. In that crowd no one would have noticed him leave, and Fey doesn't have traffic jams, and he probably had someone waiting to take him to the airport. He went back to the party the same way." Putting it into words answered another question that had been nagging me about Jondin, but for once I didn't confuse the issue by blurting out what I was thinking.

"And your proof?"

"I saw him appear out of Fey, and he said to the driver he had been establishing his alibi," I said.

"And the only person who could corroborate that is dead," Turnbow said.

David stood up. "We're done here. Unless you are charging Ms. Ellery with something, I am going to take her home."

"I guess you can take her. But don't leave the state."

David took my arm and swept me out of the interrogation room. I stumbled and he transferred his grip to my waist. The pressure hurt and I sucked in a breath.

"What?"

"I think I cracked a rib." He removed his hand. I also felt that burning, hollow feeling that absolute terror bestows on your gut. "Is he going to charge me with killing that guy?" I asked.

"No!" A single word and quite explosive. "No matter how improbable, it's clear what happened, and I'm confident that Charles will be found to have a rap sheet as long as my leg."

"What about Qwendar?" I asked as we stepped outside. It was a relief to escape the odor of stale coffee, microwave burritos, and the inchoate smell of sweat and desperation. In the east a pale line of gray and pink road appeared, outriders for the coming sun.

"You know the answer to that," David said.

"They can't touch him," I said leadenly. "But he can still reach out and touch me."

"I don't think he'll dare. If something untoward happened to you now, people would remember your accusations. And he would have me to contend with." I looked up. There was something grim in his brown eyes, and his jaw was set in a tight line. "Let's get in the car before the sun comes up. I forgot my umbrella," he snapped.

I scrambled into the car. It was a short drive to the Oakwood. As we headed down Riverside David suddenly said, "Are you hungry? You always seem to get hungry after one of these episodes."

"I could eat, but I don't want to sit in a restaurant. I can't face noise or people right now. There's a donut shop on Pass Avenue," I offered.

David turned left at Pass and pulled into the parking lot of a strip mall that contained a bank, a grocery store, a tiny Japanese restaurant, a French bakery, and the donut shop. He parked in front of the donut shop, which was doing a rousing business. He nosed the Sebring in between a pickup truck festooned with a ladder and paint cans and a truck sporting lawn mowers, rakes, and leaf blowers.

"What do you want?"

"Why don't you let me go in? The sun's almost up."

"If you hurry and tell me I can make it."

"Glazed raised, chocolate raised."

"Ah, comfort food," he said, and throwing open the door he sprinted into the shop.

He came back out a few minutes later clutching a paper sack that was already starting to show grease stains from the decadent, sinful goodness inside. By the time we reached the Oakwood the sun was up.

"Wait here. I have an umbrella in the apartment," I ordered.

I took the donuts with me and trudged up the stairs and through the door into the hall, then unlocked the door of my apartment. I then headed back down with the large umbrella. Climbing hurt my ribs, and I noticed that my legs felt rubbery by the time I reached the parking lot. I opened the umbrella and held it for David as he got out of the car. It seemed that California was, at last, going to live up to its reputation as sunny.

We got inside and I set the coffee maker to work. David pulled the blinds across the windows and sat on the sofa. As the coffee brewed he gave a deep, lung-filling sniff. "It's the one thing I really miss. I loved coffee, and the smell is so powerful and unforgettable that I can almost remember how it tasted."

I arranged my donuts on a plate. The coffee machine finished its job with a hiss, a sigh, and a gurgle. I poured out a cup and settled in the armchair. The taste and texture of donut was pure bliss. And then I started shaking so hard I shook coffee over my hand. I quickly set down the cup and the plate and clasped my hands tightly in my lap. David stared at me with concern.

"I just realized how close I came to dying last night. So everything seems extra special, from this donut to the coffee to sitting in a chair." I sat silent for a moment. "I know it's happened to me before, but those other times I was in the middle of a situation, I could run, I could try to do something. This one was worse because I was utterly helpless." I gave myself a shake and picked up my breakfast, then set it down again. "And it goes deeper than that. I'm scared, David. I'm not even twenty-eight. If things like this keep happening, will I live to see thirty? What is going on?"

He crossed to me, knelt at the side of my chair, and laid a cold hand on my shoulder. "I don't know, Linnet, but if I can help, you know I will."

I shook off the doubt, pushed back the fear, and stiffened my spine. "Well, that's good, because I'm going to hold you to that. I think there is a way for us to prove what's been happening and expose Qwendar for the murderer he is."

He pulled back a bit and gave me a wary look. "And just how are we going to do that?"

So I told him. When I'd finished he just stared at me. If he hadn't been an elegant vampire his mouth probably would have been hanging open.

"Do you see any other option?" I pushed.

"No," he admitted.

"And even if we go to the authorities no one will believe us."

"You're sure of the venue?" David asked, and he sounded desperate for me to say no.

"As sure as I've ever been of anything in my life. Think about it. It's not the Super Bowl or World Cup Soccer, and anyway, there aren't a lot of Álfar playing either of those sports, but it's televised worldwide, and gets close to fifty million viewers."

"We'd be taking an awful risk," David said.

"I know. Which is why we need help."

22

The next morning I found both Merlin and Maslin in the office sucking down coffee and sharing a box of donuts. I quickly outlined everything that happened, which left Merlin goggling at me and opening and closing his mouth like a guppy in pursuit of fish food.

"You nearly got killed." He gulped hard. "Again."

"Amazingly enough, I had noticed," I said, the words freighted with enough irony to penetrate.

It didn't penetrate. "I mean, first Jondin and now this. How do you find the guts to step out of the house? I'd be hiding under the bed."

"Yep, you would," said Maslin.

He glared at his twin. "Not everybody's like you. Trouble follows you. Hell, sometimes I think you go out and look for it." Maslin just shrugged.

"Well, I don't go looking for it," I said. "It finds me." I dug a donut out of the box.

"Maybe you should find a new line of work? Or hire bodyguards? Or change your identity? Or enter a convent?"

"Or punch you in the nose so you'll stop babbling and snap out of it," Maslin retorted. *That* penetrated. Merlin closed his mouth with an audible snap.

"This is serious and I don't have a ton of time," I said. "I need evidence, so maybe you could help me prove that Qwendar is one of the major backers of Human First."

"Already done," Maslin said. "I tried to call you with the info, but you never answered.

"Yeah, I was busy nearly getting killed." I bit viciously into the donut, and jelly squirted across my tongue.

"You told me to keep digging while you were gone so I sicced Merl on them."

"You've got a degree in accounting too?" I asked.

"Yeah. It's probably why I never get a date. I'm staid and boring." He looked up at his brother. "Not exotic and exciting."

"I still don't totally get why Qwendar was secretly backing Human First," Maslin said. "If he's all about how Álfar are superior, why let them get demonized by a bunch of house monkeys?"

"Qwendar's goal is a total retreat by the Álfar back into their own reality," I said. "He was hoping Human First would help light the fuse. I want to make sure he can't, so I want you to expose it in the most public way possible." Exhaustion had the room spinning briefly. I shook my head, fighting off the fog that seemed to be closing in on the edges of my mind. "These kind of people hate to find out they've been duped and made to look foolish. Actually, everyone hates to look foolish, but people who are fueled by righteous indignation *really* hate to look like pawns," I concluded.

Maslin tugged at his lower lip. "Forgive me, Linnet, but I don't think that's the best idea, and here's why. Humiliation will work on somebody like Cartwright; she's reasonably rational, but a lot of the members are none too tightly wrapped. They find out the Álfar have been pulling their strings, even just one rogue Álfar, and some whack job might go bug-fuck and decide to take care of some Álfar himself as payback. We wouldn't be removing a fuse, we'd be lighting it."

I sat with that for a few minutes. Remembered the faces of angry people from the news reels during integration. I found I had lost my appetite and set aside the half-eaten donut. "I see your point. So, what can we do?"

"I'll write my article and then we go to Cartwright. Use it to get her to back off and tone down the rhetoric."

I gave a quick, humorless laugh. "I might even be able to keep her from joining in this arbitration as an interested party. This thing is confusing enough and hard enough without a lot of grandstanding from Human First."

We sat silent for a few minutes, then Merlin said, "So Qwendar wants a total separation from humans. I can't say I'm all broken up about that. I worry about the Álfar deciding to go into politics."

"So do I, but that isn't exactly what he wants. He wants interactions between humans and Álfar to be the old-fashioned kind."

"Meaning what?" Merlin asked.

"The Álfar take us as slaves and playthings."

Maslin, the veteran and chronicler of countless bush wars, caught on immediately. "Ah, and for that to happen Qwendar's got to have peasants with pitchforks going after the Álfar."

"Making their only choice to retreat or die," I finished.

"That's why he needs another bloodbath—Álfar killing humans," Maslin mused. He set aside his donut. He also seemed to have lost his appetite. "Do you have any idea what he's got planned?"

"I think so. And I'm going to need your help with that, too." I paused and pinned them both with a look. "Do you guys own tuxedos?"

As I was hustling through the office heading for the doors, David caught me. "A moment, please." I followed him into his office. "What do we do about the arbitration?" David asked, once he had shut the door. "Can you face Qwendar and pretend nothing happened?"

"Do you actually think he'd show back up?"

"Yes, I do. It's how I would play it, and it's the kind of arrogance one expects from his kind. Also, he knows he's been cleared by his alibi. He runs no risk, and he might be able to rattle you."

"He probably knew I was alive even before the police came calling. Whether he ever intended to take his goon into Fey or not, Qwendar would have had to return to the Equestrian Center to either kill Charles or take him away."

David picked up a pen and flipped it between his fingers. "I should ask some of the uniforms and the crime scene people if they spotted him. Not proof of his involvement but certainly suggestive."

"And still not enough to pull in the authorities, if that's what you were thinking," I said. "Look, since he knows I'm alive, then there's no advantage to having us meet. And I've got a ton to do, so if I can miss the hearings that would probably be good."

"Do you want him to worry over what you are up to or think you're shattered by the experience and have run back to New York?"

"Much as I hate to play the victim, let's go with shattered. He's more likely to believe that anyway; he has a really low opinion of humans. Also, if he's worried, he might change his plans, and we're already working off a whole lot of assumptions about just what those plans might be."

"Yes, and that's what worries me," David said sourly. "But we can't risk spooking him, so I'll put it about that you have returned to New York."

"Qwendar knows where I live, and I think he's had people watching me, so I better be seen going to the airport. I can then double back, rent a different car, and hopefully shake him."

"Yes, that makes sense, though I am disturbed by how good you are at all this hole-and-corner behavior. Oh, I have enlisted Hank in this mad endeavor. He's a vampire and of my line, and I figured we could use the extra help." With that he waved me out of the office.

Jeff was at home. With my phone's navigation app guiding me I headed off for Newport Beach. The actor's house sat on a promontory and looked out over the Pacific. Today it was a deep azure with only small whitecaps. I drove up to the gate and put in the access code that Jeff had provided. The large gates swung open, and I drove up the curving cobblestone driveway to the house. It was an Italianate structure with the usual red tile roof, lots of balconies filled with pots of blooming geraniums. Bougainvillea tumbled over stone walls in a riot of red and pink and purple.

Once parked, I paused and listened to the deep-throated roar of the ocean breaking on the cliffs below the house. The air was moist on my skin and the smell of brine tickled my nostrils. Jeff opened the front door before I could ring the bell.

"How?" I pointed at my car, me, the door.

"Security cameras. I saw you driving in. Come in and meet Kate."

The entryway was polished flagstone. A curving staircase terminated directly in front of the door. The rich mahogany glowed in the sunlight pouring in a round, faceted window halfway up the stairs. For an instant I imagined myself in a gorgeous gown descending those steps while John looked up admiringly. I pushed away the fantasy and followed Jeff down a hall, through a modern white and chrome kitchen large enough to hold a long benched table and into a room that looked like an enclosed deck. The room was a horseshoe-shaped curve lined with windows and finished in heavy teak. It made me think of Tahitian beach houses. The ocean flexed and rolled outside the windows.

Kate Billingham sat on a window seat, a book held loosely between her fingers. She was lovely in person, with long auburn hair brushing her shoulders, dark brows, and pansy brown eyes. Without lighting and professional makeup I could see tiny crow's feet around her eyes and a few lines in her forehead. Clearly no Botox had been applied to that heart-shaped face.

She stood and extended her hand. "How do you do? I've heard so much about you from Jeff."

"Uh-oh," I said.

The hair swirled as she shook her head. "No, no. All good. About how brave you are, and I believe he called you 'sharp as a tack,' which in Midwesterner speak is very high praise indeed."

I glanced over at the actor, who smiled and shrugged. "Thank you," I said.

"Well, I'll leave you two to talk. I'll have coffee and snacks waiting in the kitchen when you're done." She floated out of the room.

Jeff indicated a window seat. I sat down, and he pulled around a wicker chair to sit facing me. "Okay, you sounded very serious on the phone. What's up?"

"First, a question. Can you get six people into the Academy Awards? And not in the nosebleed seats, but down on the main floor."

"What? Why?"

"I'm pretty sure there's going to be another Jondin incident, but with Jujuran in the starring role this time. Or some other Álfar that he can get blood from. Or maybe a lot of Álfar, I don't know, but it will be bad."

"Okay, you are officially scaring the crap out of me, and I don't even know what you're talking about. Blood? Him? Who him? Jujuran?"

"Qwendar. He's on a holy crusade to save his people from evil human influence, and he's doing it by forcing elves to kill humans. Then we turn on the Álfar, igniting a big war, the Álfar retreat back into Fey, the other Powers get worried because they're always worried about peasants with pitchforks, and we've set back human-Powers relations by decades if not centuries. And you think I sound crazy," I finished.

"Weirdly enough, I don't." He gave me a sick smile. "Maybe because I've starred in too many action movies, but it all makes a sort of twisted sense." He stood and paced, the distressed teak floorboards creaking lightly with each step. It set an odd counterpoint to the sigh and boom of the waves below us. "Was he behind Kerrinan and Jondin?"

"I believe so. I talked to someone who has lived in Fey. He said a really powerful Álfar, trained in their techniques—mental powers, magic, whatever you want to call it—could control someone's actions."

"Meaning Kerrinan and Jondi weren't . . ." Jeff stopped, snapped his fingers irritably. "What's that Latin phrase?"

"*Compos mentis.*"

"That's it. In their right minds"

Jeff crossed to me and leaned in close. "If you think he's going to do something at the Awards we've got to warn the authorities."

"And tell them what? That I think a respected representative of the Álfar Council is a murderous manipulator who has mysterious powers that can cloud men's minds and force them to do horrible and violent acts? I couldn't get a deputy this morning to believe I had nearly been murdered because Qwendar had used his powers to establish an alibi."

"Whoa. Wait. Whoa. You do not get to just casually toss out that *you were nearly murdered* and not give me the whole damn story."

I pressed my fingers hard against the skin above each eyebrow where an incipient headache was lurking. I blew out a breath. "I guess I'm just tired of going through it again and again. Suffice it to say that Qwendar realized I had figured out his game, and he decided to stage my suicide. I didn't oblige."

Jeff gave me a quick, hard hug. "Holy crap, Linnet, that's awful."

"Which is why I really don't want to talk about it anymore."

"Right, right. Okay." Jeff was back pacing again. "Okay, so if *our* authorities won't listen to us, how about we go to the Álfar authorities? Talk to this council of theirs."

I shook my head. "I'd rather not, and here's why. They might deal with Qwendar, but they'd probably just yank him back into Fey and sweep it all under the rug. That won't help Kerrinan and Jondin."

"You think the Álfar would actually throw Kerrinan and Jondin under a bus?" Jeff asked.

I shrugged. "They're the Álfar equivalent of politicians. Are they really going to want to tell the world full of nervous humans that there's Álfar magic that can turn any Álfar into a killer? Better to let the humans think these were isolated incidents with a couple of nutty actors. But if Qwendar acts again, and I can prove he's doing it, it may clear them."

"You'd do that, take this terrible risk for a couple of people you don't even know? Why?"

"Because I'm a lawyer, and I have to believe that occasionally justice prevails." I once again got a hug.

"You're sure it's going to happen at the Oscars?" Jeff asked after he released me.

"No, but I'm pretty sure. Qwendar wants a shocking incident. What better place? We're talking about a worldwide audience, a live feed, and movie stars."

"Will he have to be there to do his magic shit?" Jeff asked.

"I think so. He was on the lot when Jondin went nuts." I chewed at a hangnail. "I'd love to find out if Qwendar was somewhere in the neighborhood when Kerrinan killed Michelle, and when he made his run for Fey. Also, I think Qwendar will want to see and enjoy the mayhem."

"So we can stop him by just not letting him into the ceremony," Jeff said.

"Nice thought, but it won't work. He'll come in through Fey." I stopped. "I just figured out where Jondin's guns came from. He had them stashed in Fey and just brought them through once he had control of her. Hell, they could have been right outside the door of her trailer."

"And this helps us how?"

"It's something we need to consider. He'll find a way to arm the Álfar once he's taken control of them."

"So, we keep all Álfar out of the ceremony."

"Like that's not going to cause any problems or comment. Besides, Qwendar will use it to whip up anger against humans because the Álfar were excluded. A lot of Álfar actors are going to defy the ban and come in through Fey. Qwendar still gets his bloodbath, and we've pissed off their council. Let's not do his work for him."

Jeff gave me a rueful smile and sat back down. "We don't have any really good choices, do we?

"No," I said bleakly.

"And how, exactly, are six people at the ceremony going to help?"

"They can knock down maddened elves and protect humans."

"And who handles Qwendar? He's the guy with all the magic whammy. He's going to be tough."

"That would be me," I said.

Jeff stopped pacing, turned, and stared at me. "You."

"Me."

"All five-feet of you?"

"He can't affect me." I hesitated, thinking back on all my near miraculous escapes, then added, "And no matter what is going on around me, I suspect I'm going to be able to get through it pretty much unscathed."

We sat silent for a few minutes with Jeff just looking at me. It was one of those awkward, uncomfortable silences, but I was too tired to break it. Finally the actor stirred, slapped his palms against his thighs, and stood up. "Okay, then, it's time to enlist Kate."

He led me back into the kitchen. There was the sweet, rich scent of hazelnut coffee in the air. Kate finished arranging cookies on a plate and set them on the table. Jeff moved to her side and gave her a kiss. She smiled down at him. He pushed a long strand of auburn hair behind her ear. "Sweetie, Linnet is going to be going to the Oscars, and she'll need a gown. I can't think of anybody better to help her out."

"Oh, what fun." Her eyes raked over me, head to toe, as she walked in a slow circle around me. "Petite and very feminine. Elie Saab, I think. He made Natalie's Oscar gown, and she's a tiny little thing." She checked her watch. "It's too late today to make it over to Rodeo Drive. We'll go tomorrow, and we can hit Tiffany's for your jewelry."

"Wait, I can't afford—"

"Not to worry: unless you're Liz Taylor you borrow everything."

I glanced over at Jeff. "I'd rather not be wearing anything really valuable."

"I think no jewels," he said.

Kate looked from one to the other of us. "You both look grim."

I could read Jeff's thoughts as clearly as if I'd been telepathic. He looked at his wife. He considered what I'd said about a bloodbath. He steeled himself and took Kate's hand. "Honey, let's go upstairs for a minute. I want to talk to you."

The actress shook her head and planted her fists on her hips. Though the stance was combative, the smile she gave her husband wasn't. "You're going to tell me I can't go to the Oscars because it's too dangerous, but if what you discussed is true you're going to need me there."

"You eavesdropped?" Jeff asked.

"Yes. You were talking about the Álfar, and you know how I feel about them and about Phase Change. Look, these people are our friends and colleagues. The other actresses know me and trust me. If I tell them to move they will move. Same for you with the actors. If something happens this could easily turn into a panicked stampede. You need more help, not less. And this is something I can do to help the Álfar."

"This could be very dangerous," I said.

"I know. Which is why I don't what him to face it alone. I want to be with him, not sitting at home alone worrying." She stepped to her husband's side and wrapped an arm around his waist.

"I don't want you in danger," Jeff said.

"And I don't want *you* in danger. So, let's face it together. Okay?" Kate gazed fondly at her husband, and he took her in his arms and kissed her. I looked away.

Kate turned back to me with a glowing smile. "So, tomorrow. Shopping. We can face anything if we're in a couture gown, right?"

"Right," I said. I wondered if they made one designed for ease of running and fighting.

I collapsed in the armchair in my room at the Beverly Garland Hotel and contemplated just sleeping there. Even the effort of taking off my clothes and moving to the bed seemed beyond me. I lifted my arm and checked my wristwatch. Almost seven o'clock. Ten o'clock in Philadelphia. Late, but not enough to terrify people in their beds late, and I really needed to talk to Parlan. I staggered over to my purse, pulled out my cell phone, and called the O'Shea house. Big Red answered.

"O'Shea."

Thirty years as a cop had left him incapable of saying hello. It drove Meg wild, but then she would just laugh and call him an old war horse.

"Hi, Red, it's Linnet."

"Linnie, how the hell are you?"

"Fine. Is Parlan there? I need to talk to him."

"Yeah. He's here." There was weariness and frustration coating the words. "Parlan, pick up the damn phone—it's for you."

There was a brief silence then, "Hello?"

"Hi, it's Linnie. You said you still had friends in Fey. How do you think they would feel if they were told they couldn't cross over to the human world again, and if they tried, angry humans with pitchforks would be waiting for them?"

"I think they'd hate it. Why? Is that likely to happen?"

"That's what somebody is trying, yes, and if he can arrange for a large and public bloodbath I think he may get his wish. So, I'm calling to ask for your help."

"Sure, but I don't know what I can do."

"Can you get in touch with your friends? Tell them what's going on, see if they'd be willing to help me?"

"I can contact them. I can leave messages at ley line crossroads. Where will you need this help?"

"In California."

"How soon?"

"In a few days."

"That's going to be a problem. Rapid travel is not one of the hallmarks of Fey."

"If they'll cross over, we'll fly you all to LA." I put aside for the moment just how I was going to pay for all this. I hoped David was going to help, and it wouldn't all end up on my credit card.

"On an airplane?" he said breathlessly.

"Yeah," I said, drawing out the word because I didn't exactly know how to respond. "That's the only way we know how to fly."

"I look up at them all the time and wish I could fly on one. If I could actually get to do that it would be . . . amazing." He sounded very young now, not at all like a man in his forties.

"Well, consider it done." I hesitated, then added, "Do you know about the Oscars? What they are?"

"Sort of."

"It's acting awards. Very glamorous."

"So, I could wear some of my real . . . my own clothes?" he asked, his voice brightening at the prospect.

"You mean the clothes you wore in Fey?"

"Yes."

"I don't see why not, but you should probably be prepared for them to get messed up if you do end up protecting people. But maybe it won't come to that."

We spent a few more minutes finalizing things, then I hung up, stripped off my clothes, and fell into bed. I didn't wake up until Maslin hammered on my door the next morning.

23

Belinda Cartwright had that deer-in-the-headlights expression when she looked up from the printed pages Maslin had placed before her. She quickly regained her composure and snapped, "Speculation." I mutely handed over the research unearthed by Merlin. She read through those. This time when she met our gaze her expression was sick, and she didn't recover. "Dear God, they're everywhere, they've infiltrated everywhere."

We were back in the offices of Human First.

"No," I corrected. "This *one* Álfar has played you for a fool and built you into a tool to cause conflict between us and his people."

"Question is, what are you going to do about it?" Maslin asked.

"Expose him! Tell our members how we've been compromised."

Maslin sighed. "Wrong answer."

"Think about this, Ms. Cartwright," I said softly. "You're the head of this organization. *You're* the one who allowed this to happen. You didn't do due diligence on your donors. I'm sure Mr. Ambinder will make damn sure that little fact comes out in his final version of the article. Question is, who are your members going to be more un-happy with? Qwendar? Or you?"

Maslin studied his fingernails. "I'm betting the Reverend Trager will not take kindly to these revelations. You'll probably lose your job."

"You're blackmailing me," Cartwright said, her voice a rough thread of sound.

"No, just contemplating likely outcomes," Maslin answered.

"What do you want? For us to disband? I don't have the power." She shot Maslin a venomous look. "As you rightly pointed out, I'm just hired help. Reverend Trager calls the shots."

"Just dial it back. Tone down the rhetoric. Stop throwing gasoline on the fire." She stared up at me, her lips set in a thin line. I pulled a chair in closer, sat down, and leaned across the desk. "Look, Belinda, we're afraid. I understand that. The world as we knew it has changed. Nobody has a handle on how this is all going to work out. But this has happened many times before in our history—revolution, civil wars, depression, world wars, integration, immigration, technological innovation—and we've weathered them all. The world changes, and the people who stand against it inevitably end up being trampled because they can't stop it. What you can do is *guide* the change, soften it, make sure all sides are considered, and that's a valuable role for you to play. Whipping up anger, stoking the fear, inciting violence, that's not productive, and we're better than that as a people. The Powers are here. Let's learn to live together. We may find we can actually help each other." I paused. Her expression was curiously blank, but at least the rage had faded. "And ironically there are people on the other side who feel the same way about us, who think we're dangerous to their way of life, and they don't like the change either."

"That's rich. They've turned our world upside down."

"And we've done the same to them. A lot of the younger Álfar prefer our world to their own." I gave her a smile. "Which sort of implies we're way more awesome than they are."

She chewed on that for a moment. "So, if we don't join in this arbitration—"

"And tone down the public protests," I interrupted.

"You have one in mind?" Cartwright asked shrewdly.

"The Oscars," I said.

"So if we don't picket at the Oscars, you won't publish this story." She shoved the pages back toward Maslin.

"As much as it pains me to say this: yes, I won't publish," the journalist answered.

She stood and extended her hand. "Then we have a deal. Now I need to see about replacing a source of funding. If you'll excuse me."

We wound our way through the desks and the hardworking volunteers all diligently trying to hold back the tide and stepped out into the parking lot of the strip mall. I released a breath I hadn't realized I'd been holding. "Well, that went better than I expected," I said.

Maslin gave me a curious sideways look. "You ever considered a career in politics?"

"God, no. What made you say that?"

"You do seem to appeal to people's better angels."

"Right now I'm just trying to keep a lot of people from joining that heavenly choir. Shall we go?"

I was late meeting Kate. She was already in the Elie Saab store on Rodeo Drive, and under her guidance a couple of saleswomen were filling a rolling clothes rack with gowns. As I studied the tall, elegant, perfectly groomed, perfectly coiffed, chicly dressed women, I wanted to slink back out of the store. My professional woman's uniform—straight gray skirt, black jacket, scoop-neck pale yellow shell, sensible pumps—seemed unbelievably dowdy. I gazed at the dresses on impossibly tall, slender mannequins. I was short. Really short. I was going to look so stupid in these clothes. No one this short could possibly—

"Oh, Linnet, good. I think we've got some great choices for you," Kate said, and pulled me over. "This is Glynis and Julie. They're going to help us."

"How do you do," I mumbled. "You've got your work cut out for you," I added.

"Nonsense," trilled Glynis. "You're lovely."

Then we were into it. It was like an explosion in a fabric store. Silk, taffeta, satin, chiffon. A rainbow of colors. There was one red dress with a gathered bodice that kept the left shoulder bare, but created a wide strap effect across the right shoulder. The dress flowed to the floor and the fabric looked like it would cling to the legs. A bit of material formed a train that flowed out behind the skirt. It was gorgeous and it had me fantasizing about walking down a curving staircase to meet an elegant gentleman, taking his arm, exiting to our waiting limo—

I reluctantly and sadly put it aside. "I really need to be able to move easily. Would it be awful if I didn't wear a floor-length gown?" I asked.

"Not at all," Julie said, and she pulled down a dress of deep indigo blue with silver and white embroidered flowers.

It had a one-shoulder fitted bodice; an asymmetric hemline; beaded, stylized flowers in trapunto on chiffon. The design of the flowers reminded me of Elizabethan crewelwork, and it was done using gold and silver thread and silk embroidery floss. I had a feeling that the asymmetric hemline would leave my right leg bare nearly to the hip. My left arm was going to be bare, the right arm partially covered by translucent chiffon of a pale teal color.

I touched the material and felt it catch on the rough tips of my fingers. I snatched my hand back. "Don't worry, it's not that fragile," Kate said with a laugh. "Go try it on."

"Would you like a glass of champagne?" Glynis asked.

"Uh, it might be a little early," I said.

"I'll make it a mimosa," she said with a wink.

"Well, okay."

Julie, carrying the dress reverently draped over her arms, led me back to the dressing rooms. No tiny cubicles here. Each fitting room was large, carpeted, and lined with mirrors. There was also a comfortable armchair. "For the gentleman in a lady's life if he would like to see the transformation. Otherwise we have a waiting room in front with magazines, comfortable chairs and couches, and a beverage selection," Julie explained.

"Oh," I said, inanely. *So this was how the very rich lived,* I thought.

Glynis arrived with my mimosa in a crystal goblet. I gulped down a sip. Fortunately there was more orange juice than champagne.

Julie hung the dress, and they both stepped out while I removed my clothes. "Ready for me to help you?" Glynis called.

"Uh, yes, please."

They came back in and zipped me into the dress. I kept my eyes focused on the dressing room door. I didn't want to see. I knew I was going to look totally stupid. Julie turned me around to face a mirror. "There."

"I don't look like me," I whispered as I studied my image in the dressing room mirror.

"It looks wonderful on you," the two fashion amazons said in chorus.

"Let's go show Ms. Billingham," Glynis said, and pulled me back out into the store proper.

I stood on a little pedestal while they circled me like sharks, tugging at the material, pinching in the material at my back, pulling up material to expose more of my hip. Pins appeared to reinforce these changes. I couldn't tell if they were improvements or not. They were so subtle and I was so overwhelmed.

"How quickly can you make the alterations?" Kate asked. "The ceremony is day after tomorrow."

"We'll have them done today and you can pick up the dress tomorrow. Or we can have it messengered over to Ms. Ellery," Julie said as she plucked another pin out of the pincushion she wore on her wrist and reached for the hem of the skirt.

"Wait," Glynis ordered. "We need the right shoes." A less exalted salesperson darted away. "Open-toed, ankle strap," Glynis called after her.

I suddenly remembered trying to get out of my shoes during one of the werewolf attacks last year, and how the ankle strap had made it impossible for me to shed my high heels quickly.

"No strap," I contradicted. "I want to be able to kick them off. If my feet start to hurt," I added awkwardly.

"And a purse," Kate added.

The girl returned with a pair of silver shoes that picked up the color and sparkle of the trapunto flowers. Using Julie's shoulder for balance I slipped them on and got three inches taller. The purse was a Debbie Brooks clutch bag decorated with a multicolored rhinestone dragonfly swooping over enamel flowers. Kate reached up and pulled my hair out of its twist. If fell onto my shoulders.

Everyone clapped. "Oh, yes, definitely wear your hair down," Kate said.

I stared at the image in the mirror. I looked sophisticated, chic, maybe even a little pretty. Now, if Qwendar just wouldn't fuck everything up maybe I could be a princess for a night.

Parlan, flanked by six gorgeous Álfar, was waiting at the curb at LAX. They had a lot of luggage, as in *Oh, holy shit, that's a lot of luggage.* And of course, being me, I said just that, then added, "Good thing I got a van. But I think we're going to need a second car."

"Sorry. None of us were sure what to pack," Parlan said.

"May we meet this lady?" said the tallest of the Álfar. His long black hair was confined in a ponytail. "Though I assume her to be Linnet."

"Right you are," I said, holding out my hand. "Linnet Ellery."

"Ladlaw," he said. Then he pointed at the other five, a name accompanying each thrust of his forefinger. "Aalet, Cildar, Donnal, Zevra, and Tulan."

"Pleased to meet you. Thank you all for coming."

"Will we get to ride on the airplane going back?" Aalet asked, his eagerness and excitement showing.

"Absolutely."

"Wonderful." Tulan cuffed Aalet across the back of the head lightly and affectionately.

I recognized the behavior. "Brothers?" I hazarded a guess.

"How did you know?" Aalet marveled.

"I have one," I said.

"Condolences," Tulan said, but the word didn't match the affectionate glance he bestowed on his sibling.

I called Kobe and outlined my problem.

"I'll have a limo over to you in about fifteen minutes. We keep a lot near the airport."

"Thanks. You are a life saver."

I hung up the phone. I looked at Parlan. "Why don't you ride with me in the van? We can talk."

The limo arrived, luggage was loaded in my van, Álfar in the limo. Parlan climbed in with me and we headed out. We negotiated the long horseshoe that was LAX, reached Century Boulevard, and headed for the freeway.

"So many people," Parlan said softly. "In all of Fey I don't think there are as many people as there are in this city. No wonder they worry."

"So, you think Qwendar is right?"

"I think I understand why he wants us separated,"

"And what do you think?" I asked.

His eyes clouded with pain and sorrow. "I think that while I know I'm human, I don't want to be cut off from my own people."

"Then let's make sure that doesn't happen." We drove in silence for a few minutes, then my phone rang, but since I was on the freeway I didn't want to risk reaching into my purse. "Would you answer that for me?"

Parlan pawed through my bag and finally emerged, first with my compact and then the cell phone. He gazed at the screen and figured out how to answer. He then handed it over to me. It was Jeff.

Without salutation or preamble he said, "Linnet, I think it's on."

"Wha . . . why . . . how do you know?"

"A doc friend who works at Cedars-Sinai called me. Someone broke in—"

Memories tumbled into place. Parlan's descriptions of blood magic, Connie telling me about the Álfar blood supply. "To the supply of Álfar blood they keep at the hospital," I interrupted. Dread for what was coming clawed at my gut.

"How did you know about that?"

"The EMT on set told me about it." I beat the heels of my hands on the steering wheel in a frenzy of guilt and anxiety. "I should have thought of this. Warned them to move it, hide it." The words tumbled over each other.

"And they wouldn't have listened to you! You've done nothing wrong. If it weren't for you, we'd have no idea what he was planning. As scary as this is, again because of you, we're ready for him. We'll stop him and no one else will get hurt."

"I wish I could share your confidence," I said quietly.

There was silence for a moment, then Jeff said, "This silly case

BOX OFFICE POISON   289

that brought you out to LA—it sure doesn't seem very important now, does it?"

"Actually, Jeff. I think it's very important. It's about how we all treat each other and live together, and it means David and I better find a Salomon-like solution in this fraught atmosphere."

"Yeah . . . well, I'm glad that's your job and not mine."

The next day found us prowling through the Kodak Theatre. On stage the emcee for the event was going through his schtick, dancers were rehearsing, cameras were being set, singers were warbling through the nominated songs, presenters were parading on and off the stage. When they weren't playing for a singer the orchestra rehearsed movie themes in stuttering, disjointed snippets of music. The musicians looked like an accidental gathering of random people off the street. Instead of tuxes and long gowns the musicians wore blue jeans and T-shirts. Over all the other cacophony there was the whine of power saws and sharp staccato of hammering, sounds that echoed oddly through the nearly empty hall.

We had come in through a freight door, and we drew more than a few glances as we wandered about the auditorium. Understandable because we were a motley crew. There was David, Hank and me, Maslin and Merlin, Jeff and Kate, Parlan and the six Álfar, which Merlin remarked sounded like a '60s rock band. That earned him a glare from David and an elbow in the side from his brother. As we wandered I found myself wondering what we should call our little group of plotter-protectors. A gaggle? A herd? A flock? Or maybe a murder—as in crows. Then I decided no, all the murdering was going to be on the other side. Unless we stopped it. That thought removed any humor from the moment and had my stomach once again huddling at the back of my spine.

I was feverishly turning over every possible permutation to our plan when the flaw in my logic leaped out and slapped me upside of the head. It was so obvious and so devastating, that I just collapsed into a seat. The paper that was set on the cushion with the name of the actor for whom it was reserved crackled as I landed on it, and an official started hustling toward us.

"What?" David asked.

"Qwendar was not on the set when Jondin went nuts. He was on the lot, but not on the actual set. He wasn't in the car when Kerrinan fled into Fey. What if he doesn't show up here tomorrow night? The best we can hope for is to prevent or reduce the carnage, but we'll never tie him to the events."

The tall Álfar, Ladlaw (I was proud that I remembered his name), laid a hand on my shoulder. The long hair brushing at his shoulders was black with a green tinge, like sunlight on leaves. "Mere proximity is sufficient with a single individual. The blood enables you to ride in the mind of the thrall, holding the reins of their spirit, feeding the emotion you have teased forth from deep within them." The stilted delivery, faint accent, and florid word choice marked him as old, not all that familiar with the human side, and it was totally charming. I had to force myself to concentrate and not lose myself in the soft velvet voice. "But when you attempt to control many thralls, that is not possible. You must be able to see them in order to guide them. He will be here."

Maslin gave me a pat on the shoulder. "And just to be sure, let me take a look at some video from the car chase. With some enhancement I bet we'll spot Qwendar in the freeway traffic." So we all began scanning the theater looking for that vantage point.

Jeff pointed to the rear of the theater, up toward the ceiling. "The light booth. That's got to be it. Since Linnet is convinced he can't effect her, we station her up there."

"But it could be in the upper level of seats," Merlin countered.

"Or on the stage," Kate added. "You can see the entire hall from there. I know, I was a presenter last year."

"So we leave Linnet in the audience and hope she can make her way to him," Maslin said.

David looked down at me, and his expression was aggrieved. "I don't know why you won't give that job to me. I'm stronger and taller, and it's very hard to kill me. Unlike you who are—"

"Small and weak?" I interrupted.

"And mortal," he interrupted right back.

I decided against mentioning my seeming ability to walk unscathed through most situations. I settled for a more reasonable and logical argument. "And for all those reasons people tend to discount me and overlook me. If he sees you coming, he'll throw everything at you to try and hold you back. I can slip through. He might not even see me coming, small human worm that I am." David's eyes narrowed. I gave him back a limpidly innocent look.

"You'd try the patience of a saint," he growled at me.

"Sorry."

"No, you're not," was his response. His attention was suddenly caught by an elderly woman who had joined the emcee on stage, and for several minutes he forgot to breathe. Which meant that when he turned to Jeff and started to ask a question there was no oxygen in his lungs, and what emerged was a wheezy squeak. The vampire forced air into his lungs and tried again. "Is that . . ." He seemed unable to continue.

"Yes," Jeff said. "She's still amazing-looking, isn't she? And she's past eighty."

"I saw all her movies," David said in almost reverent tones. He had told me he liked movies, but it was kind of sweet and sort of incongruous to see him starstruck.

"We'll make sure you get introduced," Kate promised.

"That would be . . ." He fumbled for a word and finally said, "Excellent."

Jeff led us over and showed us our seats for the ceremony. They were all on the aisle and directly behind the nominated stars and their guests. Parlan spoke up. "You can remove some of those. Ladlaw and I will be in the auditorium, but the others will wait in Fey. Ladlaw will cross over if they should be needed."

"That's probably smart," Maslin said. "If Qwendar saw a lot of unfamiliar Álfar, he might twig."

"But what if they end up hanging out in the same space over in Fey" I asked as a new worry intruded.

"The elder one is about to try a spell of great complexity and difficulty. He will not wish an audience or distraction, and my companions will be a most rowdy and drunken distraction. He will choose to make magic well away from them."

We all chuckled at that, and the five other Álfar looked smug. Parlan cuffed one of them on the upper arm. "Don't decide to actually *be* drunk, Zevra," he said.

"But I am ever so much more charming and effective when inebriated," the golden-haired Álfar responded, to general derision from his companions.

"Okay. I guess we're as ready as we'll ever be," I said. "Oh, how do we get in tomorrow?"

"Front entrance like everybody else," Jeff answered.

"But what if Qwendar sees me?"

"If he's doing a magic spell over in Fey I doubt he'll be watching the Oscar preshow," David said.

"Wanting to check out what everyone's wearing on the red carpet," Hank snorted.

I held up my hands in defeat. "Okay, okay, okay. I guess we can't outguess every contingency. We've just got to roll with whatever happens."

"Remember, Linnet, no plan ever survives contact with the enemy," David added.

Jeff blew out a breath. "Well, on that cheery note . . ."

24

We wanted to time it so our car pulled up to the red carpet right in front of a major celebrity. That way all the press and attention would be focused on the star and not on us. But traffic patterns and tinted windows made that impossible. One thing in our favor was the weather. The rains had returned, which meant umbrellas would be a large part of the landscape, and just in case Qwendar was watching we would have some cover.

As our car inched forward David gazed out at the crowds lining the street and shook his head. "Why would they do this? Stand for hours in a cold rain. And for what? To see an actor?"

"And you weren't absolutely tongue-tied when you met—"

"That was different," the vampire interrupted before I could speak his idol's name. "She was an artist."

"Oh, David, sometimes you are so funny." We were almost at the dropoff point. I gave my hair a fluff with the tips of my fingers.

"By the way, you look very nice," my boss said gruffly.

"Thank you. So do you." He did: he wore the very classic old-style tuxedo with an ease rarely seen in modern men. The other thing that wasn't common with modern men were the scars twisting across his features.

The car rolled to a stop and an usher opened the back door of our limo with one hand while keeping a large golf umbrella ready to cover us as we stepped out. I climbed out and watched as hundreds of cameras were lifted and pointed in my direction. Then, like a retreating wave, they all dropped again when they realized I wasn't anybody. The eyes were already straining eagerly toward the next car in the queue. My ego having been effectively deflated, I took David's proffered arm and we walked into the Kodak Theatre.

Inside I felt goose bumps rising on my bare arm because the air conditioning was going full blast. I supposed it made sense. There were going to be a lot of bodies in this space for a number of hours and it would probably be warm, but right now it was freezing. I also wondered how much of my shivering was due to nerves and the air conditioning was just my excuse. Since we'd explored the theater two massive replicas of the Oscar statuettes had been erected on either side of the stage. The giant figures stood on a film reel; with their smooth heads and joined legs they reminded me of Egyptian statues. When you added in the long crusader's sword it gave me a sense of eerie otherworldliness hovering just beneath the shallow glitz that exemplified Hollywood.

As we walked down the aisle toward our seats it seemed like the Kodak was a box filled with gems. Not just because of the amount of jewelry sparkling at throats and on wrists and fingers, but the dresses themselves. The gowns were shimmers of rich color. Black for women was definitely not in this year. Then I realized why men wore tuxedos. It made them the perfect foil for the women's finery.

We took our seats. Parlan and Ladlaw were across the aisle from us. Parlan was dressed in Álfar style. It didn't look as good on his powerful, barrel-chested form as it did on his companion's willowy frame. We settled in for an hour and a half of incredible tedium. The only thing that made it bearable was watching fervent air kisses and man hugs being exchanged, and evaluating each new dress as more and more people arrived. To David's disgust Hank was right in the middle of the air kissing and man hugging. When the orchestra began to tune we knew we were getting close, and then the cameramen began making final adjustments to their cameras. It was time.

The orchestra played a long drumroll and fanfare. Across America and around the world people gazed at their televisions as the announcer boomed out. "Live from Los Angeles, it's the Academy Awards!"

The ceremony began. Sometime, probably an hour in, I realized my muscles were cramping from holding myself at rigid attention. Ready to leap out of my chair, ready to move, to react. The theater darkened even more and a large screen rolled down. It was time for In Memorium. A good time, I decided, to make a run for the ladies room. I turned around in my seat to whisper in to David, "I'll be right back."

"Don't rush," he growled back. "I'm dead and I feel like this has gone on for an eternity."

I wasn't the only person who had the same idea. As usual the women's restroom had too few stalls for too many full bladders. I joined the line snaking through the door and into the bathroom. I found myself between a famous TV actress and a star of screen and stage. "I should not have drunk that bottle of water in the limo," the movie star moaned. "I'm about to pee my panties."

"If you had any on, dear," said the older TV actress sweetly.

"I guess when you get to your age you don't care about panty lines," responded the younger woman.

"Yeah, don't you wish you were on my side of the divide?"

"Oh, God, yes," the younger woman sighed. "This double-sided tape is chaffing my boobs something awful."

I had wondered how she was keeping her famous breasts inside the confines of the plunging décolletage of the gown. Now I had my answer. I also realized that what had seemed like nasty sniping had actually been shared amusement. Hollywood really was like a funhouse mirror. I finally made it into a stall and tried to pee, but nerves had me so tense I could barely go. At the sinks I washed my hands and watched as the women to either side of me refreshed lipstick, added more eyeliner, rearranged their breasts, pulled up pantyhose, and fussed with their hair. I just left. I had been away for too long already.

Nothing had happened in my absence. I sank back in my chair and sighed. Thirty minutes later David leaned forward and placed a hand on my shoulder. "What?" I whispered. "Do you see something?"

"We're getting into the Best Supporting Actor and Actress. This is when a lot of people will tune in. To see who wins the big awards."

"You big fraud. You watch this. I bet you watch it every year," I said.

"That's enough of your sass," he growled.

The Best Supporting Actress cried and thanked a lot of people no one had ever heard of, but included her lawyers in the list. Merlin leaned across the aisle and said, "That's sort of nice. We don't usually get singled out for thanks. Usually we get roundly cursed by everyone."

"Shhhh," I hissed because the presenters for Best Supporting Actor were tearing open the envelope, and since an Álfar was nominated for the first time I wanted to hear. The breathless young actress leaned in close to the mike and squealed—

"And the winner is Jay Williams!"

The hall erupted in cheers. A tall, older man stood, shook hands with the people all around him, kissed several of the women, and started for the stage. I was watching Jujuran who was three rows behind me and across the aisle. He had been on his feet, clapping like everyone else, but as I watched, the actor's face went slack, then blank, and he suddenly pushed his way out of the row of seats.

We weren't as fast or as agile as an Álfar, but we were all in motion by the time he reached the foot of the stairs. From the corner of my eye I saw Ladlaw shimmer and vanish. Parlan was on his feet. Maslin and Merlin left their seats. Hank shoved his way out of his row. I kicked off my shoes and jumped up to stand on mine, scanning the room, looking for Qwendar. David, in an amazing display of grace and balance, used the backs of the chairs to run toward the stage.

Williams was on the steps leading up to the stage. Jujuran caught up with him, seized the human actor by the arm, and threw him into the orchestra pit. The cheers turned to screams, there was a harsh jangling as the actor fell among the instruments, and then Jujuran was on stage. He wrenched the statuette out of the hands of the pretty young presenter. She made the mistake of resisting, and when she lost the tug of war Jujuran, armed with the heavy Oscar, swung it like a club at the head of the actress. Her companion, acting more on instinct then planning, threw up an arm to block the murderous hit. The eight-and-a-half-pound, gold-plated statue connected with his forearm, and he screamed in pain as the bones broke. The actress tried to run backward, got tangled up in her train, and fell down.

There were other Álfar scattered throughout the audience, and they were turning on the people next to them. As I watched, Palendar grabbed the actor next to him by the throat and began choking him. A panicky crowd started pouring into the aisles. Merlin and Maslin were trying to reach an Álfar actress who was clawing at another woman's face, but the crush of people was making it hard.

Jeff shoved people aside. I saw one famous actor's toupee go flying at the rough handling, and amazingly he stopped to try and recover his rug. Jeff looked like all the action heroes he had ever played as he reached Palendar, grabbed the slender Álfar by the back of his coat and the seat of his pants, and hauled him off his victim. Jeff threw Palendar bodily over three rows of seats. The Álfar hit the chairs with a sickening crash. He regained his feet, but from the way he gripped his side it looked like a few ribs were broken. He was undeterred. He climbed over the seats and attacked Jeff.

Kate cupped her hands over her mouth and yelled over the screams and cries of alarm. "Ladies! Kick off your shoes. Use the fire exit on the left. Everyone, go, go!"

It was clear the woman was a stage actress. Kate had projection down. I was sure they could hear her in the topmost row of balcony seats. I could also see why she'd picked that direction. There was only one Álfar in that section.

People were trying to run in all directions and ended up creating a massive jam of terrified humanity in the aisles. Kate began grabbing some of them and shoving them toward the fire exit.

From my vantage point I watched Merlin and Maslin, like two maddened hobbits, double-teaming the elf actress, who was a head taller. Maslin tackled her at the knees and knocked her down. Curling her fingers into claws she ripped at the journalist's face. Merlin ripped the train off her dress and wrapped it tightly around her wrists to stop the assault on his brother.

Palendar had his arms around Jeff, immobilizing Jeff's arms while the Álfar smashed his head against the human actor's face. Then Parlan waded in and cold-cocked Palendar with a sharp blow to the skull above the elf's right ear.

On my left was the actress from the restroom who had been bemoaning her sticky tape. It was clearly no longer doing its job because her breasts had fallen out of the restraining fabric. She was frantically shoving at the backs of the people ahead of her either unaware or, wisely, unconcerned that her breasts were front and center.

There was a boom camera with an operator and a producer just off to the side of the stage stairs. The operator was looking down at the producer. I heard him yell,

"Should I turn off the camera?"

"Are you nuts! Those are Angelina's boobs!"

The Álfar actors who were not presently beset by our crew shimmered and vanished. They returned all too soon, and now they had guns. Gunfire, like angry coughs, cut through the screams, and the smell of cordite was in the air. The screaming rose even higher. Hank threw people aside as he moved toward the armed Álfar. Nausea clawed at the back of my throat. Despite our best efforts people were going to get hurt, maybe killed. Should I have warned the organizers of the Oscars? I shook it off. They would never have believed me, and there was no time for recriminations or second-guessing. I had my job—find Qwendar—and I needed to do it. I gazed with growing desperation around the room. Where? Where?

David was wading through the crowds at the foot of the stage trying to reach the stairs so he could get on the stage and deal with Jujuran. But when the shots were fired he turned his attention to the gun-wielding Álfar and switched directions. He headed back up the aisle toward Hank and the shooters. They were the right men for the job. A gun was not going to hurt them.

A flash of motion toward the back of the stage caught my eye. It was the telescoping pedestal toward the back of the stage that had been used during a performance of one of the nominated songs. It placed the singer high above the dancers that twirled beneath him, and now it was slowly rising again. There was a figure standing on the top. *Qwendar.*

There was no way I was going to make it through the central aisle. It was crammed with terrified people, but I was only two rows from the front. My legs weren't long enough, and I didn't have the unnatural grace of a vampire, so I couldn't balance on the backs of the seats. Instead I had to climb awkwardly over each row. I reached the front row and used my foot to push back down the cushioned seat so I had a place to stand. Hoards of people separated me from the curving stairs that led to the stage.

It was terrifying to contemplate crossing that seething mass of people, but I had to get to the stage. I steeled myself to jump down, then screamed in pain as something struck me in the back. Slewing around I found myself face-to-face with an enraged Álfar actress who clutched her stiletto-heeled shoe in her hand. There was a smear of blood on the heel and I felt the warm trickle of blood down my back.

Out of the corner of my eye I caught sight of the Oscar statue falling toward me just as the Álfar actress raised the shoe again, aiming for my face. I flinched from both the statue and the shoe. The giant Oscar statue landed facedown on the seats next to me. A number of people were under the plywood and papier-mâché figure. It formed a perfect bridge from the front row of seats to the stage. There was no time to worry if it would hold my weight, I jumped on it and ran. The wood flexed beneath my feet and the gold coating cracked and split. With each gasping breath I felt my cracked rib shifting in my side. My Álfar attacker was right behind me, but there was a sharp crack, a scream of dismay, and when I glanced back she had fallen through the exterior of the statue and was trapped by the wood inside.

I jumped onto the stage just as the statue broke in half. Jujuran was straddling the actress who'd tried to hold back the Oscar and punching her over and over in the face. I started toward them, but suddenly a vast section of air shimmered and six Álfar on horseback entered from Fey. That got everybody's attention including Jujuran's.

Cildar spurred his horse and hit the actor with the hilt of his sword. Zevra rode up behind him, and leaning down, pulled the human actress onto the horse in front of him. Her face was a bloody mask and both her eyes were already swelling and blackening, but she clasped her arms around his neck and gazed up at her rescuer in amazement.

I remembered John telling me that everything the Álfar did was bigger and more dramatic. "You weren't kidding," I whispered.

I raised my eyes and looked up at Qwendar. He looked back down at me. Then he gestured, and I saw his mouth move, though I could hear nothing over the screams. I looked out across the audience. The seven Álfar actors, four of whom held guns, began moving toward the stage. They were totally focused on me. I gulped and turned my back on them. I had to trust that they couldn't hurt me.

I realized that the hoof beats of the horses were unnaturally loud. Then I spotted the wireless microphone laying on the stage. It had been picking up the sound of the hooves, and since at least one camera was still broadcasting, it meant the sound system was on too. As I ran toward the back of the stage I swept up the mike and carried it behind my back.

There was a sound like an enraged bee passing close by me. Bullets had been much in my life over the past weeks, so I didn't mistake it for anything but what it was. Qwendar's zombies were shooting at me. The muscles in my back tightened in anticipation of a bullet. I couldn't help it: I looked back over my shoulder to see David bodily throwing people aside as he rushed my firing squad.

Then my view was cut off as the giant screen that had been used for the In Memorium dropped down behind me. If I couldn't see the Álfar, they couldn't see me. It was my chance. I darted off to my left as more bullets punched through the screen where I used to be. The screen began going madly up and down. Then it broke loose and crashed to the stage.

I was safely backstage. Whatever it was that made me a unique human had come through again. Somewhere there would be controls for the pedestal. Qwendar was for damn sure not going to be able to stay above it all. Then I realized if I lowered the pedestal he would be able to step into Fey, but as long as he was thirty feet above the floor he couldn't. There probably wasn't an equivalent tower just waiting on the Fey side which would mean he would fall down and go boom. Which meant I needed to go up.

I scanned the catwalks that crisscrossed above the stage. There was one that ran pretty close to the pedestal. I could make that jump . . . I hoped.

Backstage I found the ladder leading up to the lighting catwalks. I started to climb. The metal rungs on the ladder were painful on my bare feet, and now my rib was screaming its objection. I reached the top and swung out onto a walkway. As I did I caught the single sleeve of my gown on a protruding hook. The rending sound of material tearing had me wincing. I ran down the catwalk, switched to another that ran horizontally across the stage, and switched again to the one that would bring me within feet of Qwendar's aerie.

He spotted me and, bending down, he swept up a remote control box that rested at his feet. This close I could hear the clunk as the gears engaged, and the pedestal began its slow descent. There was no time to dither or fear. I jumped across the intervening two feet and hit the platform. I let my knees take the shock, but the moving platform made it hard. I was starting to fall. I managed to get my shoulder down and rolled. My rib went on strike, and for an instant I wondered if I could climb back to my feet. Gazing at the toes of Qwendar's polished shoes I saw him draw back his foot to kick me. Pain or no, I had to get up.

I staggered with a groan onto my feet. Only inches separated us. Qwendar's face twisted with rage. Somehow I had managed to keep a grip on the mike. I swung it like a billy club, and it connected with his wrist. He dropped the control box. We both lunged for it, but I got there first. I hit the stop button and then threw the controller off the platform. It hit the stage floor some twenty-five feet below us, and the plastic case shattered. I retreated to the opposite side of the platform well out of his reach, and we glared at each other.

"I should have killed you long ago. The moment you began questioning Kerrinan's guilt, I shouldn't have wasted time on subtlety," Qwendar said, and then reacted when he heard his voice booming out across the theater.

"Yeah, because he wasn't guilty and you knew it. You took control of him. Just like you're controlling them." I swept my arm out to encompass the theater. I noticed that the camera I had run past was no longer focused on the seething crowd. The single lens glittered in the stage lights. Out in the audience the sounds of conflict were dying away, as were the gunshots. It looked like David and Hank had reached the firing squad.

"Prove it," he said.

"Okay. I bet once I knock you off this platform, and you go splat all over the stage, those Álfar are going to return to normal."

He blanched and flinched. "You would not dare! You are a defender of your laws."

"And you just threatened to murder me. I'm pretty sure this would fall under the self-defense rule." The moment I finished I took a step toward him. I thrust the mike at him. "Tell everyone what you did. Or . . ." I made a pushing gesture with my other hand.

"Or I will kill you first," the Álfar gritted, and he lunged at me.

I knew it was coming, so I was ready for it. I jumped to the side and swung the mike against his temple as he plunged past me. *Don't break, don't break,* I implored the microphone. Qwendar pulled up short, spun, and managed to land a punch on my ribs. The world seemed to flare red, and nausea clawed at my throat. I couldn't help it; I doubled over.

Blinking, I realized I was facing his crotch. I knew from one night of lovemaking with John that Álfar had the same plumbing as humans. Would they be as tender as humans? I took a few staggering steps and head-butted him in the stomach while I brought up the mike and jammed it into his balls. Qwendar clutched himself, screeched, and doubled over. Looked like they were as tender as humans. I spun the old man around, wrenched his arm up behind his back, and started shoving him toward the edge.

"Talk!"

"All right, all right. I took Kerrinan's blood. I had him kill the wife. I accosted Jondin in her trailer and cut her."

"Where did she get the guns?"

"I pre-set them in Fey."

"Now let them go," I ordered, and gestured at the hall.

He just stared at me. The hatred in that look was so great that I almost felt it like a blow against my skin. There was still a gun being fired. This had to stop. I slammed the mike against his temple. I had to hit him twice before he fell unconscious. The moment he did the sounds of fighting stopped. Now all I heard was sobbing, people crying in pain, the whoop of approaching sirens, and . . . applause. Of course they clapped—it was Hollywood!

25

Since I'd broken the controller they had to get a cherry picker onto the stage to pluck us off the platform. Once down, we were surrounded by police and the six Álfar. The idea that there was going to be a tug-of-war over who took custody gave starch to my spine. I got right in Ladlaw's face.

"There is no way you get him," I said. "He's going to answer for crimes committed in our world *in* our world."

He stared down at me, and I could see his expression closing down as he prepared to argue. Parlan stepped in and touched his friend lightly on the arm. "She's right. The world has seen us . . . your kind attacking humans tonight. If you carry him away to a realm where they can't follow, they will never believe that justice was done. They'll assume we . . . you let him off and the suspicion and resentment will continue to grow until there is a war between our people."

For a moment it hung in the balance. Then Ladlaw looked down at the old Álfar, and an expression of disgust flickered across his face. He met the gazes of a policemen. "Very well, you may take him. But keep him unconscious until you have him safely locked away."

I looked out across the auditorium, searching for my friends. It was quite a sight. Six horses stood in the main aisle tied to the arms of chairs. EMTs moved through the hall caring for the people who had been injured. Policemen were escorting the uninjured out of the hall. Tatters of torn fabric lay on the floor where trains and bows had been ripped from dresses during the frenzied stampede. I even spotted the forlorn toupee looking like a dead squirrel on one of the chairs.

Jeff had an ice pack to his eye. The twins looked tousled, and one arm was ripped off Maslin's tuxedo jacket. Hank was talking volubly to a burly man in a policeman's uniform which had a lot of stripes and medals. He looked terribly official. Kate was holding a young actress and rocking her while the girl sobbed against her breast. Kate's expression was bleak, so I had a bad feeling the tears weren't just a reaction to sudden and terrifying violence. Someone close to the girl was either hurt or dead: there were a few black body bags being zipped shut and rolled out of the theater. We had done our best, but we hadn't saved everyone. I couldn't find David, and it felt like my lungs were closing down.

Then I spotted him. He wasn't out in the hall. He was sitting on the stairs on the right side of the stage with an EMT bending over him. I ran over in time to see the EMT lay a pad over the bullet hole in David's chest and a matching pad on the exit wound just below his right shoulder. The slow leak of pale, translucent liquid was staunched.

"Could you hold those in place while I rip off some tape?" the EMT asked.

I nodded and knelt next to David, one hand pressed against his chest, the other against his back. Exhaustion had me wanting to lean against his shoulder, but he was the one who had been shot, so I forced myself to remain upright. There was the sharp tear and then rip as the EMT pulled off a long strand of medical tape and ran it around David's torso.

I helped David to his feet and he gave an experimental shrug. "Thank you, that feels better," he said to the EMT.

"I can offer you a pint now," the EMT said. "You should eat. You lost a lot of blood."

David made a face. "Thank you, but no. I hate the taste and texture of cold blood. I'll be fine for now." The EMT shrugged, snapped shut his case, and went on to help the next person. David squinted down at the bulge where the pad covered the bullet hole.

"Another scar. Life with you is certainly . . ."

"Dangerous and uncomfortable? I suggested.

"I was going to say interesting." David looked around. I realized what he wanted and picked up his shirt. It had matching holes in the front and the back and was faintly stained with his pale vampire blood. He put it on. He then looked around the interior of the Kodak Theatre.

"I'm sorry," I said.

"For what?" he asked. "You were right."

"But people still got hurt . . . and killed."

"And it would have been so much worse if you hadn't suspected and put a plan in place."

"I just didn't want anyone to get hurt." I hung my head.

David put a finger under my chin and made me face him. "That was unrealistic, and you know it. We did all right. We forged an alliance of humans and Powers, exposed a plot, and prevented a bloodbath."

His words made me feel marginally better. I gave him a small smile. "Hey, we're a pretty good team."

A strange expression flickered across his face and was gone. He stepped away from me and located his tuxedo jacket. "Yes. Well, now we have to do it again. We still have the arbitration to resolve."

Two days later we were in David's office. I was reclining on the sofa with my high heels kicked off and my head on the arm rest while he paced and tried to figure out when to resume the arbitration. Once again events had led to a cancellation.

"I'm quite sure when we do resume Gabaldon is going to demand we be replaced," David said. "We didn't exactly show neutrality when we showed up the Oscars and started whaling on Álfar."

I shook my head. "I don't think they will. There's a big kumbaya vibe going on right now. I think everybody looked into the abyss of war between humans and powers and took a very fast step back. Which makes it the perfect time to make a ruling in the arbitration."

"Lovely you think so, but I don't have a fucking clue how to resolve this," the vampire snapped back. I knew he was pissed because he rarely cursed, and I'd never heard the f-word out of his mouth before.

"I do."

"You do?"

"Uh-huh."

"So, are you going to tell me?"

"It has always been the case that people have a right to maximize their talents and abilities when they compete in our free marketplace," I said.

Expectant faces stared at me from all around the long oval table. McPhee looked sleepy, but there was a glint of interest and calculation in his half-lidded eyes. Barbara Gabaldon sat tensely erect. She laid a hand over Palendar's and gave his a squeeze. The bruises on Palendar's face had turned interesting shades of green and brown, and he sat stiffly and carefully because of his broken ribs. LeBlanc looked worried and Missy looked sulky. Brubaker and his gaggle of suits were impassive. Jeff was back in his usual seat in the back of the room, his chair pushed up against the wall. He seemed relaxed and confident. I was glad he felt that way. I was incredibly nervous.

Because David had decreed that I would offer the settlement. "So I can take the blame when it gets rejected out of hand?" I had asked that afternoon in his office.

David's reaction had been to turn an Olympian frown on me. "No. I'm trying to show you respect and not steal your thunder. It's a damn good solution and you thought of it; it's an excellent solution, so you should present it."

I pushed aside the memory, took a breath, cleared my throat, and resumed. "But that doesn't mean that certain people should have an unfair or undue advantage over others." Palendar stiffened. "It's not in dispute that the Álfar are not human. They possess abilities beyond those of human beings. The ability to enter a different world that only touches ours, and which is closed to humans unless that human is brought there. The ability to do what we'll call, for lack of a better word, magic. Tragically, we all saw that on display three nights ago at the Academy Awards."

Palendar's looks of outrage vanished, replaced by one of guilt, and he seemed to shrink in upon himself.

"It's clear from the testimony that the place where the Álfar are consistently beating their human colleagues is in the casting sessions—because the Álfar actors have an advantage. An ability to cast a glamour on those around them. To be fair, I don't think they do this deliberately or with malice aforethought. For an Álfar this power is as natural as breathing. They cannot simply turn it off. But it does give them an advantage, one which my associate and I feel is unfair."

"So what are we talking about here?" LeBlanc interrupted. "Quotas? Parts being carved out for the humans?"

"No," I said.

"And if you would let Ms. Ellery finish, you would have the answer," David said, vampire snark dripping off every word. The lawyer subsided.

"It has been clearly established that the Álfar ability does not manifest on the screen. Therefore, we feel that the way to alleviate this problem, and offer a fair competition for both human and Álfar actors, is to require that all Álfar auditions be filmed or taped, and that the audition tape be reviewed outside the presence of the Álfar actor by the people who will actually be casting the movie or television show." I folded my hands on my notes and looked from face to face. "Whether SAG chooses to institute the same rule for human actors is up to that organization, but that is the judgment and conclusion of this arbitration."

Brubaker was nodding sagely. McPhee had a crooked smile, and he shot me a subtle thumbs-up gesture. LeBlanc and Missy and Palendar and Gabaldon had gone into a huddle, and Jeff was on his feet, giving me his thousand-watt smile. Brubaker and McPhee whispered to their clients, then McPhee rose to his feet and said, "This proposal meets with my client's approval."

"And mine," Brubaker added.

Gabaldon looked up. "Ms. Ellery, might my client and I have a private conversation with you?"

"We'd like to speak privately too," LeBlanc quickly popped up.

David and I exchanged glances and nods. David went off with LeBlanc and Missy to his office, and I took Gabaldon and Palendar into a smaller conference room. Palendar started to pace, but gave a gasp, pressed an arm against his side, and sank down into a chair.

"Ms. Ellery, if you had brought us this proposal a week ago, I would never have agreed to it," the Álfar said. His light tenor was like a song in the room. "But after the events at the Academy Awards—" His voice broke slightly. He coughed and continued. "When I once again had control of my own mind I looked at what had happened— what I had done; what I had been forced to do—and I realized this was different only in degree then what I was doing in auditions. I hurt people who are my friends and colleagues. Who knows if they'll ever accept me, or any of the Álfar again? Now that they've seen an example of our power they'll never trust us unless we make the first move. I'd like to take this back to the other Álfar members of SAG and present your proposal. I think there will be overwhelming agreement."

This was the longest string of words I'd ever heard out of Palendar, and I rethought my conclusion that he was stupid. This showed a lot of foresight, and a lot of class. I said as much to the Álfar actor. He gave me a sad and rather rueful little smile.

"Yes, well, but I'm not looking forward to it. Now I'm going to have to actually learn how to act."

Chris Valada and I waited for Kerrinan in the reception area at the county jail. Through the bulletproof glass I could see the actor gathering up his possessions from the box. He was out of the orange jumpsuit, and his clothes hung on his slender frame. He had lost a lot of weight while in jail. He stuck his cell phone in his coat pocket, slipped on his Rolex watch, gathered up his keys and wallet. For a long time he stared down at the box, then he lifted out a gold wedding band and slid it on his finger. Finally he passed through the heavy doors to join us. He walked like a man carrying a heavy load.

"Your car is in impound. I'll drive you over there," Chris said.

"This doesn't feel right," was his response.

"What do you mean? Why?" his lawyer demanded.

The Álfar's haunted eyes were locked on mine. "Because I did kill Michelle."

"No," I said. "You were the weapon. You're no more to blame than a gun is to blame. It's the person who uses the weapon, who pulls the trigger who's guilty."

"You're kind to say so, but the fact remains: I killed my best friend and the love of my life. How do you live with something like that?" He gave me a wan smile. "But still, I thank you for what you did. At least I know I'm not crazy, and maybe someday I'll forgive myself."

I watched the lawyer and the Álfar walk out the door, and I wondered if the long years of an Álfar's life would help to dull the guilt and ease the pain. Or would those years stretch out before him like a desert wasteland?

Now that the crisis was past I was able to concentrate on a private little mystery of my own. I had placed Vento in one of the sun pens to roll and bask in the sunshine. The rains of the past weeks were forgotten and it was eighty degrees. Just in time for me to finish and leave, the weather had finally matched my expectations. I took a breath and stopped stalling. It was time to get answers. I pulled out my phone and called Jolly.

"Linnet. My dear. Once again you are all over the news."

"I got through twenty-seven years without this happening to me. I'd really love a return to anonymity."

"I can understand." There was a pause, then Jolly asked, "They're not going to put down my horse for being a maddened killer, are they?"

"No, once they got a look at the dead guy's rap sheet, and after what happened at the Oscars, my story suddenly got a whole lot more credible."

"Good. I really didn't want to try and spirit my horse across the border."

"I'm betting Vento could get himself across the border," I answered, but my tone wasn't jocular, and Jolyon picked up the serious undercurrent in my voice.

"What are you saying?" he asked, sounding tense.

"That there's something unusual about a horse that can figure out if he twists a clip he can fatigue the metal and cause it to break. Then slide open a door and run down a man."

There was a nervous laugh from the other end of the line. "Ah, well, you know horses. They can get up to the darnedest things."

"Jolyon, cut the crap. My phone didn't purse-call you like you told David. If it had, there would have been a record in the calls-made section. It wasn't there. There was the notice that I had a missed call from David while these goons were driving me up the freeway, but no indication you called. But you told David you heard horses and the sound of my voice and I was frightened. How did you do that, Jolly? How did you know I was in trouble."

Now his tone matched mine in seriousness. "This is not a conversation to hold over the phone, Linnet. When you return to New York I promise I will give you some answers."

"But—"

"No! Believe me, it's better and safer this way." And he hung up.

Jeff and Kate threw a farewell party for David and me. They included what Kate had dubbed the Scooby Gang so Merlin and Maslin, Hank, Parlan and the six Álfar were also present. Five of them had decided to stay in California—not in the Fey version of California but in the traffic jams of human LA. Parlan and Ladlaw would be flying back east with us. Ladlaw wanted to report to his queen about the events and accept whatever punishment she decided to mete out. I already hated the woman for what she had done to John, and this just intensified the feeling.

There had been pretty much wall-to-wall press. I had tried to duck most of the interviews, and David was his usual brusque and snotty self, refusing all interviews, but the Álfar eagerly embraced the notoriety, as did the twins and Parlan. I wanted to both bless and damn them all because they kept bringing me up and giving me the credit for figuring out what was about to happen and taking steps to prevent it. Of course it wasn't all praise; there was some blame thrown around too.

The authorities castigated us for not coming to them with our suspicions, but most of the press were pretty blunt about asking them if we would have been believed. The answer was a lot of hemming and hawing. What did make me happy was that all these interviews showed humans and Álfar working together to prevent a tragedy. And another happy result was that polling on the Human First proposition showed a significant drop in support.

So now we were all out on the terrace overlooking the Pacific while the sun sank slowly toward the rolling waves. Jeff was turning steaks on the gas grill in their outdoor kitchen, and Merlin was mixing up a pitcher of margaritas while Kate tossed a big salad. Everyone seemed a little giddy. I sat on the wicker love seat and nursed a glass of red wine. Even with the propane heaters it was chilly on the deck, but nobody wanted to move inside as evening came on. The smell of cooking meat and sea air was lovely. I shivered and felt hands arranging a suit jacket over my shoulders. I looked up and back to see David. He had given me his coat.

"Thanks."

"You're welcome." He joined me on the love seat.

"You seem pensive," he said.

"No, just thoughtful." I took a sip of wine.

"Want to share some of them?"

"They're pretty inchoate, but I'll try." I tucked my legs up under me to sit cross-legged, facing David. "I enjoy working for IMG—"

"I hear a *but* in there."

I shook my head. "No, I guess I just really enjoyed building a team that combined both humans and powers. I'd like to continue that. I'd like to find a way to practice law that builds consensus between all of us rather than makes us adversaries."

"Even the hounds?" David asked with a sly note in his voice.

"Yes, even the werewolves. I admit I haven't had the best luck dealing with them so far. There was that asshole in that divorce case and, of course, Deegan."

David touched the ropey scars on his face. "Yes, I'd call trying to kill you more than a spot of bad luck."

"But Brubaker was a good lawyer, and my father's stock broker is a hound, and Jeff really likes his agent. Really there's nothing intrinsically good or bad about *any* group of people. It always comes down to the individuals, doesn't it?"

He looked down at his clasped hands, glanced over at me, and then looked away. "You are a rather unusual person, Linnet Ellery. Did you know that?" But he abruptly got up and walked away before I could answer.

"You are a very strange human, Linnet."

Qwendar's words echoed in my mind. I shivered, then Jeff sang out,

"Chow time!" and people began gathering up plates and forming a line at the grill while David leaned against the stone wall of the terrace. I shook off my sudden chill, and joined my friends.